PENGUIN BOOKS

THE LOVE BEACH

Leslie Thomas is one of Britain's most popular writers – a best-selling novelist, a travel writer and a television and radio personality.

He was born in 1931 of a South Wales seafaring family. At the age of twelve he found himself in an orphanage following his father's drowning in the South Atlantic during a U-boat attack on a wartime convoy and his mother's subsequent death within six months. His experiences were recorded years later in his first book, *This Time Next Week*, quickly followed by his first bestselling novel, *The Virgin Soldiers*, which became a highly successful film.

Leslie Thomas has now written twenty novels, including his bestsellers *The Magic Army*, *The Dearest and the Best*, *The Adventures of Goodnight and Loving*, *Dangerous in Love* and *Orders for New York*, all published by Penguin. His travel books about the lesser-known parts of the British Isles, *The Hidden Places of Britain* and *Some Lovely Islands*, in which he explores some islands off the British coast, have also been published by Penguin. *A World of Islands* is another of Leslie Thomas's lyrical travel books, and he also wrote and presented a television series, *Great British Isles*. There have, in addition, been television adaptations of his novels *Tropic of Ruislip* and *Dangerous Davies, The Last Detective*. His autobiography, *In My Wildest Dreams*, was published in 1984 by Penguin.

Leslie Thomas lives in London and Salisbury, Wiltshire, with his wife Diana and son Matthew. He has three children from a previous marriage. His hobbies include cricket, photography, philately, music and antiques.

LESLIE THOMAS

THE LOVE BEACH

PENGUIN BOOKS

PENGUIN BOOKS

Published by the Penguin Group
Penguin Books Ltd, 27 Wrights Lane, London W8 5TZ, England
Penguin Books USA Inc., 375 Hudson Street, New York, New York 10014, USA
Penguin Books Australia Ltd, Ringwood, Victoria, Australia
Penguin Books Canada Ltd, 10 Alcorn Avenue, Toronto, Ontario, Canada M4V 3B2
Penguin Books (NZ) Ltd, 182–190 Wairau Road, Auckland 10, New Zealand

Penguin Books Ltd, Registered Offices: Harmondsworth, Middlesex, England

First published by Constable 1968
Published in Penguin Books 1992
10 9 8 7 6 5 4 3 2 1

Printed in England by Clays Ltd, St Ives plc

To

VINCENT MULCHRONE

who first gave me

the notion to go

to the South Seas

'Young girls in groups of eight or ten, dancing a very indecent dance . . . singing the most indecent songs and using most indecent actions in the practice of which they are brought up from the earliest childhood. In doing this they keep time to a great nicety.'

Captain Cook's *Journals in the South Seas*

I

There was a bulky bird of some sort, an albatross or an eagle or that variety of thing, Conway thought, trailing the mast. It followed the knob at the top of the mast everywhere, dipping with it, swaying with it as the ship swayed with the moving sea, trying to kiss it with its beak but ever that couple of inches short. He's really trying, Conway thought: trying, but not quite hard enough. Just holding something back in his wings as if he knew that the moment he got his beak to the mast all he would get would be a mouthful of splinters.

Conway genuinely did not know whether it was an albatross or an eagle and he didn't care. He knew nothing about birds. It could have been a great swollen sparrow for all he worried. It had come to his attention only because he was on his back on the deck and his face was pointing in that direction.

Apart from the bird, the mast and the great liquid sun there was nothing in the sky. The Melanesian boys had washed the deck down only five minutes before, and he had been annoyed because he had to move then, but the boards were white and dry as stale bread now. Conway was wearing only a pair of stained and faded khaki shorts. He had a wide chest, and he could feel the skin under the hairs burning from the sun.

Davies, dark and small enough not to have to stoop as he came up and out from under the hood of the companionway, almost furtively, and stepped onto the deck. He was wearing grey flannel trousers, white shirt, tennis shoes and socks. He had been sizzled pink by the sun in half an hour the day before.

Near Conway's head squatted a sagging lifeboat, welded with rust to her foundations, nested in ropes and tackle, looking as permanent and fixed as anything on the ship. More fixed than the funnel.

Davies had a Welsh voice. It was the low Welsh, not the high piping note. But it still annoyed the Australian Conway. 'I heard them swilling the deck,' Davies said, conversationally. He carefully chose and sat in the blot of shade provided by the lifeboat. 'Did they make you move today?'

'Aw, I moved anyway,' muttered Conway still looking at the albatross or eagle. He wondered whether he wanted to know the identity of the bird sufficiently to bother to ask Davies. He thought he didn't. 'Yesterday I wouldn't move and the fuzzy wuzzies got shirty, then the old man got shirty, so today I saved myself trouble and I moved. I can't be bothered with bother.'

Davies said: 'Years ago when I was on a troopship . . .'

Conway said: 'What were you in?'

'South Wales Borderers.'

He saw Conway screw up his eyes.

He said defensively: 'Eight V.C.s in one battle.'

'Did you get one?' asked Conway casually.

'It was in the Zulu war,' said Davies. 'That's when they got them.' He looked uncertainly at Conway, who was looking down at his own chest. Then he said: 'On this troopship they asked for Welshmen to report to the entertainments officer. And we thought we had to sing. But they made us peel hundreds of stinking leeks.'

Conway blew his nose with his finger and thumb which nevertheless remained dry. He regarded them with some surprise. Then he said: 'Well then?'

'What?'

'About this troopship. It wasn't about the leeks was it?'

Davies stared. It was very hot. 'Oh no,' he remembered. 'No it was about washing down the decks. At night, it was so hot that we used to sleep on deck . . .'

'That's a new idea,' muttered Conway.

'Yes, and the first night I slept right next to the bell, the one they ring for six and eight bells and all that, and they banged it just when I had dropped off. By Christ, I jumped out of my skin! And this was the point about the washing down the decks, I'd just gone off again, just closed my eyes, and a bucket of water came whoosh across the deck. All over me. I said to myself "Issy", I said . . .'

'Why are you called Issy?' asked Conway bluntly. 'That's a Yid name. You're not a Welsh Yid are you?'

Davies said. 'Issy's a Welsh name. Short for Isslwyn.'

'Easier,' commented Conway dryly. 'You have to sort of spit to say the other one don't you? What sort of bird do you think that is?'

Davies had been watching it too. 'I'd say it was some kind of seagull,' he said. 'At a guess.'

Conway said: 'That's what I thought.'

They stopped talking and both looked earnestly at the fulmar petrel. There were some other birds wandering about the ocean, keeping their distance from the ship. A minor wind went musically through the ropes and stays, and there was the dull washtub sound as the old bow hit the Pacific every few feet.

'We must be near land if there's birds,' said Davies. He had only been to sea once before and that was on the ten pound immigrant trip to Australia. The sun had shrunk the shadow in which he sat, so he shuffled his seat back. 'New Caledonia,' said Conway informatively. 'Full of Frenchies. Colonials but still Frenchies. Fifty miles over there. Ah, there she is.'

'Who is?'

'The missus. The Captain's. She just shifted up there and I saw the top bundle of her hair.'

Conway nodded towards a canvas addition to the ship's bridge, slightly lower than the superstructure on the port side, and with an extra section of canvas sewn onto the walls to make it higher.

'She gets in there, sunbathing,' said Conway like a garden gossip. 'Naked as a baby. Not a stitch. That's why the sides are built up, so nobody on the bridge can get an eyeful.'

Davies said reasonably: 'How do you know she's nude then?'

'The boys say. The crew. The bloke on the wheel reckons that if he gets a good hard to port—that's funny. Hard to port, see?'

Davies nodded. Conway went on: 'If he gets a good hard to port and pushes the wheel right over, and leans right across with it, he gets a glimpse of her left-hand tit.' He laughed roughly. 'He said he all but rammed a schooner once, doing that.'

'I wondered why this thing was always tipping one way then the other,' said Davies. 'I couldn't make it out when the sea is flat. And it's just so some dirty bugger can see a nipple. He'll capsize it one day.'

'What do you sell?' asked Conway. The bun of blonde hair had vanished now and he had gone back to looking at the cruising bird. 'What are you reckoning to get rid of in the islands. Outboards, guns . . .?'

'Butter and fats,' said Davies.

Conway snorted. 'Hah! Funny! That's good. You know, I was saying to the mate, last night, that you are a humourless bastard, but that's *all* right. Butter and fats!'

'It's true,' said Davies miserably. 'Butter and fats. And I'm not humourless, mate. It's just I've heard all your jokes before.'

'You could have,' said Conway. He did not get annoyed. 'But butter and fats! All this way . . .'

'There's a market,' said Davies stoutly. Then less surely: 'I hope. There had better be or Trellis and Jones, wholesale grocers, exporters and importers, of Circular Quay, Sydney, will throw me out.' He found he was leaning forward into the sun again and it was burning his ear, just the rim, and his arm. He shuffled back. 'Up to now,' he continued, 'the people in The

Apostles have got all their dairy stuff from New Caledonia. But it's irregular because of the boats. On the other hand this thing, this ship, turns up every two months without fail. You wait, I'll be selling frozen butter and lard by the ton.'

'They've got cows of their own,' said Conway. He had looked away from the bird in the deep sky now and was regarding Davies with a little interest.

'The grass is lousy, and they haven't got enough animals anyway. And they're too lazy, or it's too hot or something, to try and do anything about it.'

Conway nodded: 'That sounds like them,' he admitted. 'I've heard they'd sooner sell their kids to slavery and their wives to whoredom than do a bit of extra graft.'

'The natives are like that, I heard,' agreed Davies. 'Just idle. It must be because it's so hot.'

'Natives?' grunted Conway. 'To hell with them. I'm talking about the British and the French.'

The half-dark of the Pacific night was leaning on the ocean. The sea swelled around the ship like bales of velvet on big rollers. Stout stars showed; the splendid Southern Cross, Lupus towing its planets like shining barges, and Centaurus throwing its bright net. The small constellation, low on the horizon, to port, were the lights of the highest brothel in the Central Pacific: on top of Mount George in the South Hibernian group.

The Melanesian helmsman knew this, so did Mr Curry, the mate, who had been navigating by them, with occasional recourse to the heavens, since seven o'clock that evening. Tomorrow they would round the coral hem of these Apostle Islands, find the gate in the reef, and ride into the harbour at Sexagesima, the capital, about the same time as the British Legion club bar opened its doors to the warm air of the Equatorial morning.

With her familiar ill-temper the 3,000-ton trading ship butted even the most innocent rollers. She was called *The Baffin Bay*.

Only an Australian could call a South Seas tramp steamer after a place in the Arctic, Davies thought, but he did not bring it up because it was too much trouble in the heat and Mac-Andrews, the captain, was the type to be touchy. It certainly had a cool sound in a hot ocean.

Davies thought he saw Greta MacAndrews giving Conway a funny bitter look at dinner that night. She was a red-faced blonde, going to fat. MacAndrews hardly said anything at meals, simply ploughing through whatever the Polynesian cook had put before them, pushing his spoon or fork under the lower edge of the Sydney *Daily Mirror*. It was always the same copy and MacAndrews read it from the beginning of the voyage until they reached The Apostles. Curry said that on the way home he did the crossword.

There was a joke on board, which had been running for eight years, about Curry, the mate, and Rice, the chief officer. MacAndrews always made the joke to new passengers, the first night out, and spoke hardly another word for the remaining two weeks of the voyage.

Davies was thirty, uncertain of himself mostly, but sometimes violent in a Welsh way when someone upset him. He had a thoughtful Celtic face, with deep dark eyes and thick hair. Sitting next to Conway he contrasted with the Australian's great shoulders, his thick neck and big muscular face. Conway was affable, very certain of himself, uncaring about much judging from his nonchalance in any table argument. He had a scar running the length of his left arm, stitched like a railway line.

With them was a Belgian, Pollet, square, getting plump, with cultured grey hair, thick glasses, and a peaceful face. He had been in the Pacific Islands all his life, and he knew them, the beaded strings of Polynesia, Micronesia and Melanesia, as well as any man. He sold patent medicines to the natives and bought

14

village carvings and other ornaments which he sold to collectors on the West Coast of the United States.

'Sexagesima,' said Pollet separating and spitting out two individual lentil seeds from the soup that night. 'Is the wettest place in the world when it's wet, and the hottest when it's hot. It is the capital of the Apostle Islands and has a thousand white people British and French, who would mostly like to get out, but cannot. Even when they do they go back. Like me.'

'A hellhole,' attested Greta MacAndrews. 'A shoddy, muddy, dirty little dump.'

'A considerable description,' nodded Pollet. 'You don't like it?'

'At this time of the year the people crawl about in mud and pouring rain, and when the season changes they crawl about flattened by the heat. Give me Sydney any day.'

'I'll buy it for you,' mentioned Conway.

'Thanks,' she said looking at his scarred arm. 'How did you do that?'

'Crocodile bit me,' he lied.

'As long as it wasn't a woman,' she said easily.

'The Portuguese discovered The Apostles,' said Pollet. 'The British and the French colonised them and fought over them. And they still fight over them—each one trying to get rid of them on the other. They produce nothing of worth, they are not strategically placed, they are not the sort of location to drop a test H-Bomb, even. In a word, they are worthless.'

'There's St Peter's and that's the main one, right?' asked Davies. 'What are the others like?'

'St Mark's is the home of a peaceful pagan tribe,' said Pollet, ticking it off on a finger. 'St Paul's is inhabited by mad Christian natives, completely barbarous. Then there is St Luke's, a sweet island I think, St Barnabas where there is an active volcano, St Matthew's and St John's, which have primitive tribes, and some smaller isles, just rocks really, in between.'

Rice, the engineer, said across the table, 'Those pistons will need doing this time.'

'Time enough,' said MacAndrews not looking over the paper.

'You said that last trip. We'll be under sail before we're finished.'

Davies, thinking of his butter and fats, said: 'There's no chance of you not continuing to sail to The Apostles regularly is there?'

'Till we sink,' sniffed MacAndrews glancing away from the page. 'It's the only sea-route known to our navigating officer, Mr Curry. The day we go anywhere else, Mr Davies, we're in trouble.'

Greta turned and looked directly at Conway who was separated from her by Rice. Rice, an obliging man, leaned forward out of her view. The mess steward was bringing around beef stroganov. There was a lot too much pale sauce for a meal on a pitching ship. 'Mr Conway,' said Greta, 'why are you going to The Apostles?'

Rice was stabbing his stroganov with a leathery piece of bread. 'He's on government work,' he said as though protecting Conway from further questions.

'What work is that?' she pressed. She started to eat and made a face at the food or at her reading husband, the sour expression starting with one and finishing with the other. 'It's time we got a cook aboard who can cook,' she said.

'Dull government business,' Conway grunted answering her first remark. Davies thought that was a lie for a start. If something was dull Conway was the type to shine it up when it came to talking about it.

Rice said: 'Which dull government is that for?' He was the oppressed little man who thinks of a pun once a month and hopes that everyone will laugh, is never surprised when they don't, and they don't.

'The dull Australian one,' said Conway. 'Nothing to get excited over. The Apostles, anyway the British half, not the French, gets orders from London, but just to keep us colonists happy the natives in one of the outer islands, St. Paul's, come under Australian trusteeship. We look after the blacks there.'

'You've never shipped with us before,' said Greta. She was now making a continuously unpleasant face at her food.

'My first trip. I don't always wet-nurse them. It's somebody else's job.'

Davies said: 'You've been in Vietnam, haven't you?'

Conway had his fork half-way to his mouth. He let it drop back. 'Where did you get that?' he asked. He stopped reacting immediately, as if he became aware of it, and pushed the ashen meat into his mouth.

'You went on about it the other day. On deck. The first day out of Sydney.'

'The day we split the rum,' said Conway remembering. 'Just romancing. I was there with the Aussie army but I got invalided home. Rheumatic fever.'

'Great place for rheumatic fever, The Apostles,' said Pollet. 'Especially now, in the wet.'

'I won't be there too long,' said Conway. 'Not long enough to catch anything—except what I want to catch.'

Davies was lying on his bunk in the way a dead man is fixed in his coffin, arms across the chest, feet touching. It was a narrow bunk. Conway was moving about in the next cabin. It was three o'clock in the morning and the ship was rolling heavily in a near-placid sea. Directly above Davies was the wheelhouse and he could hear MacAndrews banging about on his big feet. You could never hear the Melanesians because they had no shoes and Curry, the mate, who was the only other person ever to be on the bridge always wore basketball boots, so he was no trouble. But tonight the skipper trod heavily. They were waiting to go through the reef and into the lagoon of St Peter's Island.

Davies heard Conway move out of his cabin. He more or less knew where Conway would be going. He was surprised when his own cabin door was pushed open. Conway put his head in, saw Davies was awake, and stepped in like a large burglar.

'I'm going to have a chat with Mother MacAndrews,' said Conway.

'I thought you might be.'

'Well, she's lonely. Christ, she's only about thirty and she gets nothing.'

'She's been giving you the agony?'

'No. She hardly mentioned it. But the way she looks. Well, you know mate, it's *there*. She's only getting all that fat on her because she's eating too much. Compensation.'

'While her old man's on the bridge.'

'Yes, that's about it. She says he always goes up to see the tub through the reef. These are the sort of nudges she was giving me after dinner tonight. Wasn't that meat stuff bloody awful?'

'Couldn't touch it,' said Davies. 'The beef I mean, not Mrs MacAndrews. So why are you telling me?' He looked cautiously at the Australian.

'Help, just a little help. That's what I want,' smiled Conway. 'You can hear the old man thumping about overhead, can't you? You will also be able to hear him coming down from the bridge. Well if he does that while I'm in there, jump across the corridor and bang on the door. It's only a few yards.'

'God, you've got a cheek,' said Davies.

'Old MacAndrews doesn't care,' said Conway to pacify Davies' puritanism. He was unsure whether Davies didn't like the object or the method, or both. 'As long as he's got his batting averages and all that he's happy. She's told me so. He wouldn't like to walk in on it, that's all.'

'It wouldn't be cricket,' suggested Davies.

'A great humorist,' commented Conway. 'Is that okay, then?'

'I'm not sure it is.'

'I've got lots of influence in the islands,' said Conway. 'Official influence, you know. I'll introduce you to plenty of people who need butter and fats.'

'Get stuffed,' said Davies mildly. 'Anyway, how do you know I won't drop off?'

'You wouldn't do that,' said Conway. He went out and left the door open. Davies closed it, then got up and opened it again. He listened for MacAndrews' footfalls above. He was still walking the bridge.

It was not unusual for him to lie awake at night, anyway. Now he was doing it for Conway, and indirectly, he consoled himself, for the well-being of Trellis and Jones, wholesale grocers, exporters and importers, of Circular Quay, Sydney, and through them the well-being of Isslwyn Davies, and the natives of the Apostle Islands who would be getting their butter and fats on time for the first time in their turbulent history.

MacAndrews was still above, sounding like a man laboriously using a big wooden mallet on the boards, hesitating between strikes, have a puff and a blow, and then continuing for a while before stopping again.

It was funny, wasn't it, he thought, that last Sunday at home, before he had gone to catch the ship for Australia. After all it was November and it was all the wrong time to go to the beach. But the children had wanted to go and Kate had said that it would be all right as long as it didn't rain.

'It's all very well going to Barry Island in August and it rains,' she said. 'At least you can get in and have a cup of tea somewhere but there's nothing open now.'

'They want to go,' Davies had said looking at the children. 'And it's the last day.'

That last day. The words kept on being repeated all the time, didn't they. He said them, and Kate said them, and David and little Mag. The last day. The last time they would be together in Wales, of course, is what everybody meant. And they weren't sorry about that. After all Australia had more sun than Wales, and better houses and much better beaches, and it was cheap at ten pounds each. Almost as cheap as Barry Island.

They got the train from Newport and there was hardly anybody on it, not like a summer Sunday. David and Maggie pushed against the window, the boy standing and stretching, the girl kneeling on the plum railway upholstery. He and Kate sat on opposite sides and smiled at them and then at each other. He became aware that the cuff of his shirt was still frayed. She had promised to mend it too. She saw him looking at it and grinned. He could see her sitting back there now, her nice face and her hair done up by herself. It looked all right too. Her coat was getting old, but she wouldn't need a coat in Australia. She would get a nice tan too, going out on the boat, and he would meet her in Sydney, and they would be able to start again. He had answered her smile and nodded for her to come across to him and sit beside him. Sometimes they were a bit too much like parents. Doing that he felt a little childish, it was like trying to get her in the back seat of his old car when they were first going out together. They did not have that any longer either.

Lying in the bunk, with the thin mattress all lumps beneath him, Davies smiled up at the ceiling on which Captain Mac-Andrews was still bumping. Kate had refused to go across the gap in the compartment and he had laughed and had surrendered and gone across to sit by her instead. He had held her hand while the train ran through the marshy Welsh plain that goes down to the Bristol Channel.

It was a solemn day, grey but mild, with no stirring on the marshes and the ships in Newport Docks sitting up in the distance as though they were voyaging on the grass and reeds and mudflats.

'Mam,' said David, 'is that Dad's ship? Is that the ship for Australia?'

Davies remembered answering for Kate. Kate had told Mag to be careful not to fall from the seat. Mag, who was four, said: 'We are going on the ship too! We're going too!'

20

'Soon,' he had assured them. 'Quite soon. When I write a letter to Mam.'

Kate had put the little girl on her lap and showed her the sea-birds from the channel who had come to winter in the marshes. They went through Cardiff, Bute Street trying to get its Sunday morning eyes open, and then to Barry where they got a taxi to the beach because the little seaside station was closed at that wrong end of the year.

What a day that had been. What a wonderful last day. He had never realised the beach was so big and he had been going there all the years he could remember. All the rubbish of summer had been taken away by the huge tide and by the corporation workmen. The sand was flat and damp, the sea grey and tired, and there was no one there but a man taking a mongrel for a walk. The road made by their footsteps went clearly along the sand into the remote end of the beach and up there the man could be seen throwing stones for the dog.

Davies and Kate, hands held, each holding the glove of one child, walked the empty beach. David and Mag wanted to go into the sea or make sand castles. Kate told them they could draw pictures and write their names in the sand. Davies walked her on a little way. A dozen oyster catchers, strangers, black and white with orange beaks, hobbled about like men on crutches.

'Never see them down here in the summer,' he had said.

'Don't blame them,' replied Kate. They seemed to have less to discuss today than ever. He was going to tell her again, how good it would be in Australia, but he stopped himself. He had already said it. The funfair was all closed up and covered with sheets of tarpaulin and canvas, like an exhibition waiting to be unveiled. The cafés and the hotels across from the beach looked out to the slate sea and the cold ships moving on it, speechlessly and with blind, shuttered eyes. No one, it seemed, had anything to say.

'We'd better go back,' she had suggested, half turning as she said it. 'We can't leave them too far behind.'

'No, of course,' he said. The children were drawing and digging by the shore and had not looked up. Davies turned and as he did so caught Kate and clumsily folded his arms about her. She was a bit taller than he was and it had always embarrassed him to embrace her standing up. It had probably looked just as odd on the beach, on that last day, but there was no one to see or to laugh. He put his lips to her cheek and turned her head so that they could kiss properly. It was not timed very well, not very successful he thought now, but they kissed anyway miles from anybody but David and little Mag.

'It'll be all right, you know,' he had said. 'It will, truly Kate.'

'Yes,' she had answered.

It had been a wonderful last day.

Conway pushed against the cabin door. 'Didn't go to sleep on me did you?' he said.

Davies turned. 'I didn't,' he confirmed. 'Did she?'

Conway breathed a laugh without any sound coming out. He angled his head to hear the boots of MacAndrews. 'Still navigating eh? He's a fine skipper that.'

'And you're a fine bastard,' said Davies.

Conway said: 'And you're a great butter and fats salesman, not to mention adulterer's look-out. Thanks.'

'I wasn't sleeping anyway. The boots keep me awake. Were you well received, or is that being a bit indelicate for a mere adulterer's look-out?'

'Very well received,' nodded Conway. 'You should try it yourself. She's open all night.'

'No thanks. I'm married anyway and I keep to it.'

'Do you?' said Conway as though Davies had revealed some strange hobby. 'Where's your wife. In New South Wales?'

'No, the old one.'

'Oh, I forgot, you're one of those bloody Taffy people.'

'And adulterer's look-out.'

'You should try it sometime. Help you a hell of a lot. You wouldn't be so worked up and intense.'

'I told you, she's in South Wales.'

Conway said: 'That's a long way to go for a shag.' He went out and closed the door. Davies heard Captain MacAndrews clump down from the bridge and he realised that the ship was riding still in calm waters.

II

George Turtle left his bungalow at 15 Laburnum Avenue, Sexagesima, at eight-thirty. It was the last month of the rainy season, a hot, brown and grey morning with one rattling shower just tailing over St Peter's Island, heading for St Barnabas, and another coming in with the certainty of a train on time from the seaward direction of St Paul's and St Mark's.

It would be like that for most of the day, and every day until April when the last of the rain trains would pass the islands and the ocean sun would be left to itself in the ocean sky. Mr Turtle had only gone a few yards towards the lean-to which sheltered the green Morris Minor he had shipped with him from Isleworth, but by that time his shirt under his plastic mackintosh was breathing heavily with the day's first sweat. It must be eighty already, and before noon it would be ninety or more and there would be four hard showers in the morning, and a further seven before nightfall. There would also be an electric storm.

He unlocked the fading Morris with keys sticky with moisture. Inside the car it stank like a humus heap. Mr Turtle could not decide whether to steam in his plastic bag as he drove or whether to take it off and have to get into the uncomfortable cocoon again in five minutes when he reached the radio station. The rain was banging down on the roof of his lean-to. He decided to leave the mackintosh on. He started the car and backed it out into the thick wall of rain. It drilled frighteningly on his roof and he couldn't see through the rear window. But it also

24

meant he could not see Minnie waving from the bungalow window and he would not have to wave back. That was something anyway. She had received a letter from her sister in Isleworth in the consignment of mail newly arrived in *The Baffin Bay* and Minnie was upset because it had been snowing in Isleworth. 'Poor things,' she kept saying as she went about the bungalow. 'Poor things.'

George had bright eyes and no hair. He was one of those men who shows photographs of army groups taken at Aldershot in 1944 and challenge you to guess which is him. No one had ever guessed right. He had bushy hair in his military days and it gave him added height. Even he had not realised how small he was until he went bald after meeting and marrying Minnie.

Going cautiously down the running red mud of the hill which fell from his bungalow to the radio station, the windshield wipers pathetically losing their battle with the Pacific rain, George had a quick thought that he had moved from Isleworth because of the weather. But he felt guilty about it, and thrust it away with an annoyed twitch of his head. It was like having a short steamy dream about an old mistress. Not that George had any mistresses, old or otherwise, although he did occasionally have short, steamy dreams. He did feel guilty about them, but the guilt never lasted. After all with Minnie he felt he deserved some recompense somewhere.

Snow in Isleworth. Poor benighted devils. He could picture them now sliding about on the pavements, trying to claw their way onto buses, jammed like pigs in the underground, trying to make some progress in their cars through the freezing slush and the frozen traffic. Hah! He was lucky to be out of that lot. Rushing to get to their offices; little cups of tea, wet coats and shoes, neon lights that sent you blind by the time you were forty-five. My God, how fortunate he had *seen* it all as it really was, and in time too. *In time*, that was the important thing. He was only forty-three and he had seen it all *in time*. What fools they were, those Isleworth idiots, those Dagenham dolts, those

Twickenham twerps, those Russell Squares even. He took one hand from the wheel and smugly patted the back of the other, congratulating himself on his alliteration. He really must write a book one day. I Went To Paradise. Not bad. I *Ventured* Paradise. Much better. A good title that. It had that sniff of arrogance, bravery, romance about it. I *Ventured* Paradise. Very good indeed! He would definitely start writing this time. That evening. After the British Legion meeting.

Not that you could see much of Paradise today. The outer islands had been gobbled by the rain, the lagoon lay like waste water from a miner's laundry. *The Baffin Bay* was out there riding irritably at anchor while the little boats went out to get her cargo. She had been a whole day late again which had put everyone on the island in a filthy humour. MacAndrews' fault obviously, hanging around on the journey. No adventure, Mac-Andrews. Everyone agreed on that. And a day late again.

As the Morris was slithering the final few yards to the base of the hill, a wild pig came out of the wall of undergrowth at the side and gave the car a violent blow with its backside as it went by. George braked as soon as he saw the shape through the rain on his windscreen. Not through any particular humanity towards wild pigs, but through some remnant of suburbia, some deposit of Isleworth still left in his instincts, which made him react like that. It annoyed him immensely and he hoped that another couple of years among the islands would see the flaw eradicated. Kendrick and Hassey and a lot of the others were always driving up to the British Legion Club with something or other they had hit sticking like a trophy to the front bumper. Dogs, chickens, goats, and Hassey had once turned up with a very old man from one of the native villages trans-fixed there. That had cost him twenty-three pounds ten shillings one way and another.

Mind, you had to be going at a reasonable speed to get the better of a wild pig on a rainy morning. He got out of the car into the almost solid rain. It beat on his plastic mac, with its
26

pixie hood, making him feel as though he were in a paper bag. There was a dent in the mudguard. These pigs were getting troublesome around the town. He got back into the car. The rain funnelled down the creases of his mac and made an infantile pool around his feet. Something ought to be done about them. He would bring it up at the next meeting of the Roads Committee of the Sexagesima Town Council. Feeling through his outer covering was like rummaging through wet cabbage leaves. But he made it with as little discomfort as possible. He took out his Apostle Islands Horticultural Society Diary and wrote in the memorandum with a ball point pen.

The British Governor of the Apostle Islands, Sir William Findlay-Stayers, watched the rain pebbling the water of the lagoon and shivering the palm trees just outside his study window. He thought how much heavy rain made palms look like old, ill men, heads bowed, arms hopelessly dangling.

If Sir William had been afforded a choice of islands upon which to live he would not have chosen this one anyway. Luing, in the Inner Hebrides, was more his place, or Seil, where you could walk to the highland mainland over a flower-thick bridge across the narrowest neck of the Atlantic Ocean. He was not fond of sea travel and if it were possible to walk to an island he preferred it. He liked cold, wet islands, too, not hot and wet.

He went to his study window again and looked grumpily over the cut-up water to *The Baffin Bay* unloading her cargo. So far no official mail had arrived, but this was not unusual. The Chinese shopkeepers in the town invariably got their letters before his arrived. On Her Majesty's Colonial Service meant nothing to the postal service, but since it was run by a Jew, the only joint public operation in the entire archipelago, this was to be expected. In fact he shrewdly suspected that the French Governor perused the British official dispatches before

27

he did. That is why they were always so late. He had, on one or two occasions, heard Etienne Martin, his French counterpart, drop accidental remarks at social affairs which could only have been the result of reading the British letters. Still, Sir William was disinclined to make an issue of it because relations were never less than strained, and, in any case, through some addressing error the monthly consignment of excellent French liqueurs and brandy unfailingly turned up on the doorstep of British Government House, and Sir William enjoyed them.

'Funny game,' he muttered to himself thinking around these things. 'Aye, a funny game.' He was in the tradition of gaunt highland Scots, his face like a retired sparrow-hawk, sharp and powerful but having lost its hunting look and aggressive intentions. He yearned for home, for the bald brown hills and the winter waters of the Lorn, for fat cattle and fat women, and for great roaring fires. After he had been Governor of The Apostles for two years he had abruptly surrendered to an orgy of nostalgic patriotism, had ordered a stone fireplace to be built at his residence, and, when it was done had, regardless of the terrible Pacific heat, sat alone, kilted and dirked, before a huge blaze, drinking toddy and singing the songs of the islands, sweet and rough. After this he had been in hospital for three weeks suffering from severe dehydration and the fire had not been kindled since.

Marge, his dear highland wife, was dead, five years gone, back in Scotland. After a violent Burns Night party she, a democratic woman always, had driven a new Rolls-Royce, loaded to the roof with gamekeepers, dairymen and other sundry workers, dramatically and with tremendous finality into the deepest depth of Loch Lorn.

By the following Burns Night he was below the Tropic of Capricorn, in the hot Apostles—an Anglo-French Condominium, a curious, pantomime situation. Only in the New Hebrides, north in the ocean, did it exist elsewhere.

'Worthless dots!' Sir William remembered the condemnation by his irritable predecessor Dugdale late on the night of his first arrival.

Sir William recalled him sitting in the big study with made and unmade jig-saw puzzles all about the room. 'Man needs a hobby here or he'd go mad,' Dugdale had bawled at him as they sat down after dinner. 'The very act of putting together a thousand pieces of, say, Shakespeare's England or Dover Castle has saved me from going out and killing the entire native and British and French populations of this awful damned place.'

'Dots!' he repeated at Sir William. 'Nobody wants 'em now. No economic, no strategic value. Nobody in London or Paris admits it of course. They still issue their inane little Condominium postage stamps with pictures of natives spearing fish and all that palaver. Hah! Just imagine a place like this having *two* administrations. You wait until you see them rubbing away at each other, telling prep-school tales, lining up on Armistice Day and all that to-do.'

His eyes swivelled craftily to the desk again. Swiftly his hand pecked at a jig-saw piece. It was like a heron picking up a small fish. He tried it, turned it, and regretfully rejected it. 'Two Public Health departments!' he continued. 'Very little public health, though. Two Highways and Cleansing departments and what for?—five miles of filthy roads. Our dual Education Authorities have spectacularly raised the standard of illiteracy among the native and the white populations. And our two splendid Police Forces had a pitched battle last New Year's Eve.'

Sir William was glad to see the back of the testy old devil going up the companionway of *The Baffin Bay*, even though the ex-Governor's last gesture had been to push a native porter violently down the steps and into the lagoon as a finale to his rule. But since then the truth had reached him too. The Apostles were indeed worthless dots. Warm, wet, wearying, worthless dots. He too would be glad to depart.

His relations with M. Martin, the French Governor, had

never been harmonious. They lived on the most distant opposites of the island and never met unless they could not avoid it. Sir William disliked the way that the Frenchman always appeared so cool, composed and well dressed. He liked to refer to him privately as 'the tropic dandy'. Nevertheless the white business shorts of M. Martin always fitted splendidly, even sexily, while Sir William's khaki drill were always starched like a bread board and often cut him painfully below the knees. On formal occasions the decorations, both gallant and distinguished, attached to M. Martin's breast and dangling from his masculine neck looked like a brilliantly flowering garden compared with Sir William's miserable window-box. His slim Latin moustache and his eyebrows were like triplets; his tie and his dry martini were always at precisely the right angle.

Nor did the Frenchman ever throw away an opportunity to score off him. Only the previous week they had been at a cocktail party given by the Sexagesima Amateur Art Circle. 'Our navy will be paying us another visit soon, perhaps in a month or so,' M. Martin had said. He emphasised the word 'another' so slightly that it hardly jumped out of line at all, but Sir William heard it. He was not feeling in a diplomatic mood.

'You mean that little gunboat of yours is coming across from New Caledonia,' he suggested.

'The patrol vessel *Auriol*,' corrected the French Governor. 'The red pom-poms will be in the streets again! I thought *you* were expecting a naval vessel at some time.'

'A destroyer,' said Sir William defiantly. 'A big destroyer.'

'Let me see, H.M.S. *Sandpaper*, was it not?'

'Sandpiper,' glared Sir William. His starched shorts were cutting his legs again and he was getting angrier.

'Sold for scrap,' murmured the Frenchman triumphantly. 'Three months ago in Sydney.'

The British Governor had not been told. 'Was she?' he grumbled uncomfortably. Then lamely, 'Oh well, we'll get another, you'll see.'

Sir William's uncomfortable memory of that exchange was interrupted by the arrival of his official mail bag. Everything came in it, government hand-outs, Foreign Office letters and reminders from the Colonial Development Ministry to keep out of trouble with the natives. He also received, each five weeks with the boat, a complete list of Premium Bond winning numbers none of which, so far, had ever been his, copies of *The Times* and *The Scotsman* and, in this particular consignment, a letter from the Prime Minister.

It would have been no more surprising to Sir William to receive a note from Santa Claus. But there it was, a personal one-pager, saying how glad the Premier was that Her Majesty had chosen to visit the Apostle Islands during her forthcoming tour of the Pacific dependencies, and that everyone at Number Ten was sure the visit would be a happy and successful one.

At first Sir William did not believe it. The French were playing a joke, taking him for a ride. Then, as though seized with some instant madness he dived into the mailbag and began tearing through its contents. Newspapers, personal letters, lists from Harrods and Foyles, flew about the room. His Premium Bond numbers received only a quick glance. Then he came up with the sealed envelope.

'Cooper,' he called like a boy on his birthday. 'Cooper, come and see what I've got!'

Phillip Cooper, his watery A.D.C., came in anxiously as though expecting Sir William to be displaying symptoms of a vile disease. He was relieved to see the Governor merely madly tearing the seal away from a big Whitehall envelope.

'What is it, sir,' asked Cooper. 'Exactly what is it?'

'Exactly, it is tremendous, Cooper!' answered Sir William impersonating the drained voice of his assistant, an occasional lapse which Cooper disliked intensely.

'Tremendous sir,' said Cooper. 'Exactly how, sir?'

Sir William was shuffling through documents, papers, letters. The look of the hunter was in his eye again. 'We, dear boy,' he said, slowly now as though to make the relish last, 'are going to have a visit from Her Majesty. It's very sudden. On her way back from Australia she is coming in here. What about that, Cooper! What about that!'

A spot of colour appeared on each of Cooper's small cheeks. 'Exactly sir,' he chortled. 'What about it!'

Sir William was hopping about on one leg. 'The Queen,' he breathed. 'Our Gracious Queen. Here in The Apostles. Hah! Now we'll tell those Frogs what they can do with their piffling gunboat.'

When Bird rolled up the shutters of her shop the rain had cleared for a while leaving the sky clean and immediately very hot. The street outside her establishment, The Parisienne Hair Style and Beauty Parlour, was glutinous red mud for the entire rainy season and a trench of rising dust at any other time of the year. She had always tried to affect a little chic in her business, hair driers from Australia, the best French lotions and sprays, her two Melanesian assistants in fetching pink pinafores, and coffee in the daintiest cups. The effect, however, was undoubtedly spoiled by the fact that the customers either came in layered with mud like soldiers from the trenches or with dust, red and potent as pepper, lying on them. Even when they arrived by car or taxi there was an area, a sort of no-man's-land, between the actual street and the shop which needed to be crossed and, if anything, this was muddier or dustier than even the street itself. Madame Butol, wife of one of the French government officials, always made her native chauffeur carry her across the trap.

Bird was three months short of eighteen. She had been born on St Luke's Island, one of the minor members of the group, where her Australian father was a planter. He had died and her mother had returned to Sydney having sold the house and plantation. Bird loved the islands, wet or dry, and would not leave. So her mother went without her, leaving her enough to buy the shop and begin her career. She was dainty and dark with magnificent long hair and nose too broad but a suitable pedestal for her bursting brown eyes. She had a tooth missing, but it did not show unless she laughed widely, so she usually merely smiled which made some people think she was deep and enigmatic.

Her Australian parents had called her Nola after an aunt in the Dandenongs, near Melbourne, and Betty after her father's mother. Fortunately the naked pidgin-speaking natives on St Luke's Island had better taste and re-named her as 'Little-narrow - one - who - make - hop - hop - in - the - early - morning - and - calls - like - tree - bird - until - she - tired - and - cries'. This was decently abbreviated to Bird and by that name she had been known ever since. She had been educated at the French Convent on St Peter's and had there caught a strange low-spoken half-Gallic accent. She played the guitar and sang folk songs on Saturday nights in the Angelique Café off The Love Beach Road.

Having dealt with the shutters Bird looked directly over the estuary-like road to the orange-coloured shop of Bhu Vin Lee, an aged Vietnamese who had a cracked face and a dead beard hanging onto it. She did not like him very much because he frightened her every afternoon by sitting just inside his doorway, half concealed by shadow, and staring across at the Parisienne Hair Style and Beauty Parlour. He had never done anything but stare, except on one occasion when he actually picked his way across the street to suggest to her that they ought to organise a petition about the state of the road. Nothing had come of that, however, and Bhu Vin Lee had retreated into his private shadow and continued staring.

A Melanesian woman, all hips and hair, came out of the shop, which was a general grocer's, carrying a paraffin can and a packet of washing powder. Bird remembered that *The Baffin*

33

Bay had arrived which meant that all the shops would be stocked up for a while and that her consignment of curlers, lacquer, beauty creams and magazines should be coming up the road that morning.

Some men, Mr Hassey, the mad planter, Mr Kendrick, who kept the cycle shop, John Livesley, who had the only neon sign for a thousand miles above his baker's shop shouting 'Bread' in three alternating colours, and some others were sitting under the umbrellas at the café.

The café was next door to Bird's salon, with its apron of flagstones projecting out to the street. The men were on their first drinks of the day, taking the break in the rain to meet, the steam from the last shower rising about them. They looked as though they were sitting in the middle of some inferno or grouped fatalistically inside a large cannibal cooking pot. She knew them all well, from childhood. Mr Livesley who was immensely proud of his neon sign which could be seen flashing for two miles out to sea. BREAD—BREAD—BREAD it went in red, then white, then blue, across the Pacific night. Dahlia, a girl who had come to work at the Angelique, lived in the flat over the shop and her rent had been reduced by Mr Livesley because her curtains were only muslin and the flashing colours of his advertisement gave her nightmares.

Mr Kendrick she remembered because he was the first person to ever attempt to assault her indecently. It happened when she was twelve and her father had come over to St Peter's to buy her a bicycle. They had gone to Mr Kendrick's shop, which always prospered because a bicycle was the best way to get about the island, and her father had gone across for a drink while she selected her present. Mr Kendrick, who was a very clean looking man, had put his hands all over her bottom and other places while he helped her on the cycles. She chose a really strong machine and three days later ran over Mrs Kendrick's blue Persian cat killing it with one powerful thrust of her front wheel. She had taken it to the shop and laid it solemnly, silently,

34

across the counter, like some sort of offering or sacrifice, which
it was in a way, looking steadily into the sanitary eyes of Mr
Kendrick as she did so. Mr Kendrick had burst into terrible
tears, much to Bird's surprise and pleasure, because he was
wretchedly afraid of Mrs Kendrick who in turn was pas-
sionately attached to the cat. Bird had turned triumphantly and
left. Outside, as she mounted her cycle, she could see Mr Kendrick wailing over the stretched cat, trying to shake some life
back into it.

Everyone knew Mr Hassey was mad, but Bird liked him. He
had arrived in The Apostles thirty-eight years ago for a two-week
visit. 'I had only come to ascertain the fucking natives,' she
had once been fascinated to overhear him say. 'Then I thought
I'd ascertain the other islands. And here I am. Still ascertaining.'

Bird's initial customer that morning was to be Mrs Flagg
who with her husband Bert spent months of the year among
the gentle St Mark's natives, studying their untroubled
paganisms, ancestor worship and collections of skulls. The St
Mark's tribe had the picturesque custom of wrapping the male
sexual organ in a great covering of banana leaves until it
assumed huge proportions and was then tucked into a leather
thong tied around the waist like a girdle. Bird had seen the tribe
at different times and when she was very young she had
always imagined that each man had a pet hedgehog or raccoon,
or some such creature, which hung onto its master around the
waist.

Mrs Flagg was always cheerfully punctual. Her husband's
Land-Rover squelched down the street and she jumped down,
clad in Wellington boots, denim trousers and a shirt in lumber-
jack check. She was a bulky blonde, red cheeked, in her thirties,
striding and strident. She entered the shop on her massive rub-
ber boots like a hippopotamus quitting a watering place, giving
the Parisienne Hair Style and Beauty Parlour its first muddy
splattering of the day.

Bird sighed. Mrs Flagg took off her boots, sat in the chair

35

with men's socks stuck out in front of her, and said boisterously:
'Righto, Bird, my dear, give it a good scrub. Those fleas on St
Mark's don't get any better.' Bird grimaced mildly at the
tangled scalp. Mrs Flagg said: 'Just imagine, dear, what happened this time?'

'What happened, Mrs Flagg?' asked Bird dutifully beginning to lather the screwed hair.

'We've got Tom Ya-Ya, the chief, to agree to six of his chaps
to come over to stay at our house so that we can really study
them at first hand over a long period. Isn't that bewitching!'

'Bewitching,' agreed Bird. 'Are they going to put any clothes
on themselves? All the natives here on St Peter's wear
something.'

'A delicate point, dear,' admitted Mrs Flagg from under the
froth. Lumps of tree and creeper, other jungle debris, and an
insect with a million legs, had already emerged from her hair.
'Bert said they should wear shorts. But I say they are quite decent enough, a trifle exotic of course, but that is why they are
so worth our study. They have their baloots, their banana wraps
you know, and these do quite effectively cover them up. As I
said to Bert we would never get shorts that would fit them
around the waist while they retained their baloots, and they
most certainly would not abandon them, even if we wished
it.'

Bird switched on the radio. Like everyone else in the archipelago she sensed that it was ten o'clock and reached to hear
Radio Apostle which had only enough power to broadcast for
two hours a day, an hour in English and an hour in French.
George Turtle read the English news, local and international,
the latter sometimes nearer history, and then played some record requests before going home to Minnie for lunch.

On days when *The Baffin Bay* arrived there was a good deal
more news than usual because Captain MacAndrews brought
the Sydney papers with him, so George broadcast an extended
bulletin. There was no other station in the Pacific strong enough

to reach Sexagesima, except Honoraria in the Solomons when freak receiving conditions were prevailing.

The station always played itself in and out with the two National Anthems. This always embarrassed Bird a little but she encouraged her customers to remain seated, particularly if they were under the hair drier, unless they insisted on doing so. She more or less knew the ladies who liked to stand to attention, and there was a small determined group of them, pre-war dual colonists for whom the monarch, or the President, the flag and the anthem were more important to life than even dry gin. Mrs Flagg, despite her name, was not one of these and she remained round and bowed under Bird's working hands while the various small travellers from St Mark's evacuated her hair like animals leaving a blazing forest.

But Bird heard the scraping of the chairs in the café forecourt outside and knew that Mr Hassey, Mr Livesley and Mr Kendrick were stiffly standing, the rain steam still rising about them, looking squarely in the general direction of London, and ready to raise their morning glasses to Her Majesty the moment the radio record ground to a stop.

Today they were surprised by the music being snatched away far more quickly than usual, while their eyes were still far away and their glasses only ready at the waist. George's voice rushed onto the air before The Queen was properly remembered and toasted. Mr Hassey looked at the red plastic-covered transistor radio on the table with some disagreeable surprise.

'This is Radio Apostle broadcasting on 243 metres,' gabbled George Turtle. 'And here, immediately, is the news. Some special news. I—that is we—have just received a message from Sir William Findlay-Stayers, the Governor, that a special meeting of the Anglo-French Condominium for the islands, *and* the Sexagesima Town Council, has been called for this evening at seven o'clock in the assembly building. The meeting will be open to the public. The Governor has an important announcement to make.'

37

No one around the damp little table heard any more. The three men regarded each other like card players who have simultaneously turned up six aces. Mr Hassey stuttered first: 'They've sold us,' he said. 'S-sold us, the rotten buggers. I've already ascertained the situation. Sold us to the French.'

'Or the Japanese,' suggested Mr Kendrick.

'G-God, don't say that,' said Mr Hassey. 'Even in joking.'

Mr Livesley said: 'I think it's an H-bomb test. Right here. They'll blow everything to dust, or mud. And I've just got my sign up.'

Inside the salon Bird rubbed at Mrs Flagg's scalp. 'What could it be?' she said.

'Perhaps,' said Mrs Flagg with a sincere gurgle, 'they've heard about our natives coming over.'

III

There were three violent, ten minute rain storms during the afternoon, and a session of thunder and vivid lightning during which the roof of a hill house was struck while a committee were discussing the next display of the Sexagesima Scottish Folk Dance Society. The committee, mostly ladies, were considerably shaken by the explosion and the sinister smell of smoke that followed it. Some thought it might be something to do with the imminent announcement the Governor was due to make, a premature attack perhaps in a war they had as yet heard nothing about. There was always that risk when you were tucked away in a fold of a large ocean. But when the smoke had cleared and the houseboys had inspected the minor damage it was generally realised that it was, after all, just another wet season thunderstorm, and the meeting proceeded.

When the third storm had rolled out over the sea Davies took his hired bicycle from the porch outside the South Pacific Hilton Hotel and rode along the chocolate road to the sea. The Hilton was the only hotel on the island. It had been established in 1933 by Cornelius Hilton, an escaped Irishman, and had been operated by his son Seamus ever since it was recovered from the military after the war.

Seamus, a fine fungusy young man who spent his time inventing new drinks and playing his own fruit machine, had written a bold letter to the other Hilton Hotel Group protesting that his family had been in the business for more than forty years and did not intend to be usurped for any late starter.

39

The hotel had begun life as a pleasantly white building, topped with wood and local concrete which meant that by the end of the first rainy season of its existence it was letting in water at every pore. It had mothered many miscellaneous extensions over the years, a little here and a little there, but the prevailing damp spread throughout these additions also and sometimes one would fall down. The rubble was simply left untouched—unless, of course, human beings were trapped under it—and the little dead structures leaned and piled against the main building. This itself had sighed and settled, drooped and discoloured, over time, and the day that Davies arrived the hotel resembled a pale grey stodge like a bread poultice.

Davies rode his bicycle uncertainly along the gummy road, noting as he went the shops he intended to visit on the following day. They were set up on a wooden side-walk clear of the road, like the buildings in a Western film. There were some European-owned but most were run by Chinese or Vietnamese who had wandered the Pacific looking for somewhere not overpopulated with other Chinese and Vietnamese shopkeepers. The windows of their establishments were small and crammed like dustbins. Gross flies sat on the inside of the panes and blinked at the hard sun that had followed the rain. Dogs and children squatted in new warm puddles in the road. High above the children, bending and moving rhythmically like manipulations of marionettes, were the tall Pacific palms, and beyond them the recently reformed sky, smiling and innocent.

The shops and the town ended with the road. It then became a sauntering path through congregating trees, past giant bushes thick with rainwater and sweet orange flowers. Steam was moving about the roots and the lower trunks of the palms as Davies pedalled; snaking out across the path, moving everywhere, occupying the limbs of the forest. His white shirt and his cream tennis shorts, which he had bought in Dock Street, Newport, clung to him as though needing his protection in this foreign heated place.

He went through a placid village after a mile. Its palm-knitted houses were pushed half-way into the trees, just their noses sticking out, reminding him, in a sudden, nostalgic burst of the way people in South Wales used to leave the noses of their cars poking out of their garages, just to show off.

There seemed to be nobody about. Some bright washing was fidgeting on a rope line outside one house and there were several slim legs of smoke moving up from behind some of the dead brown roofs. The houses had little patches of vegetables set around them like skirts, hens and chicks investigated squares of sunlight, and masses of wild flowers pushing into the clearing from the trees were trimmed and gathered so that each dwelling place had its own brilliant cushions of colour. At the centre of the settlement there was a wide track, much broader than the one which had brought Davies there. It cut the place in half and was eaten up by the trees beyond the most extreme of the houses. A carved wooden figure, a tribal God about the size and attitude of a small jockey, stood by the track, and a few paces away a bus stop, properly painted and with a waste-paper basket around its middle as though to keep its modesty. The sign said : 'Sexagesima Transport. City Centre Service. Queue other side.'

He left the village at an ungainly circus pedal watched by six wide Melanesian women who came, sedate as wooden ships, to the centre of the road as he turned away. They watched him, discussed him, and then turned and voyaged back to the places from which they had emerged.

Walled jungle closed about Davies, pressing the wet heat close to him. He was wearing his British woollen socks with ugly open-thonged sandals and it seemed to him that the sweat was dropping from the points of his toes as he worked his legs.

Then, with theatrical suddenness, the trees and undergrowth fell away, he rode on to soft white sand, gently bumpy, looked up and stopped amazed. The beach was bowed over by courteous palms and spiky pineapple trees. The ocean, churned by

41

the storm, tripped over the outlying coral reef and ran quiet and shame-faced onto the beach. And lying, lined, and littered along the beach were the dead rusted bodies of great steel invasion barges. The bevelled snout of one reared above his head as soon as he emerged from the forest to the beach, petrified in its death attitude, jammed into the island in the place where it had come ashore twenty-three years before. Its brothers lay straddled the whole length of the beach, most of them the same shape and size, but some smaller and three or four gigantically bigger.

Davies felt as though he walked among monsters. He placed the cycle against the first barge, touching its flanks feeling the surface rust powder away in his fingers. Then he went slowly along the battlefield. He felt choked, strangely frightened, to see them left and lying like this. Their square shadows were thrown forward by the late sun, some reared up, their prows high, others nuzzled the ground in the manner of a dying bull at the fight. The landing flaps of some were down, others had never dropped. Here and there painted numbering and lettering, the square cornered 'U.S.', had survived to show who had joined the battle that mattered nothing now.

He walked the length of the line of metal ghosts. Half-way along the head and shoulders of a small pointed-bowed vessel sat sunk in the sea like an old man taking a decorous bathe. Beyond it the white tape of the surf falling over the coral and the ocean journeying out to the horizon. The retreating storm was still on the far edge of the world, black below and topped with pink, yellow and purple clouds, fluffed and fancy like a celestial ice cream.

There was a short metal ladder thinned with corrosion, fixed to the side of one of the big barges. Davies tested it, felt it flake in his fingers, but found it held, and carefully climbed it until he reached the level of the deck. He did not know what he expected to see, decomposing tanks or even strange crouched men, but all there was for his gaze was the great hold of the creature carpeted luxuriously with fine sand, inhabited by crabs and other lodgers from the sea. Nothing else, only a close silence, with the engine-sound of the reef far away and subdued, broken by the small thud of his own sandalled footsteps on the corrupted deck.

He was glad to get down to the beach level again. But he continued to walk, like a lone visitor to a museum. He half expected to hear hollow echoes. He remembered quite oddly and for the first time in years, the massive whale which had once been exhibited in the fairground at Barry Island.

His father had always grumbled at paying to see the whale which he alleged was a clever imitation made of wood. It certainly seemed like that to the touch, like dry hard wood, but the fairground man had denied any fraud and claimed it was an extraordinary feat of preserving mammal flesh. They also had a foetus whale, about two feet long and looking very pale and unborn, which was supposed to have been found inside the big whale when they cut it open. Davies had always felt very sorry for this little innocent whale and until he was eight years old and had adjusted himself to things, he had great difficulty in stopping the tears on each occasion he viewed it.

Walking under the barges on the beach was like standing under the open-mouthed surprised expression of that exhibit whale of long ago. He almost felt its shadow on him, and knew once again the firm feel of his father's hand around his.

Some of the barges on the further reach of the strand had come ashore higher than the others. They had nudged into the sand only a few feet from the trees and with that insatiable curiosity of all tropical growth the plants had sent their tendrils to reconnoitre. These had insinuated themselves into, and wrapped themselves around, the dead hulk until they had, over the years, thickened into a cocoon of greenery and flowers, giving each little ship of war a decent burial.

'Why leave you then?' Davies asked aloud. 'Fancy not clearing away after them.' He felt as annoyed and hurt as if some old men had died in the park and nobody had bothered to do anything about them.

He continued walking about the invasion barges and had turned the corner of the last one when he came upon Bird walking out of the sea. It was early closing day at the salon and she had gone to swim while the rain was away.

She wore a black bikini and as she came out of the quilted lagoon her long hair was stuck to her neck and shoulders. She freed it with a careless feminine movement and then twisted it cruelly, like a wrestler twisting an opponent at his back, wringing the water from it and then shaking it out.

The action made Davies feel strangely embarrassed as though he should not have witnessed it. Bird did not see him until she started up the beach. She stopped, then walked again.

'Sorry,' said Davies, not knowing quite why he apologised. 'I was just looking at this little lot.'

'You came in on *The Baffin Bay*,' she said.

'Yes,' he agreed and then added as though it were some kind of naval protocol, 'Captain MacAndrews.'

She smiled, strode up the clean sand a few yards to where her bicycle was parked against a tree and took a towel from the handlebar basket. She rubbed herself down as though doing a dance. Arms, neck, legs, flat stomach. Davies stood uncomfortable again. He said : 'Well, I'll be going, then.'

'Please,' she said. 'Please wait. I will be only a few moments.'

'Oh, yes, of course,' he said. 'I thought . . . well, with you drying and that . . .'

'You've got a funny voice. Where is that from?'

'Wales,' he said. 'The one next to England. Not New South Wales.'

'This is called The Love Beach,' she said. 'It's a shame isn't it.'

'Why don't they do something about it? Get rid of all these?'

She shrugged : 'Why don't they do something about anything? I don't know. They don't that is all.'

44

She folded the wet towel professionally and replaced it in the basket. She had brought out a native parau, vivid flame and white flowers on the linen, and this she wrapped gracefully about her, tucking the final end into the earlier fold of the material that covered her small breasts. He fetched his bicycle from the landing barge and they walked and wheeled towards the path through the trees.

'How long have you been here then?' he asked.

'All my life. I was born on St Luke's, one of the little islands.'

'You have a funny voice too,' he said carefully.

'I know. I went to the French Convent for years. When I was young I spoke French and Pidgin much better than English. My parents were Australian and on St Luke's we only had natives on the plantation, so I grew up speaking like the natives. My father is dead now and my mother has gone to Sydney. My name is Bird.'

He laughed. 'Bird?' he said. 'Just like that.'

'Like that,' she said seriously. 'They all call me Bird. I've got other names but nobody ever uses them. I have a hairdressing salon.'

'I saw it,' said Davies triumphantly. 'Parisienne something, wasn't it? In the muddy street.'

'Parisienne Hair Style and Beauty Salon,' she recited proudly. 'The only place it is possible to get a perm for three hundred miles.'

'Business must be good then.'

She shrugged; 'I think it is,' she said. 'Why are you here?'

'I sell . . . well I'm trying to sell . . . My name's Davies.'

'What other names? Not just Davies.'

'Well mine are difficult too. Very Welsh mouthfuls. Isslwyn is one of them. People call you Issy then, and that sounds like a Jew doesn't it?'

'You could be a Jew,' she said seriously. 'You are dark and you have quite a big nose.' They had reached the path through

45

the close trees now and she mounted her cycle and went off first, swaying and winding with the muddy path.

'You wouldn't mind being a Jew would you?' she shouted over her shoulder. 'Would you?'

'No,' he lied. 'No, I wouldn't mind at all.'

She pedalled on. 'What do you sell?' she called. 'You did not finish.'

He was glad he had not made a joke about the Parisienne Hair Style and Beauty Salon, and its muddy street. 'I'm selling butter and fats,' he shouted.

'*What* and fats?' she called back. They were getting close to the village now. He could see the houses slit and split by the thinning trees.

'*Butter,*' he shouted. 'Butter and fats.' He wondered if she were laughing. She had moved forward over the handlebars, almost crouching, and he thought she might be. But then his machine stuttered over some stones and he thought she could have crouched because of them.

'Business good?'

'Not yet. I'm starting tomorrow. It poured down today, didn't it?'

'It will tomorrow too. You must not wait for the rain to end.'

They rode from the trees and into the village. A mass of natives on bicycles were advancing down the breadth of the thick road. A bus was at the stop and more natives were jumping, toppling, falling out like people abandoning a ship. Some wore shorts and shirts, some just shorts. Others were semi-uniformed in khaki drill, and one or two wore suits and bore funny brief-cases. Some boys were rowdy at a game of football beside the road and smoke was pushing up sinewy columns from the houses. Dogs yapped and children pounded their feet in the red mud.

'Rush hour,' sighed Bird. She had stopped her bicycle at the verge of the road. Davies rode up beside her and straddled his

46

machine. 'Every night,' the girl said. 'It gets like this. The roads are hopeless for the traffic.'

'Looks like it's all one-way. I never thought I'd see this here, mind,' said Davies. He had thought of Newport Bridge at five o'clock with the cars and the buses choking its throat and the muddy Usk gurgling below. The warehouses cowering and cold along the coal-coloured banks and the castle stuck like an old tooth between the road and the railway.

They started pedalling again, Bird going first. They rode close along one kerb, while the tide of bicycles went in the other direction. 'Surely they're not all from that village,' Davies said. 'There's hundreds.'

'Oh no,' she said. 'There are four more villages on this side of the island. They all work in 'Gesima.'

He had heard people all day naturally abbreviate the capital to 'Gesima. He supposed they could hardly call it anything else. To take the first two syllables would have been ridiculous. The girl had turned along a secondary track now, away from the road, and curving like a bow along by the sea again. She was very slim on the old heavy bicycle. Her feet were still bare and the gobs of mud that jumped from beneath the tyres had reddened her feet and spotted the lean backs of her legs.

There was a yawn of wind across the lagoon, as though the weather was tired after a hard working day. It stirred the sheeted water, now an evening grey but rouged in rounded areas with the diffuse reflection of the ballooning copper clouds still piled and climbing on the perimeter of the sky. In the shallows, mooring poles and net fixings projected from the skin of water and reeds paddled, some bending as though to examine their own feet in the mud. A pair of casual birds flapped low across the sheen, reflected and slightly distorted twenty feet below.

A great evening clearness had come across the island. It was as though the focus had been adjusted. Davies could see squared houses and other buildings on the other arm of land, beyond the lagoon, individual tall trees, and almost against the distant sea-line, the splendid shape of a motionless sailing ship. He could only tell it was a sailing ship and an old one too, by the shape of the hull, thick and bulky but tapering to an elegant bow. She had only one and a half standing masts, the smaller one behind like a thin boy following his thin father.

'Bird,' he said conscious of using the odd name for the first time, 'what is that? A schooner of some sort?' She stopped her bicycle on a lip of land overhanging a primitive jetty used by native fishermen. He stopped his machine, pulling it up awkwardly with his feet because the brakes were weak.

'A hulk,' she said unromantically. 'They use it for storing the copra, you know the coconut oil, until the collection every six months. Years ago, before my parents came to The Apostles, three of them were towed up here for that use. It is good, I believe, to keep copra stored where it can do no damage if it catches fire.'

'What happened to the others?'

'They are still in the islands. Being used the same. One is at St Mark's and the other at St Paul's. The natives store their copra in them.'

It was six now and some of the thickness had been pressed out of the day. A wandering wind strengthened from the sea and ushered away the depressed dampness. The two short people stood by the shore.

'Why do they call that beach The Love Beach?' asked Davies. 'Is it one of these ancient names?'

Bird shrugged. 'It goes back to . . . oh the old customs of the first population found here.'

She laughed then. 'They had some er . . . strange sort of rituals.' Then primly: 'Dancing and such things, you understand.'

'And that's where they had the dancing and such things.'

She still looked out to the sea as though seeking an arriving ship. She laughed again. Some dogs were still baying in the

48

village behind them but apart from that and the stirring of the water and the trees there was no other sound, but her laughing. 'At school,' she said, 'we used to learn all about the history of these islands and of all the South Pacific from Captain Cook's Journals. But it was a convent, you will remember, and the nuns did not like to read some of the things and would not let us read them. We lost half of history like that. But, of course, all the girls read the sections they were not supposed to know.

'There is a passage, a strange one, written by Captain Cook— . . . Young girls in groups of eight or ten, dancing a very indecent dance . . . singing the most indecent songs and using the most indecent actions in the practice of which they are brought up from the earliest childhood. In doing this they keep time to a great nicety.' She turned to Davies. 'Do you like that?'

He was laughing. 'That's very good,' he said. 'Keeping time to a great nicety!'

'One day,' she said, 'you must watch the dancing on the beach. Then you may understand Captain Cook.'

Davies went to his room at the South Seas Hilton, climbing the steaming stairs, and finding the room laden with heat despite the arrival of evening in the street. He took his paints from his suitcase. They were in an old rugby sock, oils in little tubes. The children had bought a beginner's set for him for his last Christmas at home. He liked to think he could paint, but anyone could have told him that he couldn't. He had been to Art for Pleasure classes at Newport Technical College and he had carried his brushes, his paints and his canvases to the Southern Pacific. After all Gauguin had sailed there unrecognised. Davies thought he would like to paint The Love Beach if all those grotesque invasion barges were not littered there. Perhaps some girls doing that dance on The Love Beach and keeping time to a nicety.

Meeting the girl had stimulated him, not sexually really, but in some way. She had talked to him and accepted a bicycle ride alongside him and had pointed out some of the bits of the

49

island. She was young and small and he felt more comfortable with small people. He hated to have to look up at a woman. Once he had asked a seated girl to dance at a Community Centre Social at Coogee, near Sydney and she had looked at him quizzically from her chair as though questioning his daring. He asked again. She nodded and uncoiled from the chair, going up and up like a snake from a charmer's basket, until she hung like a threat over him. He had been trawled around for a humiliating three minutes, begging God that the musicians would stop, and finally falling from her near the exit into which he bolted as soon as the tune had ceased.

Ten months now he had been away. He wrote to Kate twice a week doing little sketches for David and Mag at the foot of the letters, pictures of ships and bridges on the voyage, and later a kangaroo and an aboriginal, although he had never seen either. Kate's answers would sometimes take a month, but then he might get three short letters in a week apologising for not writing, saying the children had been sick or the weather had been cold. As soon as he got really settled, perhaps if he managed to make a really successful thing of the Apostle Group sales idea, they would come to him in Australia. That was certain. In every letter he said it. On Sundays in Sydney he had gone the rounds of the estate agents' windows to see what they were offering once he had saved enough for a deposit.

He lay on the bed, feeling its natural dampness at his back. There was a gekko near the ceiling probing for a fly, and another petrified a few inches away, like tiny dinosaurs. They were part of the hotel service, cold running gekkos in every room, two or three little lizards to each ceiling to eat the flies, and insects, or some of them anyway. His old toffee-coloured suitcase with its stout belt around its waist was on the stone floor in the corner, flat, with his paints and brushes spread out on its lid. It was a stiff, practical, provincial suitcase, and there was a railway sticker on its flank, prosaic black and dirty white which said 'High Street, Newport'.

That last day at home, the Monday after they had been to Barry Island on the Sunday, he had stood choked with sadness in their bedroom when he had gone to collect his case. He had looked out of the small-paned window across the red and black tiles of the familiar roofs, to the sauntering smoke from the engine sheds and beyond that the winter grey-green of the park. He looked for the final time into the wardrobe although he knew he had nothing left there. Something made him glance down and in one of Kate's shoes he saw the yellow cylinder end of a roll of film. They had taken some photographs of the children in the park in the late summer and they had not been developed. Taken suddenly with the idea he thought he would take the film with him, to Sydney, and then surprise them by sending the film back. He smiled, picked up the roll of film and put it in his pocket.

IV

Because the Highways Department had not been able to find resources to extend the St Peter's Island road as far as British Government House (although it went neatly past the front door of the French Residence), and because it was considered unbecoming that Sir William should have to take to foot or bicycle, the Governor always made the journey from his home to the town by launch.

Government House was on a point of wet green land extending into the lagoon and sheltering the harbour. A small, dignified landing stage had been constructed below the voluptuous garden and distant Whitehall had provided an equally small, dignified pinnace to take Sir William on his journeys. It was manned by a Melanesian crew who wore white bellbottoms, matelot jackets and the squared hats of Nelson's sailors. They handled the launch very well and the British were proud of them. 'It gives the population some sense of pride in our armed forces,' Phillip Cooper, the Governor's liquid A.D.C., used to say.

Conway was waiting on the town landing stage for the launch to pick him up. He was glad the storms had moved away. The rain in The Apostles was warmer than in Sydney, but he harboured an un-Australian feeling that rain ought to be cool if not cold. For his meeting with the Governor he had put on a dark, lightweight suit, ill-fitting, that in the humidity seemed to be gathering itself up and crawling into his armpits and into the cleft between his legs. He wriggled and flapped his arms impotently as though to shake the thing away, but after a minor retreat, it advanced again into its former bridgeheads.

Conway had a plastic brief-case under his arm and his hair crisply parted. He had shaved twice that day. He felt altogether uncomfortable. The launch parted the flat cloth of water in the lagoon, throwing up a short, tired bow wave, pushing a chevron of ripples out to either side. The sailors from South Hibernia Island far south of The Apostles, their black faces fixed with a picturesque patriotism, turned the nose at the exact inch. Although they had never voyaged their craft anywhere else at all, not even in a different direction across the harbour or the lagoon, they knew the five hundred yard trip intimately, the helmsman touching the wheel to port immediately the fuzzy head of the petrified bosun blotted out the vivid yellow blind of the Kai Tek Chinese Fish Shop on the distant waterfront.

They came in like some small working shuttle of a big machine, slotting into place at the jetty. The bosun saluted and the sailors bounced to attention in the pinnace. Conway was about to throw up a smart hand in acknowledgement when he remembered he was not in uniform, so the military movement became a lame raising of an apologetically crooked finger. He sat on the corded cushioned seat, his brief-case uncomfortably upright on his knees. He felt embarrassed about anything formal, even anything as formal as a brief-case or a suit. He pulled the nosing trousers away from his crutch again like a man impatient with an inquisitive dog. The boat moved away, the helmsman watching for the red roof of Mrs Flagg's cottage, the point where he could persuade the craft to starboard and make straight for the Governor's landing jetty.

Phillip Cooper waited there, stiffly, conveying his chief's annoyance, he hoped, at this abrupt, unannounced, visit by an Australian on an official mission. From his seat in the launch Conway thought the young man looked like a wireworm in white.

'Afternoon,' said Conway formally affable as the boat lost

movement and touched the poles of the Governor's jetty. Observing the rigid expression on Cooper's face he was tempted to add an exaggerated Australian 'mate' to the greeting. But he desisted.

'Good afternoon,' returned the A.D.C. His mouth became only a tiny hole when he spoke and his eyes raised themselves a little. Conway was sorry he had not called him 'mate', but he made up for it by pretending that he had difficulty in getting out of the launch. He extended a begging hand towards Cooper, waggling it for assistance. Involuntarily the young English official moved forward with his hand to help, then stopped, shocked and annoyed with himself and impatiently motioned one of the black sailors to help Conway from the boat.

'Us Colonials,' grinned Conway towards the wooden Melanesian. He stood firmly on the landing stage. Cooper sniffed. In England, Conway thought, the youth obviously suffered from sinus and sore, wet nostrils. He gave Cooper's hand a hard Australian squeeze and noted the wince that jumped into the unsteady blue eyes.

They turned up the path towards Government House. The rain had excited all the crowded plants making them throw their deepest, dampest, scents. Great clouds, hills and hummocks of tropical flowers thick and brilliant, congealed about the path. Silver stems of water ran from the higher trees.

'Pretty little garden,' observed Conway.

'The Governor is *very* busy,' sniffed Cooper. He walked very upright, staring straight ahead, moving at almost a marching pace, but, with instinct it seemed, cutting around any streams of rainwater descending from the trees.

'I'm sure he is,' said Conway, matching the youth's marching. 'There must be a lot to keep him going around here.'

Cooper did a quick right-face, like a guardsman going by a saluting base. Conway smiled encouragingly. Cooper faced the front again. The Australian wondered whether there was a secret place in England, the sort of stud farm the Nazis used to have for producing their master race, where long, urine-coloured, young men were spawned and fostered for the British Colonial Service. He had to admit that Cooper had a certain power. Even over him. He was now carrying his plastic brief-case sideways up, hiding it around his backside and wishing it were leather.

Government House came into view suddenly, wide windows, minor colonnade, spectacularly white in the repentant sun; its lawns the most startling green, the Union Jack hanging thick and limp from the summit of the flag mast set in the garden.

Cooper glanced at the flagging standard. He sniffed and surprised Conway by saying conversationally: 'This rainy season is such a damned nuisance, you know. It *really* is. Soaks the flag through half a dozen times a day. It's so wet it won't *flutter*. And then the damned sun comes out and dries it and then it gets soaked again.' He sounded like a housewife complaining about the Monday wash. Conway glanced at him.

'Rotten,' asserted Cooper. 'Completely *rotten*. We've used four Union Jacks up since the season started.'

'Problems, problems,' blinked Conway. He could think of nothing else. They walked almost to the door. Conway thought of something. He said: 'How do the French manage about the Tricolour? That gets wet too, doesn't it?'

'That's the damned trouble,' retorted Cooper. '*They* have as many flags as they need. They could wear a different one every day if they wished. We get six for the whole year. Typical, of course. Simply typical. The Governor's in his study. This way.'

Conway followed him to the door. 'Mr Conway, Your Excellency,' he heard Cooper say, and a voice reply 'Good, good,' from within.

The Australian was surprised at the huge emptiness of the room. Sir William, slightly stooping and sharp-faced, walked a great brown carpet at its centre looking like a cage bird pacing its captivity. The Governor glanced up abruptly and muttered 'Come on in' then continued his walk. Conway ventured to the fringe of the carpet. He felt like a man standing at the edge of a field. Cooper sniffed and bowed his way out. Conway hid his plastic brief-case behind his back.

'We're busy, Mr Conway,' said Sir William suddenly advancing on him and thrusting out his hand like a threatening sword. 'We've got a special visitor coming to The Apostles. A very special visitor.'

The Governor waited for Conway to ask who the visitor was, but he didn't. 'Sit down. Have something, will you?' said Sir William.

'Thank you.'

Sir William pulled an old-fashioned bell rope. There was a profound silence. Conway strained his ears and saw that the Governor was doing the same, his hawkish head turned on its side. They caught each other's eye.

'Never know whether the blamed thing rings the other end,' confessed Sir William. 'Sometimes it does. Sometimes not. It depends a lot on the humidity.'

Nothing happened. They sat uncomfortably. 'Damn it, I'll get them myself. Otherwise I go blaring about the place and it doesn't do to lose your temper in front of these people, you know. What is it?'

'A beer,' replied Conway.

'Good God.'

'Do you have beer?'

'Yes, yes, my dear chap. Beer, of course. I give it to the dogs sometimes because every now and again the water gets contaminated. Beer! Oh yes, we have beer.'

He found the bottle and attempted to open it, making such a panic of the operation and making several darts towards the bell-pull, that eventually Conway stood up, took the bottle and opened it himself.

Sir William laughed. 'Easy!' he exclaimed. 'Just shows you there's an art in everything.' He had delivered undiluted whisky into his own glass. They sat down again, Sir William behind his desk. 'Heard a man at a reception some time ago asking for a whisky and *coke*. Civilisation's going to pieces.'

They raised their glasses, Sir William gazing apprehensively at the pale column held by Conway. He shrugged resignedly and they drank. 'Now,' said the Governor. 'What the hell have you come here about?'

'St Paul's,' said Conway.

'What about it? It's still there. Out to sea. First island on the left.'

'The Australian Government, or more accurately, the Australian War Department, want to try something out on St Paul's.'

Sir William looked over the top of his glass like a sniper. 'Australian War Department,' he said slowly and suspiciously. 'I don't like the sound of that.'

'An experiment,' said Conway uncomfortably. He was surprised to find his self-confidence, his exterior, evaporating before the old man. 'They want—well, to be honest, *we* want, because I'm in this as well—to get the natives over there to help in a sort of public relations exercise.'

'Public relations?' whispered Sir William as though madness were near. 'Public relations? Good Christ, what will they think of next, my dear boy, those tribesmen on St Paul's only know one sort of relations and they've only just finished the habit of eating them. Sometimes I suspect they still do it.'

Conway grinned with discomfort. 'I know there will be difficulties, sir. Our Trusteeship people . . .'

'Trusteeship!' suddenly bellowed Sir William. 'Don't let the Australian Government send anyone here to The Apostles talking about their Trusteeship. They've done damn all for St Paul's Island since they've had it. Sent some bloody fool to look at the natives teeth or their testicles or something about a year ago, and that's been the sum of it. So don't come here preaching . . .'

'*We want the natives for Vietnam,*' said Conway with quick bravery.

He thought Sir William was going to tip over the back of his big chair. The old man's eyes sagged, then his face, then his entire head. He rallied himself and leaned forward shakily on the desk.

'Where?'

'Vietnam,' said Conway. Then lamely: 'You know . . . the war . . .'

Sir William's voice became flat. Only his face showed his tremblings. 'What will they do there? Fire napalm arrows?'

'Jungle trackers,' announced Conway. 'Auxiliaries for the Australian forces.'

A mad laugh flew from the old man. 'Jungle trackers! Tarzan of the Apes. Whoooooooooooo . . . ooooooo . . . ooooo.' He jumped up and began to beat his breast. Just as abruptly he sat down and thrust a stony face on Conway. 'Out of your heads, all of you,' he muttered.

Conway said: 'The British used Dyaks in Malaya.' The old man's face seemed to expand, then contract. 'Hannibal used elephants in the Alps,' he retorted. 'But that doesn't make the poor devils on St Paul's ripe for Vietnam. Mad, you're positively mad. Have you been over there? Have you seen them?'

'Not yet,' said Conway. He felt better when Sir William shouted. 'I'm going over in a day or so.'

Sir William leaned forward. 'They've never heard of China, let alone Vietnam. Take them away and they die. They're infants, savages.'

Conway said: 'The Trusteeship people said that they are a Christian Community. They were the first tribe to be converted in these islands . . .'

'They're probably more Christian than your Trusteeship idiots. I'll grant you that . . .' He waited, got up and looked out of the window. The lagoon was luxurious with evening colours, purple, reds, deep blues. The palms on the shore-line were silhouettes, black feathers against the dulled sky, small lights were showing in the town and Mr Livesley's neon sign seared out the word 'Bread' in three alternating colours.

Sir William, his back still to Conway, shrugged to himself. 'Christians!' he laughed quietly. 'And so that qualifies them to fight a war.' Wearily he turned to the Australian. 'Mr Conway, these people believe that their island is the *world*, you know, the whole world. They believe that nothing of importance ever happens outside it, or has ever happened. They hardly acknowledge that we exist. Christians? If you like, but very odd Christians, I can tell you.'

'Odd?' asked Conway.

'Very. You see, you don't know. These people believe that the whole Bible story happened right there on their island. They will show you Jerusalem and Bethlehem, and Calvary, and Noah's Ark jammed on Mount Ararat. It's all there *now*. They won't be shaken from that. And, on top of it all, they're awaiting the arrival of a special sort of Messiah, a prophet called Dodson-Smith who will bring to them all the luxuries of life which they do not enjoy now. Mr Conway, listen to this, please. *They believe that he is going to arrive by motor cycle . . .*'

He thrust his glare towards Conway pleading for comprehension. 'How could you attempt to throw such children into a battle they could never understand. It's difficult enough for the rest of us.'

Conway looked carefully at the seam along his brief-case. 'They have a cargo cult, have they? Well the Trusteeship people didn't say anything about that.' He was feeling better, more assured again. He looked firmly at Sir William. 'Cargo cults are common enough, of course, in Borneo and New Guinea.' He grinned. 'One lot are saving their money for the arrival of a re-incarnated President Kennedy.'

Sir William said sadly: 'Well if you know about them, you obviously know how completely impractical, not to mention

59

inhuman, any sort of upheaval would be to them. How would you expect . . .'

'The Dyaks were very good in Malaya,' interrupted Conway. 'The British used to let them take the heads of the Communists, you know.'

'A lie,' said Sir William angrily. Then, dropping his tone: 'It's almost certain to be a lie. Anyway, damn it, the Dyaks are jungle people, marvellous trackers. St Paul's is an island . . .'

Conway had done his homework. 'It's a big island,' he said. 'Thirty miles long. Thick primary jungle over a large area, eighty per cent, swamp, and steep hill country.'

'Vietnam,' argued Sir William, 'isn't thirty miles long. What the hell is the sense?' He paused and became quickly upright and formal. 'I want to hear all this *officially* before I listen to you for another instant,' he said.

Conway shrugged. 'Sir William, I bear full authority from the Australian Government. My credentials, my letters, are all intact, and here for you to inspect. You will be getting further correspondence, more information. But I'm here to get this thing rolling and that's what I'm going to do.'

He handed a fold of letters across to the Governor, taking them from his plastic brief-case, about which he no longer felt ashamed. Sir William unwillingly took the papers and went towards the window where he stood stooped against the final light of the day. Conway could see the 'Bread' neon sign regularly hitting the water of the lagoon. There seemed to be a small wind loping through the garden. Sir William was several minutes. He returned to Conway and handed the letters to him.

Sir William said: 'The games we play in this life. I don't know who thinks up such twaddle.' His voice was quiet, without his previous anger. He looked at Conway. 'They'll die,' he said. 'They'll most surely die. Then where will your precious stunt be?' Putting the papers back untidily into the brief-case Conway looked at the Governor. 'Stunt, I admit, sir, is the word,' he said. 'But because it's a stunt, a public relations campaign if you like, there is a good chance—more than that, a very good chance—that the St Paul's boys will never get any further than dear old Aussie. It will be a free trip for them, just a chance to look around . . .'

'Australia,' said Sir William gloomily, 'would probably frighten them a good deal more than Vietnam.'

Conway swallowed. 'Well, anyway, we're going to do it. Some way or another. If we can get about a dozen or so of them to Sydney, doll them up in uniforms, and say they are going to join the Australian forces in Vietnam, that's probably as far as we'll want to go. I'm not certain, but it's my guess.'

'What,' asked Sir William, 'is the object of the whole business? If they are not going to the war, why take them at all?'

'Promotion, public relations, the image, all that sort of dazzle,' said Conway. Then he added: 'But this is between you and me, Sir William. Outside this room the St Paul's natives are being recruited as trackers for Vietnam.' He got up and walked a few paces on the brown carpet. 'People these days, *need* something new, something to stimulate them.'

'Not the St Paul's people,' said Sir William.

Conway stopped and looked up sharply. 'Not them,' he said. 'The Australians I'm thinking about. Even sending soldiers to war has to be dressed up in a package these days. People don't like it. We like to let people know—*everybody*, all the people in the world—the contribution we, the Australians, are making in Vietnam. Too often we get overshadowed, forgotten, because we only have a small force out there. This will give us some good exposure.'

'Package! Exposure! Your picture in the papers! Just for this you would injure or destroy a primitive people?' Sir William walked towards the door, dejectedly, slowly.

'No one is going to be injured or destroyed,' said Conway.

'Have you been to Vietnam, Mr Conway?'

'Yes. I was invalided home. They gave me a job in Military Public Relations.'

'Thinking up nightmares.'

Conway did not answer. Sir William was waiting for him to go. He walked from the big room. A servant went like a shadow through the entrance hall, but no one else was about. Sir William said: 'I shall be in touch with your government and attempt to stop this nonsense.'

Conway said: 'In the meantime I ought to make some sort of reconnoitre trip over to St Paul's. Goodnight, Sir William.'

'Goodnight,' said Sir William. 'I hope they eat you.'

V

The Assembly Building of the Apostle Islands, the official meeting place of both the Anglo-French Condominium and the local government council, was Chungking Chinese in style, with elegant oriental curls to its many roofs, overlaid upon each other like multiple skirts. It was exquisitely festooned with golden dragons and fiery red dogs. Its exterior walls were whorled and worked with coloured patterns, its windows willow tree screens and its front door powerful with immense posts and lintels like the entrance to a modest temple. Above the door were deeply engraved Mandarin characters.

'This is the Dream House of Foo' translated Pollet for Davies and Conway. The Belgian had been in the outer island villages for two days selling medicines and collecting antiques, and, on returning to the South Seas Hilton, he had suggested they should go to the special assembly called by the British Governor.

'A great big embarrassment for both the British and the French,' he continued as they walked with the crowd in the evening. 'But it's the only building, apart from maybe a warehouse, that is okay, big enough, you get it, for a meeting like this. Ah, the Condominium pretends the térrible thing isn't here. One meeting in the house of the British Governor and the next at the French Governor's place. That's how they work it. The town council—well, they get together wherever they can. The British Legion club usually. This place is only used for big meetings, although maybe if a big epic film arrives on the boat and everyone is mad to see it they put it on here. Like *Ben Hur.*'

'Who was Foo?' Davies asked.

'An architect from Chungking,' said Pollet. 'Before the war he came here and said he would build this place very cheap, you understand, for the Condominium. He wanted to try out a new plan for a building in his home town and maybe he was not sure whether it would fall down. So he came here and he built this like, as a model. Of course the British and the French Colonial offices, tight with the money, shouted joyfully to have something for nearly nothing. They needed a meeting building and this Chinese thing is what they got.'

Pollet giggled. 'Tonight I think you watch Sir William and M. Etienne. When they are here they pretend they are somewhere else. They do not see what is around them. It is the only matter upon which they have some accord. You see, they will stare straight ahead, pretending not to notice all those fire monsters hanging from the ceiling nor the scenes from everyday life in Chungking on the walls. Ha! They are both very ashamed.'

Within the building the crowd was pushed together in a thick stream and directed at a dark shuffle down a low, carved corridor and then up a gilded staircase to a balcony curved and shaped in the manner of a Peking Palace swan. Attendants pointed out places. Pollet led Davies and Conway to three seats in the second row back, clear of the view blockage caused by the thick base of the swan's neck. Around them the seats were all being taken, women wearing hats and feathers and men hot in European suits.

'Foo forgot the air conditioning,' said Conway. 'It's going to be close as hell in here before long.'

'Stinking,' admitted Pollet. 'Always it is like this. I saw an epic film here—*Quo Vadis* I remember, very good too—and every twenty minutes they had to open all the doors and the attendants came around with huge feather fans and swept

64

them about above the patrons' heads. Maybe they do that tonight.'

Davies looked over into the main well of the big room. The dais at one end was clear, but the rows of seats below were all occupied. He saw Bird wearing a sweet blue dress at the end of the third row talking to a woman with red hair.

Pollet said: 'The girl is called Bird. That is all the name she has, so they say. Just Bird. She has a coiffure establishment in the town.'

Davies said: 'Yes, I know her. Met her on the beach. Down by the old invasion barges.'

Conway and Pollet looked at Davies. But he was searching further over into the hall. 'Looking for prospective customers,' he said, still leaning. Then, in a mock shout: 'Anyone want fresh butter and fats.'

'The woman with the rusted hair, next to your friend Bird, is called Mrs Flagg,' informed Pollet. 'Her husband is next to her—the other side. A very unorthodox type of English they are. They have much interest in the natives of St Mark's, the tribesmen who wrap the penis in banana leaves.'

'Jesus,' said Davies. 'Is that what they do? Banana leaves, eh?' Conway said: 'And Mrs Flagg is interested in this er . . . habit?'

Pollet said: 'Fascinated by it.'

'And Mr Flagg?' asked Conway.

'He likes it too.'

Davies leaned back and said to Pollet: 'Who else do you know?'

'Most people,' answered the Belgian. 'I have been skitting around here many years. There is Mr Turtle. He is the man who runs the radio station. He goes for only an hour a day so he is not very busy. He is a Vigilante—how do you put it—he is the leader of the Ratepayers. He wants to put parking meters in the middle of Sexagesima. His wife cries a lot. She is next to him. See how red-eyed. She has been crying quite recently.'

Pollet frowned at the tops of the people's heads just below them. 'The man perspiring in the hairy sports coat is called Mr Hassey. Thirty years ago or more he came here for two weeks to ascertain the natives, which is his expression.'

'Next to him is Mr Livesley who is so proud because he has that neon sign above his baker's shop. It is the only sign for hundreds of miles, and I think perhaps the only one in the world that says "Bread" in three lovely colours, always changing. He sent a photograph of it to the Pacific Islands Monthly.'

The Belgian looked along the rows below him. The building was noisy with conversation and the shuffling of chairs. The seats were all filled by now and the late-comers were standing around the walls completely blocking the scenes of everyday life in Chungking.

'Ascertain some more natives for us, will you?' requested Conway.

Pollet smiled : 'Ah yes,' he agreed. 'This is probably the meaning of Mr Hassey. Well, Mr Kendrick is there, by Mr Hassey and Mr Livesley, his friends. He has the bicycle shop. People do not know it here in the islands, but a few years ago, about five, in Sydney, he was convicted by magistrates of squeezing a lemon in a prostitute's eye at King's Cross. I was in the city myself at the time and I read it in the newspaper. A most strange man.

'Colin Collins, the Reverend Colin Collins, an American missionary. He is down there. From a very minor religious group. He is their only missionary and they sent him here. He is a very good man as far as his church operations are concerned. Excellent. He has a Polynesian wife—from Tahiti, I think and she allows him to sleep with her and her five sisters all together in the same night. I understand that they have lashed two beds together for this purpose. But he told me one day that he prefers Japanese women.'

The building was now uncomfortably full. There was something different about the people, Davies thought. He searched for the reason, looking about him, watching faces and eyes, listening to sentences or half sentences, hearing people laugh or cough mildly, looking at their clothes. Then he realised that they were two generations short, that something of the movement of life had not yet reached this place. They reminded him of the grown-ups he had known in South Wales when he was a child before the war. He wondered if living in this corner had done this to them or whether they had come to the islands because they were this sort of people anyway. Had they come here to hide away?

One of the ornamental Chinese doors, to the right of the hall, opened with a creak like a falling tree, and a small, bald-headed man in a voluminous kilt, strode in, followed by a line of ten other men and four women.

'Mr Rob Roy English,' whispered Pollet. 'Chairman of the town council. And the others—they are the council.'

Davies said : 'Why the kilt?'

Pollet shrugged : 'He is proud. Nothing helps nationalism like exile, my friend. And, so I believe, he has never recovered from having that unfortunate family name. His father tried to compensate with the Christian names, but it is not the same. I can understand that.'

The councillors sat on the back row of chairs on the dais, Mr English pulling his kilt modestly over his small knees. The heavy sporran hung between his short legs like a horse's feeding bag. One of the Chinese lanterns caught the dirk handle in his stocking with silver light. Davies looked along the line of the council. They were mostly ill-at-ease, some arrayed in suits, some in open-necked shirts and grey flannels, including one of the women in khaki drill, and one in a tropical dinner jacket with white tie.

A man in uniform appeared at the flanking door and in marched six men in suits who took their seats three each side of the two central chairs.

'The Condominium,' whispered Pollet. 'Three and three. Very strong enemies.'

'Pray rise for His Excellency M. Etienne Martin, French Governor-General!' shouted the officer at the door. Half the people rose to their feet.

'The French,' whispered Pollet to Davies and then, turning to Conway repeated the identification.

'Pray rise for His Excellency Sir William Findlay-Stayers, British Governor-General.' The other half of the people stood up.

'The British,' said Pollet unnecessarily.

Everyone sat down. Davies thought Sir William gave a quick glance at the Chinese hangings and appendages above and around him, and a shudder flew across his face. The first of the six Condominium men, one of the British three, stood, and said: 'Sir William Findlay-Stayers, the British Governor-General, will make a statement.'

At the other extreme of the sextet a moustached man stood: 'Sir William Findlay-Stayers, le Gouverneur-General Britannique va faire un exposé.'

Pollet sighed: 'All the way through they will do this. Everything has to be translated or the other partner becomes offended. But almost every person in these islands speaks French and English very well.'

Sir William stood. He bowed with obvious enjoyment to his French opposite. 'Your Excellency, Members of the Condominium, ladies and gentlemen . . .' he began.

The French interpreter was immediately on his feet: 'Votre Excellence, Membres du Condominium, mesdames et messieurs . . .'

The British Governor looked at the man sourly. '. . . fellow islanders . . .' Sir William continued.

'. . . concitoyens de nos îles . . .' said the interpreter.

Sir William made a quince face. Then like a single, sour, cavalryman charging a platoon. burst through his momentous

68

message at a gallop, unpausing at the conclusion of a sentence and allowing the shallowest intake of breath at the end of a paragraph. He told them, at 250 words a minute, that Her Majesty the Queen would be visiting the Apostle Islands in six weeks' time. He completed the statement in one minute fifty-three seconds, whirled about to enjoy the outraged looks of the speechless French interpreter and the entire French echelon, and sat down breathlessly to wild and delighted applause from the British colony.

M. Martin raised a shadow of an eyebrow in the direction of the interpreter who, having shrugged, stood, and gave an ill-tempered delivery of the statement in French from a prepared text handed to him by a disdainfully smiling Phillip Cooper. Again the British cheered and some of the French people clapped politely.

Then, nothing happened. A silence swirled around the Chinese hall. No one seemed to know whether they should go away or stay. Sir William looked calmly ahead towards the carved swan, but not as far as it. The French Governor made a minute examination of the creases in his trousers and then turned attention to his shoes as though suspecting that they were odd. Eventually Mr Rob Roy English rose and moved forward, his kilt heavy about his hips, his sporran shaggily swaying.

'Your Excellencies,' he began, glaring towards the two Governors and then throwing his face dramatically back towards the audience again. 'Since no one has thought to establish a chairman for this gathering, and since it is imperative that someone says something or everyone will just go away, I would like to take the liberty of saying that something.'

There was a scattering of understanding applause. Mr English spoke in a wide Scots accent, rasping then guttural, then winging away on a sweet syllable, before descending into another croaking note like an engine after the changing of a gear.

'How long has he been here?' whispered Davies. Pollet

shrugged: 'Twenty-five, thirty years, I suppose. A long time anyway. He nurtures his accent, my friend, by listening to special long-playing records he has sent from Edinburgh.'

Both Sir William and M. Martin nodded relieved encouragement at Mr English. The kilted chairman of the council acknowledged their support. Then he said: 'We will be forming committees, of course, to make detailed plans for Her Majesty's visit. There are many things we must do . . .'

'Decorate the streets! Decorate the streets!' exclaimed George Turtle's quiet wife Minnie excitedly. Her husband whirled to her in astonishment, as though she had suddenly been struck with a fit. Other people looked and pointed at her.

'Decorate the streets,' repeated Mr English politely. 'What a good idea. Now who would have thought of that?' A ripe plum colour had gathered on Mrs Turtle's face. People were still stretching around their neighbours to see her.

With a borrowed feminine movement Mr English smoothed down the pleats of his kilt. 'There will be committees formed,' he said smugly returning to his theme. 'But we *must* get moving. There is not much time before Her Majesty—a bonnie Scots lass of course—arrives.' The chairman allowed a proud smile to work across his little face. Then his expression fell with seriousness. 'But,' he warned, 'one thing *must* be decided even earlier than anything else.' He stopped, his body remaining dramatically still and his head moving fore and back with a regulated clockwork nod. 'Yes,' he repeated, pleased with the suspended silence and the bated looks of all the people from the twin governors down. 'There is *one* thing.'

'What is it?' It was Mrs Turtle once more bouncing in her seat. George swung on her again, gaping at her public boldness, examining her face closely as though seeking a twitch of drunkenness, some symptom of malady. She smiled timidly at her husband and wrung her fingers.

From Mr English came a bleak Highland smile. 'I was just going to tell you,' he said. 'When you interrupted. Where was

I? . . . oh, yes, one thing we *must* do.' He looked about him as though ready to repel another interruption. Then he scurried on : 'We must arrange for The Queen to *open* something. We must have a wee something that she can unveil or name, or at least there must be a foundation stone she can lay. Anything would do.' He looked threateningly at Mrs Turtle. 'Don't ask me what,' he warned. 'Because I dinna' know.' He stared about him, his face up, travelling around like a searchlight to every part of the assembly. 'I ken we could do with a new building to replace this one,' he said. 'But we hardly have time to get that going in six weeks. But there must be *something*. We canna' allow her to be awa' without some permanent memento of the occasion.'

The chairman sat down. The silence came back like something on a string. Nobody moved. Half the audience pretended it was thinking, others fidgeted and looked towards the doors. Davies and Conway looked inwards at Pollet who shrugged as if to say it was nothing to do with him.

When the vacuum had become so thick that it seemed it would explode, the Chinese doors were flung open and the two governors, the members of the Condominium and their staffs, started up and thankfully marched out. At the door, Sir William half turned towards the seated Mr English and said in a shouted whisper. 'We'll get her to plant a tree. She's used to doing that.'

'Plant a tree!' hooted Mr English, displayed, kilt astride, in one of the toffee-coloured wicker chairs at the Sexagesima Hilton bar. Then, in a reduced voice, a groan : 'Plant a tree.'

Davies said : 'Well, it's easy, I suppose. I mean you won't have any difficulty in getting a tree, will you?'

'A Welshman,' stated Mr English tilting his small, pointed face, as though explaining the inanity of the statement.

Men, all men, no women, were wedged in the bar following the Governor's meeting. They filled the walls, crammed the chairs and tables and hung sweating across the bar while Seamus worked on the drinks. The place was stuffed with heat, night heat so oppressive that even the two senile electric fans moving on the ceiling felt its weight and slowed in their turns.

'Yes, I'm a Welshman,' admitted Davies. 'Davies.'

Mr English sniffed with apparent suspicion. 'At least ye've got a Welsh name,' he said. 'Ye're not doomed with a handle like "English". D'ye no' think that's a terriba' thing?' Davies noticed that, when he took thought, he plunged into deeper Scots vowels and consonants.

'I don't think it matters does it? Especially out here,' shrugged Davies. 'We're miles from Wales or Scotland.'

Mr English looked as though he considered springing out of the chair. 'But that's the point, laddie!' he howled. 'Miles away. But we ken them don' we. We sing about them. Think about them. Aye, even here.' He was getting a bit thick and drunk. He changed his posture in the chair, pedantically rearranged the kilt, and glared into his glass. 'Plant a tree,' he said. 'No, Davies, there's no great trouble in getting trees, as you so well point out. The one thing we've got in plenty on this bloody island is trees. So when the Queen comes we get her to plant another. Ho! Plant a tree!'

Rain began coming down on the windows and walls of the bar, playing at first but then so violent that the men's voices had to be raised above it. English turned his head to the sound. 'We might as well get the lass to inaugurate a rain-making machine. That *would* be useful, Mr Davies.'

Hassey had been standing to the right of the councillor's chair, his live old eyes fixed on the far wall where two teams were clumsily playing darts. With a disjointed, almost a robot movement, as though he had been awaiting a cue, he turned on Davies and thrust out a hand that seemed to Davies to be all bones. 'Hassey,' he introduced himself. 'Came out here thirty-

72

eight years ago. Just to ascertain the fucking natives, old boy. Still here.'

Hassey looked around and down at English mooning lower in the chair, his drink still held out in front of him like some suspect specimen. Carefully, like an analytical chemist, he tipped a thread of whisky over the side of the glass and watched its yellow contact with the coconut matting.

'I'm still here, too,' English said to Hassey without looking up from the floor. 'We all are. Every one of us.'

Davies took a quick drink of his beer. Hassey said steadily : 'Better than a tree-planting I thought we might get Her Majesty to perform a launching ceremony. I always think they're damned impressive. Whoosh, down the slipway, flags and bands and everybody cheers like hell. Very good for the workers too, I always feel, even those Communist devils in the shipbuilding yards. They may have their strikes and their sabotage, but when it comes to the launching and the ruddy bottle breaks, they all cheer with the rest. I suppose it shows that under the skin and all that . . .'

'Shut up, Hassey,' said English sourly. 'For God's sake man, I suppose ye ken that we neither have a ship to launch nor a place we could even build a ship to be launched, even supposing we had six years instead of six weeks. Talk sense, will ye?'

'Ah,' said Hassey cleverly. 'I'd thought of that. The Governor's pinnace is only a few months old, hardly got its bottom wet. If we could get it out of the water, hoist it up on a slipway, give it a lick of paint and a bit of spit and polish, then the Queen could launch it, couldn't she?'

English seemed to consider this. Then, bitterly, he said. 'No she couldn't. Everyone would know it wasn't a new boat, ye damned fool.'

'But,' argued Hassey, 'only the people *here* know. None of the visitors would know. The Queen wouldn't, for a start. Everyone would have to keep mum about it . . .'

'It's cheating,' said English firmly swigging off the last of his scotch. He stared at Hassey who obediently took the glass from him and went towards the bar. 'Native of Northamptonshire,' English said to Davies nodding his head at Hassey. 'Launch a boat! Ha! Old Livesley is putting it around that the Queen should inaugurate his measly neon sign, that "Bread" monstrosity. Says it's encouraging local industry.'

Hassey returned with the chairman's glass. English grunted low and tasted it, stared into the amber, and resettled himself in the chair. He looked at Davies seriously. 'The trouble wi' a place o' this nature,' he said, once more deeply Highland, 'is that the longer ye stay the more ye lose ye bearings. There's wee lunacies planted in the mind by islands and places like this. Ye suffer some awfa' imaginings, ye ha' strange bogy ideas. An' yet here ye are, stuck in the middle of an ocean, and here, as sure as God, is where ye'll be buried unless ye get out while ye can. We're all like Hassey says. We all came to The Apostles to ascertain something. I meant to be awa' and so did Hassey here and so did almost every man steaming in this room. But then ye think there's time enough tomorrow to be goin', and then ye leave it until perhaps the next day or the next year, and that's how it accumulates. Nothin' to be done about it.' He shook his head and flopped his sporran up and down like a heavy fly-whisk. 'Gradually ye go a wee bit crackers. We all do.' He nodded across the floor. 'There's a man over yon, George Turtle, a native of Isleworth in the County of Middlesex, who would like the Queen to inaugurate a system of parking meters in the centre of our town. He's read about them in the papers from home, ye understand, and he wants to have the same benefits here. He'll be after having us blow up this beer balloon plaything next. How many motor cars on the island Hassey?'

'Twenty,' said Hassey immediately, 'and two motor-assisted bicycles.'

'Parking meters,' repeated English sourly. He looked quickly at Davies. 'What's your business here?'

'Butter and fats,' said Davies. 'Selling butter and fats. Trellis and Jones, Circular Quay, Sydney.'

'How long have you been there?'

'Oh only a year. Since I came out from home.'

The final word seemed to move some thought in English. 'Have ye seen a lot o' the Queen?' he asked.

'Me?'

'Don' be flustered man. Nobody wants you to curtsey with a bouquet.'

'Well, no. I lived in Newport, see, and she wasn't down our way that much. In fact, I've only seen her on the pictures and on the television news and that.'

'We'll have the television out here some day, so George Turtle says,' said English gloomily. He had now dropped the Scots voice almost completely. His tone was flat and, Davies thought, with a touch of Lancashire. 'God knows how or when. The batteries only allow the radio to work for two hours a day as it is. One English, one French. What is it like?'

'Television?' said Davies. 'All right, I suppose. The kiddies like it.'

English said, slowly at first but then brightening and quickening : 'We could have a tomb of the Unknown Soldier! By Jesus, that's it!' He seemed, once again, to be bound to leap up from the chair, but he fell back and took reassurance from the whisky. He turned on Hassey. 'Now *that* is something we could really manage.'

'They do find them now and again,' admitted Hassey.

Davies was aghast. 'Unknown soldiers?' he said.

'By the dozen, old boy,' said Hassey. 'Jungle is full of bones, full of 'em.'

'Not full,' argued English patiently. 'But it does happen that people going pig hunting or something come across skeletons in the jungle. There's only a few miles of it but it's very thick and the fighting in this part of the world was very fierce. It's a good idea, isn't it?'

Hassey looked worried. 'But they're only bones,' he said. 'It's not often you can tell who's side the bones were on. They could be Japanese for all you know.'

English sighed. 'That's the whole bloody point of an unknown soldier. You don't know *who* he is. He's a symbol. That's all that matters.'

'Even if he's a Jap?'

'Even if he is.'

English finished his whisky, looked towards Davies, then changed his mind and handed his glass to Hassey again. It was as though he were locked in an invalid chair. 'What a bonnie idea!' he hugged himself. He had reverted to north of the border again. 'What a fine wee notion. We'll have a grand memorial made and a bright everlasting flame . . .'

'I can sell you the oil for that,' said Davies cynically. 'Trellis and Jones sell some good Everlasting Flame oil.'

English, still savouring his idea, missed the tone. 'We might do that too, young man,' he said. 'Local volcanic stone, and flowers all the year round. Hee! Hee! All we want now is a body.'

Hassey gulped on his glass. His eyes jumped. 'Where could we have it?' he asked. 'In the square? By the harbour? Where do you think?'

'On The Love Beach,' said Davies. He was surprised to hear his own unforced voice, and how readily the words came to him.

Hassey and English both cried out: 'The Love Beach!'

'My God, laddie, that's a marvellous notion,' enthused English. 'What better place than among the machines and the trappings of war. The Unknown Soldier! The Love Beach! It's grand! It's really grand!'

'Get three of the invasion barges moved into three sides of a square,' said Hassey, his eyes screwed up but brightly shining through the cracks. His words began falling over each other. 'Make a chapel from them. Have the open side facing the land so that one of the barges can be like a breakwater!'

English began to shiver with laughing excitement. 'I know! I've got it! We'll get the Queen to open the chapel or whatever you do with a chapel . . .'

'Consecrate it?' suggested Davies.

'That's the word. Consecrate it. Religious you Welsh. Well, when she's done that we'll have another ceremony and she can re-name the beach!'

'Re-name The Love Beach?' whispered Hassey.

'But it's ancient, isn't it?' added Davies. 'Traditional. It's been called that for centuries.'

'Time for a change,' said English firmly. 'It will be re-named Sandringham Beach, or Buckingham Palace Beach, Balmoral Beach. Something after that fashion anyway. Especially to mark the visit.'

Davies blamed himself for starting the thought. Many of the others had crowded about English and his wicker chair now, leaning forward, asking what it was all about. English finished his drink and held up both hands.

'Wait! Hold it, all of ye,' he said. 'I have come up with a wee idea for Her Majesty's visit.' He told them all about it. Davies watched them, sweating in the humid bar, listening like children caught with a fairy story. When he finished English added: 'All we need now is a body, or at least a skeleton. And that should not be too difficult.'

'I still think the inauguration of a parking meter system would be better,' observed George Turtle to those close about him. He made sure his voice did not carry to English. But louder he said: 'How can we be sure of getting an old body? They are not found that often now. They used to be, I know, but the source seems to be giving out.'

English eyed him. 'We'll send out search parties. We'll find one. There must be plenty still in the jungle.'

Hassey said: 'I think it is also essential that we check to make sure it's a proper genuine body. Last year, you'll remember, some fool brought a skeleton back and it was all but buried with full honours before we spotted it was a damn monkey.'

Davies began to laugh and he saw Conway, on the fringe of the crowd, laughing too. But the islanders grimaced at him so he stopped suddenly.

'Instead of searching for a body,' said Kendrick, the bicycle dealer, 'why don't we use an old one. I mean one that's previously been brought in and buried. We can dig it up, reverendly, of course . . .'

'Disinter it, laddie,' said English.

Kendrick bowed. 'Yes, disinter it, and use that. I mean, one lot of bones is much like another.'

'That idea appeals to me,' said English. Kendrick looked pleased. 'Where's the telephone? What's the Reverend Colin Collins' number? He's the clergy.'

The telephone was handed across the bar by Seamus. Little pocket diaries were consulted and someone shouted the number. English asked the Sexagesima operator to connect him and breezily greeted the voice of the missionary. He explained his idea with bubbling enthusiasm, then waited. His face descended and set into a miserable frown. Eventually he put the one half of the telephone back on the other half.

'He won't hear of it,' he said to the men all around him. 'Damned nuisance. He says if we want an Unknown Soldier we'll have to go and find one. We're not digging anybody up.'

Misery seemed to settle about them. 'I didn't think he would take that attitude,' admitted Hassey. 'After all it's in a good cause.'

VI

It was a heavy night, lumpy with clouds, hot and uneasy. The ocean, dulled and depressed by the closeness of the sky, moved wearily against the reef, and the island trees bent like tall hunchbacks. There were not many lights left on in the town when Pollet drove Conway and Davies out through the eastern street, although 'Bread' was still sending its coloured message across the Pacific from Livesley's shop.

'Anyone with the imagination of a stale turd could have made it "Cakes" or "Pies" or something like that,' complained Conway looking at the changing hues thrown upon the inky lagoon. 'Even "Cakes" might give you some romance. What sort? Iced or sugar? And you *might* want to know what's in his pies. But, dear God, what can you ask about bread?'

Pollet drove gymnastically, putting the elderly French car into turns and skids that carried it noisily through the contortions of the track they were now following. 'Here in Melanesia,' he said. 'They believe that the simplest mode of doing anything is the best. Bread means bread. The Melanesian girl always makes her flower designs the same way, clever but monotonous, and she will not, she cannot, move from that. It has been with her since she was a baby. She dances like that, also, and makes love the same way. It has a sameness about it.'

Davies quoted : 'Young girls dancing, indecent dances, indecent songs and the most indecent actions in the practice of which they are brought up from earliest childhood . . .'

Pollet laughed: 'You almost have it correct. "In doing this they keep time to a great nicety".'

'That's right,' said Davies in the dark. 'You know it.'

'Captain Cook and his old maid's philosophy,' laughed Pollet, swinging the car through the dark. 'It is a well-known quotation in these islands. He never understood the people of the Pacific. He was murdered while telling his men not to shoot at the natives. That is always a fatal mistake, my friend.'

The car shuddered like a loose tin along the track for a few minutes more, dipping like an aged boat in a changing sea. The track became narrower and trees and bushes brushed and sometimes banged like fists against the side. Then there blinked some lights through the overgrowth ahead, yellow and red lights. 'The Café Angelique, the Moulin Rouge of the Apostle Islands,' mocked Pollet. 'Presenting—for this year only—the Jap Olsen Ensemble.'

They cleared the trees and ahead they could see that the lights were isolated, standing out on a jut of land that merged black with the molassic sea just beyond.

'He is a real, a live Japanese,' said Pollet. 'He was a soldier in the occupation force here and for years after the war lived over on one of the atolls behind St Mark's. He says he didn't know it was over—one of that sort—but maybe he did and could not be troubled to find out who won. When he at last came across here to St Peter's he was wearing the last rags of an American army fatigue suit with the name "Olsen" sewed to it. So he called himself Olsen and all the citizens called him Jap, and that is how he began.'

'And now he runs the nightspot,' said Conway.

'Well,' shrugged Pollet. 'He has an interest. Not that it pays too good. But he plays the clarinet okay because he studied it when he was over on his little atoll. He says somebody left it behind in the rush at the end of the fighting, so he sat alone on his beach and learned to play it. People leave some strange things behind in war, don't they?' Pollet paused while he skidded the car between two palms that closed in on them through the night. 'Ha!' he said, the manœuvre completed. 'A clarinet! Imagine, an abandoned clarinet!'

'An abandoned Jap to play it,' said Conway.

Pollet half-circled the car in the mud outside the low building, a sluggish pirouette that brought them alongside a jeep and a tethered donkey. A brilliant white light from one of the windows was shining directly into the donkey's eyes and the animal had them screwed up in protest. Pollet considerately unhitched him and turned him in the opposite direction, tying him to the rear bumper of the jeep.

'That's a bit dangerous,' suggested Davies. 'If the people with the jeep don't notice him they'll drive off with the donkey dragging behind.'

'And that thing would never be able to keep up,' added Conway looking at the animal.

Pollet finished securing the donkey and kindly scratched the long white patch of its face before leaving it. 'No problem,' said the Belgian. 'Jap Olsen—the jeep and that bloody thing belong to him. For short journeys, and always at night, he uses the donkey. He is mean about gasoline and the headlights on the jeep don't work. Tonight when he goes home he will drive the donkey.'

They went in. Davies' immediate thought was that the room was like a Welsh working men's institute, oblong, depressed, boarded, just chairs and tables and a poor bar, with a slightly raised entertainment platform at one end. In a corner was a dead-looking woman hanging onto a cello in the manner of a drunk hanging on a lamp-post. Beside her was a florid trumpeter, a man with a permanent stare, like a fat owl rudely woken in daylight. These were supported by a young Melanesian boy behind a complex drum kit, gleaming, Davies thought, like a Welsh fish and chip machine.

'The band,' whispered Pollet, nodding towards the three. He led them to a table near the back, in the shadow. There were about a dozen other people in the dim place, hunched like poker-players around the tables, drinking but talking very little. A vivid silver spotlight that would have been the pride of the ceiling of the Milan Opera House, a searing beam descending from the low roof, lit the dais. It was raised only six feet above the stage. It was obvious that the customers were waiting for something. A waiter, a Filipino, appeared and Pollet said: 'Three,' and the man brought back three beers.

'What time do they close?' asked Davies. 'It's not very exciting is it?'

Pollet shrugged. 'The place goes on until late,' he said. 'At midnight, however, the old lady with the cello always leaves because she has a long walk across the island and she has to take that heavy instrument.'

'Good God!' said Davies. 'The old crone takes it with her?'

Pollet said: 'That's a good word. Crone. What is that?'

'Old dear,' said Davies. The Belgian's English was so assured the query surprised him. 'Old lady.'

'Old crone,' said Pollet. 'Hmm. Old crone.' Then he said: 'She—the old crone—has a little cart behind this building and she lifts it onto that. She will not leave the instrument here because she says it is very ancient and valuable and she trusts no one. So every night you will see her dragging it along the jungle road to her house. She's a widow and she's perhaps a little strange, you know.'

The violent spotlight, designed for a lofty roof, still burned down on the floor, though the fidgeting semi-silence continued to rustle in the room. No entertainer had appeared, but then through the light, briskly striding, came a fat man swinging a clarinet.

'Jap Olsen,' said Pollet. The man came to them. 'Good evening Mr Olsen.' The Japanese wore a grubby dress shirt and a cringing bow, and one tail of his long formal coat was several inches shorter than the other. He smiled a wide smile and shook hands with the other men, bowing to each. He had far open, un-oriental eyes, like fat boats.

'Spotlight vel' good ah?' he indicated proudly. 'Special from Blisbane, Aussie, see. Jesus it hot too. Jesus it sure hot.'

'It was making your donkey sightless,' commented Pollet. 'Burning in his eyes. I turned him around.'

Olsen blinked a long blink. 'Like cabaret that donkey,' he said. 'Like look into nightspot. He don' mind light.'

'What time is the show?' asked Conway.

'He come soon,' replied Olsen. 'Don' like change clothes here. Say it no good. Change in 'Gesima. In hotel. Here now . . . I hear.' There were the lights and the sound of a car outside.

The Japanese went from their table towards the bright stage light again, vanished through it like a man magically walking through a waterfall, and reappeared a minute later to introduce his cabaret, a baritone from Fiji, a mountainous chocolate man with high springing hair and an expansive face. He was resplendent in full dress, black frock-coat, brilliant white shirt and tie, sparkling diamond pin, and giant patent leather shoes. He walked into the spotlight at Olsen's introduction and the musicians struck a hesitant three-chord greeting, joined by the owner's quickly picked up clarinet on the third chord. The singer's name was Samuel Smart and he made a short ducking movement as he entered the hot spotlight and felt its force, like a boxer avoiding a heavy right cross.

Bravely he tried to look into the source of the light, but turned quickly from it, his eyes screwed up painfully and water immediately dripping down from his large Fijian cheeks. Stepping smartly from the hot circle he sought out Olsen with still half-blinded eyes and eventually detected him sitting phlegmatically almost at his feet. The singer pointed towards the searing beam, but Olsen had given the signal and the musicians were already beginning to play. Olsen joined in and the big baritone, after a moment's indecision, stepped once more into the white spotlight.

He sang well, a beautifully rounded voice, in the tradition of the best English baritones with no trace of any accent that would have sounded out of place in a Sussex palm court.

He sang 'I Left My Heart In an English Garden', 'Rose of England' and 'Old Father Thames'. He then collapsed very heavily on the stage, a fall as final and dramatic as a rhino caught in the brain with a powerful bullet. The trio and Olsen played on with professional gallantry. The audience were petrified into attentiveness, unsure, unable to move. Davies thought it might be part of the act. Mr Smart lay, a sorry black hump in the pulsating spotlight. After a full thirty seconds the music dragged to a standstill. Someone in the dim back of the place began to applaud, but the singer did not move.

Olsen waved his clarinet towards Pollet and the three men went hurriedly forward and heaved the deadweight baritone across the platform. Davies was staggered by the heat of the light as he bent forward to help. Mr Smart was pumping rather than breathing, gigantic panic movements of his deep chest beneath the white shirt now soggy as papier-mâché with his enormous sweat. His black face was wet and small gasses were escaping from his open mouth and his fine big nostrils. They carried him to the back of the building where he began to revive. Suddenly he sat up and let out a great wet roar, staggered from the bench where they had rested him and rushed towards the exit. The door banged back and forth on its hinges for some time after he had gone into the close night. They heard his waiting taxi start up. Then they heard the donkey snort.

'The bastard kick my donkey,' said Olsen.

They had been drinking for another hour, the deep bitter beer made in the islands, when Bird came in and sat on one side of the dais bent over a guitar, playing and singing in almost whispered French. Davies did not think she had seen him. She did not seem to be aware of anyone else in the place. She played without stopping, just running from one song to another, all of a like tender tempo, her fingers only suggesting that they were touching the strings, her voice low and sometimes lost, her black hair falling in a long arm, hiding her face.

More people came in. At midnight the grey lady cellist suddenly stood and marched defiantly away with her fat instrument upright by her side as though it were walking with her. Davies went to the window and saw her shadow trundling it through the mud on the ghostly handcart. Pollet went to Jap Olsen and they stood against the bar laughing. The girl from behind the bar, introduced by Pollet as Dahlia, came over and Conway bought her a beer. She was a tall girl, heavily framed, with a dark face coloured and creamed with thick make-up. She said she had been in Montreal, at the exhibition, then in Mexico, then in Honoraria in the Solomons, and Vila in the New Hebrides. Then she got to Sexagesima and caught a fever. One day she was going home to Wanganui in New Zealand. One day.

Nobody seemed to drink anything other than beer. Davies had taken a lot. He could feel it swollen inside him. The place felt damp, like a cave, and dark like a cave too. There was a candle in a rose-coloured jar on the table. He took out his wallet and spread eight photographs in the rosy light, fanning them out like a fortune-teller fans out cards. The awful loneliness fell upon him immediately. He felt like a man who had failed to resist the recurring need for pornography. He had tried not to take the pictures from his wallet. But he always did.

What would they be doing now? A Tuesday in February at —he looked at his watch and deducted ten hours—three-thirty in the afternoon. She had gone to get them from school now, he thought, yes, just now she'd be at the gate to see they didn't get run over when they ran from school. Probably raining.

Yes, probably. February was a very wet month in Newport. So was March and April, of course. May wasn't too good either, and August when they were away from school was always indifferent. September wasn't too bad. They'd always gone down to the sea at Barry in September because the weather always seemed to repent about then and the sun would shine decently. That was one of the reasons they were all going to leave Wales for Australia, of course, because of there being a lot of sunshine in Australia and too much rain in Newport. If it were raining then Kate would have her blue coat on with the hood. It looked nice that coat. It made her face look enclosed and good and sweet with the hood around it. By now though she had probably got a new one. It was a long time.

He pictured the children inside the glass door of the school, all pressing, waiting for the moment of the bell, the instant of freedom when they could run out into the rain and go home with their mothers. Kate would take Mag and David home under her umbrella and they would have tea in the little living-room and watch television, and the paperboy with the *Argus* would come around in the rain, propping his bike against the lamp, and then the lights would all be splashing on the wet roads and pavements and the men would come off the buses home from their work. But not him because he was an adventurer in the South Pacific, working, making a new life, listening to a girl singing love songs he did not understand.

Then he realised that Bird had stopped singing. She had walked to him through the warm darkness of the room and stood beside his table, the guitar resting at an angle across the opposite chair. Conway had moved over to be nearer Dahlia and Bird was standing looking at his spread of photographs. He laughed uneasily.

'Just snaps,' he said. 'Pictures from home. Takes you back a bit.' He had to pick and choose the words with care, making him realise that he was drunk.

She sat down, moving the guitar over, putting her young

head between her hands and looking down at the pictures. It was almost as though she were in a booth, her hands shielding her face both sides, her full hair thrown back, only the gentle tip of her nose visible to Davies sitting at her side.

'What are their names?' she said.

'Mag is the little girl,' he said. 'Margaret really, but she's always been called Mag. She's six. Last month. And the boy is David and he's a couple of years older.'

She pointed : 'I like this one on the see-saw. The sun is nice. I thought you never got sun in England.'

He laughed sadly : 'Oh, we do sometimes. Anyway this is in Wales.'

'Same thing,' she said. 'Your wife looks pretty. This is nice where she is laughing.'

'Kate,' he said. 'Her name's Kate. She's twenty-seven. I haven't seen them for more than a year. It chokes me a bit sometimes.' Bird moved her left hand to the photographs and half looked at him. 'It's a long time, a year,' she said. 'Who is this man?'

Davies thrust his hand out towards the end picture and his fingers touched its edge, but he stopped there, recovered himself, and said : 'My brother. Dilwyn, that's his name Dilwyn. He's about twenty-five.'

She looked at him curiously and he withdrew his hand from the edge of the photograph. 'He looks a bit older than that,' she said. 'He's proud of his car, though, isn't he? Look how he's standing alongside it. And how it shines. You can even see that in the pictures. Even in this small light.'

Davies stared at the photograph. 'Oh yes,' he mumbled. 'He's very pleased with that motor. Very pleased. Nice little runner it is too.'

With deliberately separate movements he picked up each of the photographs and thrust them with overdone firmness into his wallet. He felt sick with drink now, dreary and tired with it too. 'Would you like to dance with me?' he asked vaguely.

'They don't play any more,' she said. 'Everyone is going now.'

'Are you going too?'

'I can't stay here,' she smiled. 'I came up by taxi.' Pollet was walking unsteadily from the bar with Olsen. 'Monsieur Pollet,' Bird said. 'Have you some room for two more into 'Gesima?'

Dahlia looked from around Conway's head. 'It's all right Bird,' she said. 'I've asked. We've got a lift.'

They were the last there. They went out into the night, which was easier now, settled and much cooler with some queenly stars sitting above. The three men were very drunk, Pollet almost fell into the mud and had to be brought to his feet by Conway and Dahlia hanging onto his armpits laughing and staggering.

Pollet, hoisting his stomach, rolled behind the wheel, and jerked the engine. Davies, heavy and sick sat with him in the front, and the happy Conway was between the two girls in the back seat. Pollet revved the engine violently sending birds screaming through the darkness of the jungle trees. He let go an elongated laugh and jolted the car forward.

'Lights!' shouted the three in the back seat at once. 'Lights!'

'Ah, pardon,' smiled Pollet. The car was already careering along the skinny road, with the jungle on either side. He turned the light switch as they went, opening up the colours of the mud road ahead of them and the bright curling green at each edge.

Conway began to sing hideously, a howling pseudo-song of the Australian outback which he had never seen and did not want to see. He thrust each hand, like the blade of a fat knife, between the upper legs of each of the girls flanking him. Bird spitefully pinched the skin on the back of his hand and he removed it. Dahlia let the other hand remain, enjoying its human feel and its animal movement provoked by the jumping of the car. There were some big holes in the rough road and Conway tried to judge the moment when the front wheels began dipping into each one causing his thumb to jump at the same time and collide with the mossy collection within the nylon at the girl's isthmus. It suddenly, and curiously, reminded him of touching the bags of lavender that his mother used to buy in the street when he was a boy. Dahlia stared straight ahead. Conway stopped his song and looked at her and in the uncertain light imagined she was smiling. He smiled too.

Davies hung, miserably drunk, in the front seat beside the bouncing Pollet. The crowding green of the jungle caught in the lights of the pitching car whirled before his dazed eyes like weedy water in a restless pool. He could hear movements from the seat behind him and wondered what Bird was doing. He reached into his inner pocket to take the pack of pictures from there, intending to sling them from the window. But he could not get his fingers about them and, his resolution dying, he let his hand drop hopelessly. He heard Conway's short laugh and Dahlia saying something softly. The car bumped on. Over the trees now, like a mirrored forest fire, the red reflection of the bakery sign touched the night. Then the brilliant blue and the glaring white.

'Home sweet home,' said Dahlia.

'Where is home?' asked Conway wriggling his hand like a barracuda.

'There,' she nodded towards the sign. 'The bakery.'

'What! In the bakery?'

'Well, one floor up. Didn't you notice how shagged I look? It's nothing nice caused that, mister, it's those bastard lights.'

Conway hooted like an astonished owl. Dahlia said: 'Go on, have a scream. It's not as though the fool switches them off at a decent hour. He hasn't got over the novelty yet so they flash like that all night.'

Bird said: 'But he reduced your rent. He was kind.'

Dahlia sniffed. 'Kind! He only did it after I threatened to sue him—in Sydney. That worried him. He wasn't sure whether I could do it or not. So he knocked the rent down.'

89

'That's something,' said Conway.

'It's nothing,' the girl argued. 'Not when you're kept awake all night with red white and blue flashing across the room. Red, white, blue. Red, white, blue. If it went out of sequence, *white*, red, *blue*, just *once*, I'd run out hollering into the bloody street.'

'Curtains,' suggested Conway. 'Good thick curtains.'

'And suffocate,' she added. 'That's it. You either cut out the air or you get red white and blue waving over you all night. I have nightmares where I'm being flogged with a Tricolour.'

They had run into Sexagesima now. Empty, the streets stretching out like skeleton bones, a curious night-time brownness over everything. The neon sign flashed defiantly at a thin grey cat sitting in the road staring at it, mesmerised. The cat did not see the car until it was three feet away. It did an agile back-leap, and sat down again. The bonnet of the car, which had now stopped, blocked the full view of the sign for the cat. It moved a couple of yards further up the road, sat down, and continued staring from there.

The four passengers left the car and Pollet waved to them as he prodded it forward through the hollow street. They stood on the pavement. Bird was standing next to Davies. Conway had pins and needles in the hand which had been trapped between Dahlia's legs. He rubbed it solicitously.

'I'll make some coffee,' said Dahlia, but without much enthusiasm. Bird said politely : 'No. We'll go on.'

Davies blinked. 'Yes,' he agreed. 'We'd better. See you again. Tomorrow.'

He and Bird walked down the street, untouching, a channel between them. They didn't talk.

Conway put his thick arms about Dahlia's easy waist. They watched the other two going.

Dahlia said : 'Your friend is slow.'

Conway shrugged : 'Married,' he said. Then : 'And very slow.'

They walked along the main street. It was like walking in a huge cave undiscovered for centuries. Everything was still and crouched in the oppressive night. The dainty stars had gone now, smothered by the rolling of another great bank of Pacific rain clouds. There were no lights in the street but they could somehow sense the flashing of the neon sign now far behind them down the town.

Davies sounded a dry laugh. He was still drunk but he felt steadier now he was out of the car. 'Years since I've walked a girl home,' he said.

Bird nodded. They still strolled a distance apart, shyly, very conscious of it. Bird said in her curious way : 'I do not suppose you have if you became married. It's one of the things you have to surrender.'

'Oh yes,' he said. 'I realised that.'

'Haven't you taken any woman out since you left?' she asked. 'Not in Australia?'

'Went to a couple of dances,' he answered. 'But just to dance, you know. I didn't do much of that either. Then I met a prostitute once . . .' He was astonished to hear himself say it. He had never told anyone. Bird didn't turn her head to him suddenly, but just kept walking in the same way. He knew because he turned his eyes to watch her.

'I didn't know she *was*, mind,' he said. 'I'm a bit stupid like that.'

'You are,' agreed Bird.

'Well, she was sitting in this pub in Sydney and I went in for a quiet pint after work. She had a round homely sort of face too, and when she started talking to me I thought she was just being sociable. We had a couple of beers and then she gets this list out of her handbag, all printed beautifully and everything it was, like a price list. All the things you could do to her were printed out, and alongside were the prices for each thing. She frightened me out of my skin.'

Bird exploded with astonished laughing, looking at his

91

innocent expression in the dimness, bending forward and holding her hands over her mouth. 'Oh Davies,' she gurgled. 'To you of all people. Whatever happened?'

He stared at her for a moment, then began laughing himself. They laughed and danced a little dance of laughter in the street. They stopped. 'God help us!' he said. 'Now you come to think of it, it must have been funny!'

'Funny!' she said. 'You didn't think before . . .' He could see her eyes were wet. He still could hardly believe they were pantomiming like this in the street. He giggled again. 'No! No! It never dawned on me before . . .'

She stopped and held out her hand to stop him. It touched his hand and he felt it tender as a child's. 'Wait now,' she said. 'Wait a minute. Tell me what did the list *say*. What *sort* of things . . .'

'I couldn't!' he exclaimed seriously. 'I couldn't tell it to you.' But he knew he could tell her. A sudden bravado was filling him. He thought it was the beer being stirred up by all this laughing and prancing about. But then he looked at her, a young girl, standing grinning at him and he knew from where the release had come.

'Go on,' she encouraged him. 'I *must* know.'

'Well,' he grinned. 'There's some very rotten words in it . . .'

'I've heard all the rotten ones,' she laughed. 'I say them too. Go on, Davies.'

He smirked. He felt like a boy who had suddenly discovered the way to ride a bike, or to kick a ball, or play something on the piano after millions of years of practice. He said: 'Well, she handed me this list. All lovely and printed . . .' She burst into merriment again. 'Shut up,' he said. 'Or I'll never tell you. And on the top it said in big letters FIONA'S PRICES . . .'

'Fiona!' exclaimed Bird. 'Yes . . .'

'Then, underneath it was all set out like a menu. French and all. The first thing said "Fuck Ordinaire . . .".'

Bird collapsed on the pavement and sat holding her face in

her hands. 'Oh, Davies,' she laughed. 'Exquisite. Fuck Ordinaire! Oh, my God. Sit down, Davies, please sit down.'

He squatted down opposite her on the stones. Her laughter was still making him laugh. 'Then there was "Fuck. Three different positions".' Bird didn't look at him. She kept her head down. 'Then?' she asked. 'What then?'

'Some others. I can't remember them all . . . Oh, yes. My God, Bird, there was another one which said "Upright Fuck", and it had little elaborate brackets after it and the words "Against Interior Wall" in them.'

He tried to remember. 'She had all sorts of positions printed down and all this French, and you can imagine *me* looking at them. At the list I mean, not the positions themselves.'

'I believe *that*,' said Bird. 'She might as well have shown it to the Archbishop of Canterbury.'

'Oh, I'm not *that* bad,' he protested. He stopped and suddenly realised what he had said.

'You mean, you're not that good,' she said quietly, looking intently down the vacant street as though she saw someone coming.

He felt all the laughter drain from him. 'You don't know Bird,' he said. 'How I have felt. I sometimes think I'm the only bugger in the world who feels like this. Everybody else seems to be like old Conway. Like it says in the thing—keeping time to a nicety—remember?' She nodded and smiled. He said: 'I wish to God I was.' There was some damp dust on the pavement where they sat. Davies drew a little meaningless map in it with his finger.

'I love Kate, you see,' he said. 'And those kids . . . well, they brought a sort of freshness to me. I never wanted anything outside that.'

She drew a second anonymous island in the dust and joined it to his with a causeway made by a single stroke of her finger. 'Who was the man with the car, Davies?' she asked. 'Not your brother.'

He looked at her. Her young bright face was composed, perfect; interested and concerned. 'It showed, didn't it?' he said.

'Very much,' she nodded.

'No, it's not my brother. I haven't got one for a start, and my mother wouldn't have called him Dilwyn, anyway. That's my old man's name and she couldn't stand the sight of him. No . . . I've never met him.'

He took the pictures from his pocket with difficulty still because he wasn't doing anything right, and set them out on the ground, like playing cards once again. The photograph of the young man with the shiny car was laid out last.

'That's the joker,' said Davies. He looked at the photographs again. 'See, the day I left home to go to Australia, I found this film in one of Kate's shoes. I thought it had just got there by accident. But I knew which film it was, because we didn't take many. A couple of rolls a year. We never had a lot of money to chuck about. Anyway I remembered taking these snaps of Kate and the kids in the park, on the swings and all that, and I thought "Ah, I'll take these to Australia with me". I was going to get them developed and then send them home as a nice surprise, see.'

Bird nodded. The cat which had been watching the bakery sign had torn itself away and came sauntering up the street towards them. It rubbed itself for comfort along the channel of Bird's back and she softly caught its thin tail and let it run through her hand.

'Well,' said Davies. 'It was *me* who got the surprise. One of the chaps at work does photography as a hobby and he said he would do the developing job for me. When he came back with the prints, I was all keen and eager as you could imagine.' He laughed without humour. 'I was in such a bloody rush I dropped the things all over the floor at work, behind my desk, fortunately, because the boss came in and started telling somebody off about something; so I couldn't pick them up from the floor for a minute. They were down there, scattered about, and the picture of the chap with the car was on top. I sort of stared at it, trying to make out what it was, because I was still standing up, you see. I could see this snap quite clearly, but the others were either hidden underneath it or had fallen face down on the floor. Naturally I thought "Old Harry's given me the wrong photographs". I thought he'd got them mixed up with somebody else's.

'Then Mr Trellis went out and I dived down and picked up the bunch. They were mine, all right. All except that one. The others showed the kids on the swings and the see-saws, and there was just the one of that smug-looking bastard in his new suit and his crappy car.'

Davies looked up dizzily. The heavy sky had gathered around them. 'Looks like a bit more rain,' he said. 'We'd better get on.' He took Bird's hand and helped her up. They walked apart onwards down the dumb street, the cat following with puzzled walk. 'Even then I thought that Harry had mixed this one in by mistake. But he said it was on the roll, and he wouldn't be shifted from that. I didn't know the bloke in the picture, never saw him in my life. But you can see the number plate of the car, see, and one of the blokes at work had a diary with all the registration letter codes in it—all the one's in Britain, that is. He's from London and he brought this over to Australia with him. Anyway we checked and those letters are a Newport registration. I sent off to the County people in Newport and they turned up the address of this bloke. He lives about half a mile away from us. Well, from Kate.'

Bird stopped walking. 'This is where I live,' she said. 'This is the shop and I live up there, over the top.' Davies stopped awkwardly on the pavement. 'There'll be another downpour soon,' he said turning his head up. 'Doesn't stop for long, does it?'

'Not at this season,' she said. 'Did you write and ask her about the man?'

He said softly: 'No. I didn't have the guts. I keep thinking that everything will be all right and she'll bring the kids out to Australia. I've got just about enough for us to start again now.' He stopped there and they stood without speaking. Then: 'Goodnight, Davies,' said Bird.

'Goodnight,' he said absently. Then starting forward he continued with a rush of words: 'It's a funny thing, you know, but I should have realised there was something fishy the day I left home. It struck me at the time, but I didn't think any more about it. Or hardly. At Newport, you see, the railway bridge crosses the river almost alongside the old road bridge. There's only a couple of hundred yards between them. And that day when they all came to see me off, Kate and David and little Mag, I kissed them all at the train, got in, and it moved off pretty quickly from the station. They were all on the platform when it pulled away. Well, it was a false start. The train waited a bit, just stopped outside the station for a couple of minutes for the signal or something, and then went off across the river bridge. And I hung out of the window hoping that with any luck they might have walked as far as the bridge and would wave. Well, they were on the bridge right enough—right at the far end—waving to me. I was a bit shattered at the time. I thought "Well how the bloody hell did they get that distance in a couple of minutes, out of the station, along the street and on to the *other* end of the bridge". It was like a conjuring trick. And, thinking back on it, there *was* a car standing not very far from them, which is unusual because they won't have parking on the bridge in Newport. That's how they got there. In his car.'

Bird said: 'He must have been waiting outside the station then.'

'Yes. He didn't let the grass grow under his bleeding feet did he. Goodnight, Bird.'

'Goodnight,' she said again. She watched him walk down the sloping street towards the hotel. As she did so heavy gobs of rain fell. Davies began to lope, at a jog, his shoulders hunched.

96

VII

'I think I like you best in red,' said Conway. He hung back across Dahlia's bed, considering her, his shirt, his trousers and his shoes off, two toes, blinking at the light, poking from a hole in his black sock. Dahlia was standing in the centre of her room, tall and naked, a bottle in her hand, caught delicately by the neck. She had been returning from her drinks cupboard when he stopped her with a policeman's upright hand. She had a very strong body, with big steady breasts, and her hips, pelvis, navel and crease forming a perfect heart. Each time the neon light changed outside it threw its garish reflection through the net curtains at the window and coloured her flesh, now red, now startling white, now blue.

Conway thought it was very erotic. Somehow it electrified her shape, the blue turning her icy, the white making her like an apparition, and the red making her flesh burn. The moon shadows under her breasts and in her other hillocks and pits were deep as wounds each time the light changed.

'It suits you, that red,' continued Conway casually. 'The blue is a bit cold and the white makes you look like you've got no clothes on.'

She said: 'I haven't got any on. Can I move now?'

'Oh yes,' he replied waving his hand. 'Carry on. Don't let me stop you pouring.'

She went towards the glasses on the bedside table. 'You're a born bastard,' she said without malice. 'Really, I've ordered some heavy curtains, you know. I've been hanging it out, not knowing whether I was going to stay here in the island another week or another year. But I need my sleep. So I've sent the measurements to Noumea and told them to make the curtains in velvet or something heavy. Nobody in this dopey island is capable of making them even if I could get thick material here, which I can't.'

'Stand there a minute,' said Conway abruptly leaning towards her. She was quite near. She stood. She mimicked uncertainly: 'Stand here, stand there. You sound like Van Gogh or someone.'

He rolled over on his stomach, his white backside in view from beneath the end of his longish singlet. He rested his head and eyes on one arm and put the other out, seeking her. He got his fingers rolled in the thick hairs about her point and began to gather them together, pulling them gently down and arranging them into a sort of Frenchman's beard.

'Jesus,' she breathed. 'Now what are you doing?'

He began to tug at the beard firmly, but not hurting her, with a milking motion, his face still buried in the curve of his other arm. 'This,' he said, eventually answering her. 'It's called Fud Tugging.'

She began to bend forward tenderly. 'Excuse me,' she said. 'I can't take too much of this.'

'Take a bit more,' he suggested. 'It's very difficult to get the right rhythm and the correct control to a little perversion like this. Finesse, that's what's required. It's an art . . .'

She was looking at him with full eyes, half pulling away from him, half pushing herself towards him. Her hands moved eloquently, but she remained helpless. Conway still didn't look at her. 'I can't stand much more,' she repeated the warning, speaking very low.

'They should have this Fud Tugging in the Olympic Games,' he muttered. 'Better than hop-skip-and-a-jump. Better than the pole vault or any of those events. Just think of doing this on an international scale.'

'Con,' she began again. 'Stop . . .'

'I know who'd get the gold medal,' he said rolling over and displaying to her what the exercise had achieved for him. She looked down at him. 'Australia,' she whispered putting out her hands.

'Steady,' said Conway stopping her. He lifted the front end of his long vest and hung it over the top of his penis, like a shroud. 'Ladies and Gentlemen,' he intoned. 'We are here to-day to witness the unveiling of a statue of one of the most important members—members, get that?—of our community. He has stood erect among us for a long time . . .'

'Stop it,' said Dahlia seriously, not laughing.

He smiled officially at her. 'Lady Dahlia,' he announced. 'Looking lovely as ever in alternating red white and blue will now perform the unveiling. Lady Dahlia!'

Conway applauded politely while Dahlia, the wild lights still flowing over her skin, stood and made a speech. She had found some control of herself now and she purposefully went on for some time until Conway looked up uncomfortably and whispered: 'Hurry up then. There won't be anything to unveil in a minute.'

They made varied love after that, at intervals through the night, with the neon flashes bouncing upon them on her bed. Then the dawn peeled over the ocean, first, then the lagoon, and then the town, clear and yellowy after the rain, and the sign lost its power and went on blinking pathetically in the growing day.

They did not sleep much, but lay quiet mostly, talking sometimes, for they were both wanderers, both adventurers. They had loved in many places. Late in the night Conway said: 'Who would you say knows St Paul's the best? Is there anyone gets across there regularly?'

She was lying in the bend of his arm, her big breasts pressed into his flank, the rest of her half underneath him. 'When are you going?' she asked.

'Tomorrow,' he said. 'No, I mean it's today now. Today.'

'Abe Nissenbaum goes across pretty regularly. He does deals with the natives over there. He has a motor boat and he takes stuff across to sell to them. He does a great trade in religious things, prayer beads, and crosses and all that stuff.'

'He fixes the crucifixes eh?' said Conway.

'As a matter of fact he does.'

'With a name like Abe Nissenbaum?'

'The natives don't know the difference. He's very popular over there.'

'You wait till they find out that his lot had the hammer and nails.'

'He means to make sure they don't. Old Colin Collins, the Yank missionary, you know, he gets very mad at Abe, but he doesn't do anything about it because he's scared to go over to St Paul's himself and Abe is always generous when the mission church has a collection for anything.'

'Have you been over there?' asked Conway.

She stirred against him. 'Once,' she said. 'It was creepy. I didn't breathe till I got away from the place. They think it's the Holy Land, you know, the natives. They tell you that Jerusalem is there and the stable at Bethlehem, and all that junk from the Bible. And, the time I went over—that was with old Abe—it was near Christmas and they had a sort of play in the middle of the main village.'

'What sort of play?'

'Well like a religious play, except they truly believe it's all happening. And they're just savages, really, and they look it. But they go through all this rigmarole and it's frightening. Abe just laughed but I was terrified. They let this woman have her baby on some straw in a stable with an ox and a donkey standing there and the Three Wise Men turning up and everything. I mean, it was a real thing, this woman giving birth and she had a hell of a terrible time, but everyone stood around watching and singing carols.'

Conway said quietly: 'They're as gone as that, are they?'

She laughed quietly. 'Gone, gone, gone. They very nearly sent me too. The trouble is it's a long time since a real missionary has had the guts to go over there, so everything they know has sort of got mangled up. The tunes and half the words of the carols are unrecognisable. You should hear them sing "Hark the Herald Angels". It's like a war dance.'

'What about the cargo cult?' said Conway.

'Oh, they're waiting for this new Messiah. What do they call him. Dodson-Smith, that's right. Dodson-Smith. They're expecting him any time, and when he arrives a new life is going to begin for them. They're going to be in milk and honey, honey. Abe says they've got an old American army bike stored somewhere up on the volcano waiting for this chap. When he rides down among them that will be it. He's their God and King.'

'Dodson-Smith,' said Abe.

'Yes,' she said. 'Not much of a name for God, is it?'

Conway rolled on top of her. He kissed her nose luxuriously, getting his mouth right round it, and pushed his big hands under the cushions of her bottom.

'Again?' she murmured. 'You're in good shape.'

'I'm a hungry man,' he said. 'Not eaten for weeks.'

'Apart from Greta MacAndrews on *The Baffin Bay*,' said Dahlia.

Conway stopped what he was doing. 'How did you know that?' he said.

Dahlia shrugged and wriggled more comfortably beneath him. 'She told me,' she said simply. 'She's very obliging, I know. And the captain rather enjoys her telling him all about it afterwards. They always pick out one passenger for her. They do it together like choosing a carpet or chair. This trip it was you.'

'It's a funny place this,' commented Conway beginning to move to her.

'Hilarious,' she said, moving too.

At ten o'clock in the morning Abe Nissenbaum stood by his work boat in Sexagesima harbour. It was steamy hot with a mixed sky of clouds and open holes of brilliant blue. Not much was moving, just a native boat going out to the moored copra hulk loaded high with husked coconuts, and the British Governor's launch cutting a fine ridge across the harbour as it went to collect that morning's milk. Four cows were properly tended and fed under an Anglo-French agreement so that both Governors and their immediate echelons could have fresh milk every day.

Pollet's car shuddered around the corner of the main warehouse on the waterfront, scattering some native women who were vending melons and breadfruit. A breadfruit rolled like an orange football until the car's rear wheel exploded it into a splatter of pips and water. The Belgian waved backwards in apology and then slowed and drew the car alongside Abe with all the elegance of a royal chauffeur. He smartly opened the rattly rear door for Conway and Davies.

'Gentlemen,' said Pollet, still formally. 'This is Mr Abe Nissenbaum. He'll take you across to St Paul's and look after you.'

'It's not my day to go,' shrugged Abe eloquently. 'But, hell, I'll take you. Sure. And for just the normal rate. Not a shilling more. I'm like that.' He looked aggressively at Pollet for confirmation.

'Certainly,' agreed Pollet. 'He's like that. He won't charge you a shilling more.'

Davies looked with interest at the Jewish trader. He was a remarkable human specimen. His face was more gypsy than Jewish, Davies thought, and in this he was accurate since Abe claimed to be a Jewish gypsy. One of the few, he said. He was average in height and build, but from the middle of his body, thrusting out suddenly, dramatically, against all the laws of balance, was an extraordinary paunch. It was not the gradual mound of a well-fed man, it wasn't the low-slung belly of a

102

woman with child, it was a balloon, an oval balloon, pushing straight flat out from under his ribs and having done a sudden downwards curve, diving straight back home for his pelvis.

Conway and Davies climbed into the big untidy motor boat. Abe remained on the jetty laughing and shaking hands with Pollet. Davies sat uncomfortably. 'God knows what I'm doing here,' he grumbled. 'What's in this for me? It's *you* who wants to go over to the island.'

Conway tutted. 'Come on, boy,' he said. 'The natives over there are just screaming out for fresh butter and fats. I've been told.'

'Who told you?'

'Dahlia did. Last night.'

Davies looked at him doubtfully. 'You talked about butter and fats?'

'Some of the time,' admitted Conway modestly. 'We talked about the island and that's how it came up. You have to *talk* sometimes, you know. That's part of the game. It's no good just keeping screwing away and keeping your trap shut.'

'I don't need any lessons, thanks,' grunted Davies. 'I'm a married man, remember. I've done it all.'

Conway grinned. 'Oh, God help me, so you are. I forgot.'

Abe came down over the side of the jetty, his back to them. He was wearing a sweat shirt, blue trousers and rope shoes. From behind he looked like a fit man. He turned, rather majestically, on reaching the deck, guiding his stomach with great care around a rope.

'I told you didn't I that it's not my day today for St Paul's. Next Friday, that's my day. But I'll take you. Aw hell, I don't care. I'm very good like that.'

'You mentioned it,' said Davies flatly. Abe didn't appear to notice.

The boat began tiredly, pushing with protest against the small flow of the sea into the harbour. But it seemed to stir itself as they made for the feathered reef, heeling in an elderly

103

but graceful attitude as they met the run of the ocean coming through the gap in the coral.

'God is very thoughtful,' said Abe suddenly in the manner of a man beginning a set lecture. 'He's a good man. Good businessman, what's more. He thinks of everything. He makes a reef from coral to protect his interest, the island and the people and the things they make and buy and sell, and all that sort of thing. Then He arranges it so that the coral won't live in fresh water, and then He fixes a river to come into the sea at a certain place and to flow out and keep a gap in the reef so that people can get in and out. Now, that's ingenious. Just about as ingenious as, shall we say, sexual intercourse. That's a good business principal too. You want productivity so you get the people to enjoy what they're doing and you get the output. If we produced crops instead of babies by intercourse then nobody would be starving in the world, would they? There would be plenty all round, and more. My God, this island would produce enough to feed half the Southern Hemisphere.'

'How long have you been here?' asked Davies. The boat was beginning to paw at the water as it met the inrush from the gap in the reef. He moved more to the centre of the wooden cross-seat.

'Few years,' said Abe squinting professionally at the two teeth of surf marking the extremities of the gap. 'I'm Jewish, you understand. A refugee.'

'Where from?' asked Conway looking at the gap too. It seemed narrow and difficult, but Abe was leaning negligently on the wheel scratching the dome of his stomach.

'From Israel,' said Abe simply. 'I'm a refugee from Israel.'

Conway made a face at Davies.

'There ain't many of us,' agreed Abe. 'Jeeze if you knew what I did to get *into* that place. I got on board one of those clapped-out freighters with millions of others, all crying for our homeland. And we went in, and the dirty British tried to drown us, and we waded ashore, and kissed the beach, and all that palaver. Aw, it was great, just like a movie. Women, half their clothes off, crying and carrying on and putting their arms around everybody because they'd arrived. I enjoyed myself, I can tell you. I admit it. I used to go down to that beach after that, quite a lot, waiting for the illegal migrant ships to come in. And when they did all these half-naked women coming in on the waves, wading and swimming and falling. If was great because I used to wade out to help them and pull them in, and there were some great beauties among them too. Jeeze, you should have seen the tits on that beach. I used to really put myself into that. I liked the work.'

They had reached the mouth in the coral now, the external sea pouring through it, smooth and curved as a turquoise tongue, spreading out and flying away towards the harbour and The Love Beach which Davies could now see stretching along the eastern flank of the island, the landing barges piled like crates and boxes on the sand.

'That's The Love Beach,' said Davies to Conway.

'Like you said, it's a mess,' said Conway.

'Great opportunity for a scrap metal merchant there,' said Abe, not looking but pushing the motor boat expertly up the hill of the sea, and rolling it down the other side like a big dipper at a fairground. They were suddenly through the gap and into the open water. 'Unfortunately the civilisation here has not advanced far enough for there to be a need of scrap metal merchants,' he shrugged. 'Good, that I should be around when it is. Still, you know they're going to get the Queen over there. They're going to have an Unknown Soldier's Grave and a chapel made from the landing barges. That will be homely.'

He seemed to remember something and dipped into a paper bag on the boards of the boat. 'My God,' he said. 'I'll forget my neck next, and off will come my head. Take these and wear them on St Paul's. It makes you more welcome.' He handed to each of them a wooden crucifix, crudely worked, on a beaded loop. They took them suspiciously. 'Don't worry,' said Abe. 'It don't commit you to anything. Look, I wear one too. I always do, it makes it much safer even if you don't fight under them rules, if you see what I mean.' He hung his about his neck. They did the same. 'That's twenty-five shillings each or fifteen Pacific francs, whichever you like,' he said. 'They're a bit cheaper today. To you anyway.'

'That's very Christian of you,' commented Conway.

Conway paid for them both. They sat feeling the sun burning now, for the sky had cleared, and the sea threw up the heat at them. Davies fingered his crucifix self-consciously. 'There couldn't have been much of an outlet for this sort of trade in Israel,' said Davies.

'Exactly,' said Abe with conviction. 'No room for private expansion, enterprise, or anything like that. Take it from me—if that was my people I'd rather be among some other people. I got into trouble because I was selling little building kits to the kids. Harmless things. "Build Your Own Wailing Wall" I called them. Instructive too. After all these children had never seen the Wailing Wall, and I thought this was helping in their education. But the old dead-beats didn't like it. And they've even buggered up the little trade idea now by getting the proper Wailing Wall back into the country. Stolen from the Arabs.'

They could see the two other islands now, dull bruises on the brilliant sea. 'St Paul's,' commented Abe nodding to the form rising on the port bow. 'St Mark's,' he added looking over the silk sweep of the ocean to the other side. 'Yuk, it turns me, it really turns me. Surrounded by the New Testament all the time! You'd have thought those idiot sailors who found this place would have had more flare, more imagination. All right, have a few Christian saints. But what was wrong with Moses or Aaron or Hosiah, or one of those? Why not, tell me?'

'They're called the Apostle Islands,' Davies pointed out.

'So they wasn't called that at the start. All right, call them The Bible Islands. Genesis, Deuteronomy, Leviticus . . .' He hesitated and considered. 'Yeah, Leviticus, and why not? It's a great book! Pity no great Jewish explorers got this far down.'

'How did you get here?' asked Conway. The question was over his shoulder. The Australian was watching the volcanic peak of St Paul's growing like a wickedly humped back.

'Stowed away in the end. Went down to Eilat, on the Red Sea, and tried to get on a ship there, but those Israeli bastards kept a watch so close, you would have thought it was money they were watching. So I walked along the beach and stepped over the wire and went across to Jordan, to Akaba, and—just easy—got aboard a Japanese tanker there.

'They were very good, very civilised, the Japs. I went to Yokohama and then down to Fremantle and then, in dribs and drabs, bits and pieces, up through the islands and this is where I am now. It's not much, but it's better than Israel.'

Conway said: 'Who is the boss over on St Paul's now? They have a kind of tribal chief don't they, someone who speaks for the rest.'

Abe nodded. 'Sure, sure,' he said. 'The old one, Lazarus, died and they waited round for weeks for him to be risen from the dead. But he stayed dead, and he got more dead as the hot days went by, so they had to put him under. Big disappointment for them, though. The new chief is more nutty, really. He's called Joseph of Arimathea, so for Christ's sake ask him to take you round his garden. He likes people to do that.'

Davies said: 'Do they ever get away? From the island I mean. Or do they stay there always?'

'One or two have been over to St Peter's, but they got frightened over there,' said Abe understandingly. 'The traffic and everything scared them. So they got back quick. When the war was on the Japs were wise enough to keep away from St Paul's. They had all the other islands at some time or another, but they left this little lot alone. The Americans didn't. They used it as a jump-off for getting at the other islands. They brought stores, you know, gasoline and chewing gum and dirty books and all that stuff, and then this cargo cult—this Dodson-Smith thing started. The natives liked the good living and they're waiting for it all to come back again.'

Davies had never heard this before. 'They're what?' he asked. 'Waiting for who?'

'Dodson-Smith,' said Abe. 'He's the new Messiah boy, and they've got a U.S. army motor bike waiting up on that mountain for him to ride down in glory. Ha! There'll be weeping and gnashing of teeth that day.'

They were heeling through the sliding sea towards the island's reef now. Conway spotted the copra hulk in the lagoon, almost identical with the old ship moored off St Peter's. He turned a half circle and looked at St Mark's sitting like a slug on the sea, four miles to the east.

'St Mark's?' he said.

'The same,' agreed Abe. 'Nice people. Not Christian mind, but nice. They never cause a niggle of bother; just live and die, tie their cocks up in banana leaves, so they look three times the normal size, and—what else?—oh yeah, collect the skulls of their ancestors. But nice and agreeable.'

Conway looked at Davies. 'Glad you came?' he asked conversationally.

'It's a lovely outing,' said Davies. 'Joseph of Arimathea, Christ on a motor bike, and all that rubbish, and the other buggers tying their dicks up in banana leaves. It's different to Newport.'

'What about the St Mark's copra ship?' asked Conway.

'In the lagoon, like this one,' said Abe. 'They're getting near being rotten now. Few years ago I sold them some stuff to stick in the leaks—a mixture of sawdust and custard powder. I bought a job lot of the custard powder in Noumea and I got left with it on my hands, so I mixed it with the sawdust and brought it over and did the business. It's lasted very good, I think, but it must be wearing thin now.'

'Custard powder does,' agreed Conway. 'How long now?'

'Twenty minutes,' grunted Abe, suddenly seeming to lose his good humour at passenger's impatience. 'It don't do to rush it here. But if you'd like to get her in a bit smarter, mister, then you're welcome to try.' He twirled his wooden crucifix as though cooling himself.

'Wouldn't dream of it,' said Conway unruffled. 'You know the road, friend, you take your time.'

'Thanks,' said Abe. He did some additional, largely unnecessary manœuvres with the boat, to show how intricate the passage was. 'See the different coloured water,' he said in an immediately better humour. 'Blue, and deeper blue, nearly black, and then this green and the pretty blue green, and the nice fringe of white. Ah, it's a good place. Pity it ain't a tourist area. One day, maybe.'

'There's people on the beach,' said Davies. 'Running along.'

'They spotted us miles out,' said Abe. 'They're excited, see, because I've got a harmonium for them.'

'What have you got?' queried Conway his face twisted sideways to hear.

'A little organ, you know—a harmonium. Half a piano half an organ. They saw a picture in a missionary magazine I brought over a few months ago. It had the preacher playing the thing, somewhere in Tahiti, and all the Christians standing around singing. The boys over here like that because they go in for a lot of hymn singing, and frankly it ain't much good. I know because I've heard it. They reckoned that if they could get one of these they would sing better.'

'Have they got anyone to play it?' asked Davies.

'Details!' waved Abe. 'They're tone deaf anyway. They wouldn't know whether it's Handel or Footel. It's down there under that tarpaulin on the deck, lying flat, which is the best place for it, because you ain't never heard anything so flat before.' He chortled at his joke. 'Picked it up in Honoraria, in the Solomons. Demolishing the Missionary Chapel to build a bowling lane, or something Got it for a song.'

'I bet you're not selling it for a song,' said Davies.

'An oratorio,' admitted Abe. 'Supply and demand, my friend.'

The boat baulked nervously at the scuffling sea running through the reef gap, like a horse refusing at a fence. Abe talking a little in Yiddish and twirling his crucifix, coaxed her round with one hand on the wheel, turned her, and pointed her in the right direction. She seemed to take courage from his firm encouragement and went in on a long wave to meet the opening, taking it in style, and flopping rather heavily into the lower water of the lagoon. A short discord of notes came from under the tarpaulin. Abe laughed. 'First complaint she's made,' he said.

They ran quickly in towards the beach. It was spread out before them now like a brilliantly lit stage, populated by a hundred or more natives, some in robes, some in loin cloths, some handsomely naked, and at their centre a tall man naked to the waist but wearing plum-coloured Bermuda shorts and long woollen stockings. 'Joseph of Arimathea,' said Abe guiding the fat boat into the shallows. 'Don't forget to ask about his garden.'

There were women and children on the beach, standing with the tall man. It was a silent black crowd, not at all threatening, but merely standing and waiting. Joseph of Arimathea pulled up his woollen socks. He made a sweeping motion with both hands pushed forward and a dozen of the men moved out in formation, walked into the green water and handled the boat to a mooring. Davies and Conway waited, both looking at the assembly with some doubt and misgiving. But Abe knew what to do. He stood on the bulwark and suddenly, like an obese child launched himself into the powerful arms of the nearest tribesman. The man grunted a little on receiving the weight, but straightened immediately and proudly bore Abe through the shallows, carrying him like an infant and setting him gently on his feet just in front of Joseph, the chief.

'Oh no,' muttered Davies when he saw what was expected. 'Not us, as well.'

'Jump,' said Conway callously. 'He won't drop you.'

'And you think I'm going to sell butter and fats to this mob?'

'If he can sell a clapped-out harmonium, you can sell butter and fats,' grunted Conway. The native who was to carry Davies was waiting in the water and glancing up impatiently. Davies sighed and jumped the sort of jump a boy makes into a sand-pit. The hard arms caught him easily, giving slightly under his weight, but springing back smoothly. The tribesman smiled horribly at him with red-stained teeth and bitter breath and Davies nodded a small, nervous acknowledgement. He looked backwards and saw Conway leap, feet up over the bow, and heard the carrier grunt spectacularly and give at the knees as he took the Australian burden. He heard Conway giggle and shout 'Thank God for the lifeboatmen!' He then began to sing raucously:

'Eternal Father, strong to save
Whose arm doth bind, the restless wave . . .'

The native who was carrying Davies suddenly joined in, singing lustily and dreadfully out of tune. Conway's bearer was also singing, and then the rest of the natives in the water, and finally the entire array of the tribe on the beach, starting with miraculous spontaneity as though they had been holding themselves for the cue. The chief swept out his arms joyfully, conducting them:

'Who bids the mighty ocean deep,
It's own appointed limits keep . . .'

It was such a terrible assault, such a huge discordant mixture, that no true words could be heard, just a rush and bellow of sound blaring along the beach. Davies, his starkly white face only inches from that of his carrying native, could hardly pick a remembered syllable from the gabble. The words were run into each other, howled and bent and twisted into a terrible gibberish. It was not as though the whole congregation stretched along the strand sang the same distortion. There were fifty different distortions, all flung out with the same religious venom, like some fantastic, drunken, mad Eisteddfod.

Yet no matter how high or low they screeched or bellowed, or whooped, everybody finished the verse at the same moment. Some were stamping on the sand in their verve, some holding their hands out to the sea or to the sky; some had closed their eyes with the excitement and ecstasy of it, several were on their knees, hands clasped. Children howled as loud as the rest.

It was only twenty yards from the boat to the place where the first native had set Abe upon his feet, but the men carrying Davies and Conway declined to let them go. They remained in the shallows, clutching their burdens like sacrifices, and singing greatly with deep fretting tones, great mouth openings and vigorous colliding of gums and teeth. Conway looked far away out to sea, as though he expected a vision at any second. Davies, paralysed with fear and embarrassment, hung in the tribesman's arms and felt the full furnace of the singer's overpowering breath on his face. The tribesman, without stopping his bellow, nodded at Davies in a demanding way, and Davies meekly began to sing too, picking up a phrase here and a sentence there and squeaking them in a boy soprano voice which he found was all he could attain.

Eventually the hymn's five verses ended. It was like a door closing or a choir falling down a cliff to instant and massive death. The seas washing became deafening in the utter silence and the movement of the palm trees fringing the beach was like a beating of heavy carpets, Davies could hear his own tremendous breathing. His bearer paused, walked the remaining paces up the sand, and set him down beside Abe, with the smile of a man returning a dancing partner to her seat at the conclusion of a waltz. Conway followed and all three stood before the chief, Joseph of Arimathea.

'Happy Crucifixion,' said the chief shaking hands with them.

Davies thought afterwards: I used to read books like that and I used to toss them away and laugh and say how far-fetched and ridiculous they were. Nobody ever existed like that. The adventurers, the explorers, just made it up, faked it, so they could raise enough money to go on more adventures and further explorations.

He said to Bird: 'I couldn't believe it was happening. We forgot it was Easter—well Good Friday—see, until this chief, Joseph of Arimathea, said "Happy Crucifixion". It was bad enough them carrying us ashore like little kids, and everybody singing like mad, except they all yelled out different words. Well, I suppose they were words. And no one quite got the tune straightened out.'

It was ten o'clock in the evening in Bird's salon. Davies was connecting the wires of a new light fitting to three tails of flex projecting from the ceiling. At home, from necessity, he had always done the small jobs, or tried to do them. But he had never had the logical, practical approach of the good handyman. He sometimes made up for it with some measure of adaptability or even inventiveness, but, when he ever made some attempt at a home repair it usually fell apart or blew a fuse within a couple of days. He would laugh at it and Kate would go quickly into the kitchen or out to talk to the woman next door. He was never much good at mending. Anything.

He was arched on a doubtful step-ladder among the chairs and hair driers. Bird was gripping the vertical pieces with both hands and turning her face up to see him. Once he looked down at her and involuntarily stopped what he was doing. Her clean, solemn face was looking up the ladder, her eyes full of doubt about how he was proceeding with the task, her back arched inwardly so that her bottom stuck out neat and round and her legs were divided by the step-ladder. She saw the way he looked and smiled uncertainly. He went back to finding the right wires.

'I used to pick up a magazine in the barber's at home,' he

113

said. 'Or in the canteen at work. And there would be these yarns about people in jungles, or lost in mountains, or living some funny life on islands, and I used to think they were made up. They were just like comics for kids.'

'I would never go over there to that place,' admitted Bird. 'Not many people from this island will go. Even the missionary, Mr Collins, he won't. Mrs Flagg has been, naturally, but even she and Mr Flagg like best the pagans on St Mark's. They think they are safer.'

'They're right,' agreed Davies. The backs of his legs and his fingers were aching. He said: 'I'll have a breather. I'll get them all connected to the right bits next time. Honest.' He backed down the ladder bringing the heavy light-fitting with him. It was stainless steel and had arrived with him on *The Baffin Bay*. Bird said it was to add distinction to the salon.

Davies set it carefully on the floor, like an archbishop placing down a crown. He brushed his hands together. It was a thick, hot evening, the last downpour now rising again in quiet steam from the muddy area outside the window. He could feel the sweat scampering down the front of his shirt. Bird playfully wiped his forehead with a towel and gave it to him. He unceremoniously wiped down inside his shirt and around his neck and face. She walked away from him towards the back of the shop. 'Beer?' she asked. 'Or shall I make some tea?'

'Let's have a beer,' suggested Davies. 'It's quicker. I can't wait for the kettle. That's a hell of a job getting that thing up there. It's so damned heavy.'

She hesitated. 'I'll get someone from the builder's to do it, if you like,' she said genuinely. 'They will do it tomorrow or the next day, I expect.'

'Oh no,' he protested. 'I didn't mean it like that. I can do it, Bird, but I'd like to get the right wires fixed to the right wires.'

She brought the beer to him. It was in a patriotic mug, with a crown and a faded portrait on its side. Davies laughed quietly. 'Jeeze,' he said. 'These have travelled round a bit. Coronation mug, 1937. I remember getting mine at school. I ran home with it, clutched to me, scared stiff I'd drop it, and some other kids chased me and I thought they were going to try and smash it. I've never run so fast. I got in and slammed the door and stood there on the mat, panting and sweating and clutching the mug. You'd have thought it was the Holy Grail.'

'That makes you very old,' she said examining the side of the mug as though for the first time.

He mimicked an ancient's voice. 'Aaah ever so, young woman,' he said. 'Very, very old, I remember . . . I remember . . . No I don't. I've forgotten now.'

She laughed and he grinned, suddenly realising the release she gave him, the way she lifted his spirit and his energy. He looked down at the yellow disc of beer in the mug. She had been drinking from another cup and she turned abruptly and took it to the small kitchen at the back of the shop. There was silence in the place. A native went up the darkened street, painfully pedalling a bicycle through the sticking mud. A dog was singing somewhere across the town.

'Listen to that,' said Davies. 'He ought to go over with that mob on St Paul's. He could be lead tenor.' He heard her giggle from the other room. She came in quickly. 'Davies,' she said, almost whispering in her enthusiasm. 'Tell me again about the harmonium. That Abe! What next will he do!'

Davies grinned, still looking down. He was sitting uncomfortably on the second rung of the step-ladder. She swung herself easily into one of the swivel hairdressing chairs. She whirled it gently, her legs trailing like a child sitting on a river bank.

'The harmonium,' said Davies. 'The-big-box-fellah, him have black-white-teeth, you-hit-them-he-cry.'

She smiled at the attempt. 'Nearly right,' she said. 'One day I teach you Pidgin.'

'It's marvellous,' said Davies. 'A laugh in every line. Have you heard Abe? I don't know how I didn't choke when he started talking to old Joseph. It wasn't Pidgin-English, it was

Pidgin-Yiddish! He kept saying "YUK!", you know that expression—"Yuk!", it's a great word for disgust. It sounds so disgusting. And then he'd come out with a stream of Pidgin and stick "already" or "my life" on the end!'

Bird said: 'Abe has a degree in Pidgin from the University of Australia.'

Davies glanced up to see if she were joking, but she was not. He said: 'The best bit was where Abe got them to unload the harmonium from the boat and they dropped it!'

Bird hooted: 'That was funny, darling. Tell me again. Please.'

He was laughing himself. 'Abbott and Costello,' he said. 'The kids at home used to queue up in air raids during the war to see that on the pictures. I mean, they'd carried us off the boat —even Abe and Conway who are heavy—singing at the tops of their voices, and it was all right. But they got so excited getting the harmonium off, and they were all crowding each other and trying to help and everyone was gathered around giving advice. So they dropped it. Crunch! Right into the water, which did it no good at all and just to help a bit, it must have struck a lump of coral because it went all squew-whiff, all the joints bent over . . .'

Bird was laughing behind her hands. 'And it made a noise,' she reminded him. 'It made a sad noise. Tell me that again.'

'A very sad noise,' he said. 'A sort of wet groan. It was like an old lady falling into the sea. And what a panic. They all rushed and lugged the thing out, all shouting and blaming each other for it. Then they got it on the beach and it looked in a bad way there. Oh, I forgot to tell you before. When they put it on the beach, they stood it upside down!'

'Oh Davies no!' Bird was all delight. He thought how much like a child she was. The next time she called him 'darling' even accidentally he wouldn't take any notice.

'It was leaning like a drunk to one side where the bash on the coral had knocked it out of shape,' he continued. 'And they all stood around it and poked their fingers at it, and tried to figure it out. It looked very sad. Abe was making all sorts of noises about cargo not being insured once it had left the ship and Conway was trying not to laugh too much. Anyway I used to play the piano, once years ago, and I thought this thing couldn't be that difficult. So I went up to them and got them to turn it the right way up. It was in a terrible state. What with the sand and the sea-water, and the keys all knocked out of joint by dropping it. One of them dropped out as soon as I touched it. Anyway I started to pick out a tune on it—a hymn tune because that's what I used to play back home in Wales when I was a kid.'

Bird said quietly: 'You played for them? That was very kind.'

'I couldn't think of anything else to do. They were standing around like a lot of infants when Father Christmas hasn't turned up. I didn't play, really, I just sort of picked out the notes as best I could.'

'And you made them happy.'

'If I'd been Albert Schweitzer they couldn't have been more pleased. The box was actually making a tune. They went mad. They nodded along to it for a bit, following it. Then they realised what it was—it was "There Is a Green Hill Far Away"—and they all began howling again. Christ, what a row! But it was marvellous in a way. And then . . . well, you'd never believe this . . . I forgot to tell you before . . .'

'What else? You forgot to tell me a lot,' she protested.

'I came to fix this light,' Davies pointed out looking at the ceiling. 'Anyway I was a bit uncomfortable standing up playing this harmonium so I sort of looked around for something to sit on, a box or anything. But I couldn't see anything. Then Old Joseph realised what I wanted and said something to one of his warriors, and the next thing I know this chap is down on all fours and making himself into a stool so I could sit on his back. I didn't want to, naturally, but they insisted and they wanted some more tunes, so I sat down on him, as lightly as I could mind, and carried on playing. What about that! And all the time I was sitting on him he was singing too, I could feel him singing away underneath me!'

Bird stared at him. 'He was like a stool for you?' she asked unbelievingly.

'Like a stool,' he confirmed.

'And he was singing too?'

'Yes. I could feel his lungs going in and out under my backside and I could hear him too.'

She began to laugh again, almost hysterically. 'Oh, that is not possible,' she pleaded. 'Look you make me cry with laughing. Look at my eyes. They are all running.'

'Here's a handkerchief,' said Davies politely fumbling. She waved it away and picked a tissue from a holder by the shampoo basin. She turned from him while she wiped her eyes. He looked at her. The gentle moulding of her back showed through the cotton dress and her hair was running all over her neck. Her legs were brown and bare with the creases behind her knees like slim white channels. She turned. 'What happened then?' she asked.

'Well it stopped being funny for a start,' he said. 'They took us up the village, first. Just huts, like on this island, wood and corrugated iron and palm-leaf thatch, roughly set around a square full of chickens and kids; children I mean, not goats, although they had some of them too.

'Joseph said they had a very important procession to hold, being as it was Good Friday. He took us to his garden which was supposed to be where Christ was buried, as it says in the Bible. He's got a cave there and a big stone in front of it and he said this is where it all happened.'

'They believe that,' she nodded seriously. 'This I have heard before, of course. They think that the whole of the Bible is about their island. Did you see Noah's Ark?'

'Well they pointed out the mountain where they said it stuck when the flood went down and they said we could go up and see it some other time, but they wanted us to watch the procession just then. But they did take us up to see the motor bike, just above the village, all ready to bring this new Saviour, this Dodson-Smith, down to them when he arrives. It's an American army relic, but it's in great condition. They keep it clean and tuned up and full of juice and everything. One of them gave it a kick and started it up for us. It's amazing how they believe that this bloke is going to arrive among them. It's frightening too.'

'They have faith,' she said. 'Are not we as Christians looking forward to the second coming of Jesus? We're supposed to if we have faith.'

'Of course,' he said caustically. 'But not on a two-stroke motor bike. I swear they'd have cut our heads off if we'd laughed. Anyway then we did a round tour of Bethlehem, Jericho and all the other tourist places. And they told us that their village was the original Jerusalem. All we could keep doing was to nod our heads as though we were agreeing with them. It was like trying to humour the people in a loony bin.'

'They are very strange,' she agreed. 'That is why no one will venture there. I would be most afraid.'

'So was I,' said Davies. 'And I felt worse when they began this procession. They enacted the whole thing; Pilate washing his hands, Jesus carrying the cross, and the people spitting on him and striking him. We sat there drinking some native beer stuff that they'd brought to us, and watched it all going on. Joseph sat with us—we were on the little veranda at the front of his house—and he was lying back in a sort of horse-hair armchair, just like the ones you used to see in the houses in Wales. All the stuffing was coming out of it. God knows where he got it, but he thought it was great, and he sort of lounged back and watched the business going on, just like a man watching television. He said he wouldn't be taking part until later. Oh yes, I forgot, the whole thing was done in silence. Absolute silence.

All mimed and not a sound from anywhere or anyone, and the whole island population was there. That's what made it more frightening. Dead silence. Every time Conway took a swallow of beer it sounded to me like somebody flushing a toilet.'

'Jesus, I mean *their* Jesus, the man carrying the cross, what was he like?'

Davies raised his eyebrows at her. 'Yes,' he said. 'You're thinking like we began to think,' he said. 'It didn't occur to us, right then when we were sitting there with the chief drinking the beer. It was hot as hell, the sun really burning down, and no rain all day, for once. The chap who was carrying the cross was in a sort of blanket and his hair and his beard were long. He was the only one with whiskers, so he had obviously been prepared for the part. Anyway it went on for hours, it seemed. The whole ritual, and in dumb show. And as I said it was terrible and hot and they kept bringing us these bowls of their beer and before long I was well on the way to being plastered. I thought it was the heat at the start, because the square, with the sun really white on it, started to get hazy and all the black bodies began to wriggle in front of my eyes. They looked just like a swarm of tadpoles.'

He could see she was about to ask him what tadpoles were, but she changed her mind and did not interrupt.

'I thought it was just me, but it wasn't because old Conway was well gone. He started putting his arm around Joseph of Arimathea and saying to him "How would you and some of your lads like to go to Vietnam?"'

'What!' Bird exclaimed. 'Vietnam! Why did he say that?'

'God only knows, but he kept on. It was awkward for me, I can tell you. He was well gone, worse than I was. Yes, just leaning over as though he was in a pub at Woolamalloo and asking if they'd like to go to Vietnam. Plastered out of his mind. Fortunately Abe hadn't drunk any of the native grog and he could see things were getting out of hand. So he got us up from our seats, shook hands with Joseph, and made us do the same. The old boy smiled quite agreeably and didn't seem to mind us going. Jesus, or the man playing the part of Jesus, was carrying this whacking great cross through all the people by then, sweating under it and dragging his feet in the dust. Joseph just nodded to us and when we slipped away he was sitting back there dead pleased, in his armchair.

'We didn't have to go through the crowd. We skirted the house and Abe took us through some palms and we found ourselves on the beach again. I never thought I'd be so glad to be away from anywhere. Abe seemed to be as scared as we were, or perhaps he was just annoyed with us, because he didn't say a word. He just hurried and got the boat out of the lagoon and headed back here. It wasn't until we were well out of the way, and I was feeling sick as the devil, what with the beer and the sea getting a swell on, that anyone said anything. Conway was looking green, really terrible, and I had the thought that had been there in my mind all the time. I said to Abe: "Abe, what are they going to do with that man? They're not really going to crucify him are they?"

'Conway looked up and he looked awful. He said to us, "When they did the Christmas pantomime they actually had a baby born. I was told that!" So I asked Abe again. "Are they going to crucify that man?" and Abe turned around, really grumpy, and said: "How the hell should I know. It's your bloody religion, not mine."'

VIII

The long ranges of cloud that for weeks had grown successfully on the eastern sea, bringing the thick rain to the island, became small foothills, then little mounds, and eventually failed to rise at all. The wet season was over. Within a few days dust was piling in the streets of Sexagesima and both Governors had broadcast a warning of an impending water shortage. 'Every year the situation is the same,' said Pollet to Davies. 'In March the place is a swamp, by the third day of April there is a drought.'

'It must be really bad for the Governors to have to broadcast,' said Davies.

Pollet blew out his cheeks and hunched his shoulders in a continental gesture. 'It's no different, my friend. In fact every year on this day it's the same speech. The Governor records it and George Turtle puts the record on on April the third at eleven in the morning. The French do the same when they have their hour of broadcasting. You could call it a fixed feast. Next week Mrs Flagg will have a garden party and there will be Scottish dancing led by Mr English, the leader of the council, you remember. That is also a fixed feast. It is the beginning of the summer here in The Apostles.'

Almost every day Davies went down to The Love Beach to swim, sometimes alone, sometimes with Bird, when the salon was not busy, and occasionally with Conway and Dahlia. He liked to go in the late afternoon best because then the children from the village would come from the school and run down on to the sand, roll and jump into the sea in the sun, and then sit about under the shade of the landing barges and sing sweet songs.

A strange feeling of carelessness had come over him when the sun had arrived in the islands. He felt it soak into him, slowing his thoughts and movements, his ambitions too. His campaign to sell butter and fats had not been in the least successful. Some of the shopkeepers, the Chinese and Vietnamese particularly, had been polite and even encouraging, but his order book remained full of nothing but half-promises. Since he considered himself a trained failure the sight of his plan draining away was no surprise, but this time the savage disappointment was not there. Somehow it did not seem to matter enough to hurt him. The sun had burned his body hard brown within a couple of weeks. He took his paints and his canvases into places in the interior spending hours working alone, high up above a village with the sea at its door, trying to convey its domesticity among the green wildness, the smoke from the houses, the people moving about, and throwing nets from the beach. Once he took his bicycle to the back of the island and sat under some rocks working at his canvas all day while two men fished with circular nets into a heavy surf. Another day he painted a village market, and then some natives working at the coconut gathering. At some of the villages they began to recognise him, to welcome him, and to congregate with polite curiosity as he went about his art. Children, at the front, men and women behind, they would form an orderly gallery, very quiet, but occasionally pointing out details on the canvas to their companions.

In the painting of these things he felt a set contentment he had not experienced before in his life. He was, he realised, and he told everyone, merely waiting for the arrival of *The Baffin Bay* to return him to Sydney where he would report the utter and dismal failure of his business mission to Trellis and Jones of The Circular Quay, and would doubtless then get the sack.

But that was all to come. There was plenty of time, another month, to consider all his difficulties. In the meantime he would sit like Gauguin, and paint.

Davies, however, remained the worst artist in the world. Conway told Dahlia that he thought the Welshman was colour-blind and didn't know it. Bird was always politely encouraging, but screwed up her face when she looked over his shoulder. He had no feel for his subjects, even if he thought he had, no romance, no flair, not even the compensation of bold technical efficiency. His only attribute was absolute blindness to his own incompetence. There was nothing else.

Once while he was asleep after lunch on a heart-shaped coral beach in the north of the island, a Melanesian from the fishing village purloined his easel and proceeded to paint the scene with gusto, and with a vivid colour sense such as Davies would never have. When Davies woke up he was very angry with the man and told him he must not interfere again when an artist was at work near his village. But he let the man have his daub to take and hang in his house. 'After all he didn't know what he was doing,' he said to Bird.

Each time he went out on one of his painting expeditions he would get Seamus at the Hilton to make him up a bundle of sandwiches and wrap up some fruit, and he would take with him a bottle of native beer. When he had worked through the morning he would sleep for an hour after lunch and then continue until he considered the light had changed. Sometimes he took two bottles of beer and his afternoon sleep lasted longer.

One afternoon, lying in the shade of the barges on The Love Beach, snoring into the black sand, he dreamed, as he had often done, of little Mag and David and Kate. But, for the first time, he had difficulty in focusing them. In his dream he could not see their faces, and when he came to look at their clothes he could not recognise them either. He strained to hear their voices, forcing himself deeper into the sand in his sleep, but they were only whispers with Welsh accents. He couldn't catch what they were saying. Where were they going, moving away from him like this? What had happened to the clear lines of their noses and the light in their eyes? Kate was the same, even worse, just a shadow in an oatmeal costume and a spot of rouge on her cheeks. In his dream a commentator kept explaining to him that the reason they had altered and he couldn't see them properly was because he had been away so long and they *had* changed; they were different and he was different, and they could not be expected to remain faithful to him—any of them—because he had been away so long and they were not sure they knew him properly any longer, any more than he knew them.

He awoke from his dream with the sun beating down on his face, clear away from the shadow where he had gone to sleep. He was rolling in the sand and it was sticking to his sweat as he rolled. He awoke shouting: 'Ghosts! Ghosts! Ghosts!' His raw voice jerked him to full consciousness and he sat up in the black sand on the empty beach, and stared out to the aching brilliance of the sun on the lagoon. Above him the arms of the palm trees were stamped out against the full blue sky. The sun was burning, and the only sounds were the rhythms of his breathing and the tired washing of the sea.

'Ghosts!' he repeated to himself miserably. He thought about the dream and felt he might try to get back to sleep again to search for his lost wife and his children. He would hold them still and close so that he could see their faces and so they could recognise him. But he knew that would be useless. When he thought about it he had very little more money now than when he set out to Australia all those long months ago. He would go back home to Wales, to seek them out and tell them he was their father, not any other man, car or no car, and he would claim Kate again. Yes, he would find the money and be with them again.

When *The Baffin Bay* arrived, that was.

It was recognised that Mrs Flagg's garden party was the opening event of the summer season at Sexagesima. Her house with the red roof which provided such a convenient navigation mark for the Governor's little sailors was splendidly situated for the event, with its lawns assembled by the lagoon and its muster of trees for shade. Mrs Flagg always instructed Mr Flagg to see that the lawns were well watered for at least a week beforehand, and for the entire morning of the actual day of the party, but to make sure that the sprinklers were turned off and hidden away before the arrival of either the British or the French Governors because they had, by then, made their water-saving appeal.

'This year we're having our little surprise innovation, dear,' Mrs Flagg told Bird when she arrived for her shampoo and set. '*You* know what I mean, don't you? Some people *know* they're here, but we're just hoping that the news hasn't travelled too far.' Bird made a lined puzzled face in the mirror. 'Oh come, dear,' said Mrs Flagg. 'Don't say you've forgotten. I *told* you, now didn't I, when I sat in this very chair a few weeks ago?' She looked hopefully at Bird. '*You know,*' she nudged. 'Our native friends from St Mark's. We've got six of them.'

Bird realised. 'At the house?' she said. 'Now?'

'Yes, dear, of course. They're going to serve the guests at the garden party.'

Bird watched Mrs Flagg in the mirror. 'Have they . . .? You know, Mrs Flagg, have they got . . .?'

'The banana leaf wrappings, their baloots, dear?' Mrs Flagg gurgled. 'But, of course. They wouldn't be St Mark's if they hadn't got them would they? They're jolly interesting, you know. They've been with us three days now and they're completely fascinating. I could watch them all day. Mr Flagg and I have been making copious notes.'

'Where are they living?' asked Bird suspiciously. She started to work on Mrs Flagg's hair again.

'In the grounds. They've built a nice hut. It doesn't take them long, you know, and they're settling down very well. They

126

brought over their own bedding and cooking utensils and that sort of personal thing and they've got their ancestors' skulls all lined up outside the front door.'

Bird stopped working again. 'They brought the skulls with them?'

'But naturally, dear,' said Mrs Flagg. 'They wouldn't have come under any other circumstances. It was quite amusing really, quite amusing. When they were lining up the skulls they had quite a nasty argument among themselves about which order they ought to be placed. One said this skull was third in line, and other said no, it was this one, and the third said it wasn't either, it was this one because it had a spear mark just behind the ear.'

'They should have numbered them,' suggested Bird.

'Next time they will, I expect,' said Mrs Flagg. 'It will save all the arguments. But, you see they're just *not* used to moving. Quite frankly, even now they're not at all sure that all the grandfathers and grandmothers are in the right order. There was quite a bit of bad feeling about it at the start, but I think it's all simmered down. I jolly well hope so, for the sake of the garden party.'

On the morning of the event Mr Flagg was seen going from the harbour in his neat blue motor boat. He returned before noon bringing with him from St Mark's one of the tribal elders, an old man with flabby gums, who was reputed to know by sight the skull of every ancestor of every family on the island. 'He really was marvellous,' related Mrs Flagg at the garden party. 'He came in without any fuss and they had a sort of identity parade of the skulls outside the hut. He had a look at each one and muttered something or other, then he shuffled them about a bit, moved one up a couple of places and another further back, and said that was the right order. It was like that gambling game they play with upturned tea-cups, where you have to find the dice. Anyway my boys seemed to trust his judgement and abide by his decision. He really saved us an *awful* lot of bother. I feel so grateful to him. There he is now, over there, drinking tea with the Reverend Collins.'

Almost every European on the island was at the garden party. The sun was glassy on the brilliant lagoon and on the vivid lawns skirting it. The rain was finished, the summer had come to the island. The people, French and English, convivial for once, drank tea and ate cakes and talked in little formations that moved, separated, stayed, separated again, and rejoined, with all the elegance and good taste of Victorian formation dancers.

Mrs Flagg's houseboys caused a sensation only among a minority of guests. Others were diverted but many had lived so long in the Apostle Islands that no tribal idiosyncrasy astonished them. The six little men busied themselves with good humour serving the guests. Each one had his penis mummified in the case of banana leaves and tight bindings, brought up his stomach, and tucked neatly into an army webbing belt which Mr Flagg had purchased specially for the occasion.

'How amusing,' commented Mrs English, the wife of the council chairman, when the St Mark's men first entered with their trays. 'How absolutely amusing.'

'Sweet,' agreed Mrs Haskin simpering at her tea. 'Quite sweet. Mrs Flagg certainly has some jolly ideas.'

The little men were amused themselves, staring at the ladies in silk and nylon dresses with strange shoes and delicate parasols, and the men in their well ironed white suits and school ties. Sir William sweated painfully in a badly over-starched shirt and hard plank-like trousers. M. Martin looked cool and unofficial in a fine lightweight blue suit and cocky little hat. He had received a new consignment of silk shirts from Paris by the last boat which pleased him, although he was still at a loss to know where his wine and liquor consignment had once again vanished.

'Everything is good for the visit of Her Majesty?' asked M. Martin.

128

'Oh certainly,' said Sir William. 'We've got plenty of paint and bunting, and the band has been practising like fury all the week.'

'This I know well,' shrugged M. Martin. 'They are playing the same tune at each night from the club of the British Legion. The sound flies up the valley to my terrace when the breeze comes in from the sea in the evening.'

'Nothing to touch a little music for relaxation,' countered Sir William bravely. 'I wish I could hear them.'

'It is, I understand, a composition called "Annie Laurie". This I have been told by my foreign experts. I wish you could hear it too, your Excellency. Perhaps we could, how do you say it, swop houses; yes, swop houses, that is right, until they have consumed sufficient practise.'

'Fine old Scots air,' said Sir William. 'And they must get it right for the Queen.'

'You know our navy is coming across?' mentioned M. Martin. 'There will be a salute of twenty-one guns.'

'That gunboat of yours from Noumea?' queried Sir William testily. 'I didn't know.'

M. Martin sniffed over his cup. 'Maybe our liaison officers do not liaise enough, Sir William. They must meet more often. Yes, the warship—the *Auriol*—is coming.'

'That thing hasn't got twenty-one guns,' argued Sir William.

'It will fire its six-pounder twenty-one times,' said the French Governor with triumph. 'I undestand that there is to be a chapel of the Unknown Soldier consecrated on The Love Beach? That is a good idea. Very romantic and very economical.'

'That's their idea,' said the British Governor indicating the kilt-laden Mr English and other members of the town council in a clique at one fringe of the lawn. 'All they have to do now is to find an Unknown Soldier. I gather they've sent search parties out into the jungle to try and get one. Frankly it floors me, old man. They'll go out en masse to find a mouldy skeleton but if some poor devil is genuinely lost out there you can't get the so-and-sos away from the whist drive at the British Legion. Don't you remember that idiot who came down from Honoraria last year who got stuck in the bog ten miles up the coast? Fool had a native guide who had no sense of direction whatever. He nearly got drowned in the mud before anyone could be raised to go and look for him. What was the excuse then? Oh yes, it was August Bank Holiday.'

'It is not a holiday the French celebrate,' said M. Martin piously.

'One of the few,' grumbled Sir William. 'I can never get any of your people for half the year. Always some saint's day or other.'

'But you have a holiday without even the excuse of a saint to bless it,' returned M. Martin. 'By the way do you like Mrs Flagg's little pissens from St Mark's?'

'Not the best choice of words,' said Sir William. 'Your colloquial English lets you down sometimes, old man. You could hardly call what they have got "little" now can you?'

M. Martin laughed. 'A very funny way you have with you, Governor. They are most strange at a garden party, are they not? I understand Mrs Flagg is making a study of them.'

'So is every other frustrated female here,' mumbled Sir William.

Mrs Minnie Turtle at the fringe of a group of clinking tea-cups was saying: 'Fancy displaying yourself like that at a garden party.' She wriggled half around and glared at Bird and Dahlia.

'What goes in Europe is not always in the best of taste here,' agreed Mrs English. 'I hope they keep their wretched mini-skirts in their wardrobe when Her Majesty arrives. I want her to see that we preserve some standards in The Apostles.'

George Turtle was saying: 'It's a tragedy that the Queen won't be here long enough to make a broadcast. Now that would be a marvellous thing. And we've got our new microphone now.'

Rob Roy English, his kilt rubbing a little sweaty red seam like a garter across the top of his leg on this hot day, said to Conway: 'The people will all line the pavements and give the royal lass a fine cheer.'

'Pavements?' asked Conway rudely sucking in his tea. 'Which pavements?'

'Well the sides of the roads,' said the council chairman reacting to the slight. 'We're not a wealthy authority, you know. We can't have everything in Sexagesima.'

Conway smiled agreeably. He said: 'Why don't you get some of the natives from St Paul's over for the visit? Say a dozen. A sort of guard of honour.'

'Good idea,' said Mr English. 'We'd have to ask the Governor, of course. But it's not a bad notion at all.'

The mention of the Governor depressed Conway immediately. 'I shouldn't worry,' he said. 'They're a bit unusual, the boys over there, it might spoil things.'

Mr Livesley said to Davies: 'Do you like the buns? I think they're very good. They're mine.'

Davies said: 'You should put a new neon sign up saying "Buns". That would be dramatic.' Bird, who was standing with them, nodded: 'That would be a most effective switch in your advertising campaign, Mr Livesley,' she said.

The baker regarded them with a narrow look. They drank their tea and Bird accepted another syrup bun from one of the St Mark's natives who jolted by with a tray. Mr Livesley decided they were serious.

'I've had thoughts about extending the sign,' he puffed. 'The trouble with this royal visit is that it will be all over by the evening and the ship will have gone. My neon advertisement, I'm the first to admit, looks nothing in the day. I'd like to have a similar sign put up on the top of the mountain. Perhaps in just one continuous colour. Not flashing. In red I think. At night when you could not see the mountain it would look as though it were hanging in the sky. That's what happens with the statue of Christ the Redeemer at Rio de Janeiro, you know. So I've read. At night you can't see the mountain but the statue is floodlit and it looks just as though the Saviour is floating above the city.'

'Interesting,' commented Davies. 'What will your advertisement say?'

'The one on the mountain? Oh, I haven't thought about it yet. It's all in the air. Ha! That's a joke isn't it!'

'Yes, it's a joke,' agreed Davies. Bird nodded.

Mr Livesley reverted to his big business voice. 'Bread,' he said decisively. 'That's what it will say—"Bread".'

'Bread of Heaven,' suggested Davies. 'That would be good stuck on top of a mountain.'

'That's got *something* about it,' admitted Mr Livesley. 'A sort of ring.'

'It's a hymn,' said Davies. 'A Welsh hymn tune. They sing it at rugby matches.'

Conway walked over the lawn, his feathery tea-cup balanced ridiculously in his big hand. He nodded to Mr Livesley. 'Why don't you switch that sign of yours off after midnight?' he asked. 'No one wants to buy bread at three in the morning and the thing keeps people awake.'

'Now *wait* a minute,' argued Mr Livesley. 'I don't consider that sign merely of commercial value. It is, I believe, something of a landmark for this town and, indeed, these islands. It can be seen for miles across the sea you know.'

Davies burrowed in quickly. 'Mr Livesley was telling us about the statue of Christ at Rio de Janeiro. It was very interesting.'

'Yes, fascinating,' confirmed Mr Livesley. 'At night when it is illuminated and the mountain is hidden by the darkness the statue seems to float in the air. I read about it in *Reader's Digest*. I gather its very sobering.'

'It doesn't have that effect on Rio,' said Conway.

'I suppose you can get used to anything,' said Bird helpfully.

Then with relief 'Ah, look. The Scottish dancing is to start.'

Davies had thought that nothing more could surprise him in The Apostles. But now Rob Roy English had seized a squealing set of bagpipes and imprisoned them like a pig under his arm. His pallid wife had roped a side-drum around her neck and was rolling the sticks with fine competence over the skin. The big crowd divided and backed away making a space in the centre of Mrs Flagg's lawn, a green sunlit space, hot in the afternoon, topped by idle palms and breadfruit trees and a huge Pacific sky. Into this tropical arena came the Highland Dancers.

Four were women middle-aged, dry women, with set faces and hard necks. Three were thin, two short, one tall, and one was red and big and fat, bursting from her Stuart Hunting Tartan, pounding up and down on her buckled shoes, her calves like footballs in her woollen socks. Four more were British colonial office personnel, clerky men with inky expressions all puffing with overweight and the heat, except one who had a bristled ginger moustache, and a white worm of a body.

The other eight members of the Highland dancing group were Melanesian natives, four men and four women, shining ebony people with great arms and trunk legs. Their kilts and tartans lay about and over them in giant folds and they winced with the pain of the buckled shoes as they danced.

'Good God in the sky,' whispered Conway. 'I don't believe it.' Davies nudged him silent. The piper was playing the lament 'The Flowers of the Forest' and the sixteen dancers, black and pale, pawed their way through the dirge dance, a sad look upon each face, large and small, and powerful wooden grace in the way they swung arms and legs.

The lament was followed by a reel performed with dedication and vivacity, the tribesmen bounding, bouncing and whirling with the rest and emitting guttural Highland exclamations. When it came the time for partners to be swung the watchers became tense. One of the big native women clasping the stringy man about his little waist with a mighty arm, and being clasped by his white hairless forearm, swung with energy and it seemed that the European would be catapulted away.

Strangely it was the natives who sweated. The white dancers whirled and swayed, stepped daintily in the vivid sun, without discomfort. But the Melanesians, hung about with their Scots trappings, encased in shoes, socks, kilts weighing pounds, bouncing sporrans and hairy hats, ran floods of black perspiration and stood heaving at the conclusion of each set.

At the finale the hundreds on the lawn applauded, the little baloot clad men from St Mark's applauding too for they had never known music and dancing like it. Mrs Flagg stepped into the bright green circle and thanked the puffing natives and the sedate white dancers, then called for Auld Lang Syne. There were too many guests for one circle, so those who could cross and join hands did so around the lawn and the others clasped hands where they stood and lent their voices to the famous old song. Mr English fought the pipes, Mrs English rolled her side-drum, and the voices, of all manner of shades and accents, joined in. Sir William and M. Martin self-consciously crossed hands with the ghostly A.D.C., Cooper, on Sir William's right and M. Martin's aide to the right of his chief. It was a moving display of comradeship far out in a remote place. Some eyes glistened and the words did not come easily to many a throat. The sun, now late in its path, lit the colonial sight; the people, the trees, the tropical flowers all about Mrs Flagg's lawn, and the full-coloured sea in the background.

One of the joiners, an elderly man called Albert Coxly who had retired to Sexagesima from missionary service in Wallis Island, died while they were singing. The people on either side of him, clasping his friendly crossed hands, did not know he had passed away. He was very light and fragile and they hardly noticed his moribund weight. When, on the second verse, all the people moved inwards to the centre of the circle, in the traditional way, the dead Mr Coxly was dragged with them,

134

and then when they moved out again he was trawled back. Nobody noticed. The circle expanded and contracted half a dozen times as the song was louder sung. And he went with it. To and fro, to and fro. Eventually they stopped and laughed and applauded and walked away leaving Mr Coxly lying dead on the lawn. They returned to him, of course, when he was observed, and the doctor pronounced him extinct. 'Heart,' he grunted professionally. 'Couldn't stand up to it.'

Davies turned to Bird and saw she was crying. 'He was a nice old man,' she said. 'It is a pity he had to die. And like this.'

'It's a pity anyone has to die,' said Davies. He said to Conway: 'What a way to go.'

Conway said: 'More queer things happen around here than at King's Cross on a Saturday night.'

IX

Conway walked into Davies's room at the Hilton without knocking. Davies was having an early evening sleep, transfixed on his bed, snoring mildly. A gekko ate some flies petrified on the ceiling, sticking them to his tongue like a man wetting stamps at a post office. The blind was down but there was a dagger-shaped tear in it that admitted a slice of late sun. Conway walked around, like a connoisseur at a gallery, pulling faces at Davies's paintings which were standing around the walls. Davies rolled and woke.

'What's that supposed to be?' asked Conway hearing him wake and not turning round. He pointed his toe at one of the canvases. 'This one.'

'Let's have a look,' said Davies, he did a neat movement off the bed and looked down. 'Can't you see?' he said. 'It's The Love Beach. I would have thought even you could see that. It's plain as anything.'

'Sure,' agreed Conway with politeness. 'That's it. The Love Beach. It's the . . . it's the . . . well, you got a different angle to it, that's all. Maybe you'll get that in the Melbourne Art Gallery. That's a good one, that is mate.'

The Welshman looked at him suspiciously. 'Do you think so?' he asked, unsure. 'I'm very keen on that one myself. It's about the best that I've done.'

'Got any beer?' asked Conway.

'Two left,' said Davies reaching under the bed. He opened them. 'What's doing anyway?'

'I want a bit of help. A good sort like you can help me out.'

'I thought you didn't come in just to look at the art work,' said Davies. 'What kind?'

Conway drank from the bottle. His profile was against the light coming through the blind. He looked a hard man. 'Well,' he started, then drank again. 'In the first place, whether or not you decide to give me a hand, what I'm going to tell you is between you and me and nobody else. You've got that?'

'I've got it,' said Davies starting on his bottle.

'If you spout about it, mate, I'll not only have to clobber you something terrible, but if and when you ever get back to Aussie they'll put you in the nick for about ten years on top. Now you've got that?'

'I've got that too,' confirmed Davies. Then he said: 'It's about Vietnam.'

'See,' said Conway angrily. 'You've already worked out more than you should know. How did you get that far?'

'You shouldn't get pissed,' said Davies simply. 'When we were on *The Baffin Bay* you came out with all this Vietnam stuff which you later denied, and then, over on St Paul's the other day, you kept asking what's-his-name, you know Joseph of Arimathea, whether he and his lads would like to go to Vietnam. And you didn't come here to pick daisies.'

'How's the butter and fats business?' asked Conway.

'Lousy,' admitted Davies. 'Nobody wants to know about it. That idiot English, whose in charge of the big warehouse here when he isn't frigging about in his kilt or looking for Unknown Soldiers, turned it down flat. And if he won't take the bulk orders and store them in the deep freeze I'm wasting my time. And he won't.'

'What will Trellis and Jones of Circular Quay say?' asked Conway grimacing at a painting of a coconut.

'They'll say "Get out" I expect,' admitted Davies. 'I'm not surprised it's all buggered up. Nothing's ever worked out for me yet.'

'Everything works out for me,' said Conway. 'Generally it does, anyway. Help me and maybe you'll get some of my Aussie luck. You can also come on the Government pay-roll as an assistant. I can authorise that.'

'That makes it sound a lot more attractive,' said Davies. 'Except I'm not going to Vietnam. Not for you or anybody. Okay?'

'You won't have to,' said Conway. 'I wouldn't need to rope you in at all if the British Governor hadn't been so obstructive. He even cabled to get Canberra to haul me off. But they told him to shut up, which annoyed him a bit I bet.'

He drained the beer and put the bottle back under the bed. 'But I've got to have someone to give me a hand. Someone I can trust. You're not perfect, but you're about the best bet.'

'Thanks,' said Davies. 'Abe. Why don't you try him? He'll do anything for shekels.'

'No, I'd thought of Abe, and we may need him yet, but he's too much of an operator. I don't think he'd keep in line. You will. Abe might sell us out; he wouldn't mean it but he would never be able to resist his business instincts.'

'What is it then?' asked Davies.

'Well the guts of it is—I want to get a dozen of those nuts on St Paul's to Australia. I want them seconded to the Australian Expeditionary Force in Vietnam as jungle scouts.'

Davies whistled, 'Mad,' he said, 'raving mad. That lot in Vietnam!'

Conway said, 'It's just a publicity stunt. The British used Dyaks in Malaya and we thought if we could get some of our savages in with our boys fighting the Viet Cong it would be great public relations. You know, the old crap about the Empire coming to the side of the Mother Country.'

'But you're not the Mother Country,' protested Davies. 'Typical of you. We're the Mother Country.'

'Well St Paul's is our dependency so Aussie is mother to them. Anyway you can see what a job it is. Like rounding up lunatics. And the Governor says they'll all die of T.B. or home-sickness or something.'

'They probably would too,' said Davies.

'They won't. We'll protect our investment. We couldn't allow that to happen and spoil the bloody image. Mind you, that didn't stop the British carting the Gurkhas all over the place for ninepence a day, and sending them home to Nepal when they'd got T.B.'

'That's another Australian lie,' said Davies. 'So how are you going to save this lot from extinction?'

'I doubt if they'll ever get as far as Saigon. We just want to dress them up a bit and parade them around back home, just to focus attention on what we're doing in Vietnam.'

Davies said: 'What do I have to do?'

'Got any more beer?' asked Conway bending to look under the bed.

'No. I told you I only had two.'

'So you did. Well, at the moment you do nothing. Because I don't know what there is to do. I've got to find out a bit more about that mob before making a real move. I can't ask Abe too much or he'll jump to conclusions—he's bright that Abe—and that won't do. I was thinking of going to pay a social visit on Mrs Flagg. She seems to know as much about the islanders as anyone, and if she can get those little blokes from St Mark's to run around with their things done up in banana leaves at her garden party she may give me some ideas on how I can work on the St Paul's tribe.'

'Why don't you just go over to the island again, keep away from their beer, and ask them if they would like to go to Vietnam. Make it friendly but official. You might impress them.'

'I hadn't put that out of mind,' said Conway. 'As a matter of fact I thought I might suggest to them that it's some kind of Holy War, a sort of Crusade. They might fall in with that.' He pondered then stood up. 'To tell you the truth I had even dreamed up a way of taking it one stage further.'

'How?' Davies stood up and began rearranging his paintings around the wall.

Conway opened the tear in the blind a little further and looked out into the hot street. Two Melanesian women were talking with the Chinese hardware merchant across the street. 'It was the thing that old fool Livesley said at the garden party,' Conway said. 'About Rio and the Christ being illuminated and looking as though it was floating in the sky. That's an idea that could be adapted for St Paul's. They're waiting for Dodson-Smith to appear, so let him appear.'

'Riding the motor bike?' suggested Davies.

'Why not? That would give them the message. If he told them to send a dozen warriors over the sea to war then they would.'

'You couldn't do it,' said Davies shattered with the thought. 'It's the riskiest thing I ever heard.' He looked hard at Conway. 'You didn't have any idea of casting me in the role of Jesus, did you?' Conway shook his head. 'You're too short for Jesus. No, if we did this thing it would be your job to keep the escape route open.'

'If they catch on and get hold of you . . .' said Davies.

'I've thought of that,' admitted Conway. 'That's why I think we ought to try the official way first. Give them a bit of bullshit of course, but keep it more or less on the level and see what happens. But somehow I've got to do this.' He hit his palm with his fist. 'Somehow,' he said.

Davies said : 'It's that important? What happens if the whole thing goes to hell?'

Conway peered through the wedge in the blind again. 'I'll look the biggest bloody fool in Aussie,' he said. 'That's what will happen. I dreamed this one up and I want to see it's carried through. Modest though I am, as you know mate, I've got something of a reputation as a miracle-man and I like that reputation and I want to keep it. So I'm going back with those buggers if I have to drug them and blackbird them like they used to do in the old days.'

They went from the room and walked down the stairs. Each step in the flight had slipped during the years of disintegration of the Sexagesima Hilton. Each had fallen into a different direction and angle with its neighbour.

'It's a pity you couldn't get a few villagers from *this* island,' said Davies. 'They're docile enough and they'll do anything for a couple of bob.'

'I've thought of that too,' admitted Conway clambering down ahead. 'But it's not on. They've got to be the real, genuine thing. St Paul's is our only dependency in these parts and the recruits must come from there. If I get some men from this island and the Governor found out, or anyone else for that matter, I'd be right in it. It's too much of a risk.'

They went to the bar, Seamus was leaning on the wet top reading a three months' old copy of *Irish Independent*. 'One thing about livin' in a situation like this,' he said his voice still Irish, 'is that it's no good worryin' about what you'll be readin' in the papers because it's too late. It's all over and done with long ago. If they dropped the Bomb on us today we wouldn't know a thing about it until midsummer.'

Conway bought the drinks. Davies said sarcastically. 'Here's to Dodson-Smith.'

Conway said: 'Yes, he's a good sort. Here's to him.'

There was never any interruption of the sun now. All day it burned the islands with unclouded coloured brilliance. People stayed under their verandas until evening, or went to the public library to read the magazines, or found other cool places. All work in offices and shops ceased before noon and did not continue until four. Sometimes it seemed that the sun was so fierce it must burn the sea.

It was four-thirty when Conway went to see Mrs Flagg. Pollet gave him a lift as he was going to a village on the other side of the island to collect some graven heads which the villagers had been turning out on a second-hand lathe.

Mrs Flagg seemed glad to see him. She was spread along a wide wicker rocking chair on the veranda taking tea from a dainty cup that looked twice as fragile in her big hand. On the lawn where the garden party had been held the six St Mark's natives, their banana leaf baloots tucked determinedly into their ex-army belts, bent and pulled a giant roller over the grass. Conway took an offered wicker rocking chair—the twin of Mrs Flagg's—and rocked gently opposite her. He accepted a cup of Queen Mary's Nectar, from distant Fortnum's, poured and treated with sugar and milk by Mrs Flagg without diverting from her semi-lying position nor her rocking motion. She handed the cup to him and there was a minor awkward moment when they realised that her chair was rocking out of time with his, and the tea-cup transfer would be difficult. Conway put his foot over the side to stop his chair, like a man arresting the impetus of a pedal cycle, and having stopped it he looked carefully at Mrs Flagg's movement, and began his rocking again, in time with hers.

'How thoughtful of you,' she said. Conway thought she looked more handsome than he had imagined. She had a round English counties face, ruddy not tanned, with full arms and legs and a substantial bosom. Her hair was straggling today but bright corn colour. She reminded Conway of a fatter version of the girl in the Ovaltine advertisements, the one with the red dress and the arm full of wheat. In Singapore he had seen that poster, but the girl's eyes had been slanted to make her more Oriental. Mrs Flagg's looked a bit like that too. She had blue eyes, but they were narrowed at the ends, perhaps through working too much, studying the natives of the outer islands.

She nodded fondly to the tribesmen pulling the garden roller. 'They really do a great job, you know,' she said heartily. 'Now they've got their skulls sorted out they're very happy and settled.'

Conway didn't ask what she meant. The St Mark's tribesmen were sweating at their task. Once they stopped pulling, straightened up, wiped their black brows and straightened their banana leaves, before continuing with the task.

'The garden party made such a mess of the lawn,' she continued brightly. 'Mr Flagg was annoyed, but, as I told him it's only to be expected. He says they leave the lawn looking like the Somme every year. But there are a large number who turn up, after all, and the Highland dancing leaves a few holes. Did you enjoy the party, Mr Conway?'

'Very much,' said Conway agreeably. 'My friends did too.'

'I hope your friend—Mr Davies is it?—isn't being too carnal with young Bird. She's such a sweet girl and a very proficient hairdresser too.'

Conway blinked. 'Oh no, Mrs Flagg. Nothing like that. He's a married man with a family. He's not eh . . . being carnal with her at all.'

She brightened. 'I'm *so* glad. I was a tiny bit worried. Yes, I thought the party went very well. It was a pity that poor man had to drop dead. Still it was a lovely day for it. The party I mean.'

She indicated coyly that he might like some more tea. He accepted. This time she stopped her chair rocking, gave him the tea, and restarted the movement in the correct time. 'You're Australian, of course,' she continued.

'Sydney,' he confirmed.

'Yes, yes. Oh *what* a place Australia is, don't you think? All the Australians seem to try and get out of it. They even go to London.' She was conversing with plump sweetness, guilelessly, not looking for his reactions, but rocking beautifully, tea-cup poised in one hand and the other waving with a fat grace to emphasise her points. 'I always think of Australia as a sort of second-hand shop,' she continued blandly. 'It really does

143

fit it rather well, don't you agree? Second-hand ideas, second-hand culture, second-hand everything. Even second-hand people.'

Conway choked in his tea. 'Cough up, Mr Conway,' Mrs Flagg said with concern. 'Don't let's have any more accidents here. One in a week is enough.'

Conway recovered, stopped rocking to find his handkerchief and mopped up the splashes of tea on his shirt. He began rocking again this time out of time with Mrs Flagg. He had to be careful, but he said, 'There seem to be a few second-hand people around here.'

'Perhaps, perhaps. But shop-soiled I think, not second-hand. Perhaps we like to imagine that we're all rather grand in our own small way, sometimes, but we're only playing a game, Mr Conway. And we're in such a small corner that no one takes any notice of us, so it's quite safe. We can act out our fantasies and nobody in the world cares or minds. Big places can't do that. People notice.'

Conway said: 'There are places where people can go to act out their fantasies.'

'Lunatic asylums,' said Mrs Flagg brightly. 'Of course, my dear Aussie, we know that. I've never thought of the Apostle Islands as anything but. Mr Flagg and I have the most marvellous laughs at dinner some evenings when we think of some of the odd people we have here. Push lads, push!' The final sentence was addressed to the naked islanders heaving the roller across the lawn. 'You see,' continued Mrs Flagg. 'It has not occurred to them to push the thing back the other way. They have to struggle to turn it around. This sort of illogical approach to a simple mechanical process forms a particularly intriguing part of our study of the St Mark's natives.'

Conway finished his tea, stopped rocking, and placed the cup on the basketwork table. 'Have you studied the natives on St Paul's?' he asked.

'Not in the same class as these people,' pronounced Mrs

Flagg firmly. 'Not a patch on them. They were poisoned with this religious mumbo-jumbo long ago and they were occupied by the Americans during the war, you know, which was almost as bad. They've got dreadful dental trouble over there. That was the fault of the Americans. Giving them sweets and candy or whatever they call it. The natives on this island have the most marvellous teeth. The Japanese were here.'

'It could be they didn't get much of a chance to use their teeth,' Conway pointed out reasonably. 'I don't suppose they had much to eat.'

Mrs Flagg seemed to consider this a fair point. 'Well, whatever it is, they're not a very healthy bunch on St Paul's. Not at all. These little chaps from St Mark's have a marvellous culture and a happy way of life. Even their gross product figure—and I'm quoting from a Colonial Office official thing now—is nearly double that of those Christian savages across the water. Their copra hulk is always full when the collection vessel comes. Unloading the same size hulk at St Paul's takes half the time. This is why the St Mark's natives have to be in a state of readiness all the time. They're a peaceful people, but they have to have their war canoes at the ready and their spears and fire arrows waiting, just in case the St Paul's tribe turn aggressors.'

'They have to have a deterrent,' said Conway.

'Naturally. The St Paul's tribe used to make raids on St Mark's a couple of times a year. But about three years ago they got such a mauling that they haven't bothered since. Mind you, we'd take them on any time.'

'Of course you would,' nodded Conway supportingly, 'and beat them again.'

She glanced at him to decide the tone of the remark. 'You seem very interested in native culture, Mr. Conway?' she said. 'Are you making some sort of study?'

'In a way,' he agreed. 'That is why I asked you if I could come over and see you. I find the whole thing terrific and I'd like to know more.'

Mrs Flagg smiled at him like a healthy milkmaid. 'How truly marvellous,' she said. 'I'm sure I can help.' Then she added cautiously, 'Well, Mr Flagg and I can help. We were beginning to despair of anyone sharing our passion for the islanders. People here do tend to cling to traditional interests you know, the ex-service club, the Highland Dance Society, the people who save stamps and matchbox tops and all that sort of thing. But if you really want to know in detail about St Mark's . . .'

'And St Paul's,' pointed out Conway.

'Oh yes, those too,' she said slightly hurt as though he had mentioned a rival boarding school. 'We have quite a lot of material. Quite a lot. Let's see, we have all the official reports and studies of the islands, going back for literally years, and all our own material gathered over quite some time, and then there's our tribal museum, of course. We're very proud of that and we like to show it to people.' She tumbled on, her fair hair falling over her strawberry face and being brushed back by her large double-cream hand. Abruptly she pulled up and put her hand to her mouth. 'Stay now!' she said. 'Why not stay for the evening and I'll show you all the things we have! That would be most fruitful, I'm sure.'

It was a warm late afternoon and Conway looking at her in her rocking chair thought again that she was really quite a handsome woman in a big, perspiring sort of way. 'Well,' he began. 'I'd like to . . .'

'Good, good, then you shall,' she exclaimed, rocking the chair backwards violently and allowing herself to be quite gracefully catapulted to her feet on the return movement. 'Stay to dinner and then you can see all the collection.' She suddenly returned her hand to her mouth. 'Oh my goodness, though. I've just remembered. Mr Flagg won't be with us. He's gone over to see some tribal sacrifice of a goat on the other side of the island. I quite forgot. Never mind, more for us! You don't mind dining alone with a strange woman, do you?'

'There's nothing strange about you, Mrs Flagg,' said Conway politely.

Before dinner Conway spent two hours going through the sheafs of manuscripts and blocks of books that Mr and Mrs Flagg had accumulated during their native studies. Mrs Flagg closed the doors and lit the lamps in the big room. She gave him two schooners of Australian sherry, which she said she kept for special occasions and had two schooners herself. She padded about the place, arranging the table setting, and getting her Vietnamese chef and his assistant, a Wallis Islander, advancing with the dinner. The St Mark's houseboys, constantly tucking their cocoons inside their army belts with the same habitual movement as a fat man keeps pulling up his slacks, moved about the house helping Mrs Flagg.

Sometimes she moved over to the alcove where Conway was studying the papers, leaning over him like a cow over a byre letting her splendidly hanging right breast rest significantly on his shoulder. She had changed into a fresh dress, a Marks and Spencer's green and floral pattern which her sister had sent from Watford. As she leaned near him Conway could smell a peppery perfume which she had added to her neck. Some of the papers were of great use to him, detailing life on St Paul's, the traits of the natives, the history of the tribal leaders right up to Lazarus who had so disappointingly failed to recover from being dead. Each time he found some item of particular interest he called Mrs Flagg and she came over, moving cheerfully and quickly like a farmer's wife at a square dance, hung across him and discussed the point.

They enjoyed an excellent dinner of fish soup, tinned duck from Australia, yams, rice, tinned tomatoes in juice, and mangoes, with two bottles of Queensland Reisling which Mrs Flagg brought out in preference to French wines from Noumea in deference to her visitor. They had a strong pot of Typhoo afterwards and following that drank a lot of Mr Flagg's superlative Denis-Mounie cognac which Sir William, the Governor, had received in error, and passed on to Mr Flagg as a spot prize at a masque ball held in Government House. Both Conway and Mrs Flagg had a lot of stories to tell and they laughed like a crowd, sitting on the billowing cushions of the damask couch. The chef and his assistant went home to get some reasonable food, and the little men from St Mark's after busying themselves around the table and wiping up the crumbs and other pieces from the floor, went off into the deep night to talk for a while with their skulls.

Conway and his hostess laughed so much when they realised that they had finished half a bottle of Denis-Mounie, that they somehow tumbled together on the couch, and decided immediately to make a start on the second half. They were both demonstrative laughers. They threw themselves about a lot. Even if a laugh began as a snigger, with the person sitting upright and proper it was not long before a second snigger ignited the whole thing and they were rolling over each other on the stormy sofa.

'Lishen,' said Conway waggling his finger at her. 'Aussie ain't any second-hand shop. Unnerstand.'

Mrs Flagg hooted. 'Hooo! Hooooo!' she bellowed. 'I thought *that* would get in! You're all so very, very, very touchy about it. Poor old Aussie, and poor old Aussies! Who will buy? Come on, buy a lump of our sunshine! Heee! Heee! Come and buy—it's remnant week!'

Conway bravely assayed a leap to his feet at the affront, but his knees went and he fell forward heavily across Mrs Flagg's upland chest. It was good there, he thought; like falling into a warm snowdrift. He moved his face a few degrees. He thought he felt her stiffen in her stomach and she had stopped laughing or saying anything. Eventually, carefully measuring his words

148

so that they came out in the intended order, Conway said: 'I'd like to know how they get those banana things on.'

She said in a low tone: 'The baloots?'

'You guessed.'

'It's not really too difficult when you know,' she said persuasively. 'There's a proper way of course and once they're on it's very, very difficult to get them off. There's a proper way of doing that too.'

'Show me, Mrs Flagg,' he asked softly, his head still on her bosom.

She stroked his fair hair. 'You'd *really* like it?' she asked. 'You wouldn't be shy or embarrassed.'

'Oh no,' said Conway turning his face to hers and pushing the fat of her breast over with his chin. He felt her react. 'We could treat it as purely educational. That's what we'll do.'

'Good idea,' she agreed. 'Keep it very educational, even medical-clinical—if you like.'

'I like,' he said. 'There's nothing like education, Mrs Flagg.'

'Nothing indeed,' nodded Mrs. Flagg. Her round face was redder and warmer now, with the cognac and the proximity of Conway. Her hands were heavy and damp like cloths around his neck. Crickets were rattling in the garden and a sigh of night wind blew warmly into the room exciting the curtains and moving the hanging lamps.

'I'll need to go into the garden, dear man,' whispered Mrs Flagg. She began to wriggle away from him on the couch. 'There are some banana fronds hanging on the line. They have to be dried out you know and one of the little chaps was going to change his tomorrow . . . He won't miss them.' She stood unsurely and wandered somewhat aimlessly, one foot all but treading on the other, across the carpeted room, until, with a sudden resolution, she turned towards the latticed door, opened it with a bang and staggered out into the garden.

Conway enjoyed the engulfing sensation of well-being that always filled him immediately before and after a sure conquest.

The cognac helped and he poured two more generous glasses, sampled his, poured some of Mrs Flagg's into his own glass to make the levels right again, and wallowed back into the cushions. He watched the door through relaxed, splintered, eyes. A gentle laugh stuck somewhere down in his chest. He felt tempted to let it loose, but refrained. He felt happy.

Mrs Flagg came back, entering with a sort of pantomime villain's arched step, at a crouch, carrying in one hand the banana leaves. She smiled wickedly, turned and exaggerated her backward look from the door, spying out to make sure no one was coming.

Without a word, hardly a sound except for the bellows movement of her agricultural breasts, a look of honest eagerness on her face, Mrs Flagg advanced on Conway. He cowered back in pretend fear. Continuing her comedy villain's step she closed with him and began to take off his trousers. Conway felt a quick onslaught of boyish panic such as he could never remember. There was suddenly something frightening about being in the clutches of this big, healthy woman. He struggled symbolically like a virgin, his throat full of grit and his eyes wide.

'Come on now, Conway,' said Mrs Flagg sternly. 'No resistance now. No going back, eh?' She swooped with her big soft, rural hand transformed to a buzzard's claw, and thrust his brandy at him. He drank nervously. She began undoing his trousers.

In later years, in his most dismal and drunken dreams, Conway would see Mrs Flagg, blown to the dimensions of an ogre hanging over him with an awful determined smile on her face, like a demented hospital matron. He half lay across the couch like some accident victim, his eyes swelling, his smile iron-set, a deathly shivering setting into his fibres and cells where the warmth had been. He was afraid of Mrs Flagg.

She pulled his trousers away from his waist, his buttocks and his legs with a terrible efficiency keeping her face fixed on his all through the three distinct movements. 'Up!' she ordered when she had to pull them from under his behind, and Conway arched himself obediently up on the palms of his hands while she swooped the garment away from him. She drew away his shoes and socks with the same powerful pull.

'Good, very good,' she said looking down at him as though examining the progress of a wound. He looked down at himself and was astonished to see that he had a primary erection thrusting up inside his underpants making them like a small alp. For once his manliness frightened him. Mrs Flagg was terrorising him and he still had an erection! Could he, after all, be a latent masochist?

Mrs Flagg peeled off his pants, crimson in the face now with determination and crude pleasure. It occurred to the petrified Conway that he had never before been undressed first. He had never been in a defenceless state when the woman was all covered. She seemed now quite oblivious of him, uncaring about his feelings, or his participation in the event. Then, all at once and with a terrible realisation it came to him that he was not important, that this was no sex for two. She leaned over him and caressed him, making still more hospital noises, soothing but remote, looking closely at his lower half, examining him.

'I've changed my mind,' said Conway shivering.

'I haven't,' said Mrs Flagg evenly. She put a glowing hand on his stomach and held him flat. He did not attempt to push or struggle. He had the trembling feeling that even if he did so it would be useless. She would overpower him and do terrible things to him. He remained leaning back, her hands working over him.

'I'll try to enjoy it,' he promised himself as an easy way out. But he was still with apprehension. There was a mad look on her face as she bent and went on working away. He could see the sweat streaming like rain from her red face. Her fair Saxon hair was in wet tails and trails across her forehead. She was moulding away at him like a potter at a wheel. The alcohol, that coward, had run away from his brain and his body. He was helplessly sober.

She stopped and straightened up, puffed with her handiwork. She looked from his lower half to his face. 'I've no experience with white men. This is the first occasion,' she mentioned.

'Well, perhaps another time,' suggested Conway. He began to push himself up, but she fixed him with her powerful, hot look again, her cheerfully bowed lips making blowing movements at him as though to puff him back. Her hands pinned his stomach again. Somehow he could not fight, there was no move of which he seemed capable.

Mrs Flagg shook her blonde head like a Wagner heroine. 'No other time like the present,' she intoned. 'Remain still, Conway. I'll get the ointment.'

Conway almost screamed. 'Ointment!' She thrust her face down at him. 'The ointment,' she repeated threateningly. 'It is essential.'

'The ointment,' he croaked pitifully. 'Yes, of course. You must get the ointment.' He had a plan to leap up and run through the door into the garden as soon as she had stepped away. But she did not go far enough. She merely backed to a small cabinet across the carpet, her eyes never going from his face, pinning him back like a stake, and from the cabinet took a paint tin, pint-sized emulsion, with the end of a brush projecting from its open top.

'What colour?' he asked tragically.

'The ointment is colourless,' she assured him advancing again. 'On St Mark's it is obtained from the sap of the poisoning yalla tree. It sets hard on application.' Conway closed his eyes. He felt her painting him with the cheap hairy brush, and a sort of paralysis setting in in his groin regions.

She moved away from him again and then he felt her massive return. Her hands again and then the round bandages of the banana leaves. He moaned sullenly, keeping his eyes tight.

Mrs Flagg went about her task with dedication and distinction, wrapping and binding, puffing with intense gratification as she did so. Eventually he knew she had finished. He had the sensation of having a large stone resting on his stomach. Fearfully he opened his eyes and saw it, as he had feared, lying there like a prehistoric caterpillar, eyeing him with a single hole at the point of its head. That was one question answered anyway.

He looked up at Mrs Flagg and he was shocked to see her staggering away from him like a crewless ship before a current. She half turned and stared at him as though she were a murderer and he the victim. Her large breasts were rolling like waves and her face sweat-soaked. She moved with her hands in an ineffectual sort of way and mumbled, shaking her head. It was as though she had been brought from a trance into the horror of reality. She wiped at her face and her tongue came out and licked around her sagging mouth.

'Mr Conway,' she began, the syllables coming out wet and thick. 'I hardly know what to say . . .'

The liquid silence that filled the room was solidified by the slamming of a car door. 'Oh my heavens!' exclaimed the woman. 'Mr Flagg!'

Conway had faced emergencies before with the unexpected return of husbands, but never in a situation to equal this. He moved quickly, however, despite his horrid encumbrance. It swung outwards like the jib of a crane as he jumped from the couch. He swooped upon his trousers, his underpants, his shoes and socks and limped from the door into the dark garden. As he went he heard Mr Flagg coming through the hall at the front of the house. Conway stood a few yards from the door among some trees and contrived to replace his trousers. The solid trunk he now carried made it impossible for him to zip them or secure them in any reasonable way. Only the legs fitted. He hobbled into them and pulled them around him. The banana monstrosity swelled up and over the top. Mr Flagg now entered the room. Conway heard him kiss his wife resoundingly. 'Earlier than I thought, dear,' he said. 'All over in an hour, sacrifice, ritual, everything. Fascinating, positively fascinating. They really do get up to some quaint tricks, these tribesmen.'

Fortunately Sexagesima was full of its night desertion. Keeping to the more robust shadows, and hiding when he heard a noise, Conway made his way back to the Hilton Hotel. There was only a hundred feet of open street to risk, and he got across safely and swiftly running like a rugby three-quarter clutching the ball to his stomach. He bolted through the downstairs hall which was empty and dimly lit at that hour. Like a warring animal he went up the stairs and charged into his room.

He leaned on the bed, panting, moaning with anger and embarrassment. It took him three hours twenty minutes to get the contraption off, soaking it in a bucket of tepid water and using a scout knife.

The operation was so painful it brought shocked tears to his eyes. When he eventually got into his bed, sore and shivering, it was daylight. The Chinese shopkeeper across the road threw fifty firecrackers into the road at six o'clock that morning to celebrate his birthday, but Conway did not care.

X

After two weeks of plodding search through the webbed jungle of St Peter's Island the men from Sexagesima had still not found an Unknown Soldier. The hours spent recutting tracks overrun by the avid growth of the rainy season, the uncomfortable casualties through falling into concealed pools and inky bogs, and all the million red insect bites suffered by the patrols, were fruitless.

'Och,' grumbled Rob Roy English at the end of the day of searching. 'Ye'd think that aboot enough o' the brave lads were slaughtered here in 1944 to leave a few bones lyin' aboot.'

On several days Davies went with the patrols, glad of the companionship, eccentric though it was, and with the intention at the start of merely filling time. There was little for him to do in Sexagesima during the hot days waiting for the return of *The Baffin Bay* and his return to Trellis and Jones of Circular Quay, Sydney.

Sometimes he painted, in the town, trying to draw from its deep light; the great crawling shadows early, and the slim shadows of noon, the ponderous movement of its day, the dry houses and the dry people and the sun always striking at it as though it were the only open target in the whole of the world. Early mornings were quiet and dustless, and the town seemed to go about its life with renewed hope, sight and energy, like a man temporarily recovered from an illness. But noon would come with all its choking heat and the town would sweat and cough the dust from its gullet, and drink and sweat again, and finally surrender and hide in the darker places until the burning of the sun had receded again, leaving the settlement like a well-browned pie hot from the oven.

So Davies went with the patrols to look for the Unknown Soldier. They would set out from the South Seas Hilton bar at eight, a dozen or more each time, parading in an array of guerrilla outfits, bush jackets, floppy hats, cricket flannels, tough mountain boots, neckerchiefs for the sweat, sandwiches, boiled sweets to suck on the way, bottles of beer, field glasses, knives, machettes and guns. They took the guns because, they said, there was always a chance of wild animals, and because the guns made them feel good. Each day they would troop from the hotel like some determined rescue party from a war a century ago. With Rob Roy English at the van, in tartan trews and a Highland Light Infantry bush jacket, they would trudge, as though already weary but brave, as if they were returning from a battle in fact, along the main street. They did not look at the people who peered from the houses and shops but marched solidly like desperate men who have fought to all but the last of their blood and are ready to fight again and die.

Davies, armed with a walking stick borrowed from Seamus, was always towards the rear of the heroic column. He noticed how all the men before him seemed to fall naturally into the part of soldiers, that trudge, that dry stare into the fatal distance. When Mr Hassey went with them he would break line sometimes to pat the heads of little children sitting on the pavements sag-mouthed in wonder at the grim men; pat them as if to say 'We may die, but the world will be a better place for you, my dears'. A man who lived on the outskirts of the town and who had been in the New Zealand navy during the war turned up for one patrol in his white tropical naval uniform with ammunition boots and several medals. Rob Roy sent him home because he said he was making a laughing stock of the whole venture.

Conway never went with the men. He was spending a lot of

156

time over on St Paul's Island, ascertaining the natives, as he explained, and helping Joseph of Arimathea and his elders to build a new grandstand and crush barriers for Ascension Day. But on the mornings when he was not visiting the other island he would sit in his window at the Hilton, directly over the street, beer in hand, held like a urine specimen, and call encouragement and jeers to the patrol as it set out. 'Boots, Boots, Boots . . .' he would sing or 'Goodbye Dolly I must leave you'. Dahlia would be there with him some mornings for they found his room more restful than hers, and she would blow extravagant kisses to Davies and once threw a coloured streamer at him from the window.

Depending on which part of the jungle they were going to survey that day, the file would march north or east from the town. When they went north they would pass Bird's shop and she and those customers who were not trapped under hair driers would crowd to the doors to see the spectacle. The older women were either tolerantly amused or scathing, although none of their remarks ever reached the marching men, but Bird stood, fresh in her hairdresser's smock, watching solemnly. Davies always looked towards her and she always smiled.

Once they left the town the dust road began to crawl upwards and the sun came face on, when they were going east, and worked around to the backs of their necks when they were moving north. They began to puff and pant and out came the little jars of boiled sweets. This was the most difficult part of the journey, much of it was through rocky, open areas, where there was no shade, and it was too early to occupy themselves in the business of looking for a skeleton. After they had made two such journeys, Mr English began whistling Scots airs through his teeth and the others, taking heart, tramped and whistled to their boots in the best musical tradition of the British soldier.

It took an hour to reach the skirts of the upland jungle. It was a place of deep tangles and thick growth that thickened with each rainy season. It was a solemnly quiet place too, like a temple, with the sun cutting down through the higher trees, but only in columns and shafts, because overhead the leaves and branches were often sufficient to roof the place and keep the rays away. The floor was either glutted with growth, generations of it, too thick, too powerful to ever penetrate, or spread with a secondary tangle that could be cut away, or sometimes, quite miraculously, clear with all the sweetness of a fairy glen.

They concentrated on the penetrable areas, where they could make progress and where the battles of long ago would have logically been fought. They discovered a machine gun one morning, and army mess tins with a mould of food within on another day. Another afternoon, just as they were about to call a halt to the search and return to Sexagesima, Mr Hassey found a Japanese steel helmet and there was a great fanned out operation looking for the head that might have worn it, but with no success.

Davies found a strange change happening to him as he tramped with the men. He began to get the feel of the place. Of the jungle, of the hills, of the island, the archipelago and of the Pacific. He found the silence filling him with rest, the shadows full of comfort after the heat. He did not even resent the heat itself. He let it sink into his body, he let the sun assault his face and arms.

All the more he enjoyed the gulps of beer when they rested before going to search again, all the more he enjoyed the late returns when the sun was moving away. He enjoyed too the sudden rustles of small animals and the occasional flight of coloured birds that tore the jungle silence. And he enjoyed the sudden break-through, when they would emerge from the trees at mountain level and be confronted with the green body of the island spread below, the tracks and the little watercourses that were the veins, the small patches of cultivated land around the villages, the brown of the villages themselves, their quiet smoke in the air, the beaches, the necklace of the reef, and the great,

158

shining, swinging sweep of the ocean that seemed to occupy the rest of the world.

But he enjoyed most the company of the men. Odd they were, and narrow and strange, but in them in their talk and their lives he discovered something that had not been apparent to him before. These were the brave, the explorers, the colonists, the conquestors, even. These funny, odd-shaped little men, with their burnt faces, their prejudices, their suburban fears, their narrow lives, their hopeless dreams, their hate and their deep love for their homeland so far away from these islands— these were the Empire Builders, the last of them too, not the rugged, romantic imperious figures from the imagination of history books. For what Empires were worth, these were those who made them and preserved them, working under fans in oppressive offices, counting up little additions in notebooks in warehouses and stores, going home in the rain, worrying about their health and their wives, sending their children ten thousand miles to school so that they lost them forever. These were the pioneers. They couldn't even send for a gunboat, because there wasn't one.

When they sat under trees and ate their sandwiches he listened to their talk, talk of the islands, people they had known, how they came there in the first place, their ridiculous plans for putting St Peter's and the whole of The Apostles on the true map. Getting tourists and industry, getting their voice shouting down the tombs of Whitehall. Wait until the Queen arrives, they said. 'We'll show them who and what we are. Wait until she arrives.'

But to Davies it was most touching when they spoke of their homeland. It was as thought they spoke of some foreign place that had long ceased to be familiar. There were arguments as to whether Manchester was two hundred or four hundred miles from London, whether the first snow fell on the Western Highlands in November, who was the present captain of England at cricket, the extent of the area ruled by the Thames Conservancy

Board. Some believed that trams still ran along the Victoria Embankment. Some thought that Croydon was London Airport. Davies listened in wonder and pity. They were like blind men playing a guessing game. Not many took their leave in Britain, it was a habit that died away after a few years. The newspapers were always two months old. George Turtle at the radio station usually managed to hear Radio Fiji news bulletins and if something tremendous happened in the world he would report to the rest of them at the Hilton or at the British Legion Club. The Governor always received his private intelligences but they knew nothing of them, nor did they care. George Turtle's news had to be exceptional to be taken to them as they talked their talk of the islands. He usually judged whether something was of interest or not. Quite often he would go for two weeks without breaking anything to them. His predecessor at the radio station, a man called Melville who had been found dead with the earphones still on, had not even bothered to tell the people of The Apostles about the Cuba crisis. The assassination of President Kennedy was talked about for some twenty minutes and then forgotten because the volcano on St Barnabas Island began to show signs of erupting for the first time in fifty-three years. As Seamus at the Hilton had said, no world disaster ever struck The Apostles. By the time they heard it was always far too late.

On the afternoon of the third patrol that Davies had joined, a hairless man called Vicary who had a small plantation and a chemist's shop on the outskirts of Sexagesima, ran back, plunging through the waist-high growth, and shouted for Mr English. The men had fanned out in their search. Some had tunnelled into the undergrowth and vanished. When Mr Vicary called, heads bobbed up like bathers bobbing out of the sea.

Davies turned in the clinging growth pulling against it as it sought to retain him. Mr Vicary's red baldness moved through the green excitedly as he called. 'Mr English! Mr English!' The head vanished momentarily as he stumbled. It appeared again over the undergrowth. 'Mr English—I've found him! I've found him!'

He reached a plate-shaped clearing at the same time as Mr English and some of the others. Davies pulled himself from the mass and reached the open space. Mr Vicary, wearing khaki trousers tucked into red socks, panted to the others. 'In there!' he said. 'I've found him in there.'

They knew what he meant, but his words were such that no one was entirely sure. Mr English said: 'Who?'

'Who?' repeated Mr Vicary. 'Who? The soldier, of course. The Unknown Soldier.'

Mr English started forward with determination, Mr Vicary pointing the way. 'This way. Here he is.' The party stopped, up to its necks in jungle tangle. 'There,' said Mr Vicary triumphantly. 'Down there, see.'

'Machette,' grunted Mr English with authority. Somebody passed a machette and he began to hack away at the stems and fronds on either side. He made a clear area and first looked down and then bent down. 'Pig,' he said.

'Pardon,' said Mr Vicary surprised.

'Bones of a wild pig,' said Mr English. 'Soldiers don't have cloven feet like that. You're a chemist, you should know, Mr Vicary.'

They trudged back to their survey. Mr Vicary was sullen and hurt all day and did not volunteer for another search party.

'I can't see why we couldn't have packed up those bones in a bag and brought them back and said they were the Unknown Soldier,' he grumbled to Davies as they returned in the lessening evening. 'Nobody's going to notice the bloody difference.'

Davies was in the bar of the Hilton after one of the days in the jungle. He went willingly with the search parties. There was little else for him to do. He was sitting with Conway and

Dahlia, George Turtle and Hassey the planter. The place was all but empty because it was the night for the film at the British Legion. A middle-aged Frenchman played the piano like an invalid at one end of the bar and Pollet, who was propped against the wall reading a French motor magazine which he had stolen that afternoon from the public library, mimed the song's words from long ago without looking up.

There was an expansive wall mirror across the room from Davies, a great earthquake crack in it. It had been brought from Sydney thirty years before, gilded with a whorly design at its edges and proclaiming the goodness of Lyons Fruit Pies. Davies in turning to pass his beer mug up to Seamus at the bar caught sight of himself in the old glass and stopped. He realised that he hardly knew himself. His face was rough brown, burned red raw at the cheekbones and at one patch above the right eye. His hair was long, matted too; his chin black bristled because he had got up early that day to go on the search and he had not shaved. His shirt curled in horns at the collar ends, its white long sunk to grey. Bird sometimes washed his clothes for him because the Chinese laundry made holes in them, but he often forgot to take the things to her.

He'd been walking in the heat of the afternoon, mostly in the clear because they had searched some of the open highlands too that day, and three quick pints of beer had given him a gassy uplift. Yet, how strange that this should be him. He looked around at the others, talking, heads bent over the table, and he realised that he had come to look like one of them.

'Wouldn't know you in Newport now, would they boy?' he said confidentially to himself as he waited for the beer from Seamus. The long Irishman passed it over. Davies took another quick look at himself. Hell, fancy walking along Dock Street looking like that. No, much better to walk down *our* road like that. They saw plenty of tans in Dock Street, didn't they, straight off the boats? Of course they did. But say he walked down his own road like that—tomorrow—hard like he was now with a good suit on and a white shirt, and shaved of course. Kate would think that was a great thing. She was always going on about how tanned some of the men were at the swimming baths. She liked tanned men. And the kids would jump at him and ask him to tell them stories of his adventures in the horrible jungles. People would stop him in the street and inquire how he liked being back after all that time abroad. Yes, that would be marvellous, now wouldn't it? It was a pity there was no way of getting out of this place.

George Turtle was saying ponderously: 'All the values have gone now at home. Everything we fought for, Dunkirk, right through. All down the drain. Place full of blacks and layabouts. That's why I came here. Britain's no country for a civilised, go-ahead, chap. Or his family either. My brother in Isleworth tells me I'm well off out of it, and the wife. But it wasn't easy, you know, I admit that. I *was* proud of the old country. I remember in 1940 our evening institute had classes in thatching—you know thatching roofs of houses. In 1940!'

'S'pose they thought you'd be short of a few roofs,' suggested Conway soberly. 'Bombs and whatever you had.'

Turtle glared at him. 'I tell you what it showed *me*, Mr Conway. It showed me we had faith in the future. Anyone who wants to learn thatching has to have the confidence to look a long way ahead. That goes without saying. Yes, I was proud of England then. But then it all slid away. All in no time, it seemed. When Dad and my dear Mum died a few years ago I thought "well, George, now is the time to get out" and so I did—bringing my wife with me of course. But the funny thing was, the *real* thing that *finally* decided me was something the undertaker said when they put the old lady away.'

George paused and seemed to find some mystery in his empty glass. Davies ordered him another beer. 'What was it Mr Turtle?' he asked.

'What was what?' asked George. 'A beer, I said.'

'No, what was it the undertaker said that made you emigrate?'

'Oh yes, he was standing there talking on the telephone making sure of the times and that sort of thing for the funeral. I was sitting down and he's carrying on just as though he is selling two hundredweight of fertiliser or something. That was bad enough, but then he ended up the conversation by saying "Right then Fred" or Harry or Bill, or whoever it was, "Right then, eleven o'clock Wednesday—West London Crem." WEST LONDON CREM! That's what he *said*, in front of me, the bereaved. WEST LONDON CREM!'

'Sounds like the name of a drink,' commented Seamus over the bar.

George was huffed. 'It sounded like a piece of rudeness to me,' he said. 'West London *Crematorium* doesn't take much saying does it? And how much nicer. What a falling off of standards even in *that* trade. I walked out and went straight to put my name down to leave the country. That's how I did it. And I'm glad.'

Mr Hassey nodded agreement. He looked across and slightly up at Dahlia : 'Why did you come here Miss?' he asked. 'If I'm not being impertinent?'

Dahlia, who had been holding Conway's thick arm and listening absently, seemed startled. 'Me? Oh, I was travelling, moving about, and the islands just happened to be in my way, that's all. I'll get them out of my way before too long. I'll go back to Wanganui.'

'New Zealand,' explained Conway.

'And you?' Hassey asked Davies.

'To sell butter and fats,' shrugged Davies. 'But I didn't.'

'Ah, yes, I remember. And you Mr Conway.'

'Just studying,' said Conway cautiously. 'The natives.'

'That's why I came,' said Hassey. 'Thirty-eight years ago. Just to ascertain the fucking natives . . . beg your pardon Miss.

164

Ah well, I've said it now. Anyway to ascertain the natives. Been here ever since.'

'What did you do before, Mr Hassey?' asked George Turtle. Davies noticed how they always called him 'Mr Hassey', never by any familiarity. 'Go on, Mr Hassey, you've never told us.'

'Sailor, commercial traveller, general horse thief, you know,' said Mr Hassey blandly. 'Anything really. Had a little business once selling imitation jewellery in Auckland. But it was too up and down. Christmas time was all right, but it tailed off terrible at the other end of the year. Nothing to do at all. Could have done with another Baby Jesus about August.'

Abe came into the bar, straight from his boat, stood and bought himself a beer, rattling his loose change as he paid. 'A leak' he said turning to the group. 'A great, wet, seeping leak. Took all day to get that plugged.' His arms flailed about. He swam rather than talked. 'Tomorrow,' he announced. 'Is the big day for moving the barges, which you know already?'

'We know already,' said Conway. 'Dawn at The Love Beach.'

'And why not?' said Abe. 'Tell me friend how often do you get a chance to build something sacred? I'll be there too, boy. As a matter of fact I've arranged for the heavy hauling equipment —it's coming from Tahiti tonight. It'll be at the beach tomorrow, finished tomorrow night, and back on the freighter by the next day. It's very steep this stuff is to hire, you know. But just managed to hear this little item was on its way from Papetta to Honoraria, where they are building a bowling rink and where I have already done business concerning a harmonium.' He bowed towards Conway and then to Davies.

'Which fell to bits on St Paul's,' said Conway.

'Act of God, cargo damaged in shipment,' said Abe opening out his hands. 'What the hell. The way those boys sang over there, can you wonder the Almighty tried to destroy the harmonium before it got to them. *He* was the one who put it

165

together and played it.' He pointed dramatically at Davies. 'Going against the Will of God.'

'You got your money,' Davies pointed out. He was surprised now, how easily he entered into these island arguments.

'I'm glad to assist in moving the barges,' said Abe leaning forward on the counter, looking at Seamus and at the rest of them in the mirror. 'After all it's an interdenominational affair ain't it. An Unknown Soldier is an Unknown Soldier, boy. Those bones you bury could be those of a Jewish lad.'

'Or an Arab,' said Conway.

'My friend,' Abe pleaded. 'Don't never mix me up with those greedy little quarrels across the world. This is the Pacific. These are the islands of The Apostles. I would be glad, proud even, to bury Arab bones.'

They made an early start at The Love Beach, the sun just brimming the sea sending an orange flood over it, making the island claim its contours once again from the dark, making the trees have shapen leaves, the mountains form, and giving the people life.

Fifty white volunteers were on the beach before breakfast and a hundred Melanesians who were to be paid, just after. They stood around looking at the invasion barges with the interest of those who have seen something for a long time but only just noticed it. They wandered about in their shirts and shorts and sandals, probing at each barge like suburban men probe around an old or a new car, looking beneath and above, touching and talking. They talked about how the barges were made, how they must have come at a certain tide, how well the metal had stood the years of sea and sun and wind, and how they didn't make craft like that any longer.

The arrival of Mr English in Pollet's car stopped the activity. All the men stood about in the early sun.

English looked up at the tall prow of one of the barges. 'Gi'e a hand tae us, lads,' he said. Two men moved forward and hoisted the little leader to the metal nose. Today he was wearing a bush shirt and flappy shorts, but there was a tam o' shanter bulging on his small head and he wore his thick Highland stockings and heavy shoes. He surveyed them, black men and white, as a clan chief would have looked upon his warriors before battle.

'Taeday,' he began, wheeling a dramatic half circle so that he took them all in. 'Taeday we are goin' tae shift these wee monsters, friends. We're going to make a chapel o' them to receive the bones of the Unknown Soldier. When we find him. It's no' goin' tae be a simple matter, ye'll understan' but by nightfall we'll ha' done it, ye see.' He paused and looked around at the patches of upturned faces. He thrust his tammy back from his yellowed forehead. 'Unfortunately,' he continued, 'I ha' tae gi'e ye some puir news. The liftin' gear which our friend and colleague Abe had arranged for this day won't be here.' There was a groan from the men. Davies watched them about him in their shirts, hands on their hips, clerks and shopkeepers in the attitudes of lumberers.

'Why not?' asked Mr Kendrick, the cycle shop owner.

It was Abe who thickly shouted the answer. 'Let down, friends. I was let down. I arranged for the ship to call, but that captain did the dirty on me. He's sailed right past on his way to Honoraria. We watched him go.'

'Sue him Abe,' shouted someone.

'Can't,' admitted Abe. 'It wasn't that sort of contract.' He dropped his voice and directed it at the man. 'Very difficult to prove,' he confided.

Mr English threw his arms wide. 'So we move these wee craft oursells, friends,' he announced. There was a dissenting noise from the men. 'Like the Egyptians and the pyramids,' said Mr English encouragingly. 'What they can do, we can do.'

'In a day?' called someone.

'Two days,' replied Mr English. 'Let's get on with it.' Davies could see that the little man had been sizing up the leap to the ground from his oratorial position on the landing barge. His eyes had measured the distance carefully during his final sentences. Now, like a theatre midget, he leapt, crashing violently into the sand, his knees reaching it fractionally before his face. Davies, Conway and some others helped to pull him from the depression he had made. He blew sand from his mouth and dug it from the hollows of his eyes. 'Let's get on with it,' he repeated gallantly.

They needed to move two of the barges. The back of the chapel was already conveniently formed by one muscular landing craft which had slewed sideways as it struck the beach on that dawn in 1944 and had remained in the same place. Two other craft had to be dragged into position to flank it.

The men dug first, burrowing under the soles of the steel ships, undermining them, then laying out steel netting, and finally wooden rollers made from the fibrous trunks of the palms.

They worked heavily while the swollen sun hurried up over the island, the Melanesians sawing and cutting the palms needed for the rollers, the white men getting their spades beneath the barges. The task went surprisingly well and by sunset one of the barges was mounted on its rollers and ready to move. Everyone had a break for beer and sandwiches, brought from the British Legion Club where the wives were busy buttering and spreading. Then they fixed the ropes to the barge and were ready to pull.

Davies had gone into town with Pollet in the car to fetch additional hawsers from the jetty. They returned just as the men were beginning to heave. It was a strange scene, a sight like an ancient frieze. Davies stopped with Pollet, where the trees concluded and the beach began and looked at it. He felt Pollet stop alongside him and heard him drop the first coil of hawsers to the soft ground.

The sun had just left with its usual evening flamboyance, flinging violet and red across the lower sky, making the ribbed sea like the coloured wings of a marvellous butterfly, fiery at the centre, then subduing to purple and fringed with aquamarine and, in the end a spilling of sombre grey. Against this, all silhouettes, the black men and the whites pulled on the ropes that stiffened out from the prow of the landing barge. On the prow the little leader, Rob Roy English, stood, tiny legs astride, bent forward like a mighty slave driver, calling out the time of their pulling. 'One, two, three, Now! One, two, three, Now! One two three, Now!'

One hundred and fifty men bent against the ropes, becoming shaped like notes of music against the lines of the sea. The sight was outlined in black, against the brilliantly fading sky and the reflecting ocean.

'One, two, three, Now! One, two, three, Now!'

The gangs hung on to the ropes, tugged, relaxed, tugged again. Pull, pull, pull. Miraculously the barge, with its undersized rider began to nuzzle forward, like an old dry lizard come to life.

'It's moving,' whispered Davies to Pollet. The beauty of the beach, and the sky and the labouring men had filled his throat. 'What a strange sight.'

Pollet nodded. 'All the time, in the islands as nowhere else, you find unexpected things to cause you wonder. Sometimes they're nature gone mad, sometimes men gone mad. Often they are very, what you would call stunning, perhaps. Things are strange here, Monsieur. Every day they are strange. You will learn.'

Davies felt himself involuntarily wanting to protest. 'I won't learn. I won't be here. I'm going away. Home.' But something choked the words, stopped them, and he simply gazed again out on to the beach and saw the barge moving inches only, as the men strained and the hooting high voice of Mr English encouraged them from his steel perch.

'It's moving,' said Davies again. 'It's definitely shifting a bit on those rollers.'

'Perhaps it would be better if we stopped admiring the artistic composition of the scene and instead pulled on one of the ropes,' suggested Pollet.

Davies moved forward. 'Yes, of course we must.'

They dropped the hawsers they had brought because they would not be needed until the next day and moved quickly across the sloping sand towards the tugging gangs. As they got nearer they could hear the grunts of the men taking the weight of each pull, their feet forced into the sand, their arms hard under the tension. Davies began to run and Pollet followed him. They reached the end men, took up a yard of rope each and timed their pulling to the efforts of the rest; take the strain, now PULL, take the strain, now PULL.

Davies was aware of the sweat immediately wriggling down his belly soaking into his shirt, burrowing under his belt and running to his pelvis and his legs. He blinked the salt wetness from his eyes and felt the sinew of the rope biting into his hands. Pull, pull, pull. Rest. And pull, pull, pull.

They felt it coming. An inch at a time first, hardly perceptible. But then it began to roll towards them and they scuffed the sand and fell and got up again and fell down again, as they mastered it. Now it moved a foot, now another, now a whole yard. It was coming. It was going along with them. Six Melanesian men ran and replaced the rolled logs as they were swallowed under the barge, running and putting them under the belly of the thing as it lumbered along.

Abruptly Mr English called a halt. The entire barge was sitting, like a tame hen on the rollers, and the rollers were firm on the steel mesh laid above the sand. They had done it.

The hundred and fifty men, young and ageing, native and European, fell, flopped, or sat with some dignity on the sand to rest. Four long lines, like boat race crews defeated at the finish. The night had taken its possession of the sky, the sea and The

Love Beach. As they rested on the sand, most of them sitting now, arms back against the beach, the hooty Scots voice came from the conquered barge, from the thickening part of the sky. 'That's grand lads. Tha's fine! Now we'll leave her here until daylight and then we'll pull her into the place where we want her. It's been a gran' effort.'

The men applauded from the seats on the sand, then gathered themselves up and began to walk back to the beach track. Something decided Davies to walk back along the sand to look at the invasion craft, riding high on its rollers and then to look into the old cavity where the barge had lain for so long. He was alone for the others were moving in the opposite direction. In the pit, lying arms pathetically outstretched, was a pattern of bones that had once been a man.

Davies looked closer and put his hand to his neck. 'Hey, Mr English!' he called along the beach. 'Mr English, come here. Come and see this!'

Rob Roy English came at a jog across the sand with Mr Kendrick and Pollet. They stood looking down at the skeleton, dimly white, slightly phosphorescent it seemed in the greying light. Mr Kendrick, the cycle shop man, produced a bicycle lamp and shone it on the bones tracing one along and then another like a man following a street map. They were just bones, with a crushed and rusted steel helmet near them. Mr Kendrick moved the torch carefully. Other things, bits of metal, the hard remains of an automatic rifle.

'Looks like we've found our Unknown Soldier,' muttered Mr English quietly.

Davies stepped down into the pit and bent like a doctor examining a patient. 'No you haven't,' he said. 'See this—his identification tags. This here. Have a look.' He handed up the metal discs. 'Hard luck,' he said.

Anger stiffened the fingers of Mr English. He picked up the metal identity tags, held them in his right palm, and then turned and ran a bent and bandy course to the sea. They saw his outline vaguely jerk, like a fisherman casting a net as he reached the short surf. They knew he had thrown the discs into the waves. He came back at an amble, glared at Davies, and then looked down reverendly at the skeleton.

'Our Unknown Soldier,' he breathed. 'Puir devil, I wonder who he was?'

XI

By the end of the second evening the chapel was made. The barges had been dragged rolled and rollered, manœuvred into position so that they formed three sides of a square. Some of the members of the council suggested giving them a couple of coats of paint, but Mr English, with proper feeling said that they were to remain as they were, with the rust and the wounds showing, like the Unknown Soldier who was to be re-buried in their enclosing arms. A concrete cell was made for the tomb, a little box like a manhole to a sewer, Davies thought, and a cross incorporating remnants of the soldier's gun and his sadly inadequate helmet was made by the blacksmith at the native village and welded on to the middle barge. The skeleton was to be brought from the mission church and buried in the new grave on the Sunday before the arrival of the Queen. There was to be no eternal flame because, as Mr English so practically pointed out, the hard winds and the swooping rains in season would soon douse it and he, for one, wasn't going to keep going down to the beach to re-kindle it.

Having made and set the sanctuary the islanders abandoned it temporarily and went about their normal lives and with their preparations for the royal visit. But Davies went to the beach quite often, haunted by the moving colours and the strangeness of the scene that sunset when they shifted the first of the barges. He could feel it within himself, the tones and the little men against the tones. It ached to be remembered and caught

173

forever. He would have been a fine artist had he been able to paint.

He took his easel and his oils, still trapped in the old rugby sock, to the beach at evening and tried to get the sky right and the proportion of the humans tugging the barge. Disdainfully it eluded him. He returned to the Hilton with the same hopeless daubs, set them up in his room and looked at them, wondering what magic he was missing.

Bird came to the beach one evening, early while there was still gold on the sea and the sky had not begun to digest the daylight with its vivid juices. She wore a native parau, brilliant orange with the traditional curves and commas of white worked into the pattern. Davies was sitting against one of the barges, his easel set up trying to pursue and capture the place, the situation and the mood. She came smiling across the sand to him.

'If you are never a Gauguin it will not be because you did not give sufficient time to it,' she said. 'You are always here.'

Davies grimaced at the streaks like wounds on his canvas. 'I don't want to be a Gauguin,' he grumbled. 'I want to be a Davies.' He thought about it. 'Mind,' he admitted, 'it doesn't sound half so special, does it? Gauguin–Davies. It could be that you've got to have a certain sound of name to be a great painter. I was thinking of changing the paints when I get back to Sydney, perhaps I'll change my name instead.'

She stood and considered what he had worked. From his crouch he looked up at her. The parau was brought about her under her arms in the traditional native way with the end tucked between her breasts, so that her shoulders were exposed. It looked very natural on her, he thought, and she wore it unselfconsciously as a Pacific island woman would have done. Her shoulders were brown and gently shaped. She looked at him and smiled again. 'Still trying to catch again the vision?' she said. 'The only way, Davies, is to get all the men back here and ask them to pull another barge for you. And you must get Mr

174

Rob Roy English to stand on the barge like a slave driver.'
She laughed gaily at the thought. 'Then you will get the painting you so desire.'

Davies rolled his shoulders. She crouched down beside him,
squatting, looking at his poor work on the easel, frowning, pulling back her nose, shaping her eyes. Then she looked over the
top of the canvas and stood again. A group of native girls, from
the beach village, were capering in the water, making the shallows splash like feathers around their ankles. Their cries and
their faultless laughter came across in the somnolent evening.

'Davies,' said Bird slowly. 'You said once you would like to
paint the dancers on The Love Beach. Remember the ones we
laughed about, the maidens that shocked poor Captain Cook?'

'Keeping time to a nicety,' recalled Davies.

'Why don't you paint them now? There is some light left,
is there not? I will get these young girls to dance. You will
paint.'

Davies was slow. 'They'll dance?' he said.

Bird nodded. 'Yes, they would like it. They are happy
dancing.'

'Yes,' said Davies, still slowly. 'Ask them, will you Bird? I
would like to have a try.'

She walked away from his place, her feet making dents in
the beach. She went towards the distant young girls, un-
hurriedly, her body moving with the liquid sway of a Melanesian islander. Davies let his eyes go with her watching her
sandalled feet making tracks and the hem of the orange garment that was low about her legs. Hurriedly he took the used
canvas from the stubby easel and replaced it with another. He
was getting short of canvases, he thought. Never mind he
would be going soon. He would not be here. Back to Australia.
Then perhaps back to Newport.

Bird neared the native girls. They stopped jumping in the
shallows when they saw her coming to them. They stood
quietly in the little surf and watched her walk. Davies, at the

other extreme, saw her approach them and bend to talk with them. Then he saw them leap like fish in the sea as they heard what she had to say.

They followed her from the wet sand, up the climbing beach, skirting the still straddled landing craft, and went to an open part a hundred yards from where Davies crouched behind his canvas. Bird called something to the Melanesian girls, but the words were carried away over the attentive trees by the breeze coming in across the lagoon. Davies saw the girls obey her, saw them form a pattern on the beach.

And then they began to dance. They danced the special dance, the dance of The Love Beach. They required no music, just the rhythmic clapping, the bare touching of their own hands to keep time. Bird was at the front, dancing too, with a movement just as native as theirs, a melodic swinging grace that seemed to go with the breeze. They danced a story that was concerned with the going down of the tropic sun, that in its very mystery foresaw the coming of the night. Davies watched them and, mesmerised, began to paint them, the clumsy, bad, strokes going across his canvas, attempting to fill it as the evening was filled—with the sky and the sea, the island, and the brown dancing girls.

The dancers were engrossed, lost in their story, in its movements, its continuous grace and unheard music. Bird was with them in every motion and emotion. Davies watched and saw her take the tail of the parau from her breasts and lower it to her waist, so her breasts were exposed white and showing in the evening light. It was a natural movement, almost incidental. He buried his fists in his eyes because he wanted her too much for his own good. He looked again and all the young girls had brought their garments to their waists also. Their naked breasts and oiled shoulders moved to the simple music they made with their hands. The paraus hung about their hips and their legs, making a different separate movement. Davies worked his brush across the canvas, but there was nothing

176

there. Nothing he could capture, to take away with him from this place. He only wanted to watch them, and to watch Bird. Dancing like that, gently churning the sand with her young feet, moving like a child at the belly and like a woman from the shoulders and the breasts. She was a distance away, but he could see how fine, how marvellous, she was. All the many times he had wanted to touch her, but was afraid, not of her, but of himself, and his children, little Mag and Dave. He had seen her every day, working, or walking with him, singing with her guitar, laughing, being simply Bird, and he had been unable to find the courage to reach out for her.

She did not look towards him through the entire dance. The poetic details were accomplished, each movement, each indecent movement as Captain Cook had primly noted, worked out of the dancers and worked into the story pattern. They performed several dances, the first in rows remaining on a single spot, making a bowl of sand under their bare feet. Then they enacted a circular motif, moving sideways, and keeping once again the time with the clapping of their hands. Davies watched the dark bodies with their cocky little breasts, the slim necks and the faces, expressionless, far away in the demands and dreams of the dance. And among them, her skin tan among all the brown, Bird kept the same rhythm and the same intricate time, her breasts as small but vivid white, her waist bending with an easy swing.

Then they began to sing. They sang as they danced a new dance, in pairs, imitating the naked kiss, the love-stance, the growing of desire and ardour, girl to young girl. Bird danced with a tiny girl, about eleven years old, who matched every erotic movement with one of her own. 'In the practice of which they are brought up from earliest childhood', Davies thought.

He had stopped trying to paint. The brush had dropped into the sand the grains sticking to the yellow ochre he had been using. His canvas was just hapless streaks, his eyes full of the white girl among the native dancers. They were facing each other in pairs now, legs thrown apart, singing in a low vibrant key. One leg of each partner was thrust between the widened legs of the other and they worked their bodies upwards like snakes from the knees, through the thighs and the waists to the quivering breasts; the necks and chins and cheekbones set, the faces ecstatic and savage with the urgency of the dance. The girls worked their bodies close to each other, their voices flying over the beach, their hand-clapping sharp in the evening silence. Davies felt his sweat running down his face and his chest, a choking lump bulged in his throat. A massive erection arrived like a stranger and grew beneath him as he squatted. He dropped his eyes to his forearm and tried to think that he had to get away from this place and back to Newport, Mon.

The song and the clapping were cut off in a second. He looked up and, ashamed, saw the dancers laughing, the laughter of innocence and childishness. They rolled in the sand like dark clowns and crowded about Bird, gabbling to her, and giggling. They raised their paraus from their waists, covering their bodies and each one tucking the bright hem of the garment into the glade of her breast. Bird patted their shoulders and their heads as though they were her children. They were laughing again then, the almost hysterical native laughter like screaming and tumbling, jumping up, running and tumbling again, like prisoners suddenly released to a world of sand and sea. Bird began to walk back towards Davies, slowly, her head bowed like a novice, and the Melanesian girls ran in a flock to splash in the surf-line of the lagoon.

Davies watched Bird come back to him across the dimming place. The great booming evening was past the climax of its display, the colours were running across the bottom of the sky draining away and the sea was growing dark and pensive. He watched her steadily as he crouched by the easel but she did not raise her head as she came towards him. The emotion he felt for her stuck up inside him, reaching from his groins to the curls of his stomach.

178

She stopped her walk a yard away from him and looked up with her composed face. She pushed her hair away, taking it to the back of her neck and leaving her hands there, her arms bent upwards like wings, her body stretched and slimmed by the movement. Davies remained squatting by the small easel.

Bird smiled uncertainly and stepped a pace nearer, looked down and saw the few scratches of paint on the canvas. 'You have painted nothing,' she whispered. 'Didn't you like the dance, Davies?'

He put out his hands and delicately encircled her ankles. His dark hair fell forward against her legs and he pressed his forehead and then his face and his lips to the brown skin of her legs. 'I was watching,' he said. 'Watching so much I couldn't paint.'

She put her girl's hand down and touched the rough hair at his neck. 'The dance was too short to paint anything, perhaps?' she said. 'It was only for you to get a glimpse, an idea. That was all.'

Without raising his head, keeping his face against the flesh of her leg where the parau divided, Davies reached up with both hands and caught her wrists. He guided her down to the sand beside him. They were squatting like native children squat in play. He raised his face to her and Bird smiled and wiped his wet cheeks with the back of her fingers.

'You *are* like a bird,' he said casting his eyes down again. Her olive knees were thrust from the orange garment she wore and it opened in a wedge between her legs as she squatted. 'No wonder they call you Bird.'

She leaned towards him and kissed him and he kissed her very lightly. 'I have tried, Bird,' he said miserably. 'I have, haven't I?'

She moved her eyes down. Her lashes were long against the little swelling of her cheeks. 'You have tried, Davies darling,' she whispered. 'And so have I. But I cannot try always. They are so far away across that sea. So far they cannot hear you, Davies.'

Davies thought he was going to choke. Little Mag and Dave, and Kate too, his wife, what were they doing now? He tried to see their faces, screwing his eyes up so the tears were crushed. But all he felt was her fingers reaching out for his face, touching his neck, his ears, moving over his lips and his nose, running over his eyes. 'You've lost them,' she said. 'You've lost them, Davies. You must realise that. You are a good man, darling.'

He sat back involuntarily and rather comically on the sand. He felt foolish sitting down like that. She squatted easily and still smiled her serious smile. She moved forward on to her knees, in front of him and his arms went out to her, begging for her, and Bird went to him, holding him tightly feeling him enclosing her body. They kissed savagely, long, soft, then hard. They rolled in the sand and he was above her grasping at her, feeling her, touching her with all the powerful gentleness he felt. Her hair panicked behind her on the sand. He reached for it, the lovely dark soft hair he had so often watched, and wound it in his fingers, tying them prisoners. Then each inch of her young face, with his face and his lips. Hardly touching her.

The night was forming about them like the walls of a house. The village girls ran from the sea and scampered up the beach, calling to each other across the sands, making for the trees and beyond them, the settlement. They were like little black ghosts of the island but Bird and Davies did not hear them or see their going.

By eleven o'clock the temperature had dropped to eighty-seven degrees and a rough wind was coming into the island agitating the eloquent heads of the palms, piling the sea against the reef, and rushing swollen low clouds across the moon.

Bird went to the latticed shutters when they rattled, peered out like a prisoner into the streets of the town, then closed the wider of the two outer windows. She said quietly to Davies: 'Sometimes a storm comes at this season. It blows all night and rains, but in the morning it is gone.'

Davies looked at her as she adjusted the shutter. Her hair was tied in a youthful tail now. She wore a satin housecoat that was too big for her. As her hand went to the shutter cord the smooth white sleeve fell back unveiling, like a slender statue, the brown arm. There were two lamps burning in the room. She turned around at the window.

'Davies,' she said. 'Are we going to my bed?'

'Yes,' he said. 'Yes, of course, we are.'

'I've never shown you my bed have I? I never show it to anybody. It's a joke really, but I like it. It's in here, where you haven't been.'

She pushed a Chinese curtain aside and he walked into the small bedroom with her. The bed was a muscular four-poster, carved, curved and corniced. Its dark, sombre wood, the four thick posts, like trees, and its embossed side panels, were set off by the lace hangings, white perfection, the creamy extent of the bedspread, and the high pillows.

'It's seven feet wide,' said Bird. 'It is the biggest bed for a thousand miles.' She stood just before him looking at the bed and she did not look around at him. He stretched his hands to her shoulders and he felt her trembling.

'It's very wide,' he said.

'I can walk about at night,' she laughed. 'And never leave my bed.'

'Where did it come from?' he asked.

'From a colonial house in New Caledonia. It belonged to my parents. Davies will you make me have a come tonight?'

She ran the three sentences quite naturally, without a long pause. Davies turned her about. 'You didn't on the beach, did you?'

'It was my fault,' she replied. 'I was nervous and I have

never experienced a come anyway. I wonder if I perhaps have the right pieces inside me.'

'You have, I'm sure,' he smiled at her seriousness.

'Then I do not know how to work them,' she said. 'I have known two men before you, Davies, and neither could make me work inside.'

She begin to slip the buttons open on his shirt. She opened the front and scratched his chest. 'Where is your vest?' she asked. 'I left it on the beach,' he said, awkwardly. 'In the confusion. Can you manage that?'

She was trying his front zip. It stuck at first, but she jerked it firmly and it ran down. She helped his trousers down.

Davies said pedantically : 'You should unlace the shoes first. It is very difficult and embarrassing for a man to get his trousers off over his shoes.'

She was kneeling by him, putting her soft hair close to his groin. 'I have never known a man with trousers,' she excused herself candidly. 'That is my trouble. My first man, when I was fourteen, was one of the natives on my father's plantation and he never wore anything. And the second man, well, he was a boy really, only seventeen, was in the police here and he wore shorts only. This trousers is a new experience for me.'

Davies said : 'He was a native . . .?'

'No, not the police boy. He was white. Well, almost.'

'The first one?' said Davies. 'He was a native, you said.'

'Yes. He was very funny too. I was only a little girl, of course, but he was very good to me, although he was in terror of my father finding out.'

'How long did that go on for?' asked Davies. She had taken his shoes off now. He kicked his trousers across the floor and sat on a basketwork chair.

'A few minutes,' she said looking at him surprised. 'Oh, it was nothing.'

'No,' he argued. 'Now wait a second. How long did the affair go on? The whole thing?'

Bird blinked: 'Is that important?' she asked. 'Only once, it happened. He was killed by a wild pig three days later. Only once.'

He wondered why he felt angry. She was smiling at him. 'Things are different in The Apostles, Davies,' she said. 'Many things. It is not like your town, is it?'

'No,' he admitted. 'It's not much like that.'

She put her small hands to the lapels of her satin coat, opened them with a natural movement, letting the garment slide from her and fall in a drift around her legs. She was still kneeling, so beautiful he hardly dared to look at her. He swallowed his priggishness inside him, all of it. Everything. Her plantation native, her police cadet, Kate, David, little Mag, Dock Street, Newport, Transporter Bridge, Barry Island beach in autumn and Trellis and Jones of Circular Quay, Sydney. Choked them all down, stuffed them inside himself and sealed them in, bugger them.

Pale were her breasts, the roots just meeting at the lower inside slopes, swollen out from them and then coming to the quiet unused nipples. The moulding of her sunned shoulders slipped away to the long veneer of those marvellous arms. From above her, looking down the whole valley of her body he travelled from one place to another, first with his eyes and then with his eager fingers and his entire hands, his palms, his wrists, his knuckles. Her stomach was tucked back in a dark hollow, but her thighs, as she knelt, were close against each other like brown pigs buried against their feeding mother.

She moved her face into his open legs and lay there scarcely breathing until he put his arms to her and drew her up the length of his body. They kissed as the first splatter of the expected storm was tossed against the window.

'When we make love,' she asked quietly. 'Will you please talk to me all the time? And I will talk to you. It will make me feel easy, and then what I want to happen will surely happen.'

They did. They lay, drowning in the white waves of the

ridiculous bed, making the most profound love, and conversing.

'What shall we talk of, Davies darling?'

'Anything, Bird. The weather?'

'It is storming. As I said.'

'You were right.'

'Tomorrow the sky will all be all washed and shining.'

'The boat will arrive in before long.'

'I shall get a letter from my mother.'

'I shall get one from my wife.'

'That hurts.'

'What, darling?'

'That there. The thing you did then, Davies.'

'Sorry.'

'That is better. It was sore.'

'All right now?'

'Yes, very much better.'

'Sure?'

'Yes, Davies darling.'

'You're so marvellous to feel.'

'You too. Inside me I feel every centimetre.'

'I feel every bit too.'

'We must not talk too much of what we do.'

'Why not?'

'It will stop my pieces working. I will not come.'

'You still want to talk, though?'

'Oh, yes.'

'It's still raining hard.'

'Oh God, that is hard too, Davies.'

'We're back to that again.'

'Think of something different. Please.'

'I will, Bird.'

'When is Her Majesty arriving?'

'In one week.'

'It will be lovely, won't it.'

'A big day for everyone.'

'Are you going away from here?'

'Yes.'

'When? Tell me when.'

'When *The Baffin Bay* arrives.'

'That is soon. I expect a letter from my mother.'

'You said.'

'Davies, this is so beautiful.'

'Yes darling.'

'It is for you also?'

'You know.'

'Yes, we move so well.'

'Keeping time to a nicety.'

'Hah! you like that?'

'Don't do that, Bird.'

'What?'

'Say "Hah!" like that. It hurts.'

'What! Hurts you there?'

'Yes, it hurts.'

'Just saying "Hah!"?'

'Don't! I said *don't* say it!'

'And I said it.'

'Yes, you did. It hurt then, too.'

'My sweet darling, I'm sorry.'

'I'm sorry I mentioned it.'

'You liked our dancing on the beach?'

'It was very beautiful.'

'Perhaps you understand a little now.'

'A little?'

'About when I was fourteen.'

'I see.'

'I was born here. I am of these islands.'

'And I'm of Newport, Mon.'

'Now you are of the islands also.'

'Bird, quietly Bird, I must stop.'

'To rest?'

'No. I am too quick.'

'It is me. I am slow.'

'How are your pieces?'

'Inside I think they are working well. I feel strange and full.'

'Don't talk so much, darling.'

'Are you rested, Davies?'

'Not yet. Wait until I've settled down.'

'Do you think the procession will be exciting?'

'Procession?'

'When Her Majesty comes. Everyone is marching or watching.'

'Very exciting. More now, darling.'

'I have been waiting.'

'It's still pouring outside.'

'It will for an hour. What will it be like to come I wonder.'

'I know what it is like for me.'

'Dahlia told me you would make me come.'

'Did she? How did she know.'

'She is a good judge of people.'

'Good old Dahlia. Darling, I can't much longer.'

'Rest again, please then. She said a woman coming is like ...'

'Like what Bird?'

'Like eagles leaving their nests.'

'Poetic. Not yet, darling. Be still.'

'I have never seen an eagle. Have you seen a great many?'

'None.'

'But they are very big.'

'So I believe.'

'Great wings. Slow wings and then faster and soaring.'

'Bird my sweet, I must soon.'

'Inside you,' she said. 'It must be strange.'

'Bird ... Bird ... I must.'

'Me too, Davies. Move with me.'

'I am.'

'Move ...'

'I am . . .'

'Move.'

'I am . . .'

'Soon, Davies . . .'

'Now! Now Bird! Oh, Now . . .'

'Oh, me too! They are flying. Flying!'

Encompassed by her great bed they lay. She opened her eyes first and kissed him. He was almost sleeping. 'Those eagles are such big birds,' she said.

It rained, as she had said, for exactly an hour.

XII

Conway returned from St Paul's in Abe's boat. They moved sluggishly across the glassy afternoon sea, beaten down, subdued, it seemed by the persistent heat of the sun. The men felt dry and low as well. Abe was unhappy because his boat was leaking again. Conway had that morning put a clear proposition to Joseph of Arimathea that a dozen of his tribesmen should be allowed to leave the island to fight in a Holy War. It had not worked.

'You're taking a hell of a long time today, Abe,' Conway grumbled.

'It's not me, boy, it's the boat,' said Abe shortly. 'I could get there faster.'

'So could I,' agreed Conway. He felt raw burned up by the sun, his face, his scalp, his arms, his knees. He had a bush hat but he used it to fan himself. Half sitting on the bleached deck seat he looked over and down into the infinite waters of the lagoon where the coloured fish moved like children's kites.

'Shit,' he said briefly.

'Nice,' commented Abe. 'What's the hurry anyway? You ain't paying by time, mister. You ain't paid at all yet, not for any of the trips. You owe me.'

Conway tried to spit at an orange fish. 'Sorry Abe,' he said. 'It's not you, mate, nor the boat. It's something else.'

'Your girl in the big club?' asked Abe casually.

'Not on your life,' said Conway allowing himself a smile. 'That girl is a pioneer of the birth pill in the Pacific. The only regular taker between Honolulu and Darwin. She got them from a man in Hawaii.'

Abe smiled with admiration. 'That's nice,' he said. 'That must be real nice. No messing about eh? I'd like to get a stock of them baby things. Maybe I could get the agency.'

Conway continued looking over the side. 'Just one every night,' he said.

'Monday's child is full of woe, Tuesday's child has far to go,' recited Abe reflectively. 'That's what they say, ain't it? That's the sort of thing your pal ought to have been peddling, not butter and fats. Who wants butter and fats, anyway.'

'Looks like he had a wasted journey too,' shrugged Conway.

'So you did as well?' asked Abe, very Jewish. He rested his stomach on the wheel.

'Looks like it.' Conway spat at another fish, a blue one this time, a harder target. He thought he hit it. 'Listen Abe, I'm going to tell you something because I may need your help, and this boat. Anyway your know-how. You'll get paid, Abe, but you've got to keep your gate shut about this, whether you're in it or not. Understand?' He made a quacking, duck shape with his fingers. 'No talkie-talkie, okay? More people know than is healthy even now.'

'You can trust me, son,' said Abe hitching up his belly symbolically. 'If I get paid, particularly, you can trust me.'

'That island back there,' began Conway. 'That God-fearing, God-for-bleeding-saken island. That's my bother.'

Abe nodded with immediate understanding. 'I'm not one to ask,' he said with suburban primness. 'Never poke my nose anywhere that's private, but I knew you didn't get over there, among those heathen savages, just to help get 'em along with Jesus. When I saw you helping to build the grandstand for the Ascension Day thing, I thought to myself I'm buggered if that Aussie is filled with the Holy Ghost! I thought "He's after something".'

Conway told him what he was after. Abe slowed the boat

even more so that the story could finish before they reached the jetty at Sexagesima. He kept shaking his head. 'Dangerous,' he said at last, with a round whistle. 'Very dangerous. They're very touchy that tribe. Very touchy indeed. When they used to have a war with St Mark's it was terrible to see. Cutting up and bashing in, crucifying, stakes through the hearts. All that sort of business. For Christians, Aussie, they ain't very charitable.'

'I know all that,' said Conway impatiently. 'What I want to know is that when I do something drastic—and it's going to be soon—can I rely on your help in case anything goes wrong.'

'As long as I'm clear of the St Paul's lagoon and this boat is repaired enough to break the record between there and here, I'm with you,' said Abe throwing a rope to a Melanesian on the quay. 'Otherwise I ain't with you.'

Conway clambered up to the jetty. 'Get that leak plugged then. And give that engine a birthday. It's not had a rag over it in six months.'

'I will,' promised Abe laconically. 'I'll get a sail rigged up too.'

'Any beer?'

'Two left. Funny there always seems to be just two left when you poke your head in.'

Davies felt under his bed and came up with the two bottles holding them by the necks like animals. He gave Conway one. It was hot in the room again. The gekkos on the cream walls half closed their eyes in the heat, too indolent to eat the slow flies. The sun came through the break in the blind like a dagger.

'It's always so flaming hot in here,' complained Conway.

'It's a choice room,' said Davies. 'Sun all day. What did you want?'

Conway slowly drank half the bottle of beer. He checked the level, took enough to fill his mouth again and set it down on the floor. 'Well,' he said. 'It's got to be done. The business over on St Paul's. There's no other way.'

'They don't want to join eh?'

'Do they hell. The black bastards are too busy waiting for Ascension and all that crap to think about anything else. Christ, I've got some blisters helping them to put that stage up too. And nothing for it.'

Davies said: 'You asked them straight?'

Conway shrugged. 'More or less, I said it was a Holy War, but shit they were struck dumb at the idea of anybody asking them to leave when Ascension Day is coming up. You'd think it was the Melbourne Gold Cup.'

'Maybe it is to them,' pointed out Davies.

'You always were such a great big bloody help.'

'I thought you wanted my help.'

'Later. Just now don't bother.' He swigged the rest of the bottle, looked regretfully at its green hollowness. 'I put it straight to that fat fool Joseph and said it was a special invitation from Her Majesty's Australian Government and he more or less said that Her Majesty's Australian Government could go and screw itself.'

Davies had got half-way with his beer. He saw Conway looking at it, but he deliberately drank the rest himself. 'What are you going to do? Give up?'

Conway snorted: 'Aw, come away. You know me better than that. Hell am I going to give up! I told you I'll take those boys back to Aussie if I have to blackbird them.'

'So how?'

Conway licked the blisters on his hands. 'Look at those, for God's sakes, working like a black putting up their concert party stage. Look at them.'

He held up his hand like a traffic policeman. Davies nodded. 'You could get ten bob an hour doing that in Sydney.'

'You're right you could. Anyway I'm going ahead with the other thing.'

'Not the motor bike!'

'Yes, the motor bike. They're waiting for this Messiah, this Dodson-Smith of theirs and they're convinced he's going to turn up any minute and ride his perishing motor bike down to them. They won't do anything without him, let alone go to Vietnam. But if the sign came from him, son, they wouldn't hesitate. They'd be out of here on the next boat.'

'Jesus,' said Davies quietly, looking at the Australian's face, 'I always knew you were mad, but it's got worse.'

'Listen,' said Conway leaning forward. 'You can get people to believe anything. People mate, any sort of people. People in cities, in out-stations, on funny little islands. Tell them something properly—anything, tell them it's going to rain blue frogs or the sun is coming up black tomorrow, and they'll swallow it. How do you think politicians and public relations blokes get by? Telling the truth? Do they hell! They get by because the bigger the lie the more people believe it. And especially if they *want* to believe it. And over there, on St Paul's they want old Dodson-Smith to come riding down that hill on his motor bike more than anything. More than life even. They're ripe for it.'

'Couldn't you have offered them money to come with you?' interrupted Davies practically. 'Money usually works anywhere.'

'Anywhere else,' Conway conceded dolefully. 'I tried that. They said no thanks because they can manage till the copra collection. So I could stuff my money.' He looked thoughtful. 'Mind you, I did get a scent of an idea. But I'll leave that for now.'

'Well how are you going to work this miracle? And, what's important to me, where do I come in?' said Davies.

Conway picked at the stubble on his chin as though seeking out weeds. 'You and Abe,' he said.

'You've told Abe?'

'Yeah, I had to rope him in. I need his boat.'

'What about Pollet?'

'No, not yet. In a funny way I think he'd be a risk.'

'You mean he's got a decent regard for the natives?'

'If you like.'

Davies said: 'All right, what is it and when?'

Conway grinned. 'I wish it was as simple as that, sport. But it just ain't. It will need to be soon. During the next three nights, I think. We've got to get over there in the dark, get around the back of the island, the volcanic side, and climb up over the top . . .'

'*We've* got to?' queried Davies.

Conway glared at him. 'Maybe me, maybe both of us. It depends on how much help I need. Maybe I won't ask you, anyway. I can handle it myself. I need a bell . . .'

'A bell,' said Davies.

'A bell,' confirmed Conway. 'And a sort of black cloak, which is what this Dodson-Smith character is supposed to arrive in—according to all the stuff in the records and observations of the island.'

'Where did you get that?'

Conway shuddered. 'Mrs Flagg,' he said. He glanced at Davies but Davies did not react. 'The bell rung continuously is a sign that they must prepare for war. I mean, I don't intend to ride that motor bike down to the village and tell them in my Sydney accent that I'm Dodson-Smith and they've got to go off to Vietnam like good fellas.'

'That is a bit thin,' commented Davies wryly.

'And risky,' agreed Conway.

'So you ring the bell like a muffin man and they'll follow you anywhere,' said Davies.

Conway glanced at him. 'They're only going to see me from a distance,' he said. 'The whole village will go down on the beach.'

'In the middle of the night.'

'I've worked out a little diversion there—a sort of counter-attraction. Like a sign, shall we say, or a vision.'

'Like what?'

'Not yet. You'll see if you come. Anyway when Dodson-Smith turns up he's going to ride through the village—which will be empty because they'll all be on the beach—and along that track that runs just above the beach, remember it?'

Davies nodded: 'And ringing his bell,' he said.

'Right. So they know he's turned up and so they know he's sounding the war signal.'

'Then what?'

'Then old Dodson-Smith pisses off along the track for a mile to the little pebble beach at the north of the island where Abe's boat will be—with you and Abe in it—and we get the sacred bike on board via a ramp from the pebbles, no tracks or anything see—and clear out quick.'

'And the next day you'll go over there and then we get a dozen men with their bags packed, itching to get at the Viet Cong,' said Davies. 'Absolute bloody lunacy.'

'Listen,' said Conway. 'I'll bet you that they'll come with me within a few days. How much will you bet?'

Davies said: 'It's so mad. It's unbelievable.'

Conway looked at the Welshman's negative face. 'Listen,' he said fiercely. 'Can you picture that day when we went over with the harmonium. Was anything more mad, more unbelievable, than that? Go on tell me.'

'I suppose it was really. Judging by normal standards.'

'That's the trouble. You're using the wrong measure. Normal standards don't count here. I know you think the whole thing is far out but what you've got to admit is that everything is like that here. Look at this Mrs Flagg and her natives with their dicks all bound up. Look at this Unknown Soldier business. If that's not looney I don't know what is. Look at this nut with his bread sign flashing all night, and this Chinese place where they have their meetings. And the meetings. It's like an insane asylum anyway. What might seem madness in your place, what d'you call it? . . .'

'Newport,' said Davies helpfully. 'Mon.'

'Yeah, Newport, Mon., and what might seem like madness in Sydney is normal here. It works! It's got something to do with the sun and the isolation and the way the moon is, and the season. It has got everything to do with all these.'

'I still think it's barmy,' said Davies. 'God, is it worth all that?'

Conway bit his top lip into the stubble. 'It is. To me it is anyway. I never start a thing I don't finish, son. I'm known for that.' Davies got up and looked out of the split in the window blind. The ancient Chinese across the road was putting up the Communist flag of his homeland and a large photograph of Mao as his contribution to the street decorations for the royal visit. Davies shut his eyes and turned into the room again.

'What sort of chance does Abe give it?' he asked.

'Every chance. He's like Pollet, he knows this place, these islands and these people. He knows the mad things that happen, and especially with the natives. He knows their minds, the superstition, even when it's supposed to be religion.' He leaned forward towards Davies. 'Listen, people in these islands sit down and die, just like that, because somebody else says they've *got* to sit down and die. They kill their parents if they feel they've *got* to kill them. And its not just to go to the bleeding orphans outing, either. Their whole lives, mate, are built up on terrible fears, bogie-wogies, ghosts, and Dodson-Smith if you get me.

'Look, in the South Hibernian Islands the people went religion mad. They were so full of the Holy Ghost they ate all the missionaries and their wives. So brimming with the spirit that they couldn't help themelves. And that wasn't any voodoo religion, it was a substitute for voodoo, and they called it Christianity. They put everything primitive into it, everything that's powerful in their lives and the lives of their tribal ancestors for

195

donkey's years back. They call on Jesus and then lay down on a bed of red hot coals. And they get up again without a blister. I'd like to see your Archbishop of Canterbury do that.'

Davies said: 'And you're prepared to stir them up, nutty children though they are, just to get your little thing going.'

Conway said: 'Aw, now come on sport. Don't let's get down to ethics. If you like I'll give you the whole works, H-bombs, napalm, women and kids. I can recite the lot. Because I've seen it. I've been there. Ethics are no worry of mine. I just want to get these blackies on the way to Aussie.'

He took an impulsive swig at the beer bottle, found it empty, and dropped it dully on the floor. 'Are you still with me?' he said to Davies.

Davies had gone to the window again. He looked out on to the enclosed hot street. The Chinese shopkeeper was showing his flag and his portrait of Mao to his Vietnamese neighbour.

Davies said slowly: 'It seems that the insanity in this place is catching. It must be the heat or something.'

'Good,' smiled Conway. 'I'm going to need you.'

'Well listen before we go any further,' said Davies. 'First of all I want to tell you that at the first sign of murder, even if it's yours, I'm pissing off out of it with Abe.'

'Abe will be yards ahead,' said Conway confidently. 'If I have to swim, I have to swim.'

Davies said: 'Secondly, since I've turned from a butter and fats salesman to a wholesale kidnapper and southseas adventurer, perhaps we could come to some agreement about what I'm going to be paid.'

'Why not?' said Conway. 'Two hundred Aussie dollars, flat rate, is that all right?' He held his hand up to Davies. 'I'll give you a note of agreement, don't worry, just in case I don't get back. After all, mate, why should you lose?'

'Why should I?' agreed Davies.

XIII

Newport was as far away as the planets that night, Davies thought. Newport with its wet evenings and the lamps like water lilies on the pavements. The cars sizzling through the rain, and the bikes going by making whispered hissings like snakes. The neon over the Odeon, the river mud under the bridge, the copper dome on the tech gone mouldy green, the old town hall crowded by buildings all sides so that its clock tower peered helplessly out like a pinioned man. The band-stand in Belle Vue Park, the buses on the Cardiff Road, and those big ships riding in the meadows in the south, just as little Mag and David had seen them on that day.

Abe was already aboard the boat, working in an efficient manner, coiling a rope, banging his foot in a testing manner on a board, giving the engine a little oil from a can like a nurse giving a child night-time medicine. Conway stood on the jetty, looking very big in the dark, feet astride, staring over the tired sea to where he knew the hump of St Paul's squatted. There was no moon that night and there were never any lights showing from the island at that distance.

It felt very unreal to Davies; unreal and yet somehow natural enough that all this should be happening in these hot places. It was *he* who was the unreality. He, Issy Davies, South Wales factory-hand, turned immigrant, turned butter and fats sales-man, turned sailor, explorer, adventurer, and God knows what else before the morning came. But the setting was right. The dark sea heavy and warm, the stirrings of the Pacific dark; the close sky. He had just left Bird lying diagonally across her bed, beautiful, resting, her sweat cooling. How did all these things come to take place. As Conway had said they could only happen here. In Newport they would never believe you.

He put his fingers up and felt his face. The night perspiration was lying across it like drizzle. His chin felt hard. Pollet had cut his hair for him. The Belgian cut the hair of the natives in the villages, kept the bits and used them in the manufacture of Melanesian dolls which he carved from wood. He had chopped and changed and chopped again until Davies' hair was hanging around his head like tails.

Bird had loved him profusely that evening, lying on that ridiculously erotic bed with him above her, held in her soft arms. As they lay and moved together, they no longer needed to converse in their sex, big moths and other airborne insects flew in frenzy about the globe of the lamp by the bed, sending whirring shadows over the skins of the lovers. When Davies loved her, when his body was beside her and within her, he could find no room for any other thought or emotion. Only the great swollen sickness that she drew from him with her love, the feeling of it swelling up, gathering inside him, and then flooding away, leaving him clean and relieved. Then he could look from the window out to the assembled night and its staring stars, and send his thoughts away through the sky and back to distant places again. Then he wondered about the components of him that were stretching over so many thousand miles. How could a man be in two such separate places at once? She with true woman's insight, never asked him where his thoughts were. She lay and felt him, all over his body touching each part, examining him, almost, his face, his hair, his ears, front and back, his chest, his stomach, his backside, his legs, and his loving parts.

Once, as he stared from the bed to the word she asked: 'Looking for the boat?'

'The boat?' he asked stupidly.

198

'No,' he said looking around to her and seeing the pain in her face. 'No. Never thought of it. It'll come some day, I suppose.'

'No supposing is necessary,' she said firmly. 'It will be here soon. It is on the ocean now. I hope it meets a hurricane or a typhoon, Davies.'

He had laughed quietly and took her choice breasts in his hands and kissed them. 'Poor Captain MacAndrews, and Greta and old Curry and Rice,' he laughed. 'What about them in your hurricane?'

She had smiled ruefully. 'Well I hope they are saved by a passing boat,' she conceded.

'In a hurricane?'

'Yes, it will be a miracle rescue. The whole world will discuss it. But I hope *The Baffin Bay* never gets here.'

'It will,' he had said surely. 'By Tuesday.'

On the jetty he stood just behind Conway. Conway, who, he knew, would leave Dahlia very easily and she would leave him the same way. They were travelling lovers, they would never forget, but they would never particularly remember either. That was a good thing to be, a travelling lover.

Davies was wearing some sailcloth jeans and a blue shirt with one button the middle of an original family of five. He still retained his tennis shoes, although they had aged and his big toe was thrusting through the right one. He felt that his body was brown and tough. Strangely he felt as though he had grown. That night he felt he could have undertaken a fight with Conway.

Conway said: 'Ready then?'

Davies said: 'Ready. Why is Abe so keen? Have you paid him?'

'Half,' said Conway looking at Davies sideways. 'The other half later.'

'What about me?' said Davies. 'Don't I get anything?'

'Christ,' muttered Conway. 'Show a man danger and he starts counting the pennies.'

'Dollars,' corrected Davies. 'Aussie dollars. Let's be business-like.'

'All right,' agreed Conway. 'I said I'd give you a payment note, is that good enough? It's a hell of a fine time to discuss your terms, sport.'

'It's the best,' said Davies. 'A payment note will do if you haven't got the change on you.'

Conway grimaced. 'The day of the gifted amateur is over, eh? Well, as it happens I've got your note all ready here and signed. You would have got it. Do you want me to stamp your health card?'

'I'll just take the note,' said Davies. He took it. Two hundred Australian dollars. A hundred pounds. That would get him some of the way home, anyway. He folded it carefully and slotted it into the back of his trousers. 'Right, I'm ready,' he said clambering down into the boat. 'Best of luck, Messiah.'

Abe watched them studiously, especially Davies. He felt surprised at Davies. He had always thought he was a bit soft. Playing that harmonium, that morning on the beach at St Paul's, he had really thought he was a bit soft. This place changed people.

They left the harbour quietly, the vessel snuffling along the sea like a smelling puppy. Davies had not been among the islands at night, except for his arrival in *The Baffin Bay*. St Peter's slunk off astern, black except for the stark fluttering of the 'Bread' sign over Livesley's shop. It reminded Davies strangely of a can-can dancer lifting a many-coloured skirt. He watched it and hummed out the time and tune of 'Orpheus in the Underworld'.

'Cheerful,' commented Conway. He handed Davies an Australian army water bottle.

Davies looked at him and then the bottle. 'No thanks,' he said.

'Scotch.'

'Sorry.' He took the bottle and had a drink, feeling the fiery glow coming through the hard rimmed neck. He felt it fanning out quickly inside him. 'Aussie army issue?' he asked.

'For special combat assignments,' said Conway. 'This thing here is a gun. A pistol. Aussie army issue again. It's for you.'

Davies made a face at the weapon. 'I told you, didn't I? Any trouble and I'm running not fighting.'

Conway said: 'Listen son, all sorts of things could happen. If you get two hundred of those fanatical buggers around you waving clubs and spears it's no use playing the bleeding harmonium.'

'A gun won't be much better if there are two hundred,' said Davies, nevertheless taking it. 'How does it work?'

'You've been a soldier?' asked Conway. 'Don't you know?'

'*Officers* had little guns,' said Davies. 'Other ranks, that was me, had the long guns. I've never used a little one.'

Conway ill-humouredly showed him the working of the pistol, flicking it open and closed, throwing the magazine, closing it, handing it back. 'You point it this way,' he said sarcastically. 'With the little hole directed outwards.'

'Glad you told me,' said Davies. 'Can you now tell me exactly what is going to happen when we get there?'

Conway said: 'I wish I knew. Too right I do.' He clamped his top teeth over his lower lip. 'What I hope will happen is that we'll close in to the little pebble bay just around the headland from the lagoon. There's a wide opening in the reef there, but hardly anything of a beach. Enough for us though. I'll go ashore and all you have to do is to wait for me to come back. Abe knows the drill already because I've been through it with him. Right Abe?'

Abe nodded in the dark. 'I know it all,' he said. 'Just as long as nothing goes wrong, I know it all.'

Conway continued to Davies. 'We've made a wooden ramp— it's there, see?—to run onto the boat from the beach. It's pretty elevated just there and the levels shouldn't be any worry. All you have to do is to be waiting with that ramp in place for me to get back on their sacred motor bike.'

'You'll run the bike aboard,' said Davies. 'And we get out as quick as we can?'

Conway grinned. 'Simple for you, mate. Just nothing to it. I've got the hard part.'

'That's how it should be. How are you going to stop them rushing you when they see you on the motor bike? After all if they think you're the divine Dodson-Smith they'll want to grab hold of you. When they find it's only you, not Santa, they'll have your balls off.'

'They won't see me that close,' said Conway. 'Not if I can help it. They'll all be down on the beach.'

'And how can you work that?'

'I have something figured out, don't worry. They won't catch more than a quick look at me when I ride down the road through the village and then down that bend above the beach. Then I'm heading like hell along the track for half a mile, down on to the pebble beach, and we get the bike aboard this thing and we tail off as hard as we can go.'

'Still sounds as though you're out of your mind to me,' said Davies.

Conway looked quiet. 'It sounds a bit like that to me too, sport.' He sniffed around at the sky and the sea, a dark mixture all about them. 'Never mind,' he said. 'It's a nice night for it.'

He had gone ashore on the island, moving with expert quietness up the shingled stone of the beach, and sidling into the trees.

Davies sat in the boat with Abe. It stirred a little beneath them. They were in a small tightly curved bay with the eavesdropping palms close over their heads. There was little difference between light and shadow. Davies could just see Abe's face.

'What about him then?' he asked Abe.

'Lunatic,' sniffed Abe. 'Real lunatic. He'll be a great man.'

'If he lives.'

'Oh he'll live okay. Great men always do. That's part of the secret of being great—survival. If you don't live you don't make it to be great.'

Davies grunted uncertainly. 'What a thing to try, though. What a thing.'

'He'll be great,' confirmed Abe. 'Like Barber, and Wilkie Wilkins, and Sooney Petersen. Like all the world's great men.'

'Who the hell were they?' Davies glanced at him in the dark.

'You don't have to whisper,' said Abe. 'But you don't have to shout neither.'

'I wasn't whispering.'

'Shouting,' said Abe. 'That's what you was doing, shouting.'

Davies put his hand on the pistol lying on the cross seat before him. 'Do they have guards or anything at night?' he asked.

'Do they buggery,' laughed Abe. 'You don't get people anywhere so tired as this tribe. They all sleep like the rotting dead. Dodson-Smith had better make a row or he won't stir 'em.'

They squatted silently, the boat musing to itself.

'Sooney and Wilkie Wilkins?' said Abe shaking his head. 'Greats. World greats. See it depends on what your world is, sonny. Here the world is the furthest island you can see. Not much matters after that. Suva might as well be London, and Sydney, well that's the stars, and London—ha! we've never heard about it. They don't affect us, see? We hardly get to think about them. And if you come here, from the outside, you soon get like it too. Oh yes, you learn pretty quick that the whole world is just this little bit. It ends where the sky starts.'

Abe bent down towards the cabin opening. 'You want something to eat?' he said. 'I'm going to cook some tea and I've got some crab. Fresh from this morning. You want some?'

Davies agreed. Abe wriggled into the door of the cabin. 'Wilkie, now,' he said. 'Ha, you've got to be an islander to really get the feel of them. Wilkie used to run a flying boat, see, around the islands. He used to have a base at Honoraria up in the Solomons. That thing was so old there were no more spares left for it—not anywhere in the world. Nowhere. Not a nut, a bolt to fit the thing. But he flew in every day, patching it up, putting bits into it that he made himself. Everybody flew with Wilkie, son. Island to island. Honoraria, down here, St Peter's to St Mark's to St Paul's to St Barnabas. and the rest. All the tribesmen went with him. The St Mark's boys and this lot from St Paul's had a pitched fight one day in the flying boat, so Wilkie rolled it all of a sudden in the sky and tipped them all arse over earhole. What a man.'

'Dead?' suggested Davies. He took a sandwich from Abe and felt the dry salt taste of the crab.

'Oh sure, dead,' nodded Abe. 'But a *great* man. He kept tying that flying boat together, and then he was fiddling around for weeks trying to make a pipe or a valve or something that would fit it. He'd be stuck in Honoraria, which wasn't so bad because he had his woman there—Filipino she was—but sometimes he'd be down here trying to fix it, or on one of the outer islands. But it couldn't go on forever. He'd patched and welded and put so many bits and oddments in that flying boat that it just had to fall apart some day.

'It did too,' confirmed Abe. 'Boy, you should have been there. Almost everybody in 'Gesima saw it. He took off from the lagoon, great sight that was too; big forward wave and just getting gently up into the air, like a big beautiful cow. Then one of the propellors fell off and went splash. And all the people in the town, who'd been flying with him, and knew him and how he tried to look after the flying boat, stopped and watched and nudged each other saying things like; Look, there's the propellor just fallen from Wilkie's flying boat! That sort of thing you know. Just conversation. Because it seemed so natural for things to fall from Wilkie's flying boat. I mean, they was always falling off. But this time something else came away, and then another lump and then some more, until there was no flying boat flying at all. Just all bits and pieces, Wilkie among them. They all fell in the lagoon and so did Wilkie. He was by himself in the contraption that day, trying it out after putting something right. I suppose he didn't put it right enough. Anyway all the oddments fell down and old Hassey, who was a pal of Wilkie's said: "He'll never be able to put the bloody thing together now." '

Davies nodded vigorously.

'A great man, see?' said Abe. 'Lunatic, but great. It's the same thing in the islands. You come to get to know that, son.'

'I'm getting to know it already,' said Davies clumsily, his mouth full.

'Sooney,' Abe mused. 'Sooney Petersen. Ha! Came from a circus in Copenhagen or somewhere cold like that. Went over to St Barnabas and stopped the tribe over there putting him in a casserole for dinner by showing them circus tricks. He used to leap from a big high tree fifty feet or round about like that, with a rope looped around his ankle, just a bit shorter. Wham! He'd stop dead a couple of inches from the ground. Boy, that was something to see. He taught the boys over there on the island. They can all do it now. They been on the movies and television and all those things. A great man.'

'Great,' agreed Davies.

'Lunatic again,' said Abe. 'So you call this Livesley a lunatic because he's got that sign up saying "Bread". Right, maybe. But he's a pioneer, son, that's what he is. Next week maybe the cycle shop will have a neon sign saying "Bikes" and then the undertakers saying "Deaths" or "Burials" or something if you get me. I'm the agent for those signs, by the way. Then the hotel gets one, if Seamus can get himself away from playing his own fruit machines, and then somewhere else and somewhere else. In no time the whole town is flashing on and off across the Pacific! Red, blue, yellow, all the colours of the Union Jack, boy, and the ships that go passing us by will want to know what this place is with all the life. So they come, big ships, even, ocean liners, tourists. So Livesley a great man.'

Abe half stood and listened across the night. 'Nothing yet,' he said. 'But not too long to wait, I fancy.'

He returned to Davies. 'You came here selling what? Butter and fats, or something?'

'Don't remind me,' said Davies.

'Now that *was* lunatic,' said Abe. 'Only someone from outside the islands could be that lunatic. And it doesn't make you great. It was *genuine* lunatic. That's the difference.'

He listened again, but lowered his ear after a while. 'Pollet, now he's a friend of yours?'

'Yes, came in on the boat with us.'

'A great man, see. Knows about the islands and knows what to do. He can smell things. Trades with the villages, gets their knick-knacks and sells them. Right? And he knows every village and what it wants. There's one place, Uru-uru, do you know it?'

'No,' admitted Davies.

'Pollet took them a football one day. The English football, the round one. Yes? Now they play football all the time, not just the boys and men, but everybody, women, girls, babies, grandmothers. Every spare second they're hacking a ball about in the village. Two hundred of them sometimes, in the monsoon rain even, going wild. All in football shirts, all different colours, shorts and socks, but no boots. They can't take the boots. Pollet just has to take them these football things and they trade their wooden carvings, and all the rest of it. I'm the agent for sports gear in these parts, by the way. But he's a *great* man. Boy, I've seen a huge big pregnant woman kicking a ball like

206

crazy, going like a tank through boys and men. A man, ninety-eight, was killed by a ball there last year when he was playing goal. Straight in the face. It's like it all the time. In and out the houses, kicking against walls, playing inside the huts in the dark nights, they never run down. Old toothless women, two-year-olds . . .'

'What's that?' said Davies reaching for the gun.

'Something,' agreed Abe. 'I heard something.'

From beyond the trees, a mile away from the lagoon of St Paul's came a second sound, a cotton-wool thud. A spray of sparks ran above the palms. The sky glowed orange, then yellow, then a deep red. They could hear a throaty roaring.

'The diversion,' said Abe.

'No,' whispered Davies in disbelief. 'He's not set the copra boat on fire?'

'Looks like it,' said Abe calmly. 'It was the natural thing.'

'That's criminal,' whispered Davies. 'But that's bloody criminal. He can't do that. The stupid bastard doesn't know where to stop.'

'You're in it too,' Abe reminded him. 'You've got a signed promise note for your fee.' He looked at the crimson sky. 'Burning great,' he said admiringly. 'I offered to insure it for them, but they said the premium was too big. Alice and Northern Territories Mutual Protection. I'm the agent around here.'

There was one light left burning in the village when Conway was on his way to fire the boat. In the circle of that light he saw someone moving about. He could wait. He sat at the edge of the lagoon on a painful piece of lava rock, where the lava joined the coral, and waited.

He had time, so he asked himself why he did these things. It was not often he put the question but then it was not often he had to hang about like this before setting fire to a ship.

'All right then, why do you do it?'

'Because it's me. Because I like to do things in a certain way. And I like to do certain types of things.'

'Don't you think that sometimes it's difficult, dangerous and bleeding unnecessary. I mean like setting fire to these poor buggers' copra ship. It's like burning a man's bank balance.'

'You're beginning to sound like a conscience.'

'Not before time, either. Well, why?'

'Because it's a job I've fixed to do and I'm going to do it. I don't like to lose.'

'That's just about it. You don't like to lose. That's why they gave you that medal in Vietnam. That was a laugh.'

'Right.'

'But what you did, running into that village like some film star, was difficult, dangerous and unnecessary. Agreed?'

'Agreed. Right, now shut up because I want to get this incendiary grenade right in the middle of this copra hulk. I've never set fire to a copra hulk before.'

'I'm dead sorry for you son. You know this will make the poor sods penniless, don't you?'

'That's partly the idea. First to make a diversion . . .'

'So you can get the motor bike and play Jesus . . .'

'Dodson-Smith.'

'And so these savages, ignorant so-and-sos will take your money to cart them off to Vietnam . . .'

'Australia. They'll never get as far as Vietnam. You know that.'

'All right. Aussie then. So you can tell the boss what a marvellous job you've done again. They may give you another medal.'

'It's all fixed, so shut up, sport. Right, the light's gone out. Here we go. See if a drop of water will keep you quiet for a while.'

He stripped. Once he was in the warm water of the lagoon

208

he felt better. He was on his way. The whole thing would be great. He just did things this way.

Efficiently, with no noise, he moved across the dark lagoon. Animals and various birds were clucking in the jungle fringe, but they were not alarmed. He swam with shortened strokes so that the water was worried as little as possible. It rode easily under and above his arms, his legs scissored gently. The hulk, sitting placidly at its eternal mooring like a grandmother in a bed, was just ahead of him now. He wondered momentarily, if they ever kept a watchman on board. He doubted it. They were too tired.

The bow of the hulk was over his head now, like a black canopy. Little mewings came from it at water level. Creaks and strainings, and these little kitten sounds. He trod water to make certain the sounds were from the timbers. He realised they were; the old wood talking to the water. There were some carvings on the side of the hull, ancient and dulled but still there, clearly embossed in the dark. Conway wondered where the ship had traded.

About his waist he had a waterproof wrapper and within this the Australian army issue incendiary grenade, fixed to a timer which gave him thirty minutes before the fire started. He lay on his back in the supporting lagoon, unwrapped the package, checked that he had fixed the timer correctly. He had. He lobbed it efficiently over the bulwark above his head. It struck the deck boards and rattled on the wood. He waited, waited in case it rolled back. But it stayed up there. He got close to the hulk to listen for its ticking, but the water against the hull made too much commotion.

That would be all right. Thirty minutes from now. He went back to the shore, to the right-hand jut of the land around the lagoon, with the same quiet swim, watching the village for movement or light. There was none. He genuinely hoped they never got as far as Vietnam because it was not a place for tired people. Too many things happened when you were asleep.

They wouldn't, though, he was certain of that. Six weeks in Aussie touring about, big cities, and then shipped back here to tell everybody what a great time they'd had.

He reached the edge of the water, climbing out low and carefully, trying to decide whether coral or lava hurt most. He decided on the coral. There was a towel in his pack. He believed in doing things comfortably if not lavishly. After he was dry he dressed, looked back at the silent vessel in the anchorage, crossed his fingers, uncrossed them, then set off through the trees for the track that led to the hill above the village. Night noises froze him sometimes, but he made no great disturbance in the jungle. In the days he had spent on the island he had carefully judged distances and directions. He always did this kind of thing very well. Time spent in reconnoitring had never been time wasted.

The path rising to the plateau, where they kept the sacred motor cycle was steep but not difficult. He used a secondary route for the first section so that he kept out of sight of the village at all times. It took him twenty minutes. He checked his watch, looked at the motor bike and checked that over.

It was an American war-time Argosy model, standing like a museum piece there on the hill. They kept over it a cover made of thatched palm to protect it all the year. They had made the area about it like a little temple, an altar and a lectern, and un-lit candles. An oil burning torch sent out a lick of flame at one corner. That was always there in case Dodson-Smith should lose his way. Conway looked about him and felt a gleam of pity for the men who had made this place. Strange how people always put their faith in something unknown and then tied it up to something familiar and known. Like a motor bike.

He ran his hands over the old metal of the machine. He knew it would start because the islanders started it up every day at noon and kept the engine running for five minutes. Abe sold them two gallons of petrol every month for the operation. Abe was the agent for the petrol company.

210

Conway unscrewed the cap on the fuel tank and hung his finger in the aperture. The tank was almost full. It was possibly grade one too, unless Abe charged them for grade one and gave them grade three. He kept checking his watch. At the thirty minutes he sat down sedately and looked over towards the village and the lagoon. The dark trees falling down the hill in front of him, cut away in a parting down the middle, shielded most of the village but he knew that, had it been daylight, he could have seen the brown roofs from where he sat. The lagoon was a liquid shadow and on it, like a dark coffin, the old ship.

At the thirty minutes nothing happened. He stared towards the lagoon. He shook his watch but it answered with its prim tick. Nothing. Just Pacific darkness, an infant wind, a touch of inherent light from the ocean. At twenty-three seconds past the half hour the incendiary grenade exploded on the deck. Conway felt the quick excitement and the relief run through him. Those crappy timing devices. Twenty-three seconds late.

The explosion was dull and quite minor like a little bush of light suddenly grown in the centre of the ancient deck. It spurted and flared, coughed and half expired. Then it reared up like a blatant red sword, forcing its bright way through the deck wood, getting at the stored coconut oil, blowing outwards into a thousand fires. A great crack sounded over the lagoon. All the water was alive now, green and red, and orange, with the sparks shooting up into the thick night. Conway sat and thought that Livesley's neon sign would look better in green and red and orange. Much better than red, white and blue. It would be more like a bakery and not so much like a recruiting office.

Nothing had happened immediately in the village. But then there was a delayed rush from the houses, into the streets. Conway could see rapidly jolting lights. Trust them to take a candle to a conflagration. Voices, shouts and cries and native lamentations came from far below him. He sensed, from his high perch, the movement towards the beach, an onrush down to the side of the lagoon, with Joseph of Arimathea at the front. He did nothing, merely lounged there, waiting for the village below to clear. He glanced at the motor cycle on its mounting and ran his hand up the tyres. The originals had perished long ago, but Abe, who was the Pirelli agent, had replaced them twice. Conway guessed they were retreads.

'Enter Dodson-Smith' purred Conway to himself. It was strange how the most outlandish plans worked. He took from the army shoulder pack a grey robe and hood which Dahlia had made that afternoon from two blankets quietly obtained from the ambulance station. Conway had once won a bottle of champagne at an army fancy dress parade by making a monk's robe from a blanket and entering as a friar with a filthy habit. It was an easily manufactured costume and Dahlia, who still did not know why the garment should be required, made it dutifully.

That midnight on the hill it suited Conway very well. The cowl covered his head and the robe enveloped his body. It was too warm in there though, and he immediately began to sweat. Then there was the bell, borrowed, again unofficially, from the mission Sunday school on St Peter's Island. He took it from the army pack, holding it by the clapper like a veterinary surgeon holding a dangerous animal.

Folding the army pack he fastened it to the motor cycle's pillion, with the elasticated straps provided. Dodson-Smith was obviously expected to arrive with some small items of luggage and the grips had been thoughtfully provided.

From the beach he could hear the voices of the St Paul's natives howling like a newly-started wind. The copra hulk was burning spectacularly now, sending up great blossoms of flame, red, yellow and blue with green shoots sprouting over the lagoon. He pushed the motor cycle from its mounting, a simple wooden cradle, and wheeled it very easily a few feet forward. An excitement had now caught him, a tight band of it around his chest and his belly. It came back like some companion from

212

the past who had not been with him for some time. The air seemed closer and hotter around him. Within the encompassing robe he was dripping wet. All sounds that carried up from the beach brought more fever to him, and the wild crackling of the fire added to the pulsing of the air. But inside himself he was cool and efficient. Conway had never felt better.

He adjusted his robe, pulling it round him with a flying fling like a pantomime dame, and mounted the motor cycle. He tucked the blanket ends beneath him so that they were not trailing. Now he was ready. He bent and picked up the bell and it gave a small amused tinkle. He frowned at it. The noise of the voices still came up powerfully from the beach and the old ship was crackling cheerfully. Now some small canoes were standing off the burning hulk. Conway could see vaguely their splinter shapes. 'It's no use peeing on it lads,' he called softly. Then he kicked at the motor cycle starter and it growled into surprised life. He revved it violently knowing that the elevated sound would fly like the call of a fierce wild animal over the village and down to the beach.

They had kept the machine in fine condition. Dodson-Smith could have no complaints about his transport. Conway felt it vibrating beneath him as though it was experiencing a trembling anxiety to run off after all its symbolic and static years.

He pushed it forward gently, and let the gear in. It rolled off beautifully, smoother than riding a sedate Shetland pony, easy and controlled, throwing out a few snorts of smoke but making a loud happy growling. Conway went down the jig-saw path to the village. Half-way down he began ringing the mission Sunday school bell.

On the coral beach the St Paul's islanders wailing at the flames sizzling through their treasure of coconut oil, were stilled, silenced, petrified, by the first spitting sound of the engine. They stood in their attitudes, looking towards the lagoon. Even the fire seemed to be frozen. Then the jungle sound of the heavy revving roared over the trees to them. Joseph of Arimathea, in pyjamas, turned first, his great face set like a black jelly, his eyes thrown outwards, his lips dry and hard as tusks. The rest of the tribe, with a slow movement that would have enhanced some primitive ballet, turned then, from the head, then from the hips, then the clumsy feet revolving through the sand. In the lagoon the crews of the canoes stopped cursing the fire and looked over their shoulders towards the towering land.

Fear, foreboding, joy, wonder, crowded on the tribe at the same moment. Some felt the fear the most. Women covering their big jet breasts, their hands going to their throats. Children hurrying behind elders thrusting their frightened noses into the sanctuary of a buttock-crack, holding tightly on to adult legs. Some dropped with dreadful foreboding to the sand of the beach, their bodies bent as though awaiting quick death, their eyes gradually travelling up to see if the death was really coming. But a jagged smile drew itself across the old face of Joseph of Arimathea, a smile that filled his brain and all the channels of his body. His arms went out, moving as though they had been paralysed all through life and had learned how to work. Others near him felt the joy too, igniting within themselves just as their copra ship had burned from the inside. Wonder rooted some to the sand like strange stunted trees. There was no sound from the tribe, except their breathing, a noise like gas leaking from them. They were experiencing almost every emotion but disbelief. Bound by the terrible certainty of their outlandish Christianity, never considering the thought that someone might be cheating them, they looked up towards the glorious sound of the travelling motor cycle. Dodson-Smith, and no one else, their Messiah, their Saviour, was coming down the hill to his waiting people!

Then Conway began banging the bell, holding one handlebar of the jolting vehicle like an expert cowboy riding and guiding a steer. The tribe reacted with a universal jolt when they heard the bell. But they remained in their attitudes on the beach,

214

covered with their choking silence, unmoved, only waiting. The copra ship spat a great bellow of fresh flame as the fire reached some new source of feeding, but no one noticed. The canoes had been turned by the dazed crews and were floating idly a hundred yards off shore. Each man felt the new gust of fire burn his back, but none of them took their eyes from the path above the beach.

Conway descended on the pathetic people, riding the motor cycle like a bad comedian, ringing the bell like a demented town crier. He bounced, jolted, went into a half skid but righted it, and finally flew flamboyantly into their view as he travelled at forty miles per hour through the village street. Dogs, with no spiritual barriers, chased him joyfully, snapping and sniffing, leaping and falling over each other, an unruly, tumbling pack. The moment he throttled into sight of the tribe each of them fell flat on his face, the children pressed to the sand by their mother, great sobs now escaping from their black recumbent bodies. Joseph, with a vivid demonstration of humility, tore his pyjamas from about him and threw them wide away, before rolling forward, his face jammed hard into the gritting coral sand.

They saw Conway only briefly as he careered through the village, for two outcrops of trees hid the track from the beach after that. But when he turned the sharp bend above the beach hitting the bank with all the aplomb of a scramble rider, and when he began to throw the bell back and forth with tremendous dexterity, they saw him then. They lifted their faces, those who dared, and saw the robed rider taking the path just above their heads, only fifty yards away. The black garments tight about him, the carefully nurtured machine snorting as proudly as any king's charger—and the bell telling them to prepare themselves for war. They had not expected that. But anything Dodson-Smith decreed was good.

'Aaaah,' Joseph of Arimathea howled at last. 'Aaaaaaaaah.'
'Aaaah,' wailed the tribe. 'Aaaah, Aaaaaah, Aaaaaah.'

At that point the clapper from Conway's wildly flying bell, accustomed only to the gentle tinklings of the Reverend Colin Collins on Sunday afternoons, shot from its socket and went like a heavy missile ahead of the motor cycle. Conway found he was ringing only silence. 'Balls,' he cursed with no appreciation for the moment. He changed gear and roared on, along the brittle track, now once again out of sight of the natives, and heading for the pebble beach and Abe's boat.

Davies was lying, semi-conscious, on the long seat of the boat at that moment, poisoned by the bad tinned crab that Abe had used in the sandwich. He moaned and vomited and moaned again, lost in a fog of nausea and impotence. He heard the motor cycle sound coming through the trees and was aware of Abe starting up from his seat. But he could do nothing more. The crab gripped his guts from the tender inside and held him down to the deck.

Abe shouted something to him, but it was swallowed by the dreamy cocoon around him. He could not help. He could not move. Abe spat with annoyance and moved forward to make sure that the ramp they had manufactured was firmly against the pebbles at one side and gripped to the deck at the other.

'Wait,' shouted Abe. 'Too fast!'

A tail of Conway's robe jammed in the rear wheel and brought the machine round fast and in the wrong direction. With huge skill and strength Conway righted it so that it headed for the ramp again. But he was too late with his brake. The plan had been to stop the machine and quickly wheel it aboard the boat. Instead it ran snorting like a war horse, fiercely, straight up the wooden ramp and crashed spectacularly into the cabin of Abe's boat. Straight through the door it went, wedging itself and its rider in a great debris of planks and splintered wreckage.

'Mama,' howled Abe. 'What the hell you doin'?' He rushed towards Conway, who was still sitting astride the shattered machine, hunched forward, his head against the only wall of the cabin which remained. Davies was crawling from beneath a pile of planks, blinking with concern and astonishment, and speared by a renewal of his own sickness.

Conway had the presence of mind to wave his hand at Abe, in a forward movement, telling him to get away from the shore. Abe understood, pulled the ramp aboard, and clearing wreckage away started the engine. He breathed quick but true thanks as the boat responded and began to ease herself into the little bay. He went to the wheel and it came away from its fixing in his hands. The steering was jammed, but at least the rudder was straight because they headed unerringly for the wide gap in the reef and out into the dark ocean. They would soon be beyond sight of the island, far off into the the night sea.

Half a mile from the beach where they had waited, the entire St Paul's tribe was advancing fearfully along the road, following the tracks of the motor cycle, looking for Dodson-Smith, the Saviour who had arrived ringing his bell, and had gone away again so quickly.

By the time they reached the beach Abe's boat was two miles out to sea. Far away from the shore he eased up and did a quick repair job on the steering. He did enough to get them back to Sexagesima harbour and he turned his shattered boat in that direction. He began to feel happier when he thought how much the Australian Government, through their employee Conway, was going to have to pay for the damage. He might even get a new boat.

Davies and Conway, both unconscious for their different reasons, were laid out on planks either side of the wrecked cabin, like big tuna fish caught by a game fisher. Abe looked at them and smiled. He began to sing a traditional Yiddish song.

Davies, awakened, knew he was in his own room because a late-risen moon was filtering through the break in the blind making a bright knife on the wall. His stomach felt cold, vacant. His whole body seemed light as a ghost as though all the substance had been beaten from it.

'Crab,' he muttered miserably. The word and the very action of saying it invoked a shiver. He tried again, 'Crab.' He was still in his clothes, but he felt chilled in the close little room. Throwing his arm limply sideways he reached below the bed and brought up a bottle of beer. The opener was on the wicker table at his bedside. He moved across the bed on his back like a man crawling through machine gun fire. His eyes felt heavy and burning in the lightness of his body. The opener was there. Gratefully he took it and opened the bottle with his leaden eyes closed. God, how dreadful he felt. Just the effort of lifting the top from the bottle made him run with sweat. He drank the beer. It ran down his mouth and throat like flood-water washing through a dry and ancient channel and fell in a cascade down inside his cold husk of a stomach. He knew it would make him sick and it did. But after two minutes of vomiting he was much better.

Back on his bed he felt some of the outside warmth feeding back into him again. He tried to remember it all, but all that came back was the vision of the gaudy flames high above the trees from the copra hulk, and the violent, giddy sickness that had seized him twenty minutes after eating Abe's fresh crab sandwiches.

'Bastard,' he said thinking of Conway.

Then he thought about Abe. 'Bastard,' he said again.

He decided to go to Conway's room. He walked along the corridor full of strong shadows and bars of moonlight, and walked into the room without knocking. The blind was up from the window and the moon settled on the stark face of the Australian topped by a blood-stained turban made from a towel. Davies faintly remembered then the commotion of Conway's

218

arrival on board. He recalled only the violent crashing and Abe shouting obscenities, for the crab sickness had thrown him down again just then.

Now he hesitated and craned forward to look at Conway. He took a couple more steps across the explosions of moonlight on the floor. 'Conway,' he said nervously. 'Con.'

Close up he saw that the Australian had a picturesquely split lip, that there were black bruises on his cheekbones and small channels of dried blood with their sources under the towel. Conway was breathing stridently and snoring through a blood-clogged nose. Otherwise he looked as good as dead. He opened his eyes painfully and regarded the timid Davies.

'What happened to you?' he asked Davies.

Davies sat on the side of the bed. 'I'm the one that should be asking that.'

Conway ran his fingers up to his face and winced as he touched the bruises and then the towel. He put his little finger gingerly against his split and swollen lip. 'Have I lost my good looks?' he asked.

'What you had you've lost,' confirmed Davies unsympathetic now that he saw that Conway was not bad. 'You look terrible, boy.'

'The bloody motor bike didn't stop,' said Conway. 'Didn't you see?'

'I was lying on the deck, flat out,' admitted Davies. 'Abe gave me what he reckoned was fresh crab and it wasn't fresh. Came out of a tin from Australia, I bet. Anyway he poisoned me with it. I went out just like that. I've just woken up.' He looked at Conway seriously. 'You're an unscrupulous bastard, you know.'

'That's me,' agreed Conway.

'Setting that hulk on fire was a bastard's trick,' said Davies. 'And a lousy bastard's trick at that.'

'Yes it was,' nodded Conway. He seemed to find the nodding painful and stopped. 'Have you got any beer?'

'Haven't you?' asked Davies.

'Not a trickle. Get us a beer, mate.'

Without answering Davies got up and went back to his room for a bottle of beer. He hoped it would make Conway as sick as it had made him. But it didn't.

'I couldn't believe it when you did that,' said Davies. 'Honest, I didn't think even you would do such a lousy trick.'

'I did,' said Conway evenly. 'I know me better than you know me. There's no getting away from it, I am an unscrupulous bastard.'

'That's all they had to live on, that copra,' said Davies feeling hopeless at arguing with the man. 'I thought you were just going to do the Dodson-Smith act.'

Conway smiled like an actor recalling a favourite and famous part. 'I was very good,' he said. 'Terrific, in fact. I really put the fear of God into that mob.'

'The bike worked all right?' said Davies miserably. He decided not to argue any more. He still felt sick.

'A beaut. A real beaut, that bike. And the bell went like mad until the bloody clapper flew out. Ha!'

'So now they know they've had the sign from their Messiah telling them they've got to go to war?' said Davies.

'That's too right, son,' said Conway. He moved carefully around on the bed so he could hold the beer bottle in the other hand. 'No beer for you?' he asked.

'I had some,' said Davies. 'I only kept it down for thirty seconds.'

'And you hoped the same thing would happen to me?'

'Yes I did.'

'Well it won't. I feel sore, not sick.'

'You'll go over tomorrow, well I mean today now, and do your recruiting?' asked Davies.

'They'll be waiting with the old kitbags all packed,' said Conway. 'I'll pay in advance, of course, and they'll be needing some army pay now the piggy bank is at the bottom of the lagoon.'

Davies shook his head slowly. 'It really was a bastard trick,' he repeated.

'You're in it too,' said Conway. 'We've got a written contract remember?'

'Don't worry, I won't go to the United bleeding Nations about it,' Davies assured him bitterly. 'I don't want any more trouble. But you won't get me involved with any hokey-pokey like this again.'

'Quite right too, sport,' said Conway. 'You leave that to the professional shits like me. You sell your butter and fats.'

XIV

A marmalade dawn spread over the sea. The islands and the hills and trees, the coloured palettes of the lagoons, the white houses, the red earth and the ocean itself changed their tones with every new moment of the growing day.

People began moving about Sexagesima early because it was easy to do the things that had to be done before the air became swollen and hot in the streets. Abe slept only for an hour and then walked along the cool waterfront to his boat. The Melanesian women were already spreading out their fruit baskets for the day's selling and Abe bought himself half a melon for breakfast. He bartered about the price and got it reduced. He ate the melon as he went towards the boat, letting the juice fall down his chin and onto his thrustful belly, hardly noticing it because it always fell down like that anyway and he was full of the thoughts of how much to charge for the damage to the boat.

He stood on the jetty and shook a sad head at it. The motor cycle was still spectacularly embedded in the debris of the cabin, the boat's steering wheel was hanging like a fallen star, the planks and plywood stuck out like buck teeth. Carefully he performed some subtle rearrangement of the wreckage, putting a plank here and a section of shattered plywood there. The result of these touches was that the damage looked even more violent, a device which Abe excused on the grounds that he had needed to do a certain amount of clearing up when they were at sea during the night, so that he could stand and steer the boat back to Sexagesima.

Having posed the subject to his satisfaction he produced a German camera which he had stolen from a busy Dusseldorfer in Paris and which he considered as part of German reparations to the Jews. It was an excellent camera, although he told himself not nearly as excellent as his grandmother who had died in Breslau. He took an entire reel of pictures of his boat to be used as evidence in any future litigation and then proceeded to clear away the wreckage. Sections of the cabin, stray planks from the deck and bulwarks, and finally and spectacularly the St Paul's motor cycle, all went over the side and into the pale blue harbour.

On the following day Her Majesty would be arriving in her royal yacht and Abe needed his boat to take sightseers who couldn't wait a moment longer out to meet the arriving vessel. He was already fully booked at two pounds a ticket and he could not countenance losing a commission like that. Indeed, he thought, the removal of the cabin meant that he could probably be able to sell another five or six places on the deck.

The whole of the forgotten fetid little capital was making itself ready for the great tomorrow. The sagging buildings and the gritty streets seemed to feel the excitement as much as the people. Coloured bunting streamed along the paintless sun balconies of the waterfront. The streets had been swept twice that week and would be done over again quickly a few hours before the arrival of the royal party. The imitation Christmas tree which flashed on and off every year in the window of the Chinese Emporium in the main street had been produced out of season and was on display with all its little lights. Chairs from the British Legion hall had been brought down to the quayside and arranged in ranks for the accommodation of the distinguished British and French residents and the tribal chiefs from the outer islands, the banana-clad leaders from St Mark's being cunningly accommodated in the back row.

Tame flowers from the gardens had been carried in baskets, pots and handfuls to the arrival point. They sat up in tubs,

223

fell dizzily over balconies in long brilliant trails, climbed posts and the masts and rigging of the little boats in the harbour. The copra hulk in the lagoon was dressed overall, the Gover- steady journey across the harbour, the crew in their virgin uni- nor's pinnace shone like a regal swan as it made its orthodox forms and set faces performing their pattern of six familiar navigational movements.

From the peak of the Condominium headquarters on the waterfront stood out two new flags, the Union Jack and the Tri- colour, flank to flank heads down in identical limpness in the breathless, breezeless air. It was expected that the Queen would deliver at least three sentences in French somewhere towards the end of her speech.

Children's tea parties had been arranged for the school and the mission hall and there would be Highland games on the town sports field in the cool of the evening followed by a special performance of 'Judas Maccabeas' given by the Sexagesima choral union at the Chinese Assembly Hall. Speeches had been prepared, wires spread out, cars and children washed, and the police band threatened with certain dismissal if they didn't get it right this time.

Down at The Love Beach, by its caretaker ocean, the chapel of the Unknown Soldier stood in metallic solitude, set into the sand, the concrete tomb having received the poor bones, the crucifix of gun and helmet fixed. Flowers would be brought that evening by the children from the beach village and gar- landed about the rusting shoulders of the landing barges. It was Bird who had suggested to the children that they should bring the blossoms and cover the sides of the invasion craft. They would go out in the evening, a few hours before the arrival of the royal visitors and gather thousands of flowers for the barges on the beach. So that the Queen and all the impor- tant people with her would not see the shame of the Apostle Islands.

Like everyone else George Turtle was awake that lucid morning. His wife had experienced a bad night dreaming about fainting while curtseying to the Monarch and she had kept waking him up to tell him her troubles. His eyes felt sore as he left the house with his green Morris Minor to go to the radio station. But the brilliant early scenery of the island, the overflow greenness, the darting colours of the birds, the blue sheeted ocean beyond the trees, revived him. This was a splendid place. He was never so glad he had left Isleworth.

He was pleased too with the new paint on the radio building, a fine cricket white so that it looked like a nice pavilion. The aerials looked high and powerful. The Queen would come to visit the station after all, although she would not have the time to broadcast. He would have some impressive pictures to send home to his brother for the local paper. Christ, wasn't it marvellous to be *somebody*!

The station had been in contact twice daily with the approaching royal yacht and he knew it was steaming placidly two hundred and thirty miles or so to the south. Leaving his Morris on the gravel drive in front of the building he walked out to the small garden headland and looked over the sea to the saucer edge of the horizon, pointing his blank Isleworth face due south and trying to imagine he could see forever, or two hundred and thirty miles at least, and focus that grand vessel approaching these fine islands. Had he looked south-west towards the rising pudding of St Paul's Island he might have seen a few hairs of smoke no thicker than a Melanesian poisoned arrow, standing over the brow of the island.

At the South Seas Hilton Seamus stood outside in the street and nodded his approval at the final efforts of a Vietnamese boy, the sickly son of the shopkeeper across the road, to tie the cord of a large flag of the Irish Republic above the door. That was fine. As long as they were in no doubt where he stood. One day he wanted to go back to County Wexford and he wanted to make the journey with a clear conscience. It was all right to sell beer and spirits to the British, feed them, accommodate them, even be friends with them. But never let them think that you approved of them. One of the older ground floor rooms of the hotel had collapsed that morning. It had been sagging for some time and that part of the building had not been very safe since 1948 and was let at half rate because of the risk. But no one had been hurt. These things happened, Seamus thought, even in the best-run places.

At the pavement café next to Bird's salon Mr Hassey, Mr Kendrick and Mr Livesley met in the full ten o'clock sunshine for their first drink. Each sported a patriotic rosette which Abe had been selling on behalf of a French firm at Papette who had over-manufactured when General de Gaulle visited Tahiti. Since the national colours were the same there was no embarrassment.

'Never thought I'd live to see a time like this in The Apostles,' beamed Mr Hassey. 'My God, thirty-eight years in the islands. Thirty-eight years, you know.'

'Ascertaining the natives,' Mr Livesley finished for him. Hassey stared at him in an aggrieved way. 'That's why I came,' he agreed. 'Been doin' it thirty-eight years.'

Mr Kendrick said: 'Every bicycle in the place, white and native, is going to be decorated with coloured streamers. From the handlebars, through the spokes. Every single bike.'

'Some people might think I had a lot of foresight with my neon sign,' commented Mr Livesley drinking pedantically. 'It's in the most patriotic colours don't you agree?'

Some Tonkinese children bright yellow in the sun jumped along the dry street waving paper Union Jacks, jostling each other as they ran. The Chinese shopkeeper opposite threw a mild firecracker into the street to frighten them but they laughed and ran from it. The Chinese threw another behind them.

Mr Hassey turned, annoyed. 'For God's sake,' he said. 'That old fool is forever throwing those things. Chinese New Year, his birthday, his kids' birthdays—well his son's anyway—and any other excuse he can think of. I hope he doesn't chuck them tomorrow. He'll scare the shit out of the police band.'

Bird came from her salon and looked at the three men at their drinks, at the wisp of smoke from the dying firecracker, then down the yellow light of the street of bunting and flags to the Irish banner that Seamus had flown outside the hotel. From over the house-tops, already seeming lower under the growing heat, she could hear the muffled band practising on the quayside. It would be a wonderful day tomorrow. She was sure of that. Something they would always remember.

Rob Roy English went to The Love Beach very early and stood contemplating the shrine he had caused to be made from the landing craft. He seemed relieved that it was still there. He grinned savagely at it, pushing out his jaw and projecting his false teeth with the grin. It looked starkly impressive, like one of those modern art masters they sometimes showed in *The Scotsman*. The thought of newpapers made him remember that *The Baffin-Bay* was due to arrive in three days. Its appearance, always the great hinge of the month to life in the islands, had been almost forgotten in the anticipation and excitement of the royal visit. Yes, the papers would be arriving, *Scottish Field* too. What with that and Her Majesty dedicating the Tomb of The Unknown Soldier it was going to be a tremendous week.

Across the sheeted lagoon, on the terrace of her house, where the red roof projected like a sharp tongue, Mrs Flagg composed a letter to the British Governor protesting at the placing of Tom Ya-Ya, the St Mark's chief, in the back row of the official reception stand on the quayside. She made the point that since Her Majesty had desired to see the islands she ought to see them in all their aspects. It was too late to do anything now, but she felt she ought to make a protest.

Her lawn rolled down luxuriously to the indolent lagoon, touching it with diffidence as though afraid the colours would not mix. Water sprinklers danced a splashing ballet over the green, the drops splintering in the sunlight as they fell. Somewhere in the overblown thicket at the side of the garden the St Mark's natives were polishing their family skulls.

Despite her disappointment at the relegation of her islander chieftain, Mrs Flagg was firm with well-being that morning. She had been selected as one of the important islanders to be presented to the Queen and she had been practising her curtsey since the previous Friday. She had been working on a hat decoration which incorporated some of the tribal feathers of the St Mark's tribe and, since their vivid feathers were never less than two feet in length, she was hoping that Her Majesty would be encouraged to ask her about them.

She looked up after signing her letter—she contrived to model her signature in such a way that her surname was flung out in the appropriate shape of a pennant—and saw a small native boat coming through the lagoon towards her small landing jetty. It was immediately recognisable to her as a St Mark's war canoe, coming through the idle water at an urgent pace. Mrs Flagg was at once alarmed and half rose from her basketwork chair. Then she saw her own natives running towards the waterfront, dancing with apprehension. She plunged among the six natives a head and more taller than any. She cupped her hands and made a bellowing noise across the water. An answering sound came back, a single moaning hoot, followed by a gobbling chorus from the other men in the boat.

'Something terrible has happened,' Mrs Flagg said to herself, repeating the prophecy to the natives in their own tongue. They agreed anxiously. The canoe, manned by ten natives, was now only fifty yards off shore, swinging to come into the jetty. Tribal language was bellowed across the flat water so fast that Mrs Flagg could not follow it. The natives ashore became very agitated. Two of them ran off towards their hut to collect spears, ancestral skulls and other personal belongings.

Some of the phrases so rapidly shouted between the tribesmen began to make sense for Mrs Flagg. She held her throat like a shocked duchess. 'War?' she said to herself. 'That's what they're saying? It's war with St Peter's.' She swung on the native nearest her and questioned him. He began to gabble.

'Slowly,' pleaded Mrs Flagg. '*Slowly* if you will.'

He told her slowly that his brothers in the canoe had come to say that a great war fleet from St Peter's was about to attack St Mark's with the object of stealing the St Mark's copra hulk. The St Peter's hulk had been burned out in the night.

Mrs Flagg felt herself go pale. She turned from the lagoon and ran heavily up the grass to the house swerving around the sprinkler as she ran. Mr Flagg was coming serenely through the french windows carrying a Polynesian skin shield and some poisoned arrows. He turned the points of the arrows quickly upwards, out of danger, when he saw his wife closing on him.

'Bert!' she gasped. 'Oh Bert, something awful.'

'Calm, calm,' he motioned. 'Let's be calm.'

She all but collided with him, held onto him. He thrust the arrows high above his head well out of harm. 'Please!' he pleaded. 'Calm.'

Mrs Flagg halted. 'Right,' she breathed. 'I'm calm.' She looked at his startled face. 'It's war,' she said. 'The St Peter's people are preparing to sail against our lads at St Mark's. Full tribal war!'

'No,' whispered Mr Flagg. 'That can't be.'

'It can be,' argued Mrs Flagg. 'It is. The St Peter's copra hulk was burned out last night and you can be certain they're mounting an attack to steal the St Mark's hulk, or to burn it, or something.' She stamped with temper. 'Oh, how I hate them! They're such a rotten lot of sports!'

'And Her Majesty is coming tomorrow,' said Mr Flagg closing his eyes.

'Exactly,' moaned Mrs Flagg. 'Exactly.' She ran into the house. 'We must *act*,' she said. 'At *once*. We must tell the Governor.'

She made for the telephone, flopped onto the couch beside it, and asked the Sexagesima operator to put her through to the Governor. She got Cooper, the A.D.C. 'Good heavens Mrs Flagg, are you sure?' he said, his head sinking lower to his desk.

'Absolutely,' she said. 'Do something Cooper, and quickly or there will be mayhem. Mayhem!'

'Mayhem,' he agreed. He went into the Governor's office. Sir William was combing out the feathers on his white officer's hat. His best shoes had just been cleaned and were sitting obediently on the carpet by his desk.

'Fine hat this, Cooper,' said the Governor before his ashen A.D.C. could speak. 'Look at the cockade. Never had a chance to wear it before. Ha! what a day it's going to be tomorrow, eh?' He beamed up, saw Cooper and frowned. 'What's the matter man?'

Cooper swallowed. He seemed to digest some of his own face as he did so. 'Sir William,' he said. 'There's trouble.'

'Trouble?'

'Mrs Flagg, sir, she just phoned.'

'Oh her,' said the Governor turning away, relieved.

'The St Peter's natives are going to war against St Mark's sir.'

Sir William stopped as though an arrow had caught him between the shoulders. He turned. 'Dear God! When?'

'Today sir. Any moment. Their canoes are ready to sail and the St Mark's tribe are preparing to sail out to meet them.'

'But they *can't*!' protested Sir William. 'The hell of them! They can't. Not today.'

'They are sir. The St Peter's copra hulk was burned out last night. Either they think it was St Mark's people who did it or they are out to get the St Mark's copra ship. Or both.'

Sir William cradled his head. The cockaded hat slipped back over his neck. 'No,' he muttered. 'No. Not now. Why do the black fools do it now.'

'They're just contrary sir,' suggested the inane Cooper. 'Just damned contrary.'

230

Sir William stared from the window. The flags and bunting in the Government House garden hung exhausted in the sun. Across the harbour he could see the red white and blue colours lining the quay. He turned on Cooper standing pale and thin as a thermometer.

'Cooper,' he said. 'We've got to stop them. We can't have tribal war when the Queen is about to arrive. We have to stop them.'

'Yes sir,' acknowledged Cooper. 'How?'

'God knows,' said Sir William dropping his old face in his hands. He stood up consciously straight, took the cockaded hat from his head, and stared into the lagoon outside his window. He revolved again.

'Get English,' he said. 'And the other people. You know, Kendrick and Livesley. All the council people. And Mrs Flagg. Must have her.'

He looked uncertain, his brow collapsed a little. 'Better tell Monsieur Martin, I suppose. We're supposed to let the French know if any emergencies arrive. Yes, tell him. And . . . Yes, listen Cooper, get me that Australian bugger, you remember the objectionable one.'

'They are frequently objectionable, sir,' said Cooper. 'Mr Conway you mean.'

'That's him. He knows a lot about the St Peter's people. He's been over there a great deal recently. Too much in fact.' Sir William seemed to suddenly revive. 'Come on, Cooper we're going to this war. And we're going to stop it.'

In the thick mid-afternoon Conway was uneasily sleeping in his room at the Hilton, his split and bruised face lying painfully in the crook of his arm. He was sweating and there were so many flies in the room that even the gekkos had been sated and did not want to gorge any more. The flies whirred in the hot

231

enclosed air, full of their new freedom, standing proudly on Conway's bare feet, playing up and down his nose. He twitched but did not wake.

Davies woke him. Pale still from Abe's crab, he entered the room, shook Conway by the shoulder and loudly called him. Conway released a stiff eye. It seemed to take him some time to recognise Davies. 'What's going on, pal?' he asked.

'They're going to war all right,' said Davies grimly.

'Great,' grinned Conway getting up on his elbow. 'See, son, it always goes for the brave. I'd better get over there.'

Davies looked at him nastily. 'I wouldn't,' he warned. 'They're going to war against the St Mark's natives.'

Conway's face went solid. 'You're joking,' he breathed. He jumped up. 'The bloody fools, they can't do that! What the hell are they doing that for?'

Davies shrugged, enjoying watching Conway. 'Because the St Mark's islanders are their traditional enemies, that's why. And when Dodson-Smith rings his bell for them to go to war they don't go to Vietnam because they've never heard of the sodding place. They head straight across the water because that's where the usual enemies live. And what's more they've got eyes on the copra stored in the hulk on St Mark's. How are you going to work this one out?'

'Shut up and stop gloating for Christ's sake,' said Conway angrily. 'I'm in trouble.'

Davies said: 'Yes I can see that.'

'You are too, Taffy, because you're in it as well.'

'Thanks for bringing it up. Anyway the Governor wants us both.'

Conway looked upset. 'The Governor? Wants us? What for?'

Davies said patiently: 'Well it's like this, see. He's a bit worried about having a full scale tribal massacre on his hands when Her Majesty is sailing in tomorrow.'

'I bet he is,' agreed Conway. 'But he doesn't know anything

about us, does he? He can't do, unless Abe has been opening his mouth.'

'He wants us because he knows that you've been spending a lot of time over there on St Paul's with Joseph and his mob. And he's got to hear the story about me being over there that day with the harmonium and playing hymns for them. Everybody's heard that now. So he wants us to help him.'

'Help him what?'

'Stop the bleeding war I suppose,' said Davies miserably. 'Listen, mate, since you got me into this perhaps you'd be so damned kind as to get me out. You're full of plans and schemes sometimes. You *were* last night, weren't you. Well you better think up something now, boy, because we are in the shit.'

Conway got up and began to pull on his trousers. 'What savages,' he said bitterly. 'What idiots. Fancy starting a war.'

'Without you too,' said Davies without humour. 'I can't understand it.'

'How does he propose to stop it?' Conway asked him. 'The Governor I mean.'

He pulled on a khaki shirt and pushed his hair back from his forehead. Changing his mind he went to the enamel wash basin and poured a measure of water from the jug into his hand, transferring it with tenderness to his sore face.

'I don't know how he's going to stop it. Perhaps you ought to wear your Dodson-Smith get-up.'

Conway came across the room to him fiercely, angrily. 'Listen to me,' he said holding Davies' shirt in a bunch in his left-hand and closing his large right fist. 'I don't mind you taking the piss out of me, but you say one word, one breath, about last night to anybody and you'll never see Newport again. You won't see anywhere again. All right.'

'All right,' agreed Davies prudently. 'You can put me down now.'

Conway released him. He dried his face on the corner of his bedsheet. 'Never have any towels in here,' he said excusing

233

himself. 'You'd think as they put a basin and water in the room they'd think to put a towel as well, wouldn't you. Have you got a towel in your room?'

'No,' answered Davies.

'We ought to complain to Seamus. After all we pay enough. Right let's go and see how we can assist His Excellency. Have you still the gun I gave you last night?'

Davies nodded. 'Under my pillow,' he said. 'Do you want it?'

'Better take it,' said Conway. He had recovered his shell now. He was very composed, easy, good humoured. His eyes were a bit sharp, thought Davies, that was all. Davies went and recovered the pistol. He gave it to Conway who tucked it inside his shirt.

'Where have we got to go?' he asked as they went down the cool stairs.

'By the quay,' said Davies. 'He's got a sort of collection of people down there he thinks might help. I think we're going out in that pretty little pinnace of his.'

'With his Nelson sailor boys,' said Conway. 'That will be picturesque I must say. Right let's see what he's got to propose.'

'I'm not looking forward to this,' said Davies as they walked quickly in the hard sun down the street.

Conway said : 'I'm not exactly in rhapsodies about it myself.'

It was three o'clock in the brilliant afternoon when the first of the St Paul's war canoes began to move from the lagoon. Inside the reef they had assembled, surrounding the single charred rib of the copra hulk that remained above water. It stood like a stricken tree, rooted in the sea, deprived of leaves and branches. The islanders did not look at it.

Their canoes numbered a hundred and ten including the big supply dug-outs with their store of arrows, shields and spears, and the four ambulance canoes which would be used to transport the wounded back to their own island. They were painted like peacocks, but each with a large wooden cross at its prow. All the warriors wore special battle crucifixes which Abe had supplied at the time of their last emergency.

Joseph of Arimathea, regal in his Bermuda shorts, held a wide shield and led a session of community hymn singing before the tribe went to battle. They were glad to go, eager to meet the traditional pagan foe. Now that Dodson-Smith had appeared, even though he had disappeared again so briskly, they felt they were going on a blessed crusade. The ringing summons of his bell was still sounding in their faithful ears.

The warriors were armed with the traditional island weapons, the simple poisoned spear, the bow and the arrow dipped in the same potent pot. There remained on their island some wartime dumps of firearms but these had not been used by the St Paul's natives since a series of accidents had reduced their numbers some years before.

On the beach, beneath the curving trees and with the roofs of the village thrusting through the green behind them, the women and children assembled bravely and stood with their men as the canoes slid full of purpose through the water. Joseph began each hymn, selecting them at random from his memory of the Church Mission Hymnal. No one sang with anyone else, although in their uncanny way, everyone finished together. The mutilated words and terrible tunes babbled across the lagoon filling the bursting afternoon with an impressive cantata. The warriors, as they sang, rested their hands on their paddles and on the weapons they carried to the sea for the battle.

Their expressions were peaceful for they believed their cause was holy. The people left on the beach saw them go without qualm because they believed also. By evening, they were assured within themselves, the victory would be claimed and the warriors would return, possibly towing the St Mark's copra hulk as a bonus.

'God is on our side,' Joseph called out to them in their own language before they made for the gap in the reef. 'He will fight with us against the heathen.' He gave the signal for the advanced boats to go forward towards the wide battlefield of the ocean.

It took an hour before all the boats had cleared the reef. They formed up in three main squadrons, one slightly in advance of the others, with a small fourth section composed of the supply canoes and the ambulance vessels, together with the young boys and older men of the village as auxiliaries and crammed uncomfortably together in three obsolete canoes. In the high sun they made a strong array, gathered like black beetles on the moving blue of the sea.

As the ladies of Sexagesima touched their afternoon tea-cups a few miles north, the war fleet moved across half a mile of ocean and advanced on the green lump of St Mark's. The paddles moved with eager rhythm chopping the ocean, sending the slim craft urgently through the Pacific swell. There was no singing now, just a great panting and breathing from the warriors, sweat lying across their flesh, their eyes closed with the effort of their endeavour in the sun.

After three miles Joseph, standing in the foremost canoe like a prophet in the pulpit, raised his large right arm and brought his armada to a rolling halt in the sea. The warriors knew what to expect. They looked up and saw, formed and ready on the sea, half a mile ahead, all the black canoes of the St Mark's tribe, quiet, unexcited. Waiting for them.

XV

An anxious flotilla of cream boats left the tight harbour at Sexagesima at mid-afternoon, the Governor's official launch at its head, its Nelsonian sailors trembling at having to sail on an unfamiliar voyage. The routine journeys across the harbour were accomplished with fine precision thanks to the navigational landmarks such as Mrs Flagg's red roof and the Kai Tek Fish Shop, but to sail for the world's most monster ocean, and to have to go through the midget gap in the reef to reach it was full of terrible possibilities. The bosun had told Cooper that he knew his men well, and one thing he knew was that they were not capable of this refined and unaccustomed seamanship. So Abe had been chartered as pilot and he stood at the wheel, smiling fatly at the luxury of his situation, and took the launch out towards the Pacific.

Sir William and his aide stood on one side of the cabin stiff with their inherent sense of the emergency. The thoughtful Conway and Davies stood on the other side. A turgid boat owned by Mr English followed, loaded with the owner, Mrs Flagg, muttering with anger, Pollet and leading citizens of Sexagesima including Mr Kendrick and Mr Livesley.

Behind them came the Sexagesima police boat, the crew marble-faced at the prospect of becoming involved in bloodshed on such a fine day. The French officer glowered at his British counterpart pointedly blaming him for spoiling the afternoon rest period.

M. Etienne Martin, the French Governor, crisp in white

237

shirt and shorts, a ceremonial revolver with a fancy lanyard at his waist, stood easily astride the scrubbed boards of his official launch, with his crew from New Caledonia, sharp in white ducks and red pom-poms. His craft was clipping along at half speed only since the British launch was unable to move faster than she was already proceeding.

M. Martin kept patience. His moustache was straight as a pencil line and he kept his handsome eyes on the horizon for signs of the native war fleets. He wondered why the British always had such bad luck. He laughed.

In the forward launch Sir William and Cooper also watched the skyline. Phillip holding heavy black binoculars in his thin grip, Sir William through worn field glasses which he used in Scotland during remote and happy grouse seasons. Conway and Davies stood impotently, feet apart on the deck, hands uncomfortably behind their backs, saying nothing. Although no accusations had been made they felt like suspects being taken back to the scene of their crime. Abe was singing low and soberly as he persuaded the wheel. They went through the reef with the familiar water-chute sensation and two members of the regular crew were surprised by the jolt and fell over backwards. Davies, glad of something to do, considerately helped one of them to his feet. Sir William glanced around, winced and turned his eyes to his field glasses again.

They sighted the rival battle fleets low against the sun at almost the moment that they closed for the first contact of their action. The small black splinters moved threateningly towards each other across the open ocean. A chorus, the combined war chants of both tribes, howled through the sky reaching the men in the motor boats even before they could plainly see what was taking place. It was a haunting howl like a thousand begging winds. It shrieked over the ocean sending sea birds screaming away in horror, making the Melanesians in the three boats, the Governor's, the police boat, and Monsieur Martin's pull long faces of fright. Pollet picked his teeth. The other white men swallowed and stood straight. Abe said: 'Looks like we've missed the kick-off.'

The first encounter was bitter, carried through with fierce hatred and raw bravery by the men of both islands. The dug-outs of one squadron on each side ran towards each other rolling over the bulges of the sea, their warriors crying the gigantic cry, the bows ready for the first fusilade. At one hundred yards the arrows flew, hissing through the clear afternoon air, striking, killing, wounding, the black bodies on both sides. Some of the canoes skidded as the arrows hit their men, one of the St Paul's boats fell sideways as half its men were thrown into the ocean by the arrows. The St Mark's natives were just as ravaged by that first assault. Two of their fast moving canoes collided and the second flight of arrows from the St Paul's men sizzled among the crews as they grappled to get the buried nose of one vessel from the flank of the other.

Like slim birds the second flight of St Mark's arrows flew towards the other tribe. The war cries were increased with the screams of the warriors who were struck. Some were in the sea, a sea already tinted with the native blood, swimming feebly among the prancing canoes.

There was only time for two flights of arrows. Then the chanting and the shouts ceased and the spears and clubs came into the fight as the canoes touched nose to nose and rammed into violent kisses. All the ancient savagery of the Pacific islands was in the encounter, the natives closing and locking, squirming together, falling, provoking a storm from a calm sea. The clubs and the spears struck and thrust in intimate violence. The cries, the blatant war boasts across the water, were smothered in the bodily battle reduced to grunts and sweated breathing to gasps as men died sharply or to cries strangely like the calls of small children.

The two squadrons on each side, which had stood back to let the battle form, still rode the water, keeping their formation, watching with all the fascination of spectators at a crucial football match. No sounds came from them either. They floated in their canoes, witnessing with almost academic calm the struggling butchery of their fellows.

Abruptly the battle broke. No one retreated, but as though at a telepathic signal the combatants disengaged, and the canoes were briskly turned like horses being reined about. The blows stopped at once and there was no interference from either side with the manœuvring of the boats. There was even a touch of traffic courtesy as the dug-outs were guided around and away from the battle area before going back to rejoin the rest of the tribal army. A St Paul's canoe locked with an adversary was politely disentangled by the St Mark's native at the bow, and both proceeded back to the waiting echelons of their people.

The space of water where the engagement had been fought was clear of the boats within a few minutes. The tribes contemplated each other at a distance across the blue avenue of the sea. Between them floated sluggish bodies of those who had been killed in the fight, black lumps bobbing on the sunny water and with them the sharply finned backs of four upturned canoes. One of the floating men raised an arm and splashed forward in a weak and woeful swimming stroke. Then his head went forward and his body was covered over with the sea.

From the north the advancing fleet of white men's craft was now well up on the horizon. The natives from both sides saw them but made no reaction. They waited, pausing like prime boxers between rounds, for the next encounter.

There was a quaint regatta air about the boats and their passengers approaching from Sexagesima. The white and cream clothes, the caps, the binoculars, the anxious expressions could have fitted partisans at the Cowes finishing line. Everyone stood up straight and interested in the approaching spectacle apart from the knowing Melanesian sailors and police who had sunk to lower positions behind the bulwarks of each vessel. Conway and Davies remained standing, blinking with unease under the pouring sunlight.

'They've stopped, sir,' said Cooper lowering his monster glasses. 'They packed up whacking each other.'

'I can see, Cooper, I can see,' said Sir William a little coldly not enjoying his aide's enthusiasm nor his colloquialisms. 'They seem to have disengaged.'

'Waiting,' called Pollet from the boat just astern. 'They fight like that, your Excellency. In relays. They'll be engaging again in a moment.'

The Governor slyly turned to see how M. Martin was reacting. He turned away again, annoyed, because the elegant French Governor had immediately spotted his concealed movement and had graciously waved at him in a comradely manner as though congratulating him on some performance or achievement.

'Damn the man,' said Sir William under his breath. 'Damn him.' He looked at the other flank to Pollet's companions, Mr English, Mrs Flagg and the other dignitaries positioned pale as statues in their labouring launch. Only the British would stand so stiff on such a bouncing platform to watch a disaster, thought Conway, who followed the Governor's glance and saw his approving nod. They were stood necessarily grouped close together like white skittles, their heads elevated, their eyes looking out towards the gathered canoes. Mrs Flagg seemed as though she intended herself to join the battle on the side of her beloved St Mark's islanders. Her red hands clenched, unhinged, and clenched again as she squinted to see into the sun flying from the mirror of the ocean. Pollet picked his teeth and wiped his glasses.

'Are you sure they're merely resting?' Sir William asked Abe.

'Having a breather, your Excellency,' agreed the helmsman knowledgably. 'When they have a fight it's in three bits. First one lot, then another, and then the third. Then after that, whoever is left piles in for the last punch, and that more or less picks the winner. They've never had a war that wasn't finished by supper time.'

'This one must finish before that,' grunted Sir William determinedly. 'Won't this vessel go any faster?'

'Giving her all she's got now,' said Abe rolling his head. 'She'll go off with a bang if we push her any more.'

'Don't do that for God's sake,' sniffed Cooper without removing his face from his binoculars. Sir William looked at Cooper with distaste but added nothing. The war canoes were now clear, lined up in their individual patterns. There was no movement from either tribe. They sat and watched each other across the coloured swell while the motor boats came from the north. Then, like the starting of a dynamo a low hum came from the St Paul's men, taken up, but out of time, by the rival islanders. The hums moaned through the clear ocean air, rising and falling, getting louder with every new chorus.

'Haven't you got any bright ideas?' Sir William suddenly asked Conway. He lowered his field glasses and glared at the Australian. 'You seem to have a lot of influence with them.'

Conway shrugged. 'No ideas,' he said evenly. 'It would need more than a bit of influence to do anything about them now.'

Davies said, hesitating over the words: 'We . . . we ought to try and do something or other, didn't we?'

Conway turned on him. 'Why don't you sing a couple of hymns to them?' he suggested bitterly. 'Try a few choruses of Build on the Rock, mate. See if that will help.'

'Shut up,' Davies said. He stared truculently at Conway. Conway stared back, challenging him to say something more. He didn't.

They were approaching the tribes now. They could see the distant outlines of the men crouching in the boats like soldiers in trenches. In the hot air of the afternoon there was the heavy smell of death and battle. The squadron of motor boats fanned

242

out to line abreast. M. Martin loosened the many-coloured lanyard of his revolver, but only with the dignified air of a man adjusting his clothing. His face was unworried. They dropped speed, cautiously going towards the native fleet, going on a wide line for the separating channel between the two. Abe, who was reluctant to take risks, looked towards Conway and Davies and then questioningly at the Governor. 'Carry on, Mr Abe,' said Sir William quietly. 'We'll cruise through the middle. I will speak to them.'

It was the strangest procession. The motor launches courteously pushing aside the water before them, proceeded through the ranks of the antagonist armies, who remained completely still and composed, sitting in the dug-outs like invalids in wheeled chairs. Only their dark native eyes moved.

Sir William in the way of a general astride a military vehicle, inspecting an array of troops, cruised very slowly through the blue corridor of the sea. He stared to either side and met the same impassive masks of the islanders. 'They've really got to stop,' he grumbled almost to himself. He spoke to Cooper : 'Give me the megaphone.' He took the trumpet and, swinging slowly from side to side addressed simultaneously the warriors of both sides. As he did so his boat proceeded bumping several times against the drifting bodies of the natives who had been killed in the earlier combat.

Sir William raised the megaphone as majestically as a boat race umpire. In his imperfect Pidgin-English he called to the tribes. 'You fellas no kill. Fellas go home Mama. Good things they come.' He repeated it, first to one side and then the other, to the impassive and unimpressed natives. The Governor, worried that he might be boring them, varied the sentences. 'Fellas go home Mama. Fellas no kill. Good things they come.'

Everyone in the white man's flotilla watched Sir William's performance with sharp interest and differing reactions. Cooper gazed at his chief with loyalty and admiration, Conway smirked, Davies looked respectful. Abe folded his rubbery face as though he felt a deep ache. M. Martin looked across at his co-governor with one eyebrow, slim and dark as his moustache, accented above the level of the other. Pollet smiled affectionately at the Governor's attempt. Mr English, Mrs Flagg and the other councillors remained at their instinctive attention and merely inclined their heads. Mr Kendrick looked at the others and down at himself, and wondered how many British in history had died like this, hands smartly at their sides.

The motor boats, pushing their creamy arrows through the sea, moved powerfully on through the passage between the rival tribes. No movement had come from either assembly of islanders. Then, when the four white launches had reached their extremity of the open channel dividing the natives, from each set of warriors came a long growl, thickening as it sounded, full of threat, full of the eager challenge of battle again. The citizens of Sexagesima were already looking over their shoulders. They saw the left-hand formation of each tribe start forward through the silk water, the canoes thrust energetically towards the battle area, the deep-throated noise becoming more insistent with each dip of the paddles. The craft went irrevocably towards another collision, another fight, another slaughter.

They met with a grinding and a strange patient sighing from the canoes, as though they, anyway, were tired of the game, and then the men were upon each other again. To Davies watching horrified, propped against the cabin of the Governor's launch, it seemed the black men were like furious crocodiles threshing in the water all wet sinew and muscle, each entangled in the others.

Once more the clubs crushed and the spears were jabbed and turned. The remainder of the tribes sat, again impassively, witnessing the deadly display.

The second engagement was fought in the same strange half-quiet as the first. Only the grunts and the uncanny infant whimpers came from the chaos. The canoes bucked like protesting horses, turned, were overturned. Everywhere jet-black men were fighting, swimming, drowning, dying.

Sir William angrily raised the megaphone to his mouth. 'Halt!' he shouted. 'Halt! Stop it I say! In the name of Her Majesty's Government I order you to stop.'

Some of the natives paused in their conflict to look briefly at the gaunt man calling to them. But they returned to the fight immediately. Another canoe capsized into the disturbed waves and the prow of one of the St Mark's dug-outs reared into the air as though it were pawing in pain. The men in the water who were unhurt, when they could recognise members of the opposing tribe, continued the grappling fight. There were heads, and oddly, legs projecting from the sea.

'Stop!' bellowed Sir William desperately. 'Stop I tell you!'

Joseph of Arimathea squatting in the prow of his boat, waiting for his final squadron to join the battle, frowned with annoyance at the British Governor, the frown of a disturbed spectator in a cricket pavilion and then turned to watch the maul in the ocean again.

It broke up once more as magically as it had done the first time. The combatants disengaged themselves, those canoes still upright turned their snouts away from the arena and the sea settled down patiently to its normal rhythmical swell. The canoes and the bodies from the first encounter were now floating far south with the ocean current, bobbing like debris from a flood. The new casualties occupied the water between the two tribes. They began moving away obedient to the tidal flow, washing around the hulls of the four Sexagesima motor boats.

Mrs Flagg was crying quietly into a tartan handkerchief which Mr English had considerately passed to her. 'There go my friends,' she sobbed as the dead warriors floated by. 'There go my friends.' Rob Roy English himself was pinch-faced and sick. Culloden must have been like this he thought, apart from the colour of the antagonists and the presence of the sea.

245

The other councillors stood in ashen apprehension stupefied by the callous violence of these people they lived among but could never know. When the second squadrons from the islands had withdrawn there was quiet again, a full, rich, awful quiet over the easy waves. Mr Kendrick and Mr Livesley watched the canoes on both sides and the pale sweat gathered on their British brows. Pollet, pale too, repeated: 'Nothing will stop them. Nothing will stop them.'

In the police boat everyone was sitting down, unmoving, constables and officers both French and British, all gratefully impotent, merely watchers. M. Martin in his launch was at his composed stance, wondering what he would have done in Sir William's place. He was glad that, by virtue of the fact that St Paul's was an Australian Dependency, only half the responsibility for St Mark's was his, and the added factor of an impending royal visit, the worry was squarely on Sir William's back. He felt sorry for Sir William.

In the Governor's boat nobody spoke for some time after the second engagement had been broken off. Conway broke the clammy silence. He watched some bodies floating by. 'Mr English ought to collect a few of these,' he mentioned casually to Davies. 'Store 'em up in case he needs any more Unknown Soldiers.'

'You ought to be floating by with them,' said Davies but low enough to be out of the Governor's hearing.

'I might be yet,' said Conway without anger. 'You too, son. Our friend the Governor's getting ideas. Look at that British chin sticking out. He's not going to sit on his bum and watch any more.'

Davies felt cold in the hot afternoon. He tried to quickly work out the correct time in Newport. How did he get here, in this boat, in this ocean, with these mad people, and a good chance of being stuck through with a poisoned arrow? Why couldn't he have stayed at home like everybody else, gone to the Odeon on Saturdays, watched Newport County football team, played with the kids in the park, and gone down to Barry Island on fine Sundays?

'Everybody sit tight,' said the Governor squarely.

Conway said: 'I told you.'

Strangely Abe had said and done nothing. He lounged over the wheel, resting his strange monster belly on it, making shapes with his mouth as though he were chewing something particularly tough, looking with his brimming eyes at the natives. Cooper was suffering from the weight of the binoculars. Abe said to him: 'Too big, too cumbersome. I've got a pair of Hilier Supers at my place. Austrian, but very good. I think you ought to have them. I'll do you a part exchange deal.'

'These are perfectly all right,' said Cooper loftily.

'Okay, I'll sell you a nice tripod then. Something to take the weight. Pearl-Swinneton, made in the States, but very good.'

'When the bargaining is finished,' said Sir William testily, 'I will tell you what I propose to do.' He looked around, particularly hard at Conway and Davies. 'This is it. At the first sign of the third attack we in this launch and the police boat, and M. Martin if he cares to join us, but leaving Mr English and his party behind—we will go forward and place ourselves between the two groups of canoes and attempt to keep them apart. I have a pistol, so have you haven't you Cooper?' Cooper nodded miserably. 'And Mr Conway has one tucked under his shirt. So that will help. But—and this is most serious—all firing will be above the heads of these tribesmen. There must be no shooting at them. Do you understand?'

'I haven't got a gun,' said Abe. 'What do I do? Spit?'

'I shall take the wheel,' said Sir William sternly.

'It's your boat,' said Abe unwilling to argue. He stepped down.

Sir William looked a granite look at him but swallowed his comment. 'I don't want there to be any civilian casualties,' he said instead. Abe nodded in agreement. Davies found the

247

hundred pound promissory note from Conway folded in his pocket. Christ, he thought, the quicker I get the rest of the money for a ticket back to the rain and the muddy River Usk and all the rest of it, the better.

The Governor revolved and raising the megaphone with style addressed the other boats. He told them what he proposed to do, instructing the police boat to follow him, an order received with no enthusiasm whatever by the policemen, and inviting M. Martin and his pom-pommed sailors to join if they wished. The French Governor bowed a courteous acceptance, also to the plain disappointment of his crew, and loosened the bright lanyard of his pistol again.

'I propose to move forward immediately either of the St Mark's natives or the St Paul's tribe begin to do anything further,' said the Governor. He wondered how his dear late wife would have handled a situation like this. Probably by distributing woolly sweaters from the women's guild or something. Still he had to do the best he could. 'I would like to emphasise that if we have to open fire then all shooting will be above the heads of the tribesmen. *That order will be in force until it is countermanded.* Is everyone quite certain of that?'

Heads were nodded in the boats. 'Everyone's sure,' said Abe as though he had been asked to check. The Governor ignored him. Cooper glared at him. Conway grinned. Davies wiped the back of his mouth with his hand. 'Maybe we really ought to try a chorus of "Jesu Lover of my Soul",' he suggested wryly.

'Why not,' said Conway. 'Offer 'em a free packet of butter and fats at the same time.'

'Get stuffed,' answered Davies quietly. 'Your ideas don't look so good to me any longer.'

Conway stared at him. 'Now shut up,' he whispered. 'Don't try anything or you will end up floating off with the rest of the bodies.'

Davies had no doubt he meant it. 'Thanks for reminding me,' he said. 'Do you think when and if we get back to Sydney

248

your government department would help me with my fare back home to Newport?'

'Gladly,' said Conway. 'We want men in Australia.'

'Good, I'll keep you to that. Oh God, here they go.'

With their ghostly winding up sound, like the starting of an eerie engine, the tribes were swaying in their boats. The third echelon, spectators until now, began to slide through the sea. In the leading St Paul's boat was the impressive figure of Joseph of Arimathea, Bermuda shorts clad, wooden cross swinging like an anchor around his thick neck, with a tassled spear held in his left hand. The St Mark's boats moved off at the same instant, avidly eating their way through the water, the ancestral skulls bobbing on the bows, their chief, Tom Ya-Ya, a bulging man with his banana husk sheath tied like a heavy burden around his middle, astride the foremost boat. They made their war noises as they converged and to the choral ears of Davies it seemed they achieved a rare harmony, chorus from one side, descant from the other, far more musically acceptable than the hymn singing of the St Paul's Christians.

The canoes moved fiercely through the sea, the noise of the warriors going with them like a propelling wind. For a moment Davies with relief, thought the Governor had changed his mind. But Sir William then raised his arm, like a cavalry major of old, and motioned his little white fleet forward. He had taken Abe's place at the wheel and stood thin and with traditional bravery, pistol in one hand, heading his launch for the diminishing channel between the warring tribes. Abe sat in the stern of the vessel, sheltered and shutting his eyes in the sun, letting it rest on his big face, occasionally squinting to look at the reluctantly following boats.

Sir William looked behind too and saw that the police launch was dragging its feet behind him, then M. Etienne Martin's smart boat, the French Governor standing theatrically hand on pistol, and then, to Sir William's surprise and worry, Mr Rob

Roy English and his boatload of civilians. He thought of waving them back to the safety of the sidelines, but he realised it was too late and if he did perform any waving movement it was more than possible that the police boat, thankfully mistaking the signal, would beat a retreat. He did not want that.

The pretty pinnace went at a steady rate for the gap. Cooper stood inwardly shaking but with required external fortitude, beside his chief, Conway crouched on the port side and Davies sat down resignedly by Abe. He was glad it was Conway who had the gun.

'Why pick on that lot,' said Davies to Conway nodding towards the St Paul's army. 'Why not have a shot at the others.' He nearly added 'for a change' but prudently changed his mind.

'If I'm going I want it to be a poisoned arrow shot by a Christian,' grunted Conway.

'Good thinking, boy,' agreed Abe. 'If they get *me* from either side it's no consolation. I told you, didn't I, a long time ago, we should have a Jewish island around here.'

Both native tribes had read the Governor's plan with ease and accuracy even before his boat moved. They were now racing powerfully to get there first, to close with each other before the white man's vessels arrived. Their chants had ceased now, as they had before the previous engagements, and they grunted as they pushed the canoes forward, straining, each side in an ironic harmony of purpose, to get there before the launches, lunging and plunging to close the gap in the sea.

But Sir William now gave the boat more power, three-quarters, then full, and coughing in protest, it tore into the gap, its bow wave flying like a pair of feathered wings, its following boats close behind. It was a magnificent strategy. The substantial hulls of the motor boats made a wall between the native craft, beating each fleet by a hundred yards. Then Sir William slowed his vessel. The canoes hesitated, then lost way. The grim purpose of the silent warriors was abruptly replaced with frenzied anger. They shouted and jeered and gesticulated like schoolboy footballers when someone has confiscated the ball.

Then arrows began to fly. Abe heard them whistling first. 'Down! All get down!' he said in a sort of muttered shout. 'Down you come sir.' He pulled at Sir William's thin elderly leg and the Governor almost collapsed on him. Cooper followed.

'Damn you,' swore the Governor at Abe. Abe looked hurt. 'Only thinking of you, sir,' he said. 'Those poisoned arrows can give you a nasty sting.'

'Open fire!' ordered the Governor ignoring Abe now, he crouched and fired his pistol at an angle so that the bullet would fly harmlessly at the blue sky. A sagging sort of volley followed from Cooper and Conway, both of whom were keeping their heads well down, and from the police boat and the sailors in the French boat. Davies felt himself tighten with fear. The arrows sang like bees. He could not see a single head sticking up from the police boat behind them. Its course had become a ragged zig-zag which seemed to indicate that the helmsman was lying down at the wheel. The boat rolled and pitched like some ghost ship.

Abe saw it too. 'Why put your head up if you're shooting to miss?' he asked logically. The guns continued to sound, ragged and stammering. The arrows, by contrast, flew in formation. The natives howled and pulled their bows.

'They haven't hit us yet,' said Davies to Abe. 'I haven't heard one hit.'

Abe turned his big creased face to the Welshman. 'That,' he said with the air of a great strategist, 'that, boy, is because they're not shooting at us. They're all over the top. See, look at that lot.' He pointed up as though sighting a flight of birds. 'Right over. And now that lot's going the other way. There, see.'

'By Christ, that's good,' said Davies, relieved. 'I thought they were rotten shots.'

'They're playing ping-pong,' grunted Abe. 'Why waste good

poisoned arrows on a few white men. Right over the top, look, there's another lot.'

'Like King Harold and the Normans at Hastings,' said Davies suddenly comforted by the lack of immediate danger.

'Yea,' said Abe. 'Could be they read that up.'

Sir William, realising that his boat was not the target for either side, slowed the engine, and stood up behind the wheel. He watched the symmetrical flight of the arrows curve high above him, saw the men firing and falling on either flank. Looking behind he saw the apparently riderless police boat wallowing through the swell, and then, beyond that M. Martin standing aloof and observing the battle while smoking a long cigarette. The French Governor waved encouragingly. Doubtfully Sir William waved back.

At least, he thought, the two tribes were still separated. He had driven a wedge between them. Hopefully he picked up the loud hailer and called once again: 'Stop! In the name of Her Majesty's Government stop! You fella go home Mama!'

At fifty yards he presented an easy target and Joseph of Arimathea, aiming casually put a long arrow straight through the tin skin of the megaphone, through one wall and out the other, while Sir William still shouted into it. The Governor looked angrily at the arrow and then towards the bowman, who waved.

'Hell, sir, they're all coming now.' Cooper was on his feet and had heaved his bulky binoculars to his face. He dropped them immediately, not liking what he saw, then swung around to look at the mass of the St Mark's army which had been sitting watching the third phase of the engagement. 'Both sides, sir. They're all moving in.'

A hundred canoes came from the port and another hundred from starboard, rushing through the sea with their warriors arched against the paddles, rushing into the final stage of the sea battle.

252

'Tell them to stop, sir,' suggested Abe callously.' Give them a shout.'

'Stop blathering man,' answered Cooper. The Governor said nothing. He was observing the foremost echelon of each tribe, the sections he had kept apart and who had been fighting with arrows. They had, with that uncanny timing that suggested long rehearsal, stopped firing and were now moving forward again, the advance party of the main army which floated three hundred yards behind them. Again the enemies had an attitude of common purpose.

Quickly worried, the Governor spun first one way then the other and fired a warning shot from his pistol over the lines of the black heads converging on his ship. The natives took no heed.

'Prepare to repel boarders!' he ordered and was annoyed with himself because his voice had become a croak. He lifted the arrow-shot megaphone and hooted: "Prepare to repel boarders,' towards the reluctant boats astern. From the police boat several heads looked up and bobbed down again.

'Damn them,' swore Sir William. He brandished his pistol and saw that Davies and Abe had prudently armed themselves with marlin spikes. Cooper was waving his revolver dangerously and Conway picked his nose and held his gun soberly ready.

The Governor thought he felt old enough for a bath-chair in some retired English town. 'Prepare to repel boarders,' he ordered again.

From both flanks the tribesmen came, singing again their splendidly combined harmony, first and second tune, all together as confidently as if a single conductor was leading them. They were quickly around the launch.

'The first man over the side is dead,' threatened Sir William and, somewhere deep in his mind, wondered if the sentence made sense. Davies felt stiff with fright, but the marlin spike was hard and comforting. Abe was shaking his big head as though sorry it all had to end like this. He put his hand on

253

the pistol arm of Cooper which was shaking. 'Don't do that son, you make me nervous,' he said. Conway was still as cold iron, his pistol with its nose slightly in the air.

But not one Melanesian head appeared over the side. Instead the men of both tribes gathered industriously around the hull, their enmity shelved in a common purpose. They were like begging natives around a newly arrived cruise boat. They clamoured there for a while. Then selected men began to rip out the planks from the side of the vessel, using axes and spears and their powerful hands. The Governor's launch shuddered. No one moved on board. Sir William was nonplussed. It seemed impossible to shoot in cold blood at men involved in carpentry. 'Stop it,' he called over in his normal voice realising his inadequacy. 'Stop it at once. This is government property.'

'What are they doing?' asked Davies, not sure.

'Making a hole in the bloody thing,' said Conway.

'We'll sink,' said Davies.

'I expect we will,' said Conway. 'But we won't die anyway. They just want us out of their way so they can get on with their battle.'

Outraged, Sir William rose from the deck, but a pattern of arrows, shot from both sides, sprinkled the cabin just above his head. He dropped down again. 'The devils, the damned devils,' he said.

'We're all alive,' pointed out Conway. 'A least we will be if nobody sticks their head above the deck again. The worse we can do is sink.'

They sank. They sank spectacularly in a rich Pacific swirl, the sea gushing and pouring through the mouths of the holes that the natives had opened in both sides of the hull. It came in like water from a fractured main, two smooth curling necks of it, one from each side, swilling around in the boat, filling it quickly.

'Abandon ship,' shrugged the Governor. 'Everybody over the side.'

254

'The ship is abandoning us,' said Conway taking off his shoes.

'You have wisdom for every moment,' said the pale Cooper, nevertheless taking off his shoes too. He was surprised and thankful to be still alive and he felt some of his confidence returning.

'Can everybody swim?' asked the Governor sternly, looking about. They all nodded or said 'Yes'.

The Governor looked miserable. 'I can't,' he confessed. 'Never learned. The water's too damned cold in Scotland.'

Cooper and Abe helped the elderly man, now all subdued and pathetic in his anxiety not to drown, into a life jacket and assured him that they would keep him afloat. The boat was turning gracefully now as thought she were mounted on a very slow turntable. The forepeak was well down, nuzzling under the water, the lapping small waves climbing enthusiastically over the side of the boat like children entering a forbidden garden.

They left by the stern, five plops into the Pacific, the last one a slow hesitant drop as the Governor went into the sea. They were aware of other things happening, native canoes hurrying by, the grunts and other noises of another hand-to-hand battle. There were hundreds of combatants now, dug-outs slicing through the water to join the fight, cutting by the heads of the five white men in the water. Conway and Abe helped the old Governor along, hung tragically like some hunting trophy through the lifebelt, arms hopelessly stretched out, walking with his legs, spitting out the salt water. Fortunately it was warm and easy for swimming. Davies patrolled alongside the Governor and his helpers and Cooper was irritably swimming on the other side. They sensibly moved away from both the battle and their sinking boat. It was strange looking at it from water level. The two thousand fighting men, a hundred yards away, seemed like giants grappling in the sea. The noise was almost deadened at that low level and waves coming in with the swell blocked Davies' eyes as he watched. More war canoes came by them, going like business-like sharks through the water.

'Are there any sharks around here?' Davies asked Abe thoughtfully.

'Sharks all over the Pacific,' answered Abe affably. 'Around here they're not generally speaking hungry but I wouldn't like to say about today with all that blood on the water.'

The little party began to move strongly towards the boats which had been behind them. It was difficult to see very much from sea level, but they could see the white hull of M. Martin's cruiser closing on them. Davies wondered where the police boat had gone.

A swimming native policeman approached him smiling as though to answer the question. His wet face seemed stretched with the grin and he seemed glad to see them. Davies saw that he was followed by a little fleet of floating policemen, two white, the remainder black.

'They sank us too, sir,' beamed the English officer in the direction of the panting Governor. 'Crept up, sir, didn't see them coming.'

Sir William turned his wet head with difficulty in the uncomfortable lifebelt. He was feeling elderly, tired and full of salt water. 'You wouldn't be likely to see them would you,' he said, coughing violently at the middle of the sentence. 'Lying on the bloody deckboards.'

Nothing more was said. The efficient M. Martin had brought his boat to them and one by one, the Governor first, they were hoisted aboard, and laid out on the deck. M. Martin knelt chivalrously by Sir William. 'I am most sorry, your Excellency,' he said. 'I found it necessary to retire for a short distance in order that they should not sink my boat.'

'Damn good job you did,' said Sir William. 'Drat them. They're scrapping again.'

'Slaughtering each other I'm afraid,' nodded the French Governor. 'There is little to be done. The other boat, I am glad to inform you is quite safe. It seems that your Madame Flagg and M. Pollet came to some agreement with the natives and they refrained from sinking the vessel.'

From their lying positions on the deck the wet men heard at that moment the dull, awful sounds of the battle. Davies stood up, so did Abe and Conway. Three hundred yards away the huge fight was still undiminished in intensity. Two thousand men were at close quarters now; a rumbling came from them. Many were dying. The bodies floated by on the current and with them the torn canoes. From behind they heard an engine and Mr English's white boat, with the phlegmatic Pollet and the other occupants still stiffly observing the mayhem, came alongside.

Mrs Flagg had stood starched and pale as the others, but suddenly she put her hands to her mouth and screamed like a schoolgirl: 'Come on St Mark's!'

Everyone in the two boats watched her antic. She became aware of them and she turned, at first embarrassed, then defiant. Her face heaved. 'I *want* them to win,' she said.

The sinewy black battle continued, a low storm on the peaceful sea. The white gallery looked on helplessly, except the Governor who could look no more and was sitting in a wet sulk on the deck. M. Martin was positioned a little higher than the rest. Suddenly he motioned to one of his sailors for a pair of binoculars. He swung with them, away from the battle, away from the islands, looking out to the clean line of the ocean.

'A warship approaches,' he announced.

'The navy!' exclaimed Sir William rising in difficult cramped stages to his feet. 'Thank God for that.'

M. Martin looked again. 'The French navy,' he added without triumph. 'Our little warship the *Auriol* from Noumea come for the royal visit.'

'Hell,' said the British Governor honestly. He looked apologetically at the French Governor. 'But no. Hell,' he repeated.

'Why does it always rain on me?' He stared down at his clinging clothes and laughed a wry hopeless laugh. 'Well, your Excellency, will you ask them to do something about this er . . . fr . . . fracas.'

M. Martin smiled sympathetically. The triumph he thought he might feel in such a situation was much diminished by the soaked resignation of his counterpart. 'I will, your Excellency, with pleasure. Signaller.'

One of the Melanesians, suddenly full of naval strength after the sight of the warship, sprang up beside the Governor. The French vessel, a grinding gunboat which had been doddering around the islands since she became obsolete fifteen years before, was large on the sea now. She came towards the two pale boats and their people, steaming full ahead and coughing grey smoke with the exertion. If the islanders saw her they took no heed but merely continued with their bludgeoning among the canoes.

'She's in flag range now,' calculated the Governor. His naval commander nodded.

M. Martin dictated the signal and the signaller, with a sly cautious look over his shoulder to make sure that the tribes were still fighting out of arrow range, began thrusting and circling his flags. The French Governor watched for the acknowledgement and reply and then the signaller translated it.

'The gun isn't working,' he said apologetically to Sir William. The British Governor split his face with a small grin and looked down.

'But they do have a how-do-you-say-it.' He was not often lost for English, '. . . a charge for the deeps!'

'A depth charge,' suggested Cooper brightly. 'For submarines, you mean, your Excellency.'

'Correct,' said M. Martin without looking at the aide.

Abe said: 'All we have to do now is to get those natives into a submarine and drop a depth charge on them.'

The French Governor afforded him no attention. 'Unfortunately it is all that is available. The warship is on a courtesy visit,' he said stiffly.

'Pity about the twenty-one gun salute,' said Cooper nastily. 'You were looking forward to that, your Excellency.'

Abe said: 'Have a twenty-one depth charges salute.'

The Frenchman said evenly to the British Governor, 'If they launch the depth charge wide of the natives it will throw up a great reaction—a big explosion, and a wave which will upset their boats. That should result in the solution of *your* problem.' Incensed by the remarks of Cooper and Abe, he was immediately more formal.

Sir William regarded him kindly. 'I am most grateful, M. Martin,' he said. 'It will terminate this silly conflict. Please ask them to use the depth charge.'

'Signaller,' said M. Martin. The Melanesian jumped like a performing doll. His flags went through their gymnastics. The French Governor watched for the reply. The signaller spoke to him.

'They will manœuvre around us, as far to the right as is possible,' he announced. 'They will fire the charge about two hundred yards from the natives.'

M. Martin hesitated obviously uncertain whether to add something. He decided to cover himself. 'There is a possibility, which I am sure you will appreciate, that the depth charge will not explode. It is very ancient. From the war years. They have never practised with the real thing since this particular one is the only one they have.' He glanced at Sir William as though seeking understanding in a fellow sufferer. 'These islands, as you know Governor, are not always the top priority with our Governments.'

Sir William waved his hand. 'Your Excellency, I am grateful for your assistance, and of course I understand perfectly. Not only do we not have a depth charge, we have no ship capable of firing a depth charge. I am most grateful, particularly as it is your only one.' He seemed embarrassed. 'We shall reimburse you for it of course,' he added.

The ramshackle warship tottered to within a couple of hundred yards of the launches. A klaxon was sounding and on deck the crew could be seen running to their action stations around the useless gun under the bridge and to the depth charge launcher at the stern. The captain could be seen on the bridge issuing orders and clearly taking a cine film of the battling natives.

M. Martin coughed. 'I see our captain is using the sextant,' he observed. No one argued. They watched the warship curve, old but menacing. In the other boat Mrs Flagg began to call out in distress. 'Don't shoot! Don't shoot! They must not bombard! The United Nations will hear about this, Mr Governor!' She shook her plum fist at both Sir William and M. Martin.

'Mrs Flagg!' called the Governor sternly. 'There is no call to distress yourself. No one will be hurt.'

'The thing might not even go off,' said Conway under his breath.

It seemed that the tribesmen were unable, now, to quit the combat without damaging their honour. As they fought they looked over their shoulders at the circling warship with apprehension, but then returned to the fighting again using greater strength, each side seeking to conquer before they were both attacked by the white men.

The captain of the gunboat turned his vessel so that the stern faced the wide area over which the natives were now fiercely engaged. He backed it up like a driver backing an unwieldy lorry. Around the depth charge, sitting like a prize egg on its mounting, the crew waited. From the bridge came the order. They let it go. It flew high and wide like something thrown by a boy and plummeted into the sea two hundred yards short of the natives.

'I think I'll sit down,' said Conway on the launch. He sat down quickly on the deckboards. No one followed him. Nothing happened. The little barrel had been swallowed up and digested by the big ocean. The natives fought on eagerly like two football teams in the closing minutes of a goal-less match. The Sexagesima people stood grouped together in the manner of evangelists awaiting a sign. Nothing happened.

'A dud,' decided Abe loudly. 'What we going to do now. Spit?'

The answer came from the belly of the ocean. It burped up in a huge wet explosion, like a submarine mountain vividly erupting; a hundred feet high, sea green and blue, feathered at the edges, plumed at the crest, rumbling with power from the inside, sending great storm waves running over the surface.

It flung the white people down on the boards of their boats, jarring them and swinging the boats about like fairground contraptions. Conway, already sitting, found M. Martin lying across him. With stunned apologies the French Governor freed himself. The others lay criss-crossing each other, arms flung out, trying to regain a balance that, once regained, was immediately lost again as the boat plunged the opposite way and then was struck by the next hammer wave.

Davies, after rolling like a tumbler to the edge of the boat, could hear Mrs Flagg crying from the other craft. 'The poor dears! Oh, the poor dears!' Her call was swallowed by the belated roar from the depth charge; it sounded like the world splitting at its seams, deep, then loud, the sound breaking out into the sunlit day and exploding over the sea. It was a full two minutes before the boats stopped staggering. When they had settled the Governor, Sir William was first to his feet. He looked out to where the battle had been joined.

'Done it!' he exclaimed hoarsely. 'Done it, by heavens!'

The others crept up and looked. The canoes appeared as though a hurricane had been loose among them. They were scattered and capsized, floating with the running shock waves. All around there were stunned natives in the water, swimming by instinct most of them, no weapons in their hands, no breath in their chests.

'Signaller,' ordered M. Martin looking over the heavy ribs of the sea. 'Tell the captain to lower boats to pick up these men.'

'Well done indeed, sir,' breathed Sir William. 'Always rely on the navy.' He added: 'No matter whose it is.' M. Martin smiled generously. The warship's lifeboats began picking up the islanders from the sea. St Paul's and St Mark's natives sat obediently along the wooden seats like cowed children on school benches.

The bodies and debris of the battle were still floating by the launches. Mr English watched them and felt a chill. 'They are floating due south,' he said to Pollet.

'I had noticed the direction,' said Pollet. 'I wonder has the Governor also noticed.'

They looked across. They could not tell whether he had noticed. But he had.

XVI

It was night before they reached the harbour again. Sir William went to Government House, bathed, changed and had a stiff double scotch. He spent the rest of the night with George Turtle at the radio station. When he returned by car to his house on the headland the early crowds were already beginning to congregate in the streets of the shabby town ready to welcome their Queen. Sir William felt like shouting to them 'Go home, go home,' but he realised how inadequate that would be. His heart was heavy for the poor little place and its hopeful, hopeless people. He saw their flags with sadness and their new flowers loaded him with humility. The Melanesian children from the mission school were sweeping the area in front of the quay and dusting down the rows of chairs. He turned the windows of the car up so that he would not hear their happy singing. He felt old and shapeless and unable to cope with life.

At eight o'clock he sent for Mr English, who arrived at Government House arrayed in a fine swinging kilt, smiling a pinched smile. The Governor knew him too well. He could see his optimism was forced.

'Hie, it's a gran' day for it, your Excellency,' said Mr English. 'A gran' day for two Scots like o' us.'

'It's a gran' day for nothing and nobody,' returned Sir William lapsing into a little soft Scots for the sake of his council chairman. He looked sadly at the pathetic dwarfishness of the man, listened to his hooting voice, until now a bane, only with

263

a sort of pity. These people, after all, he had thought, had so little here.

'Nothing and nobody?' queried Mr English. But he knew what the Governor meant. 'Ye've called it off then?'

Sir William put his face into his big fingers. 'Aye,' he said. 'Aye, it's off, Rob Roy. I had to do it. You know that.'

He thought Rob Roy was going to weep. The little man shuddered. 'There's the whole thing is ready,' he said. 'The chapel at The Love Beach, the procession and the band, and all the people. The wives and the schoolchildren.'

The Governor went from habit and looked out of the window. He could see all the coloured activity on the quay, the boats busy, the bunting floating and flying, and the gay people. 'I saw them,' he said, 'putting up the flags and the fresh flowers. Aye, it's sad. Especially for a place like this. It might have given it just the something it needs. A little bit of . . . well, pride, I suppose. That's it. Pride.'

'It'll be a long time before she's back this way,' said Mr English. He fiddled at his crutch. 'God damn,' he muttered. 'This new sporran is full uncomfortable.' He adjusted it. 'Aye, Governor, I think it might have done a wealth o' good to The Apostles. Just to see the *owner*, as it were. That's always a good thing in a firm. See the owner now and again.'

The Governor turned from the view of the lagoon and the harbour. 'I thought you'd be angry, Mr English,' he said. 'I'm surprised. Thank you.'

'What's the use. Ye've done it, so what's the use. I guessed anyway, yesterday.'

'You can't have a tribal butchery one day and a visit from the Sovereign the next,' shrugged the Governor. 'It just cannot be. I'm disappointed too, of course, just as much as the littlest schoolchild will be. It would have been nice, just before I retired. A fine thing to recall in the years when I have time to think.' He gave a half laugh. 'Look, I even got the plumes fixed properly on my show bonnet.' He took his white cockaded hat and displayed it to Rob Roy. 'I've never worn it yet, you know. I don't suppose I shall now. Looked good on me too.'

'Put it on,' suggested Mr English kindly.

'Aye, I will,' agreed the Governor. He placed the big hat carefully on his head and regarded himself in the far mirror. 'That's grand, don't you think?' he smiled.

'Aye, gran' it is,' said Mr English. 'Like my new sporran.'

'That's fine too. Have a drink.'

'It's early, but today I will,' said Rob Roy. 'I've kept that sporran for twenty years, you know, your Excellency. Stored it up for a moment like this. Well, a moment like we thought it would be.'

Sir William poured two double measures. They stood, one in his outrageous kilt and the other in his outrageous hat, and lifted their glasses.

'The Queen,' toasted Sir William with a smile.

'Aye, Her Majesty,' responded the wan Mr English. 'May she pass this way again.' Then he added. 'And stop.'

They went together to the pier where Abe had provided an emergency ferry to replace the launch now lying three miles outside the lagoon. Abe had scrubbed and painted his craft, removing the debris of the wrecked cabin. Patriotic silks and streamers hid the dent in the bulwarks. Abe was wearing one of the rosettes purchased from the firm in Tahiti. He offered one each to the Governor and Mr English and they accepted with a smile. Then he knew the Queen would not be coming. He mentally decided to refund half the ticket money he had taken for the trip out to the harbour. Then he decided to refund two-thirds of it. Then, hell to it he thought, all of it. It was a pity because he quite fancied seeing her himself. He had never managed to see a King or a Queen even when he was operating in London because at such times as Coronations or royal funerals he was always too busy running some concession.

Neither the Governor nor Mr English spoke during their crossing of the lagoon. It would have been a perfect day for it :

the sun round and firm now, looking over the higher palms, the island rising green and proudly, the sea striped with all its colours. The embellishments that the people had made, the flags and all the other decorations, and the people themselves, waiting and bright, filled the town. As the Governor and Mr English stepped ashore from Abe's boat the steaming spectators, lined behind the barriers, ushered by shining policemen, hot in the sun, began to cheer. Sir William had retained his fine white hat, and to this he had added his smart, smooth uniform with his modest medals like a coloured keyboard across his chest.

The cheers from the Governor's landing were heard along the street, lifted and carried on to the quayside, where the police band, really in tune, played in the waiting morning.

Those who knew the form the programme was to take that important day were surprised to see the Governor and Mr English make such a premature appearance. Sir William, for all his white starch and graceful feathers, walked tiredly, without lilt or enthusiasm. Mr English looked down studying the pendulum movement of his sporran. The band performed, but on a suddenly puzzled slightly wandering note. The police conductor growled, gave more authority to his baton, and they rallied, but now the Governor followed by Cooper and Rob Roy English were on the dais where it was planned that Her Majesty would stand that day. Cooper gave a flat wave to the band and they trailed to silence.

All the area about the Sexagesima quay fell to silence with them. The sun-touched colours of the children, the older citizens, the yellowing houses and the other poor buildings, became at once a fixed pattern. There were hundreds, black and white, waiting in that enclosed place. Sir William looked out on the stilled scene and felt his heart further weighted. A small child cried out behind the school's barrier but there was no other noise the Governor could hear except the breathing of the high palm trees and his own bumping heart. They must have known it was something bad for all the flags, the Union Jacks, the Tricolours, and the ill-proportioned miniature flag of The Apostles, which had already been held and waved a million practise times, were all at once drooping, held listlessly by those who had shown them. All the faces, from the black tribesmen to the pale English maidens in flowered print dresses of dated fashion, seemed to be turned on him and watching his every expression. Nervously he reached for the microphone.

'Ladies and gentlemen, Citizens of Sexagesima and the Apostle Islands.' He left it there for a moment and the crowd stirred uneasily. He noticed how the people in the local dignitaries' seats, without the native chiefs, who were to have sat there, seemed to crouch.

He breathed slowly and continued. 'Today I am afraid I am the bringer of bad news . . .' There was a stir like a foreign wind in the crowd but no voices. 'We are all here awaiting the arrival of Her Majesty the Queen—an event to which we have, every one of us, looked forward for many weeks. A great deal of work and effort has gone into our preparations and this would have been a great, good, day for the islands.'

No movement now, not even a stir. They were frozen solid in their attitudes under the growing sun. 'Unfortunately,' he went on, 'as quite a number of you may know, there was late yesterday an unprecedented tribal battle out at sea between the islanders of St Paul's and those of St Mark's. Many men were killed before this conflict was stopped.

'Any one of you who knows anything about the responsibility of being a Governor—my responsibility—will realise at once that it is not possible to have violent bloodshed one day in a place and expect to entertain a Sovereign the following day. Therefore, during the night, by radio, I had to inform Her Majesty's advisers in the royal yacht of the state of affairs here, and they had no hesitation, indeed no option, but to tell me that the royal visit would be considered too great a security risk. I therefore have to tell you that the Queen will not be coming today to Sexagesima.' He added wearily: 'I am very sorry.'

He stood before them, his tired head now dropped a little forward. They were silenced still, as though each had just heard a sentence passed upon them all. Then the sound of their reaction swept the quayside, no shouts, no violence, just their thousand voices all talking at once. All sad, all disappointed, all agreeing that it was right the Queen should not come to that island.

Davies and Conway were standing in the first floor window of the hotel, hanging out over the rotting balcony so that they could see down into the quayside square. Bird and Dahlia were in the next window.

'You,' said Davies bitterly to Conway, 'you, mate. You buggered the whole thing up for them.'

'So I did,' answered Conway. 'What do you want me to do, go out there and apologise?'

'Why not?' suggested Davies. Conway did not reply. His eyes squinted against the sun now clearing the roof-tops across the street. He shuffled back so that the shadow of a tousled palm, higher than the red roof, took the sun from his face.

From the dais the Governor continued. 'I have only a little consolation in all this,' he said. 'First a message from Her Majesty in which she says: "Please convey to the people of the Apostle Islands my deep regret at being unable to visit them. I shall think of them and pray that their lives may be full and fruitful. In the future I hope it will be possible for me to visit your islands. God Bless You All." '

A frantic cheer, as though the visit itself had been reprieved, blew up from the people when Sir William read this message. He saw some Melanesian women from the northern villages weeping at the barrier. He cleared his throat again. 'The tea parties for the children and the other events arranged for today will still take place, of course,' he croaked. Then he laughed sadly: 'We can't waste all those sandwiches and cakes, can we?' The crowd, especially the children, laughed and cheered him and shouted 'No!'

The Governor caught a glimpse of George Turtle, with a piece of yellow paper in his hand, approaching the dais. His heart jerked for a moment thinking that perhaps she would come after all. But he knew this would not be. Cooper passed him the message slip. He read it and moved again to the microphone, silencing with his movement the buzzing of the people in the square.

'Something further,' he said. 'I understand that the royal yacht will in fact be steaming quite close to this island and that if we assemble by midday at The Love Beach we will catch sight of her as she makes her way north. I suggest we all go there and cheer our Queen.'

They shouted and cheered at that, the black and the white children jumping in their excitement and heading off immediately from the square, hundreds of them running along the coastal track in their bright best clothes, through the closer trees and the village, until they reached the beach.

As the children ran on, their shouts in the sunlight frightening the birds in the tangled trees and puzzling the dogs in the village, the other people began moving that way too. The youths and girls first, coloured and white, racing off after the shouting children, the young men, heads down, trying to show off, to be there before any of the others. Then the adults, hurrying along in their silks and their best suits, perspiring, panting, but jogging patriotically anyway towards the place where they would see the passing of the monarch.

Bird and Dahlia pulled Davies and Conway along by the hands along with the hard-breathing crowd, through the town, along the track, under the closer trees, over the village and down to The Love Beach. Davies looked around. Some of the people were laughing as they ran. Hats flew away and had to be caught, legs soon tired, some limped before the village was reached. Young men on bicycles, bells shrill, rode along the outskirts of the crowd like roundup cowboys with a herd. They shouted and teased the girls as they went. They were native, and British

269

and French, all together. The elite, the island dignitaries in their special hats and suits were folded into the crowd of the others and hurried along in its company. The band, its uniform creased and stained with the morning's sweat, began to march, but the ragged march became a run and they pounded on their hot boots, their instruments clutched to them, the piccolo player far out in front, the man with the big drum rolling it resoundingly through the dust far behind.

They streamed out onto the brilliant beach, with the ocean rearing, in apparent surprise at the invasion. It fell over the reef and flopped into the flat of the lagoon. The hundreds of bright people ran from the trees like a happy army, fanning out among the dead barges, now all beautiful with the trailing flowers that Bird and her helpers had placed there. They lined the fringe of the sea, looking out to the two blues of ocean and sky. They climbed to the flat catwalks and other places on the barges, crowding and cramming along the rusty metal strips, exposed to the fullness of the high sun.

The barges which formed the chapel of the Unknown Soldier were as populated as the rest, people lined on every vantage place, for they had forgotten all about the sanctuary and the bones of the man which were beneath the sand.

Conway saw them as he and Dahlia with Bird and Davies following went down onto the beach. They found Pollet standing looking in the same direction. He smiled and studied again the flamboyant people all over the three walls of the chapel, then shrugged. 'It is so typical,' said Pollet. 'They have now forgotten their Unknown Soldier. He was to have been the star today.'

'He's just a bit player now,' said Conway and Davies winced at his cruelness. But he knew it was true. The people of the islands, of every race, wanted this to be their holiday, and they would make it fully so. The whole beach was vivid with them now, standing and sitting everywhere, their noise like the noise of an overpopulated seabird sanctuary, a sort of mass cawing into the wind. They sat like crowded birds too, on every ledge and in every space, sitting, singing, eating sandwiches, staring at the southern edge of the cape that formed one coral wall of the lagoon. Waiting.

The band had been assembled on one of the landing craft, the police having forcibly removed the people who had climbed there first. Now, sweating heavily from their run, the clambering and the impromptu transportation of instruments, they sat, squatted and stood, launched into the best-rehearsed piece of their limited repertoire which was Selections from 'South Pacific'. Abe, with his big business smile flooded across his face, and aided by recruited helpers, distributed further rosettes to the people with an added line in wide paper sun hats, Japanese fans and sunshades. Sandwiches and ice cream meant for the mission school's tea-party were brought to the beach and the children began to eagerly eat. The native villagers competed against each other in song and dancing competitions in the sand. Wrestling contests were cheered. When the Governor arrived with M. Martin at eleven-thirty there was hardly room for them on the patriotic stand.

Cooper and other busying officials cleared a path for them and they arrived at the landing barge nearest the seashore which had been quickly cleared and reserved as their official vantage point.

Davies thought he would never come to understand these islands. He had half expected a revolution fired by disappointment when the Governor made his announcement in the square by the quay. Instead there was only touching loyalty and tears. And now these same people, black and white, the kin in many ways of those he had seen fighting so bitterly the previous afternoon, were making this beach like Barry Island on an August Monday. Bird saw him looking at their animation and smiled for she knew how he thought. She took his hands and sat him in the shade of a barge. She knew that he would not be with her much longer.

Just before noon, under the powerful sun, a great quiet fell over all the people on the beach. The singing, the dancing and the games stopped, the talking petered away, the movement of the hundreds was stilled and they stood, like a huge congregation, watching the southern rim of the sea. The emotional expectation of the people could be felt in the heated air. Sir William and M. Martin, seated on their rusty barge on hastily acquired official wooden chairs, sat unmoving. Cooper and a dozen others all round had binoculars fastened to their eyes and to the horizon. Abe, counting his takings, heard the silence come over the beach, stretched up and tried to peer over the heads of the people towards the Pacific. Davies and Bird remained in the shadow of their barge, but the people who had now risen in front of them walled their view. An inviting foot came from the deck of the barge above them. Conway was standing with Dahlia fixed very close in front of him, and with Pollet at his side. The two men reached down and hoisted first the delicate Bird and then the lightweight Davies up to the platform with them, shuffling back and making two extra squares of room on the already crowded deck. Bird had red white and blue ribbons in her hair. Her face had the eagerness of a schoolgirl. Davies looked at her carefully.

It was Cooper who spotted the royal yacht first, a reward for the aching arms he suffered holding up his boot-sized binoculars. Others were just behind him. Their exclamation flew above the crowd and immediately everyone on the beach was straining eyes and toes. 'She is coming,' whispered Bird to Davies.

'The ship of the Queen is coming,' she repeated. He touched her brown arm where the white short sleeve of her dress cupped over it. She put her fingers up and met his fingers. Conway had casually lifted Dahlia's short skirt at the back and had hooked his hard hand around the cool top of her left leg. Dahlia glanced below at the people, but no one was looking at them. She smiled agreeably and pushed backwards into Conway's body.

On the horizon where previously only the sky interrupted the sea everyone could see the growing patch that was the royal ship. Hardly an eye was taken from it. Conway said to Pollet : 'Christ, I hope it's not old MacAndrews in *The Baffin Bay*. They'll lynch him.'

'I had thought of that,' said Pollet. 'But he's not due until tomorrow. He has never been early yet.'

Davies suddenly thought : 'Tomorrow. And the next day I will be going from these strange people and this strange place. Away. Far down to Sydney and to Trellis and Jones of Circular Quay, and then home, really home, across the world to Newport. If Conway keeps his promise.'

It was not *The Baffin Bay*. The ship that appeared was too high out of the water, too noble, too fast. It was clear enough now, steaming far out, three or four miles away, approaching the island initially, but then, turning in her course and heading north.

'Good God,' muttered Sir William to Cooper. 'Is that the closest they're coming? I can hardly see the damn thing.'

Cooper said : 'I suppose they want her to keep well away in case of trouble, sir. Look she's going off again. I'm afraid that is all we shall see.'

'I suppose we had better stand,' suggested Sir William wearily to M. Martin. The two Governors stood, facing out to where the ship remained a miniature on the huge shining sea. The crowd were realising that the vessel was going away again, that she would come no nearer to their view. A muttering of disappointment moved across the beach. Sir William looked at Cooper. 'The National Anthem,' he breathed. The A.D.C. signalled the conductor of the police band and his baton flicked. The band began to humph out 'God Save the Queen' and the people stopped muttering, stood to attention on the searing sand, and sang loudly, the minor breeze from the sea carrying their voices high and wide, back over their own island.

The force of it, the disappointment, and the faithful singing of the people moved Sir William to elderly tears. The fine sentiments of the anthem sounded loud and the yacht to which they addressed them was drawing away pathetically to become once more a smudge on the sun-heavy sea. The islanders sang every verse, for every verse was always sung in The Apostles, at school, after public gatherings, after the monthly cinema show. At the end, when the vessel was hard away north, dipping below the horizon again, the Governor called for three loyal cheers and all the people of the hot, neglected, shoddy, little place, cheered loyally and loudly. Then, when there was not even a smudge to see, everybody turned and walked quietly away from The Love Beach and back to their small town and their smaller villages.

XVII

The beach, when the people had wandered away, was as dead as a desert. All the day's brightest flowers, in their garlands and vivid strings, were feeling the afternoon sun. Some had been pulled and trampled by the crowd. The invasion barges looked more gaunt than before and rubbish—sheets and scraps of paper and palm leaf which had been used for wrapping—moved around the beach slowly in ritual procession with the slight breeze. The chapel they had made for the Unknown Soldier squatted shabby and sorry on the sand.

'Just like Barry Island after an August day,' observed Davies. 'Paper and rubbish all over, running along with the wind. People are the same everywhere, I suppose. They *will* leave their rubbish about.'

He and Bird were sitting against the remote and most rusted of the landing barges, alone on The Love Beach, viewing its desolation. 'There's one difference,' Davies went on. 'There's no newspaper here. On Barry Island it's nearly all newspaper bits they leave. But there's none here to drop.'

Bird said : 'This island you always speak of. How far from the shore is it?'

He grinned : 'It's not from the shore at all, it's joined onto the shore. There's a road and a railway.'

'Then it's *not* an island.' She said it petulantly, as though it mattered. 'It's a cheat.' She got up and began to walk away from him, down the strand towards the iron chapel at the far end. He followed her with his eyes. He got to his feet and walked miserably after her, his hands in his pockets.

'They just call it an island,' he grumbled. 'There's nothing dishonest about that. It was once, I expect, but they filled in the channel.'

'It's a cheat,' she repeated. 'To say you are one thing and really you are another.'

'Sometimes you can't help it,' he said, taking her hand. 'Sometimes the channel is filled in first. I don't suppose poor old Barry Island had any say in it.'

'How sad it was today,' she said suddenly. She had stopped and looked out to the wide, vacant sea. 'It was a shame Her Majesty could not come here to the islands.'

'Yes,' he dropped his head. 'It was a damned shame. All those people.'

She turned quietly and they wound into each other's arms, loosely at first, and then closer and tighter. He could feel her gentle giving body under the material of her dress. The smell of her, the full smell of a young girl of the islands no matter what her race, came to him. He lowered his face to hers and they pressed their cheeks flat and fiercely together and then kissed while the debris of the day drifted around their feet. It was late afternoon now and the stubby shadows of the invasion barges were enlarging across the sand.

'Love me here, Davies,' she said.

'I did the first time,' he replied.

'And this is the last.'

'There's tonight,' he said with male thoughtlessness. '*The Baffin Bay* won't be in until tomorrow.'

She said nothing. She did not want to dispute with him. Turning gracefully in his hold she dropped onto the beach and pulled him carefully down with her. They undressed each other as they had always done. They were like children when they were naked. She put her small hands down to his lower valley and held him cupped there. Davies kissed her lovely, sorry face and her wet eyes, her cheeks, her neck, and the bursting pink nipples of her pale breasts. He felt himself beginning to run into her lowered hands. They lay softly together then and he went to her, knowing her now after all these days, but still finding her new and strange.

Paper and bits of rubbish piled against them as they made love. Davies pushed it away at first, but, once when they rested, for they always made love for a long time before ending it, she laughed sweetly through her tears. 'It is covering us up, this garbage,' she said. 'It is ashamed of us being here like this. It is like the leaves covering the children in the fairy story.'

They continued. His hands held her small bottom like a loving cup, she stroked the triangles of his shoulder blades and sometimes, when they lay quietly again, took small handfuls of sand and sprinkled them playfully on the crease of his backside. They were near the fringe of the sea, coming in its idle run from the warm lagoon. The fingers of water kept reaching out towards them, capturing on the way some of the day's rubbish, floating it away, and then, in one ambitious grab taking away Davies' shirt with it. They did not notice.

'Oh Davies, darling,' she whispered.

'Yes, Bird.'

'I want to converse.'

'Aren't your pieces working?' he asked close to her ear.

'They are afraid to work. Because this is the last time.'

'What would you like to talk about.'

'About today.'

'What a shame today was, Bird.'

'All through. From dawn.'

'Such disappointment.'

'Such sadness. The children . . .'

'You will get a letter from your mother.'

'When *The Baffin Bay* arrives.'

'Perhaps it will be late.'

'It will come some time.'

'This is not working, Bird.'

'To talk like this? No.'

'Why are you looking away, darling?'

'I am watching your shirt floating away on the sea.'

Davies turned and saw the white shirt moving away like an ice floe. He laughed and remained very full inside her.

'Oh Davies, that was strange,' she said.

'What was strange?'

'When you laughed. It helped me. I felt.'

'When I laugh. Just that?'

'Yes, today perhaps I need to laugh to deceive myself.'

'Well we can't just laugh. Just like that. Tell jokes.'

'I can laugh,' she said. She arched herself back and laughed, laughter full of tears. He went with her, laughing and crying at once, their bodies vibrating under the emotion, reaching a convulsive pitch where suddenly her inside bubbled and so did he and they flooded together, laughing and weeping and rolling on the little sand hills of The Love Beach.

They lay sorry and quiet after it was finished. Then he leaned his elbow into the sand and looked out over the lagoon. 'I'd better get my shirt then,' he said. She started up. 'No, Davies, I will swim for it.'

He let her. He lay on his side on the sand and watched her, slim and naked, walk to the sand's edge and then run and dive into the brilliant green. She went easily through the basin, her brown body writhing under the skin of the water, her hair slow trailing. Reaching the shirt, now low in the sea, she caught it and returned with it, coming again to the beach with it hanging from her hand like a caught fish. The water ran down the channels of her fresh body, from all her grooves, and she blinked it from her eyes, and walked towards him. She stood over him and handed down his wet shirt. Davies looked up from the beach, getting a new view of her, the fine grained brown of her legs, the arrowhead and wet hair at her loin, then the flattened stomach, the white cones beneath her breasts, the slim stem of

278

her neck and her serious deep expression on him. The water still ran from her like small, silver express trains.

She dropped beside him and pressed his nose, his forehead, his thick hair to her nipples. 'You cannot go,' she said. 'Davies darling, you cannot.'

He pushed his face into the lumps of firm flesh. 'I'm going,' he said. 'I can't stay here. I'm going when the boat arrives.'

She sobbed against him now. 'I know all you hold dear,' she said. 'And I know they are far away. But I have never asked for anything in all my life. Now I am asking for you to stay. I love you.'

He felt guilty and sick. His hand went to her face and he pushed her tears away. 'I've thought for hours and days and weeks about this,' he said simply. 'Lying in your bed I have fought with it. And I've decided I must go.'

She stood up from him and walked to the lagoon's edge again staring at some puzzled fish, orange fish, darting undecided this way and that. She turned to him quietly.

'Go then,' she said. 'Go on, go away.'

He felt himself grow cold inside. Instinctively he knew that this was the moment to leave her, while she was angry, while she was giving him the margin, the excuse. He put on his trousers and picked up his shoes and his wet shirt. 'I will,' he answered evenly. 'I'm going.' He walked away towards the path that led to the village and then to the town.

'Go!' she suddenly screamed after him. 'Get away! We don't want you here!' He did not turn around. He walked on, his eyes dry, but ready to burst, fixed on the aching sand. Still naked she began to pursue him like a woodland wraith, darting in and out of the landing barges, calling after him, suddenly appearing above his head on the metal deck of one barge, then peeping madly around the corner of another, harrying him, taunting him.

'Go away. Go away you little married man! Go back to where you belong.'

Davies squeezed his eyes together and felt the squirt of the tears. Once he swung around on her but could say nothing, so turned again and continued with his trudging walk up the beach. 'Married man!' she cried again. 'Go home to your house.' From shadow to shadow she darted, from corroding hull to rusty deck, pushing her face through skeins of flowers which she herself had placed there that morning.

'Go! Go! Go!' she cried after him. Then she repeated the call, but now she had disintegrated into sobs. He looked around again and she was lying face down on the sand.

Davies hesitated, went back to her and helped her up. She looked at him with her eyes sore with her tears and knew that he had not come back to her because he had changed his mind. He had not. She shuddered but calmed herself. He retraced his walk and picked up her clothes. He gave them to her and she dressed without looking at him. He fastened the second button of her dress, far down the back of her neck because she could never reach it. She said 'Thank you' quietly, and began to walk up the beach with him. They walked apart.

When they were near the trees a long hollow hoot came from out beyond the reef. They turned together.

'*The Baffin Bay*,' said Bird. 'For the first time she is early.'

They spent the night moving about her big bed, wandering in bitter dreams, waking each other at times to make melancholy love. It was a hot night with a great sickly moon and no breeze. Davies woke again when it was early daylight and Bird still slept. His eyes burned sorely and his body felt like a shell. He left her sleeping and went to the hotel to pick up his suitcase. He wanted to get aboard *The Baffin Bay* with his belongings, to commit himself to the return voyage, before he had to look into her eyes again. That much done he felt he could carry through the thing that he had to do. He could, somehow, if he were resolute, leave her, and get away from the feeling of these islands. He could go back to Newport where it was cool and where the moon looked round and crisp over the hard streets, not so bursting full and rotten ripe as it had been all night.

It was the first grey light of the new day. The sun, the red show-off, the great daily egoist of the islands, had not yet made its flying entrance from the lower part of the ocean. But its forerunner colours were already squeezing along the eastern sea line. Soon it would be hot again in The Apostles.

Davies told Seamus at the hotel that he would be back later to say goodbye to everyone. That he was just taking his things to *The Baffin Bay* early to stow them aboard. Seamus seemed to understand his motives. 'Get out at the first chance, me boy,' he said. 'Don't wait for a single minute or the minute will turn into years before you know it.' Davies smiled wryly at him and humped his suitcase into the grey street. The old Chinese shop-keeper across the road was squatting in his doorway, shaking his head at nothing, his unused picture of Mao and his patriotic flag fixed over his door. He made no sign that he had ever seen Davies in his life. A few other people were moving about, some men on bicycles came into the town from the village, riding in silhouette against the peach sunrise and the turquoise sea, flicking against the bowing columns made by the lines of tall palms along the waterfront.

Davies had the feeling that it was the beginning to a coloured film, the prelude before the titles, and that he had seen it many times before. Even the shuddering noise of the rolling shutters of the shops by the quay, flying up for the day's trading, were familiar to the split second, and along the street the now impotent flashes of Mr Livesley's neon sign blinked in the new daylight.

He could see the red roof of Mrs Flagg's bungalow, the thick green hem of trees around the Governor's house on the headland across the harbour, the trailing, sweet musky flowers along the harbour road, the Melanesian women setting out their fruit baskets on the grass by the Condominium office, the Union Jack and the Tricolour nudged by a minute breeze on the roof of the office, and the untiring waves rolling and spilling over the unwearing reef beyond the lagoon. He felt acutely aware of everything about the place, the smells, the feel of the warming air on his body, the creaking morning noises, the voices of the fruit women, the dry squeaks of the bicycles, dogs and cockerels sounding dutifully. He felt as though he had been there for one hundred years.

Before he reached the quay Conway caught him up, a cheerfully hurrying Conway, his heavy suitcase easily on his shoulder. 'Clearing out, eh, sport,' he said. 'Good idea too. Sometimes I didn't think you'd make it. Where's Bird?'

'Sleeping,' said Davies.

'Mine too. Better than weeping, I say. Hah, there she is, the old *Baffin Bay*. Now don't she look great?'

'Seems like ages,' said Davies. They did not stop but carried on with their jogging trot towards the jetty and the petrol-coloured water. *The Baffin Bay* was a hundred yards offshore and Abe's boat with a load of general merchandise was pushing back towards the land. They reached the steps just as he coaxed it into the side. He came up the steps to them.

'You're early,' he said studying their expressions and their suitcases.

'We thought we'd get our stuff aboard,' grunted Conway. Then he added half apologetically : 'While it's cool.'

'I mean you're about six weeks early,' said Abe. 'That thing won't be out of this harbour until then. Pistons are all buggered up. Old Rice has been warning the skipper every voyage for the last ten years and yesterday did it.'

A strange firm hand seemed to touch Davies. He stared at Abe then glanced at Conway. The Australian was leaning forward, his tan gone a quick yellow. 'Don't joke, Abe,' he said. 'She's sailing, isn't she?'

282

Abe laughed at his disbelief. 'No joke,' he said. 'The pistons are all buggered up. I told you, MacAndrews tried to get here a day early—so he could see the Queen.'

'See the Queen?' said Conway incredulously.

Abe looked as though it were a personal affront. 'Sure,' he jabbed his finger at Conway. 'He's entitled to see the Queen as much as anybody.'

'And he wrecked the engine trying to get here.' Conway muttered the words out sat on his suitcase staring hatefully at *The Baffin Bay*. MacAndrews, Mrs MacAndrews, the engineer Rice, could be seen arguing on deck. Rice had his hands spread out.

'Rice said it was the final insult to the machinery,' said Abe.

Davies said carefully : 'Can't they mend it?'

Abe snorted : 'Anywhere else it would be a big job,' he said. 'Here it's bloody nigh an impossibility. It will take six weeks— and that's the minimum.'

'No other boats coming?' asked Davies.

'There's the copra collection ship,' said Abe. 'But she's still around the Solomons somewhere. She's not due till July. She may not come at all when she finds that a third of the collection is all burned up and sunk.' He looked spitefully at Conway. 'Anyway she'll only go to Noumea from here, so you might as well wait until this old thing is repaired.'

'The warship!' exclaimed Davies spinning around. 'Where's she gone?' The Sexagesima harbour was empty of anything beyond a motor launch.

'Sailed,' affirmed Abe. 'Last night. Back to Noumea. The best thing you two can do is fly a shirt as a distress signal.' He laughed at his own jest and carried his outflung belly down the steps towards his boat. 'I'll have to wait for my claim now, won't I?' he said looking back and then pointing to the place where the cabin had been demolished.

'*I've* got to wait,' said Conway morosely.

Davies still felt stunned. 'Was there any mail?' he asked Abe.

283

'Sure, there's always mail. Even a place like this gets somebody writing to it once every couple of months. None for you though.'

'None? How do you know?'

'Because I'm the postal agent,' said Abe logically. 'The mail came ashore last night and I took the letters to the hotel myself. Nothing for you.'

'Did Bird get anything?' asked Davies not knowing why he asked.

'Yes, a letter from her mother. It's still in the office.'

Davies sat heavily on his suitcase beside Conway. 'Dahlia's pregnant,' said Conway miserably. 'Those pills were dud.'

'Pregnant! And you were clearing out?' said Davies. Nothing about Conway surprised him now.

'Well, I'm not clearing out now am I?'

'What was dud about the pills?'

'The bastard in Hawaii twisted her,' said Conway. 'He gave her three hundred baby aspirins. Pollet analysed them for me.'

Davies surprising himself, hooted with outrageous laughter: 'Baby aspirin! Ha! Oh, that's bloody marvellous! Ho! Baby aspirin!'

Conway turned to face him as they sat on their cases. He pushed his big serious head on his big shoulders forward towards Davies. 'She gave Bird half the supply,' he said. 'Laugh that off.'

The sun was clear of the world now, flinging its burning flamboyance all over the town, the lagoon, and the green islands of the archipelago. 'I'll need a job,' said Davies. 'I'm broke now and promissory notes are no good.'

'Maybe we could help Abe,' suggested Conway. 'I'm broke too. We'd better move in with the girls.'

Mr Hassey came along the quay and stopped by them, looking down at them on their luggage, and across at *The Baffin Bay*. 'Never heard of the boat breaking down before,' he said.

'Not in all my thirty-eight years in the islands.' He grinned at them: 'And what will you young men be doing now?' he asked.

It was Conway who replied. 'Ascertaining the fucking natives,' he said sullenly.

FOR THE BEST IN PAPERBACKS, LOOK FOR THE 🐧

In every corner of the world, on every subject under the sun, Penguin represents quality and variety – the very best in publishing today.

For complete information about books available from Penguin – including Puffins, Penguin Classics and Arkana – and how to order them, write to us at the appropriate address below. Please note that for copyright reasons the selection of books varies from country to country.

In the United Kingdom: Please write to *Dept E.P., Penguin Books Ltd, Harmondsworth, Middlesex, UB7 0DA.*

If you have any difficulty in obtaining a title, please send your order with the correct money, plus ten per cent for postage and packaging, to *PO Box No 11, West Drayton, Middlesex*

In the United States: Please write to *Dept BA, Penguin, 299 Murray Hill Parkway, East Rutherford, New Jersey 07073*

In Canada: Please write to *Penguin Books Canada Ltd, 2801 John Street, Markham, Ontario L3R 1B4*

In Australia: Please write to the *Marketing Department, Penguin Books Australia Ltd, P.O. Box 257, Ringwood, Victoria 3134*

In New Zealand: Please write to the *Marketing Department, Penguin Books (NZ) Ltd, Private Bag, Takapuna, Auckland 9*

In India: Please write to *Penguin Overseas Ltd, 706 Eros Apartments, 56 Nehru Place, New Delhi, 110019*

In the Netherlands: Please write to *Penguin Books Netherlands B.V., Postbus 3507, 1001 AH, Amsterdam*

In West Germany: Please write to *Penguin Books Ltd, Friedrichstrasse 10–12, D–6000 Frankfurt/Main 1*

In Spain: Please write to *Alhambra Longman S.A., Fernandez de la Hoz 9, E–28010 Madrid*

In Italy: Please write to *Penguin Italia s.r.l., Via Como 4, I-20096 Pioltello (Milano)*

In France: Please write to *Penguin Books Ltd, 39 Rue de Montmorency, F-75003 Paris*

In Japan: Please write to *Longman Penguin Japan Co Ltd, Yamaguchi Building, 2–12–9 Kanda Jimbocho, Chiyoda-Ku, Tokyo 101*

The Virgin Soldiers

One way or another the Communist guerilla war in Malaya kept a whole British army occupied from 1948 until 1952. They were the virgin soldiers – idle, homesick, afraid, bored, oversexed and undersatisfied. 'Scenes rivalling the best of D. H. Lawrence' – *Daily Telegraph*

Orange Wednesday

Codename: Orange Wednesday. The password to a black comedy of terrors for reluctant soldier Brunel Hopkins, suddenly embroiled in the complex and sinister preparations for the re-unification of Germany. 'Deliciously funny ... A sure-footed and highly accomplished work' – *Spectator*

Orders for New York

A gripping war novel based on one of the strangest true stories of World War Two. Master storyteller Leslie Thomas has woven evidence that governments tried to suppress into a tragic, bloody tale of high treason and high adventure.

The Magic Army

This is Leslie Thomas's compulsive story of the unexpected events and flaring passions of the never-to-be-forgotten spring of 1944. In it he distils the dogged endurance, the bravery, the heartbreak and the folly that went into the making of the greatest military adventure in history.

also published:

The Adventures of Goodnight and Loving
Dangerous in Love
The Dearest and the Best

and his autobiographies:

In My Wildest Dreams
This Time Next Week